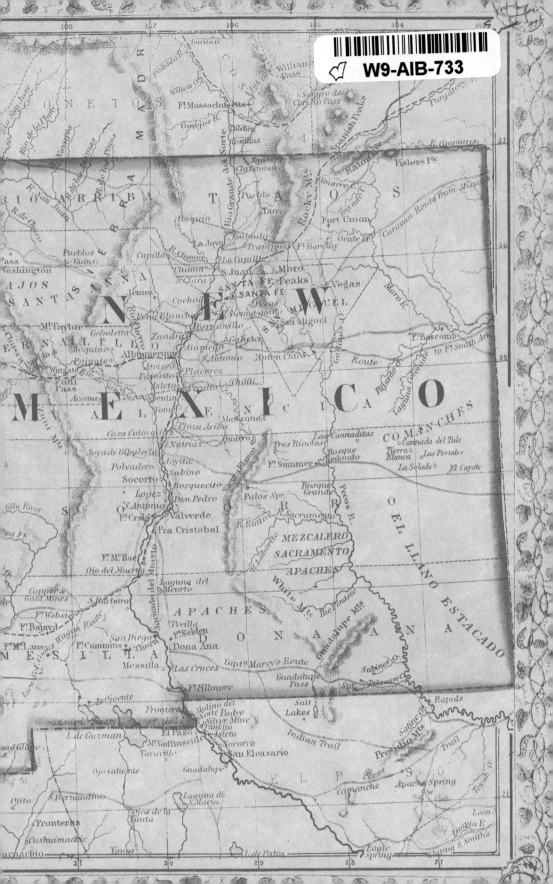

"Nancy Turner knows the land of the 19th-century Territories, as it must have been, and she knows the landscape of the heart as it was then and always is."

—Meg Files, author of *Meridian 144*

In a compelling fiction debut, Nancy E. Turner's unforgettable *These Is My Words* melds the sweeping adventures and dramatic landscapes of *Lonesome Dove* with the heartfelt emotional saga of *Oldest Living Confederate Widow Tells All*.

Inspired by the author's original family memoirs, this absorbing story introduces us to the questing, indomitable Sarah Prine, one of the most memorable women ever to survive and prevail in the Arizona Territory of the late 1800s. As a child, a fiery young woman, and finally a caring mother, Sarah forges a life as full and fascinating as our deepest needs, our most secret hopes, and our grandest dreams. She rides Indian-style and shoots with deadly aim, greedily devours a treasure trove of leatherbound books, dreams of scarlet velvet and pearls, falls uneasily in love, and faces down fire, flood, Comanche raids, and other mortal perils with the unique courage that forged the character of the American West.

Rich in authentic details of daily life and etched with striking character portraits of very different pioneer families, this action-packed novel is also the story of a powerful, enduring love between Sarah and the dashing cavalry officer Captain Jack Elliot. Neither the vast distances traveled nor the harsh and killing terrains could quench the passion between them, and the loss and loneliness both suffer only strengthen their need for each other.

While their love grows, the heartbreak and wonder of the frontier experience unfold in scene after scene: a wagon-train Sunday spent roasting quail on spits as Indians close in to attack; Sarah's silent encounter with an Indian brave, in which he shows her his way of respect; a dreadful discovery by a stream that changes Sarah forever; the hazards of a visit to Phoenix, a town hot as the devil's frying pan; Sarah's joy in building a real home, sketching out rooms and wrap-around porches.

Sarah's incredible story leads us into a vanished world that comes vividly to life again, while her struggles with work and home, love and responsibility resonate with those every woman faces today. *These Is My Words* is a passionate celebration of a remarkable life, exhilarating and gripping from first page to last.

These
is *my*
Words

These is my Words

The Diary of Sarah Agnes Prine, 1881–1901

ARIZONA TERRITORIES

A Novel

Nancy E. Turner

ReganBooks
An Imprint of HarperCollinsPublishers

Endpaper map courtesy of the Arizona Historical Society, Southern Arizona Div.-Library/Archives Dept., #100.

This novel is a work of historical fiction. Geronimo, General Crook, Larcena Page, Miss Wakefield the school teacher, and Mr. Fish at the dry goods store were real people and lived during the time at the places mentioned. Every other character, all dialogue, and plot are products of the author's imagination or are used fictitiously. Any resemblance to actual persons living or dead is purely coincidental.

HarperCollins books may be purchased for educational, business, or sales promotional use. For information please write: Special Markets Department, HarperCollins Publishers, Inc., 10 East 53rd Street, New York, NY 10022.

FIRST EDITION

Designed by Elina D. Nudelman

Library of Congress Cataloging-in-Publication Data

Turner, Nancy E., 1953–
    These is my words : the diary of Sarah Agnes Prine, 1881–1901 / Nancy E. Turner.
      p. cm.
    ISBN 0–06–039225–8
    1. Prine, Sarah Agnes—Fiction.   I. Title.
    PS3570.U725T48   1998
    813'.54—dc21   97–37622
                                             CIP

98 99 00 01 02 ❖/RRD 10 9 8 7 6 5

For everyone who has ever stood alone on a hill in a storm

These
is *my*
Words

the Northwest Territory with her folks, then with Papa. She says a move is a time for lightening your load and starting things new.

Me and Mama rolled up the dishes in curtains and packed the bedding and quilts that was finished in between her mirror and a real glass window we was taking from out the front wall. All the packing was done and we was pulling out down the road and I couldn't take my eyes off the little house sitting there lonesome looking with that window open like a mouth calling us back. Ahead of us the boys are driving the herd and behind us is our dogs Toobuddy and Bear, running and playing and chasing a rabbit now and then. Papa gave me a can of hoof black to use for writing and I have whittled some quills from our old rooster's tail feathers. He said he never saw a body more set on writing letters than me.

We drifted the herd towards the town of Prescott and started down the long mountain through the black canyon then out across the big Salt river valley. It took eight days cause the wagon broke a axle and we had to send back to Prescott before we was far out of town. It was only the beginning and I started to have this holler feeling and kept dreaming of that house with the open mouth calling us. Mama I says, its like its a bad sign.

Mama got her feathers ruffled and said the good book don't teach signs and suspicions and made me read the Old Testament out loud to her most of the afternoon on the road.

She never did learn to read but she sure wanted her children to so she made Papa teach me some letters and then I figured out words from the letters. Mostly I do right well but some of these Old Testament verses gets me addled with the words.

I hope there is schools in San Angelo that will take a girl as big as me cause I want to learn to write better! Probably there ain't.

July 29, 1881

Well, we drove up through the Valley and there is a sign at Hayden's Ferry saying it is now a town called Tempe but it is just two adobe buildings and some fence and they got a mighty nerve to call that little old cow corral a town. It was hotter than I ever knew it could be. Out across the desert forty five miles to the Gila river, and no water for all them long miles. It was the hardest travel I ever knew and I felt sore on the insides like we was riding in the dark to a brink of a canyon we couldn't see. Times like that you have to trust your horse's sense and let him have his head, as only a pony could smell the lay of the land at night.

August 4, 1881

By this time Rose is getting good and broke in. She lets me on her bare back but don't want a saddle, so in a few days I will try a blanket. She feels good and rides smooth as a canoe, and don't take to rough mouthing her, which I don't do.

We struck the river just above the Pima agency and stayed put some days to water the horses and us as well. All around the agency was Indians and Mexicans. I never did see so many brown people before and I figured the sun scorched 'em like a flat iron on a white shirt. Anyway I feel sorry they have to live in this end of the devil's frying pan.

They stared at me and I stared at them back, and then Papa said girl get in that wagon and pull your bonnet down low and quit looking.

I asked Ernest what for and he said he been following me with a shot gun all day to keep them in mind I was a lady and nothing else.

I asked him what else and he said a dead lady. So I laughed and said I seen him shoot, maybe I better carry the shot gun myself.

August 6, 1881

We traveled up the river to the old town of Florence then come to the mouth of the San Pedro river. At that point we are joined by two wagons of folks who want to throw in with us to go east. By the time Papa gets done saying all he knew about San Angelo they is ready to go there too. I don't know where he knew it from. It is Mr. and Mrs. Lawrence and their four daughters. Alice and Louisianna and Ulyssa and Savannah. They is all beautiful girls too except the middlest one whose got buckt teeth. I seen her smile at a rabbit and scare it!

The oldest girl Savannah Lawrence set about to making biscuit dough that evening and I never did see my brother Albert more taken with biscuits than that supper. He was fetching her water and stoking her a fire and had a blaze going to light up midnight and I laughed. Mama poked my ribs and said any biscuits put in that better be named Shadrack, Meshack, and Abednego. They are them fellers in the Old Testament flung into the firy furnace who walked out again without a singed hair on their heads.

All these handsome girls and their ma was dressed in black and with little caps because they is Friends which we call Quakers. They talk strange but they can quote the Bible up one side and down the other, so Mama thinks they are wonderful folks. Their Pa is scary looking to me cause he got a wooden leg and told how he lost it in the war, but he wasn't fighting but doctoring. He says Quakers don't believe in killing nor fighting of any kind. We are all thankful to know a doctor out in this forsaken land even though he says he is just a sawbones not a pillgrinder.

The other wagon belongs to Mr. and Mrs. Hoover. They keep to themselves and seem peevish about every one of us. They got a huge conestoga kind of wagon and are from back east some where, Papa 'spects it must be east of the fertherest tree since they are such tinhorns and whine and worry him so. Papa don't take to being worried, he says horses take to a calm hand, a strong backbone and a steady grip, if you give 'em a weak knee they just do wrong. He knows his horses and I 'spect I like a strong backbone better than all the tears and blushing and complaining from Mrs. Hoover.

Mr. Lawrence says there's outlaws in the mountains and Indians and either of them will take the horses from us by force, so he will help guard in shifts for the good of us all. My Papa said that's a blessing and he promises Mr. Lawrence a pick of a horse in payment for his good advice when we see San Angelo.

August 8, 1881

We traveled up the San Pedro to Mt. Graham and turned east to Willcox. There we struck the S.P.R.R. railroad tracks. We seen more white people who say we will never get to Texas with all them horses, and for us to travel as near the railroad tracks as we could all down through the San Simone valley. They said Mr. Lawrence was right about the mountains and I got that sore feeling inside again.

In trying to stay near the tracks, we have to go wide now and then where the track skirts right up on the banks of the San Pedro. It is muddy in places and even where there is not water a horse can step down and get mud. There are trees so thick and close a deer couldn't get through or even a weasel in places, and twice we got stove up on brush that looked like it led to a path but didn't. That San Simone valley was more of a desert and a wilderness than anything I had ever seen, although it was not as hot as before. Brittle brush and prickly pears are everywhere, and along the banks of the river its thick with mesquites and brambles and high cottonwoods.

That is the prettiest kind of tree there is to me. A cottonwood makes a little sound with the leaves like they are talking to each other, a gentle and soft sound. In the fall they turn yellow and copper and the ground under a cottonwood looks like it is covered with pennies. Under our cottonwood back home I used to collect the pennies and pretend I was rich. One time I sewed them onto a bonnet to be pretty, but they dried out and fell off.

August 10, 1881

We met some travelers going back the other way. It was two fellows on a buckboard loaded with mail, and five Army soldiers to guard it plus they have got three mules loaded with ammunition. They told us we were lucky to come this far, as there is terrible Apache problems all around us. We shared some water as their horses looked mighty dogged. They were grateful and wished us well.

Well, my Papa has a hand for horses better than most anyone you could name, but he don't have much hand for fixing houses and wagons and by the time we was pointing toward El Paso we lost another axle. Mr. Hoover got a spare two for himself but he can't see it clear to lend us one, so we lay up for a whole day while Mr. Lawrence and Papa rig up a axle.

Mama rolls her eyes a lot that day and says there's a dry wind coming but I don't know what that is. Sure enough, it is dry and thirsty and you can drink but it don't do no good, and before we get down to the Rio Grande Valley we is all wanting water and the horses drink our share. We had to go down some eighty miles to the old ruins of something that was called Fort Hancock. There by the banks we rest and drink and watch the horses drink a dry spot in the river.

August 11, 1881

Mrs. Hoover is carrying on about my brothers playing Indians and war party cause it makes her worrisome. Mama scolded Harland and Clover and said play it where she can't hear you boys, she is a tenderfoot and libel to faint if she hears one more war hoop or rebel yell from you younguns. Also Mr. Hoover says tonight he won't be able to take a watch cause his wife is feeling poorly from the travel. I think inside if he is worried he can watch nearby but I don't say nothing.

It is becoming fun to have the Lawrence girls to play with. I never had sisters except to pretend. They tease each other and plait their hair under them little hats into a roll and they said they will do mine.

The girl Savannah made some questions about Albert, but I wanted to talk about other things. The littlest one, Louisianna, has a hand-turned doll dressed just like her and it is not fancy but I see by the stitches it is a fine piece of work. They is fun but none of these girls rides horses bare back only in buggies and wagons and they was sure surprised when I took my rifle and Rose and went past the trees and brought back a deer for venison stew. They said so many times oh my, oh my, that I thought I might of stood on my head and sang a song it was so strange to them. Well I lived in the territory all my life and I got four brothers and a girl has got to get along.

Papa and Mr. Lawrence are thinking about moving on a bit after supper to see the pass through which we must travel tomorrow. It looks like a place of ambush, Mr. Lawrence says, and they will wait until there is but a hour of daylight left to go see the area.

Clover and Harland been shooting each other with sticks and hollering give up you rascal and I got you and give up! as if they was a outlaw or sheriff in a wild town. After supper Clover declared he was about to turn in he was tired out. He spread himself a blanket under the wagon at the tongue bracing and soon was sleeping two rows at once, he was plum tuckered.

Up come Albert and Ernest to Harland and says lets fish in the river while there's light and they do and sure enough they catch a big old ugly catfish. The boys laugh and think they are surprising little Clover and they throw the nasty thing on him and holler snake! snake! That blanket unloads Clover like a mule and he bucks his head real hard on the tongue brace and soon its blood everywhere.

Well, Mama is tendering Clover and scolding the big boys all in the same breath and it sounds like the most amazing bunch of speech I heard ever and all the Lawrence girls come over and say oh-oh over Clover. One gave him a peppermint she was saving and they patched up his head. He's got a busted head big as an egg and a bloody bandage and before long he is a marching around with Harland being soldiers and they is fighting each other and hollering take that yankee and take that reb! at the top of their lungs.

I see Albert and Ernest is sorrowful for what they did but not too much and they is trying to skin that catfish and clean it and they are moaning at the smell. Mrs. Hoover is fit to be tied she never did see such goings on she declares and sniffs her smelling bottle and goes to bed without helping with the dishes.

August 13, 1881

We all put down for the night and its a dark one with a bit of cloud on the moon, and Clover suddenly calls out I'm hurt! and snake! again and again. He has got the whole place woke and is still hollering, and Mama has a terrible time to hush him and he is crying out louder and louder that his hand hurts. Finally she gets him hushed and we sleep till daylight starts in on us, then it is Mama calling out.

Clover is in a fever and there on his arm is two big old holes like I seen on my dog Buddy from a snake bite. Mr. Lawrence comes a rushing over and they is all talking at once about what and when and what to do now. There is a look on Clover of grey and yellow like I hope I never sees again, and right away Papa takes a live chicken and slits it open and lays it on the holes, as long as the heart is beating it is pulling out snake venom he says. As soon as the chicken is good and dead they cut another and try that but its doing no good. They speculate about cutting off his arm where the snake bit is only the doctor says it is too late and the poison is in his vanes now. I don't know what that is but he says it with a look on his face I seen with my insides not my eyes.

Mr. Lawrence says he has got some laudanum and some bitters for snake bite but Clover chokes on it and can't get it down but don't seem to be in much pain except his arm. All there is to do is hold little Clover and wait. He says he is cold and Mama covers him around with her pilgrims progress quilt with the blue sprigged calico squares at the corners, then sets on the milking stool and rocks him in her arms.

The big boys is sniffing and Harland sets to bawling like a branded calf, then all the boys is bawling and the Lawrence girls and even the Hoovers. We just all set and cry sort of quiet into our sleeve and about halfway to noon Clover shivers real hard and is gone.

In the twilight I stood at Clover's little grave and sang Jordan's Stormy Banks.

He's living in Canaan now, and I wonder what kind of good times he is having. But I remember he is dead and nothing about it seems happy or blest. No one can eat. We have drank our tears for food.

Little old Clover was a top notch fellow after he got out of diapers. I will sorely miss his little puckery smile and all.

August 16, 1881

Now I got a Angel Brother to be with my Angel Sister. The boys is about to bust with feeling they pestered Clover on his last day on earth.

Miss Savannah Lawrence—that is such a pretty name, she is my best friend—is beginning to share her reader and show me to write better.

Two days after burying Clover we is still at the spot cause Mama and Papa just walks around lost like and saying they can't leave him. It is a hard time but I am making myself useful and then one morning there is uneasiness in the air. The horses is skitterish and high and even Mr. Lawrence who is used to them is having a hard time. He and Papa kept looking to the bushes and hills and that day put the wagons into a closed space hard against a hill and herded all them horses into it.

Noon comes high and hot and Mama cooks up catfish for dinner. As I am doing dishes first one arrow hit the wagon tongue right near where I am standing then another past my head so close I hear the feathers flick something and spang into a water bucket. Then the air is filled with arrows and we don't know where to turn or hide. There is surprise from us and screaming from them Indians and they are riding around and around and scaring us to our death. Dust is strangling us like a hot dry blanket and I feel sick. Then a Indian hollers at us and does a lot of pointing and yelling and then waits like he is wanting us to answer him. As soon as he sees he is getting no answer he slipped into the dust and was gone.

All is quiet as we count noses and all unhurt, not even a dog or chicken or any of Mrs. Hoover's fancy island geese. Papa and Mama is suddenly back to right and we spend all after noon loading rifles and packing shot wads and getting ready and nobody eats much supper either. I have tore a hole in my yellow gingham from catching it on an iron fire tender while running from the arrows, so I am fixing it before dark too, but the light is poor and I am purely tired.

In my sleep I see a canyon open up before me as I ride Rose full out and we can not stop and pitch headfirst over the edge and down in the bottom of the canyon is a little house with a open hole like a mouth and inside the mouth is my Angel Brother and Angel Sister. Ever time I sleep I see this over again and wake sweating and shaking like the fever so my teeth rattle together. It is a lost and mournful feeling. I won't let myself sleep any more, so I just lay here and write this by the fire and wait for daylight.

August 17, 1881

Before the first light is clear, we hear whooping that comes from the open gates of hell. It is much more terrible than my brothers a playing in the yard. We have our rifles ready and begin firing back as arrows rain in on us. They are hitting the horses and the cows and all about me is the sound of screaming. Horses are screaming, the Lawrence girls are screaming, Mama and Harland are screaming and the Indians are making sure the devil knows we're coming.

I think I was screaming too but it is too awful a noise to know and I am loading along side Mama. It just seems like it will never end. They are all about us and riding bare backed with their toes holding on, they fire arrows and a couple of repeater rifles with both hands free. Suddenly next to me Mr. Hoover takes a arrow plum in the throat and I will not write what next happened but he is gone to his reward. Mrs. Hoover is struck dumb for some minutes and then commenced to bawling at the same time she picked his rifle from under his body and shot a Indian surely in the chest as if she was a crack marksman.

My heart is aching and heavy as I remember this next, as bullets went past one went smack through my skirts and took Ernest in the leg at the knee. He hollered to make my bowels twist in a knot, and I began to think we are all going to die soon. Papa is a firing away, Mama at his side runs to Ernest and hugs him. At that second Mrs. Lawrence was hit deep in the stomach and doubled over into the dirt the scared horses was kicking up. Then sudden as the breath of death there is quiet except for Ernest moaning and some hurt horses crying.

Dear Mrs. Lawrence is gone, Mr. Hoover is gone, Papa has taken a ball clear through the arm but it is a small clean wound and not even much blood, and good old Ernest is in a frightful state as Mr. Lawrence looks him over.

He isn't sure of his doctoring, he says with such tears in his eyes, but there had been many a boy in the war who didn't live from less, and he says the leg must come off. All the laudanum that Mr. Lawrence had is broke and leaked out from a bullet that hit through their canvas and got the medicine bag and the doctor tells us to hold him down tight. It is a certain thing and quickly done. Luckily the doctor has much experience, but Ernest pleaded to God and Jesus and all the angels and Mama and Papa and everyone he knew to save him and afterward he is in bad shape.

I keep looking in on him and touching his hands and he squeezes me ever so softly, then I go so he can't see me crying over him. My head aches bad. I asked Papa couldn't we turn back and go home. He set his hand on my arm, and said, Girl, there's never any turning back in life. But don't you worry, he says. The Lord is watching over us. Then I felt real hollow and low and mean. If He is a watching us, I wish He'd lend a hand now and then.

Papa was cussing the Indians as he dug graves for our friends and it was decided to rest Ernest's little leg with Mr. Hoover.

August 20, 1881

For a nineteen year old brother Ernest suddenly seems mighty small and there is nothing for his pain so he cries sometimes like a baby and then finds a dreadful and fitful sleep. God if you see us in here please help my Ernest I love him and we need him as a brother and a good boy who never had a mean bone in him.

Besides our folks, we lost one dray horse and two stock horses and a sheep, the Hoovers lost an ox and a pack horse, and the Lawrences lost one milking cow and a calf and a dray. Mama says we should pray and so does Mr. Lawrence but I can't seem to put my mind to it much.

Mrs. Hoover is storming around like a tornado. She neatens up things and later sends buckets flying with a kick, she is fit to be tied for sure. Papa says to pack up, we will leave before sunup to get a jump on the Indians and beeline for Fort Stockton.

August 23, 1881

Fort Stockton is just a little settlement of soldiers, not a dozen souls there. As we rolled on down the Concho river we came to a creek coming in from the north called Rockey and some live oaks, and we drove the wagons under a big tree and camped. All seems hot and scorched here in Texas country. It is deader and more worrisome than the Territories we come from, and even Papa is feeling he may be wrong about San Angelo.

I am learning to write better from Savannah and I love her like a sister, she has given me a present of a reader and half a newspaper from last January which I can read without stopping. I learn to spell better from it too.

August 28, 1881

Rained in the evening and cool. Next day the mud on the trail and near the tracks is too thick to walk in or pull a wagon so we are stuck, but the air is fresh and dry and Savannah and Louisianna and the other sister I will tell about now have had a time and want to bathe in a stock tank deep among some near trees.

The water is fresh and rainy but Papa says no, not away from the wagons. We are low on food and he needs to go hunting, too, and there are signs of antelope all around, but his arm is hurting real bad from the bullet hole now. We set about to make the camp look like there's plenty of men about, pointing rifles all about us just leaning on wagon seats and such, but they are gone hunting. I'm sure they are sorry we did not think before to butcher up the cow that was Indian killed.

When they were gone Mama said for us girls to all go together and watch carefully, and bring back two buckets of water and hurry. Mama and the boys will stay at camp and maybe have a bath in a wash pan.

The girls are glad to slip quiet as a deer into the trees and quick get out of their dresses and into the water. Savannah has brought a little piece of soap in a cloth. Alice is a little noisy until Savannah's sister shushes her. I don't know why but it felt wise to be quiet. The water felt like sweet fingers on my head but it still ached inside.

Savannah's other sisters' name is Ulyssa, after General U. S. Grant, which is a name from the northern side of the line but I don't mention that. Ulyssa is gentle as a lamb and tiny as a hummingbird, dark haired and pretty as if she could be a queen. If she was Queen Esther in the Bible she looks like a king would save a nation for her. Her eyes sparkle and her skin is smooth as a white feather and I've seen every one of my brothers look at her and turn beet red. They can't open their mouths when she is around and they trip over their own feet like puppies.

I got my shimmy on and my drawers and one underskirt and I hear a funny whimper and turn around, and there with a knife big enough to skin a grizzly is a nasty dirty pair of men. They are wearing skins and wooly beards all filthy with tobacco spit. The one with the knife has got Savannah by the mouth with the knife to her throat and cuts her a little so blood drips fast on her wet skin. The other one is grinning real mean like and says, any one makes a sound my brother will gut her 'fore she's dead.

All of the Lawrence girls are whimpering and yet I notice the men are staring hard at Ulyssa. As one makes a move toward her I stepped back a bit into the bushes. Alice saw me and I pointed to her to run, but as she does, Savannah lets out a cry and there is a new cut on her little throat. Alice crouched down like a scared rabbit and I scrunch myself down low. He throws Ulyssa to the ground and punched her with his fist hard in the stomach, and commenced to taking down his pants.

In my head I am screaming fight back Ulyssa! Fight back honey!

Pretty soon Savannah is crying softly and Ulyssa is moaning but he's got her mouth under his hand and he's hard on her. Something comes into my mind from the Bible about being sore afraid and I never knew what that was before.

When he stands up he is all bloody and he takes Savannah by the hair and the other fellow gets ready to take a turn on poor Ulyssa, but he says pointing to Alice, she's next. Run Alice! Fight back Ulyssa! Fight back Savannah! But I cannot make a sound for Savannah will die as this fellow is cutting her just to watch her hurt. Ulyssa lays there meek as a dove and takes it and I am filled with fury that has no name.

Without a thought in my head that fury takes hold of me and I run back to the camp barefooted through the brush. Not saying a word to anyone I yank a rifle from a wagon seat and sling onto Roses' bare warm back. My toes curl around her and my hair is flying and my skirts are up to my waist. I let go of the reins and steer her with my legs back to the water tank and hold on like an Indian and fire that rifle first at the man holding Savannah, the one who had already hurt Ulyssa. After I get him between his eyes, the other fellow lifted his self up to see and I got him in the side, probably through the gut, and he rolls off Ulyssa. I slung myself down and grabbed up Alice and then Savannah who had fainted away hard. You girls, I hollered, get your sister into that water and clean her up.

They all three raised Ulyssa up and towards the water then Ulyssa lifted her poor bruised face and screamed at something behind me. The gut shot one was moving, and I gave him another dose. When I turned back around I nearly fainted myself for standing so close to me I could hear him breathing was an Indian man in skins and bear claws and face paint. He was tall and brown as a tree, and he looked at me hard. Without saying anything he pulled a flint knife from his belt and took a scalp from both those men. He held them toward me and shook them kind of like he was a giving them to me. I pushed them back with the tip of the rifle and he said some words and dropped them scalps and then disappeared into the bushes. Only then did I hear his pony's hoofs.

We was back to the wagons before the men, and there was a darkness in my insides like I never knew before. When Papa and Mr. Lawrence got back they wanted to know what was the shooting. So I told my Mama and Papa, and then there was the sound of the girls' explaining in their wagon, I could tell from the whispers and then the tears.

I have never felt so sorry and so angry and so ashamed all at once. Mr. Lawrence went to see the men's bodies and you could hear him roar like a stuck bull from the woods when he seen them. Mama and Papa just fret, walking around, not able to sit still for a second.

I want to run. I want to run and run and go far away, back to the Territory or off to some foreign land where there is no more sorrow. If I could follow Clover to Canaan that seems like a good spot. But I am too scared to move a muscle. I just sit here, aching to run away, and stiffened up so's my legs wobble like a newborn calf, thinking about running and yet sitting holding on to this milk stool like it was the last handle on the earth there is. Mama came and held my shoulders and patted my head real gentle. She didn't say nothing but her hand on my head did.

September 2, 1881

My face feels all pulled down and I declare I don't think I know how to smile no more. Mama is crying saying it is her fault for letting us go but it is not. Albert don't say anything to me but he pulled all my stickers out from running for Rose in bare feet, and poor sick Ernest raised himself up and told me I done a good thing and God surely knows it.

September 5, 1881

We move on like stone statues. I feel like my legs are made of wooden branches and my heart is a hard rock inside. For days I do not even tie up my hair and it flows around me like an Indian's. I can't find my bonnet and my traveling clothes are ragged and so is my soul.

Papa and I have a fever from so many mosquito bites they are about to eat us alive. They torment Mrs. Hoover and her face is swole up but she don't notice, just drives them oxes like a haunt. Worst of all, none of the Lawrences, not even Savannah, will have a thing to do with me. They turn their heads when I talk and will not walk near me. Mama said she has heard of Quakers doing this it is called Shunned, for some act of sin. I asked Mama was it a sin to do what I done, and she said no, it was the same as David slaying Goliath, it was only to save Ulyssa and the others, not because of meanness that I did it. I would do it again, too. I am not sorry, but this has hurt my heart and spirit more than all the other trials, for being forsaken is worse than being killed.

September 7, 1881

I heard Mr. Lawrence saying to Papa that he thinks these Indians are Comanches and this is their land and we are trespassers, then they get into a big argument about whether or not it is right to fight them for our very lives. Mr. Lawrence says they have been mistreated by the U.S. Government Indian Agents and I'm sure that's so, but we have no way to talk their language nor do they seem to want to listen. In my head I remember the day the Indian man came and hollered at our camp and hadn't hurt anyone yet and I think he was trying to say something, but no one will lift their eyes when I speak so I don't say anything.

Ernest says he wants to get up and sit by the fire tonight for dinner and so I am happy for the company as Albert lifts him from the wagon. Mr. Lawrence is making Ernest a wooden leg like his own and it seems to be a fine one all lined in the pocket with lambs wool. Soon he will be good enough to try it out. Good old Ernest lightens my spirit and he keeps looking at me with admiring in his eyes.

I took Savannah's reader and her newspaper and laid them on her wagon seat tonight when she was asleep. It is as if I have done something to them and I can't understand it at all.

Just as I begin to try to remember all that had happened, I see the fire sparkle in a pair of eyes in the bushes and I put my remembering away for another time and stay close to the shadows so I can watch.

We are closing in on San Angelo and should be two or three more days. It seems Papa was right, it is good ranch land, rolling hills and streams and not dry like around El Paso. It looks as if it gets good rain. There is brush and thick grass and it seems to be good grazing country. It is still rough going, and the brush sometimes hides big rocks that seem to jump up to try to smash our wagon wheels and trip our horses. Before noon, that rigged up axle broke. Papa goes to Mrs. Hoover's wagon without even asking her and unlashes one of the spare axles and commences to jack up our wagon and put the wheels on the new axle. It is a strong hard wood and too big for our wagon so the wheels will not track with the front ones, but it is sound and will keep us moving ahead of the Indians.

While he is doing that, Mama says to me to butcher a chicken for noon dinner and I picked up the hatchet and took one from the pen and walked to a fallen tree to use for a chopping block. As I lay that chicken down she stretched out her neck and calmly laid her head on the wood making little cooing sounds. I lifted the hatchet and shook her. Fight back, chicken, I said. Then I hollered at it, fight back, chicken! In a minute I was yelling Fight back Ulyssa! Fight back Ulyssa! over and over like a lunatic.

I was standing there shaking all over and crying out and I could not chop that chicken to save my life. Suddenly over my shoulder I hear these words in Savannah's voice, Well, you are WRONG, Papa! and then Savannah is there and taking the chicken and the hatchet from me. Everyone has circled around me while I was crying. Savannah says, I'll do it for you, it's all right, then she bursts into tears and drops the hatchet and the chicken and throws her arms around me and we both cry to beat all.

Harland took to chasing that chicken to have her for lunch and calling out come here, little Drumsticks, and we all smiled for the first time in many, many days. Before too long that chicken is turned to drumsticks and I felt hungry enough for two people but still had to share. Still it is a good meal and we all feel tattered but friendly again. Then it occurs to Papa that we are still in a line and easy to attack, but we are going to push on quickly and we begin to move out.

Not five turns of a wheel and we roll down a little ridge and into a wide, spread out circle of what looks like a hundred Comanche warriors with their bows drawn. As we look behind they have closed ranks and surround us completely. We have our rifles but don't want to draw down fire because we are a lost cause.

About forty Indians break from the line and come forward and calmly surround our entire herd of horses. As we sit helpless and watch, there goes our future and all our stake in San Angelo. They have bows drawn, but they do not move to attack. Then one Indian man cuts from the line and moves into the herd, weaving through the horse backs until he comes to a roan with a white nose wearing a rope halter. He scoops up the reins in his hand and pulls Rose from the bunch and starts toward us. Calm as you please he comes right up and looks us all over, rides over to me and holds out the reins. I took Rose from him and then he turned his pony like a top on hind legs and galloped away. The same Indian was the one who scalped the bad men and offered me the scalps. There was a different kind of respect in his eyes when he looked at me than anyone ever had before.

September 19, 1881

We have made San Angelo and it is just a little place of a dozen wood buildings and some tents, and within a week my Papa had grown badly infected in his arm and had a spell of pain in his chest and grabbed his heart and died. That very day I had talked to him about our plans and he said, You all will do fine, just fine, and, I'm tired, girl, just so tired. Let me sleep some and then we'll plan more. And then he went to sleep and then he roused and said he was strangling and, Help me! to Mama, and then fell down in the floor.

I have no idea what took my Papa away. How can we go on without Papa, I just don't know. He was wiry and strong and yet gentle always. Oh, Papa. I always felt like I had a hold on things when there was Papa to turn to.

My brothers are sitting around asking each other over and over what will we do now. They ask me what do I think Papa wants us to do, as we have no horse ranch, and almost no money to start up one. We would have to hunt mustangs and break them ourselves, just us four children. Likely we will all starve. Ernest says Papa would want us to stay here and last it out. Harland says he wants to go home. He don't understand how we have sold that place and have no home to go to. Albert just looks at me and shakes his head. He says what do I think but every time I try to think Papa's voice comes into my head telling some tale or giving directions about a good way to trim barb wire or such.

Albert, I says, we are about give out now, and I hate to think of traveling all that way again through all that sorrow. Yet staying here means trying to spread out our money thinner than smoke. He said to me he will ask up and down for work, but as I saw him walking off, he crossed back and forth between the buildings and I seen his shoulders hang lower every step. We have lost all and are living in a little hotel room temporarily.

Mama is just a hollow ghost of a person now and don't eat unless you make her, nor comb her hair. She just sits and holds her pilgrims progress quilt and rocks back and forth. The sound of the squeaking rocker is reminding me she is still with us and I think she will get better in time.

September 21, 1881

Mrs. Hoover sold out her wagon and gave us the money for a stake, saying she wanted no part of it and would have burnt it to the ground long ago rather than go on this foolish pioneering with Mr. Hoover, and besides she had a inheritance and was going back to Boston where she belongs. I saw her to the train and she was wearing the finest travel duds I ever saw and had four trunks of dresses she had been dragging in that Conestoga to load on the train.

Ernest is beginning to walk now, and he and Albert and I have decided it is up to us to take care of Mama for the rest of her days.

Albert asked us would we trust him with the money, so maybe he could put a clear head to it all if he knew just how much we have amongst us. He said did we agree with him that some kind of action was better than sitting and waiting our fate, which don't appear to be a good one. I for one told him that taking a quandary by the horns and wrestling with it was a better plan than expecting it to go away. So I handed him my money, and we shook on it. Harland did it too, but Ernest was mad. Finally, though, he saw no other way for us to make it in this life, so he did the same.

September 30, 1881

Today I got a wonderful surprise. Albert was gone all morning and comes back riding in like a drunken cowboy. He has gone and asked Savannah to marry him and she is going with us back to the Territory. Since he will have a wife too, Albert has bought Mrs. Hoover's old Conestoga back at a bargain because he told the livery man he could tell it had seen some rough trails.

Albert has met a man selling pecan seedlings with some apple and peach and pears, and he remembered how well trees grew in parts of the Territory we passed through. He took some of our money and bought most of the seedlings and we are going home. We are waiting for a wagon train that is being gotten up and some cavalry soldiers will guard the way. It is the first time I noticed that Albert is a man for sure, not just a brother, and I will have a sister and we will plant some trees for our children and their children. Last night I dreamed about a little house at a bend in a creek with glass in all the windows.

Albert married Savannah yesterday afternoon in a circle of strangers and our little families gathered near the wagon train. There wasn't no preacher in town nor any sign of a judge or even a lawman, so the Captain in charge of the Cavalry troops said some kind words from the Bible, but he mixed it up a little bit. He is a tall fellow, my head only comes up to his shoulder. He is decked out like for a parade for this little country wedding, and he has clear grey eyes that seem to see like a hawk. It is a fancy sight, and I wish Papa could be here and Mama could realize what's happening.

Ernest, who was standing real close behind me so he can whisper in my ear, said, Sarah look at Albert's pants and I did and you could see Albert's boots a trembling inside his pants legs. Although it was a nice ceremony and Albert looked as clean and scrubbed as I have ever seen him, every time he looked at Savannah he got this look like he was going to faint sick or something.

Ulyssa is standing a little back with a big bonnet over her face. She is pale and quieter than ever she was before and any time she speaks she is pleasant and kind but there is a cloud of darkness that slips across her face just as she opens her mouth. She only says dinner's ready or milk the cow or wash your face Alice, as if she don't see a future any more just here and now. It pains me too much to think of her sorrows so I just talk to her the same way, about mending a buttonhole or such.

Afterward there's cheers all around from the wagon folks and some music and dancing is put out by a couple of fellers. One is a Mexican man from San Angelo who plays the guitar so amazing well I could listen to it for hours. The other is a boy coming with the wagons, just a young feller like Harland but he is a fine hand with a fiddle and can hit a tune with just a person calling out the name. There is a lady with a lap harp who says she can play and does a piece but when the feller gets to fiddling she only half keeps up so sometimes she rattled spoons on her hands and it's just a fine evening for a wedding.

I never danced like they all do but everyone is feeling friendly and the soldiers all want to dance with the ladies. My Mama says no good girl would dance with a soldier and she says it with a look on her face that would scorch a man for just wanting to be a soldier. Mostly I danced with Louisianna and Alice round and round like little girls do and we danced around Harland who made some sashaying and we laughed 'til our sides hurt. Over my shoulder I watched Albert and Savannah in the middle. They are grinning at each other and whispering, and my heart suddenly feels like it is in my throat. How I would like to have a fellow look at me like that.

Some men and women made Albert and Savannah get in their new wagon and acted like the men were the horses and dragged that wagon out onto the flatland a ways. The Mexican man played a beautiful love song and sang to them in Mexican and even though the words are different I felt as if I had a knot in my throat from the sweet sound of that song. Then there was lots of crazy cheers. I know they'd never sleep with all that caterwallin and us dancing to beat the band.

The next morning it was a hard time to say goodbye to the Lawrences. Mr. Lawrence looks real old and sad and tired and kind of disapproving, but he is licked and can't keep all them daughters forever. I am sorry to leave my new sisters and I made them promise to write me as I will write them. Savannah has cried and kissed them all three times. She keeps looking back waving her hand to them. Alice gave Mama a wild rose she picked and Mama pressed it into her Bible. As they slip out of sight behind a little ridge I feel this awful pain at my eyes and can't seem to keep them from running with water, although it is not tears. The sky is heavy and low and clouds are moving much faster overhead than the wind is on the ground. Rose is tied to the cook's pantry in back. Our axles don't match but our wheels are turning.

November 27, 1881

Albert don't want his new wife to have to drive the team. It is so loaded with the seedlings that he feels shamed to ride too and wants to save the horses. It would be better if we had bought some oxes instead of horses to pull this load. Sometimes Savannah begs him to stretch her legs and so we walk together and Albert drives. It is not hard as this large wagon train ain't making good time like we did coming over. But it is safer to have all these people together and so far we have no sign of Indians. Likely they got all the horses they need now.

Savannah says I ought not to wear skirts above the ankles and Mama up and says I declare but Sarah, you are eighteen now and we missed your birthday in San Angelo. Well, it was the farthest thing from my mind but I see that I need some changes and we set out in the evening to cut a long skirt from some yard goods. It is brown and that is not my favorite color but it will be new.

Mama will add a length to my petticoat and I will be a lady. Well I don't feel like a lady so I asked Savannah about things.

She says I'm just fine and she is proud to have me for a sister but I begin watching her and see how she does just so. I have to make myself think to take small steps and not walk like I was always keeping up with Papa and Albert and Ernest in the old days. I notice she don't laugh out loud nor talk free to people but holds her peace until it seems lady like to answer. I don't know if I can get to talk genteel as she does because she has been to the tenth grade advancement and has taken a teachers' test and passed it.

We are packed to the rafters in pecan seedlings all wrapped in sackcloth bundles which we water the roots every evening. We have eight horses pulling and two more spares who aren't good teamsters but they are better than none. With Rose makes eleven but I would never ruin her by putting a yoke on her neck, even if we lost all them others.

There is a pack of travelers in our line, and some of every kind of person I 'spect there is, even two families of colored freedmen and one of chinamen, one of mormons, and some folks that look regular but don't talk our language and no one knows what it is they talk nor can talk to them in any way. Some folks started a commotion about the Colored folks wagons and the Chinas and Mormons and foreigners, but Captain Elliot gave them all a speech about how none of us could leave without anyone he had been placed in the charge of. He has a loud voice and he talks like he is used to being obeyed. Seems to me this is a suspicious lot of folks and not too friendly as they all are inclined to hate each other. I will be sorely glad when this traveling is over and we have made a home again.

November 30, 1881

Today it began to rain just as breakfast was cleared up and as the time passed it came harder and harder until the train was forced to stop. We have opened all the water barrels to collect the fresh rain, and tethered all the stock and there is little to do but wait and sew. So my new skirt is done and I am proud to wear it.

It will be a lean day and I don't like having to eat cold food left from last night as there is not a dry stick of wood in miles and there will be no fires today or tomorrow either. Folks sit in their wagons and as I look out the wagons all look deserted and empty and the train disappears off in the distance like a line of white sheets fluttering just above the ground.

December 1, 1881

At sunset tonight the sky turned miraculous colors and gold shined off everything in the land and it reminded me I have always wished for a yellow sunbonnet. Mama used to say yellow won't go with my hair which is too dark to be called blonde and too light to be brown. She said stick with a nice blue or at least dark brown to match my eyes. I have got some freckles from not wearing a bonnet often enough on this trip. Savannah is lucky.

I know my face has gotten brown from riding in the sun. The truth is there is nothing much I can do, I am plain and not pretty like the Lawrence girls. Savannah is shorter than me and has got a fine figure and I am straight and thin like my brothers, and she has all that wavy dark hair and mine is straight as a stick and cantankerous, although it is thick enough for two people to share. I know Mama would say that the heart is what is important, but I think if I was shorter and filled out more and prettier I would like that just fine. I can look eye to eye with lots of men, and mostly they want to be taller than a girl. There's nothing special about my figure, either, so it will likely be a hard thing for me to take up with a fellow. I'll bet men would stand in line to marry any of the Lawrence girls with all that black hair and those blue eyes, even Alice with the bucked teeth. If I had a yellow sunbonnet I would wear it always and keep from getting more freckles.

December 2, 1881

Today Savannah was watching me and Ernest clean the rifles and guns. I always did like the smell of cleaning guns. It is a cooling smell like a rain coming. She says to me Sarah, show me to shoot a gun.

Well, Albert was not keen on this but he can't say nothing because it don't put him out any. I told Albert how important it would be if we was set upon by the Comanches again just to have one more hand among us. Well, he says that's why we got this here army, but he agreed Savannah ought to learn at least to fire a pistol, so after dinner we set up a row of cans and sticks aways off. The pistol kept popping up in the air and she jumped before she even let fly with the trigger, so I said try the rifle, maybe that is your best shot.

Savannah says she will try and put the stock against her arm instead of her shoulder. It gave her a kick and knocked her back so she sat down and began to cry out, my arm! my arm!

Albert was all bug-eyed and made her go right to the wagon and roll up her sleeve and show him. Then he judged it was not broken but blue bruised. It was getting dark, so we went to the inside of the wagon circle for now. It quit raining but turned cold that seeps into your bones.

Our family was sitting quiet in a circle and Ernest began to talk about how Savannah might hold the rifle different but she should let her arm get good again before she tries, and she is agreeable to this. Then a fellow near by says real loud, It ain't no good for no woman to learn to shoot any how, least of all from some skinny little girl. He says this to some other fellows around and their women sit around and nod and send us mean looks like they are too good for the likes of us.

I thought maybe it wasn't lady like to shoot a gun but Savannah is darning socks by the firelight, and without missing a stitch she doesn't look up but says to our family, When those Comanches come back Missis will have to throw her knitting at them.

Then Ernest laughs low and says, That will surely scare them, he seen her knitting. We all had us a good hearty chuckle out of their ears.

December 3, 1881

My feet have paid the price of growing and walking too much at once. I will ask up and down the fires tonight if there is a shoemaker amongst us. Mr. Barston's wife is heavy and expecting to be confined any day now. She looks mighty peaked and will be glad to have that over with. She looks as rangey and meager as any spavined old mare I ever saw and being used to breeding animals by nature, we all know she will have a mean time. Even though she has three other living children, she is missing some teeth and is nearly bald headed, I saw her hair is missing in patches when her bonnet blew off yesterday.

I heard Mr. Barston talking to the army Captain about when her time comes and the Captain looked real angry but I don't know why. Then I hear some other soldier saying about how any one having babies on the trail is bound to be left behind and to take their chances.

The Captain says back he wasn't going to leave anyone in this Comanche territory but any man who'd make a baby before a trip like this ought to be torn apart by horses. Then he looks up and sees me standing there and he says he is mighty sorry for saying them words in my hearing. I was just so red faced I couldn't talk at all and I turned away with my wash bucket and hurried back with the water.

Mama must be right. Soldiers are a dirty bunch and that was a dirty thing to say. Still, I know you don't want to drive a mare in foal and it has got to be true for people too. I will stay away from that Captain Elliot as he is a coarse and mean soul.

I have been up and down the bunch and have asked about some boots to trade for some hand work or washing, or some cobbling to be done but there is none. Ernest and me are trading walking and driving the wagon. Mama can't seem to be able to manage driving it so sometimes she likes to walk with me and Savannah.

Tomorrow being Sunday we will stay put for the day but we will not rest as there is harness to mend and washing to do and all. Ernest was talking to those folks that was talking out about Savannah and me shooting the rifle. He says their name is Meyers and they are from Missouri State. They say they are the ones who made the Captain stop for Sunday and asked Ernest wasn't he glad that some folks was Christian enough to stand up for what's right?

He said back that hurrying was important with Indians and bad weather on our heels but that maybe some prayer wouldn't hurt. Then that Ernest gets to admiring that fellow Mike Meyers' fancy rifle. It is a long barrel Winchester and got some carved bird dogs on the stock. Mike Meyers begins to brag that he can shoot a tick off a dog with that rifle, and his brother Billy says he can shoot the eye off the tick next. Ernest says, that must be some shooting and tomorrow he would surely like to see some shooting like that.

Their ma is the one who looked at me as if I was low down, and she says Not on the Lord's day, but her boys whine and say it is not gambling but just a show of how fine their rifle is so she says okay. Then she says to Mama something about how a mother has to always watch her youngerns don't she, and Mama just smiled.

Mama sometimes just looks into yonder and smiles and that was the look she was wearing this evening but Mrs. Meyers nods and smiles back like she knows what Mama is thinking. I am sure she don't know at all.

Then that rascal Ernest says he got family that's a right good shot but not himself, and would they allow some contest. Pretty soon word of this spreads through the camp and then all we hear is soldiers talking about who is a good shot, farmers talking about who is a good shot, their women just roll their eyes. I think this is a way to waste lots of powder and lead because it seems now every man here is about to be shooting ticks off every dog in the country come morning. I think I will hide our dogs Toobuddy and Bear in case.

All of a sudden Mama says she will hold a Sunday School and to tell all of the children to come tomorrow. Mama has not spoke five words in a row since San Angelo but we all go to bed glad to see her with some spark in her eyes. When I bed down I hear her praying in the dark. It is a good old familiar sound, and as I write this just before I go off to sleep, I think Mama is back with us.

December 4, 1881

Sunday morning comes and it is the first clear skies since San Angelo. We got breakfast early and just like she said, Mama got out her Bible and her spectacles and sat to wait for the children. Before long there is a circle of youngerns and she opens the Bible and makes like she is reading to them. I know she has just got the whole thing in her head and can't really read it, but it is good to hear her voice. After prayers we all went to eat dinner. We are having quail roasted on a spit since it is easy and not too much work for a Sunday meal.

The Meyers are camped too near us again and they are eating cold mush and sniffing the air as if their noses could eat it. Mrs. Meyers says out loud how she don't 'low no cooking or working on the Lord's Day and we just turn our backs. I guess we been through some hard times and all are pretty thin especially Ernest who looks like a stiff wind would send him to the Territories ahead of us all, and if the Lord is going to grudge us a quail for dinner well then that's that.

I am smiling that they are sniffing the air so hard and Harland says, Sarah what are you grinning about? but I don't say nothing.

Captain Elliot has said that there will be no soldiers firing shots except at his warrant or something like that, meaning they will not waste their shot and powder. He advises us settlers, as he calls us, to do the same. This contest is plum foolishness to me, and I am sorry Ernest got to talking about it, but I feel like Mike Meyers' boasting must have been more than he could take and boys like to brag to each other.

Pretty soon the men are setting up some cans and sticks out in a line and about ten or so begin to shoot at their marks. I hear them but I don't go because I know Ernest ain't no shot and Albert is busy stitching a patch on his canvas cover. Every now and then Harland comes running up telling us who is shooting what, and Ernest is over there watching, just quiet.

I have got a line up of shirts and drawers and such drying in the sun in about an hour, and still they are shooting. I can tell they have got more careful now because there is time between each shot to aim and I can feel the air tighten up as they take aim and then bang! the shot, and I can hear if it struck a rock or dirt or a can or just the wind.

Well, then there is quiet and here comes Ernest up to me. He says Sarah get your rifle, and I made a face at him but I did. I walked up to them folks gathered around and I can see there is a big crowd, almost as big as for Albert's and Savannah's wedding.

Ernest says real loud, Look here, Mike Meyers is betting his fancy rifle that nobody can outshoot him. He done real good so far, but my sister here can drop a Indian riding hell-bent on a bare backed pony in the blink of an eye. He hands me the rifle and I see there is some kind of poison in his eyes and he is not funning he is mad.

I said to him, This here's a waste of powder, brother, but everyone is waiting and I wanted to fuss at him but instead I said, What are we shooting at.

He pointed yonder to a tree and I see Mike has set up a line of little stones on a level branch. He shoots one at a time and five out of six goes down. Some other fellow scoots out and sets up another line of six stones.

I say to Ernest, Get Albert to do this here, but he says no, take a shot. I don't like to have all these folks staring at me and there is Mama and Savannah too, and Harland is laughing in his hand. Well, I said out loud, it's no different to me, but I think I can hit it. I aim and get just air and I hear some folks chuckling.

Mike Meyers says, Aw this is stupid to shoot against a girl.

Everyone gets quiet as I aim and I stop for a second and say, Well, I never had no target to sit still for me so maybe I'd just swing around and fire.

That Mike Meyers laughs at me and his Ma is there looking haughty. So I up with the barrel and fired five times fast and they are all quiet as all the six stones are gone, one broke up and knocked the extra one down with it.

He says it don't count if I get two with one shot cause that means I didn't hit it square and only rickershaysed it off or hit the branch. The fellow sets up four rocks on the branch and Mike shoots all of them down but he takes five shots.

I asked the fellow putting up the rocks to check if there's any holes in the branch yet and he says no, but when he puts up my rocks there is one that is a little speck of a pebble and half as big.

Just as I lift the rifle Mike shouts in my ear, Don't get nervous girl! real loud and I have to wait while everyone makes some noise. Well, then I whipped up the barrel again and let go four times and dropped all four rocks. You could see them flying out past the tree and even where they hit the ground. Just as I shot the last one Mike lets out a Indian war whoop and something in my insides turned cold and scared and before I know what I'm doing I turned fast at the noise and draw a bead on his head.

People all around suck in their breaths and I put it down feeling sheepish. That war whoop is a sound makes me know I have to fight and he didn't know that but he nearly found out. Then out of the silence I hear one man laughing at the whole thing. It is Captain Elliot who has been watching it all.

Then soon it's everyone laughing and cheering and saying Mike give her the rifle. Well, he was sorely put out to do that, but he hands it over to me and I looked at the pretty stock and the metal and the long shiny barrel for a second. I picked it up and aimed it at the tree then hefted it and sighted it and gave it back to him. It is too heavy to aim and too big and ponderous to carry so I say, No wonder you can't shoot straight, with this big old clumsy thing, and did my best to look down at him.

He still had his mouth open from being mistook for a Indian and he didn't say nothing but his Ma sort of growled and says That's what you get for gambling on the Lord's Day.

Everyone laughs and we are all having a good time except the Meyers who all leave in a stew to go eat some more cold mush. Ernest is mad at me for not keeping the pretty rifle.

December 9, 1881

Passed five graves yesterday on the trail. Two more today and one was dug up by wolves. Mama cried when she saw that but we reminded her how careful we buried Clover that no wolves could dig his grave. There is a strong wind today and it feels cold down through all our clothes. My shoes are about gone but still there is not much to be done. I am going to ask around tonight if there is anyone with a piece of leather goods and I will make myself some moccasins at least to keep the rocks off my feet. We are aways from the rainy place we left two days ago and it is dry and dusty but cold. Ever since the shooting contest folks have been more lighthearted and friendly and I think it makes everybody feel good to see a bragger get his due.

I have gotten the loan of a fifth grade reader from a family named Willburn for a few days. Their boy Rudy is the one that plays the fiddle so fine so I thanked him again for playing for Albert's wedding. Savannah has begun to teach school in the evenings and there are at least fifteen children coming every day, and more will be to Mama's Sunday School.

I am very troubled that all that shooting wasn't lady like and I feel embarrassed because some of them soldiers are still talking about who could outshoot me if they had only been given the chance. One of them who is young and fresh mouthed rode up along side our wagon one day and said did I learn to shoot from Doc Holliday and did I know who he was, and that he was a personal friend of his. Across his shoulder I see that Captain Elliot watching this way.

I turned my head and didn't look at that boy. Finally, when he left, the Captain sent him to the rear of the line. I didn't try to tell that boy we just came from the Arizona Territory and know better than to go near a town as bad as Tombstone, and I do know who that Doc Holliday is and I have heard he is the lowest kind of man, drunken and dirty and carrying on with fancy women. I don't care to know any soldier boy who rode with the likes of that.

Savannah and I did up the dishes after supper and packed up the pantry real tight, taking stock of all the provisions. Then I said to her, Let's wash our hair and Mama's, and she was willing so we set up a kettle to heat on the fire.

When I took Mama by the hand and led her to the chair where we needed her to sit, she stood in front of it, just quiet and staring. Come on, Mama, sit down, I said.

She stood there and stood there. We did Savannah's hair. We did mine. Mama just looked forlorn. Mama, I said. Mama, I called out. Then I took her shoulders and made her look at me and said, Mama, come sit here, please.

Then I shook her a little, and she looked at me like a hurt lamb, and leaned her face to one side and said, Is it Sunday? Then she went right back to looking out past forever, or wherever she is looking.

No, Mama, I said. It ain't Sunday. It don't have to be Sunday for you to talk. Come out of there. Come back here, Mama. You are acting touched. Then I let go of her arms, and she got tears in her eyes, and blinked and stared, and she walked away and sat on the stool where she had ate supper. I was ashamed for what I just said, and I looked at Savannah and she just looked at me sorrowful. I wanted to throw myself down and cry like a baby, but I just said, I'm going to walk a bit. There's plenty of time to dry our hair by the fire in a while, and it isn't even very cold tonight. And I wrapped a long towel around my hair, and I walked and walked, around the camp and through the soldiers. And I looked around at all the people talking and carrying on. Some was laughing and some had crying children they was hushing, and some had gone to bed already. And all of them had their trials I 'spect, but I felt full of meanness at them all 'cause they were all talking and none of them had Mama just staring out yonder. I am surely a low down sort. It ain't Mama's fault she has lost her mind. It is only me losing patience.

Then I went back to our place and sat by Mama and put my head in her lap, and said I was sorry. I tried by wishing and praying to make her recognize me and put her hand on my head, just for a little pat, just a little sign that she could come back if she wanted to. But she just sat there. Tears ran off my face sideways onto her lap. And she didn't move until Savannah came and said, Mother Prine, come and go to bed.

December 11, 1881

Something hit my bonnet, blowing in the wind. It startled me some but I was more startled when I grabbed hold of it. It is a piece of paper, but most important it is a piece of a book. A page from a story. It is page eighty-seven, and starts with, carried far out to sea. And the little boat went on into the gale, and ends with, beautiful woman clutched the letter to her bosom in fear as she saw, and then the page is finished and there isn't no more. On the other side is a little pencil picture of a big water and a little ship. I have read it over and over, trying to wish the rest of the story out of the page.

Who would sail away from the woman and what is a gale I do not know. What was in her letter, nor why was she afraid, it does not say. Most likely there is Comanches on the horizon. She has a dress of scarlet velvet and pearls in her hair, and I don't know what that is either but it must be beautiful and someday I want a dress of scarlet velvet and pearls to put in my hair. I put this page in my cigar box to keep and I think about what kind of yard goods it must be she is wearing called scarlet velvet.

December 12, 1881

Captain Elliot had a meeting of everyone tonight and said scouts have seen Indians following us alongside in the hills. They are staying with us but not too close and he wants us to be on guard for attack. Soldiers will post sentries to watch and I figure that means just like we did on the trip out. The Prines didn't say anything as we are now accustomed to Indian fighting and know what to do and went to load up our rifles and pistols, and keep them close by us. <u>Accustomed</u> is what the scarlet velvet woman was. She was accustomed to her sorrows it said, as she had been accustomed to great riches and fine foods. We are accustomed to Indian wars and sorrows and traveling fast and folks dying.

December 14, 1881

Toward noon today with all these wagons making pretty good time for the first time, Captain Elliot has passed the word down we are not to stop for a meal but move on. Maybe some folks are afraid and it has made them move quicker, but still not much compared to a band of Indians on light ponies. Suddenly out of the noise and dust there is a woman's scream. Everyone pulls up to a stop about as quick as fifty-one wagons can, and there it is again.

There is no sign of Indians but there is another scream. The soldiers begin to holler to get moving, then the word comes back it is

Mrs. Barston's child coming. Mama and Savannah and I are walking and just as we let our breath out that it is not Indians, we see
them on the hillside. No sooner did we spot them than they spotted us, and here they come, that sound of war whoops and yells
that makes my insides all cold. There is a confusion and a cloud of
dust as the wagons stop and some don't stop enough and bump
each other. Some folks are frightened and begin to whip their
team to run away.

The soldiers begin firing back, and we have no time to circle up
as Captain Elliot is trying to make folks do even though they are
scared. They just all stand and take it. The Indians ride around and
arrows are coming in. The three of us women have taken cover
inside the wagon but the pecan seedlings have the whole wagon
and there is not much room to hide.

An arrow hits our wagon and sticks in the hoop under the canvas, and then the canvas is burst into flame. Before we can all
think, Savannah has jumped up and takes a pan where she was
soaking some socks and throws it at the flames and it is out but
smoking badly. I had my rifle by me, but there is not a good shot
and the Indians are too far away.

I see another wagon and it is in high flames by now. The family
has jumped out and just as they did they are cut down by arrows
and gunfire. An Indian jumped off his horse and is standing over
the woman who is bleeding from the mouth with a knife in his
hand and here comes Captain Elliot riding like a madman, his
horse almost on its head as he pulls up and lays that Indian man
open with his sword. He has a pistol in the other hand and shoots
another Indian at the same time. Then he plunges into the middle
of them, and it is a frightening thing. I'm glad he is on our side. He
must be fierce and wicked and brave all at the same time. All is
suddenly quiet, they have retreated to the hills. A bugle sounds
and the soldiers are moving quickly to chase them.

As I write this tonight by our fire, my hands just won't stop
shaking, and I hold my jaw tight to keep my teeth from rattling.
Every time the Indians come I am more scared than before. I
wonder how many of those Indian ponies are our horse ranch
they are riding away on.

December 15, 1881

The family that all died were the foreigners family. Suddenly it seems as if they were real important to us, but we just didn't know it before they all died. There is nothing left of their wagon to save either, except two of their horses, the others were put down because they were burned real bad. It is real sad to see the little crosses made up over their graves with no names on them. I hope when I die my marker will at least have my name on it somewhere.

All around us the horses are sniffing and high and I know what that means. They smell the Indians following us, maybe even hear the Indian horses sniffing back. All is quiet but we are nervous and touchy.

Ernest said tonight that he wants to go off and be a soldier and that when we get to the Territory, he will follow the Army to the fort instead of staying with us. Mama just nodded and looked far off.

Albert and Savannah said long speeches to him to talk him out of the plan. But I could see by something in his eyes he is set on this. He hasn't been the same since that shooting contest, and I was counting on him helping to plant the trees and all, and build a house for Mama, but he says, That just ain't how it's going to be.

So then I said, What if they won't take you because of your leg? and he threw a rock and walked away. I found out later he went and talked to Captain Elliot and signed himself up. Ernest has always been my favorite brother and I don't know what's gotten into him, but maybe if I was a man that lost his leg I would know.

Mrs. Barston had been screaming the day through, and finally, we stopped to eat and the ladies gathered around to see if any had an opinion about what would help her. The poor woman had been laboring right through the Indian fighting, and was in a terrible state. She was getting weaker and that old Mrs. Meyers says right out loud that she won't make it. It has been two days of her laboring with that child and some of the women are whispering that child might be dead by now. Her other children are all puny and starved looking, just like her.

Finally she has that child and I was there with some other ladies, but Savannah was not and I am glad. She had an awful looking child, and dead. When she saw the child was dead, Mrs. Barston just fell sort of quiet like and late after we had fed and watered the stock and watered all the trees, we heard she too died.

December 16, 1881

Now it seems as if all these folks that were so mean spirited and hateful before suddenly know they need each other to stay alive, and they are much more friendly and willing to share things. All are included, even the colored families and the Chinamen and Mormons who look just like everybody. I don't know why folks don't want them around as they talk our language and all, and call each other Sister Clara and Sister Nina and Sister Lucille. They are three grown sisters and one of them's husband, and about six children all sharing that one wagon and sleeping on the ground at night.

While Savannah teaches the little children school, I stand nearby and listen. I know she knows I'm listening and she is helping me to learn reading and writing without being embarrassed because of being full grown.

Captain Elliot has put two sergeants in charge of platoons that will take charge of groups of wagons he said. We are split up with assigned groups with each platoon and a sergeant, and now he is telling us he doesn't care who anyone is or what they do, or if they are sick or in childbirth, all the wagons will travel together, there will be no splitting off the wagon train.

Well, it is good news that all are included, because I have found by much pointing to my sorry shoes that the China people's Papa is a cobbler. As I was sitting on their tiny stool to have my feet measured, the Chinese family gathered around and talked in their little bird sounds and smiled, and they offered me a cup of tea which was very good. Well, I have got my skirt lifted a little bit for him to measure my feet, and there is that soldier boy who thinks he is friends with Doc Holliday peeking over a harrow hanging off their wagon and grinning at my ankles like he is seeing something fancy.

I said to the Chinese Mama, even though I know she doesn't understand, that he is a scoundrel and I pointed to him and made a frown. Well, she took off after him and chased that boy from their wagon like he was a snake, all the while scolding him at the top of her voice. I can see we will be friends and she looks after her children just like all Mamas and Papas do. They have four children, all very small but since the Papa is only as tall as my shoulder, I suspect they are older than they look.

It seems we are being tormented by the Indians as every morning there is someone who wakes up with their bedroll gone in the night, or their dinner pail or some such. The Indian warriors sneak in under the noses of the sentries posted, and without even waking a dog they take a blanket and go, and don't harm nobody, but it makes a body feel fully nervous and edgy. They think we are taking their land and don't know we are just passing through so they want to scare us and they are doing that just right.

So everyone wants to sleep in the center by the fires and close together, with the soldiers on the outside for safety, but Savannah begins to cry at this and blushes about twenty times and says Albert I just can't, I just can't. Well, there is rough old Albert, as ornery as any big brother a girl could have, putting his arm around Savannah and cooing to her like a repenting hound dog, and promising her she won't have to be sleeping out with other folks and that she is not common nor shameful. I watched all this and thought you just never know sometimes what's in a man's heart. When you think he is all tough nails and boards he can be different on the inside. It makes me wonder about other men I know, too.

So tonight and every night, Albert will make a little tent and fashion a door that can be tied shut and he slips in and out when he takes a watch, and hides Savannah in there so she can sleep away from other folks eyes. She said to me she is sorry there can't be room for me too, but I said it is different because she is married and too genteel, and I will be fine, but still, I figured it would be nice to be fussed over a little like that.

December 21, 1881

I have the most beautiful pair of ladies boots I have ever seen and I hate to wear them just to walk to Arizona in, they should be for dancing.

While Savannah is teaching all of us to write and read and do sums, I am helping the Chinese children to say some of our words. I am no teacher but they need to know some things just to get along, and I know their names when they say them but I cannot think of a way to write the sound of it. They call me Sarung instead of Sarah, but I don't mind because they are pleasant and always offer tea which is very sweet with sugar and they have come to our fire place and travel close to our wagon. Their oldest boy can say, I am walking, I am sitting, and some words like bucket and horse and wagon, and I think he knows what I mean sometimes. This is a good feeling, to help someone.

I talked to those Mormon sisters Sister Clara and Sister Nina who is real young, about my age, and Sister Lucille who appears to be very much older than my Mama. Now I know why people don't want them around as they are pure addled and claim they are all married to the same husband.

Pretty soon the trail got so muddy we were obliged to stop, and Captain Elliot said, Round up the train.

I saw him on his horse this morning just studying the sky and smoking his cigar and looking lonesome and sad, kind of like my Mama looks when she is thinking about yonder. I wondered if he was thinking about them Indians or the coming rain or what, then I saw him shift in his saddle and just like that he looked like a fierce man and I remembered his bloody sword and the way he went to save a woman that was already dead. He is tall and has a big Cavalry mustache that droops down sad looking as if you couldn't tell when he smiled at all, and he wears a regular hat instead of a garrison cap like most of the soldiers. He was patting Toobuddy on the head yesterday and looked real gentle, but something about him makes me stiffen up and want to be careful how I walk and what I say and where I look.

December 22, 1881

I am almost full grown now, and need to have more room in my blouses up top, and Savannah said I better fix up my hair instead of letting it hang down like a girl. My camisole is busting apart in the middle and the ribbon that used to hold the top in little ruffles just makes a ridge that holds up the camisole without any help from the straps. I am glad. Maybe I will get a figure after all. So we cut a new camisole and mended the old one, and out of my old skirt we are piecing together a blouse. We have hid the seams in the front with some embroidered flowers and it doesn't look pieced at all.

Then we decided us ladies would like a bath in the rainwater, and we shooed the men and Harland away and made them bring us up buckets of rain, so we could wash our hair and clean off. When Savannah stood up in her shimmy I saw her looking pinched and strained and then I said, Why, Savannah you need a new camisole too, and bigger drawers.

Mama looked at her hard and suddenly said, Savannah, you have plumped up like a mother hen.

And Savannah started to blush hard, and she said, Yes, it didn't take long. I saw that she and Mama were staring at each other, and suddenly I realized what they were saying. Savannah's body was plumped up in the right places and there was no mistake.

Then I thought of what that hateful Captain Elliot had said about a man being torn apart, and I thought of Mrs. Barston screaming herself to death for more than two days, and I felt sick. Mama and Savannah were all but crying with joy, but all I could say to her was, Don't worry, we will be home before it comes, and I left their wagon and went back to ours.

This isn't a good time for a baby and I can't help feeling that God sure likes to make things tedious on folks. It seems as if no one is spared a share of torment, and some will have more than their due. Lord if you see this pitiful band of travelers, please lend a hand and see us through with no more dying. I've had enough to last me all my days.

December 24, 1881

Tormented by Indians most of the day. Many soldiers are dead and some of the wagon train folks. I have no more feelings and just keep my rifle loaded and my eyes on the horizon and drive.

December 25, 1881

Christmas Day. It is cold and dreary looking out. Some of the folks want to stay put to have Christmas and Mrs. Meyers is the loudest and rudest thing and scolds at the Captain for pushing us onward. He doesn't say anything to her but orders his men around and we go on. We have pushed on and on and the wind has picked up terribly.

I wish I had a gift for my family but I don't, so I went to everyone this morning and said Merry Christmas and hugged them and told them they are my Christmas present just being alive. Next year we will have Christmas in a house I hope and have gingerbread men and mince pie and roasted goose, then I said, it will be with a new baby in the family and that is a fine gift for all of us. Well, Savannah cried when I said that and hugged me tight and said I was a wonder to her.

Mama started singing Gather at the River, but I said, Mama, sing a Christmas song. She started singing Away in the Manger and we were humming along, but in a few lines she had it confused and it turned into Hush Little Baby Don't You Cry, and she started rocking back and forth. That is the song she sang to Clover as he passed away, and it is too sad for me to bear on a Christmas day and so I got out of the wagon and let Harland drive so I could walk out of hearing up ahead aways.

I wasn't going to write anymore but I have been given a Christmas gift from the Lord and I must tell it. Around noon we came upon a deserted campsite and standing there as if the owners were coming right back was a small wagon with a canvas cover. Since our wagon is close to the front of the train, I hurried up ahead to see if there were folks around.

No sign of anyone, and in fact, the worn down places on the canvas and the scattered fire place looks as if it was deserted for the longest time. We are several miles from the railroad tracks, on a route the Captain has on a map, and although the trail looks used, this wagon is deserted for sure.

Being my share of nosey, I climbed up inside and found the dearest treasure I think I have ever seen. The wagon bed was lined with boxes of books. Books and books, stacked and packed in rows with leather covers on them and some had gold and ribboned edges. Some of them were story books, some of them seemed to be schoolbooks, and were about things I don't know of, and one is a magical book, with a big D on it, a book of words to learn to spell and what they mean. I opened it up and said my ABC's to myself and found Gale in the book and it is <u>a strong wind of high velocity usually a storm on the ocean.</u>

This wagon is a treasure chest and I am suddenly struck greedier than ever in my life. I want it so bad I am just beside myself. All these words to read and know is more than my insides can stand and I am trembling all over with excitement.

Mama, Albert, Savannah, Harland, Ernest! I shouted. I can drive this wagon, we have two extra horses, and the foreigners horses and, Rose. I cannot force her to a yoke says my heart, but look at all these books!

Well, Albert says the Army has got those foreigners horses and he doesn't want to spare the extras without a double yoke, in case they are needed by the family. And why would I want all that, he says, obviously someone else dropped it as useless trash.

These books are not trash, I said, as I know they are the opposite. They are the only thing I wanted in my life more than I could name. They are pearls in my hair and scarlet velvet gowns but I could not say that out loud because they would think I was touched.

Before I know it I am off to see Captain Elliot again. Just as I found him riding along and he tips his hat to me, I feel like I must fly back to that wagon and find out what a velocity is before I can go another step. Captain, I said, has the Army got the right to those killed settlers horses, or are you just keeping them for spares?

Well, he wasn't used to being spoken to so directly by a woman, I 'spose, because he kind of laughed and looked at me queer again. No, we don't have the right to them, Miss Prine, he says, but they need to be fed and I guess we could keep them if we wished since the Army is feeding them.

Well, I said, I wish for someone else to feed them. Me. I have found a wagon, a good, sound wagon and it is loaded with good books someone left behind and I need just two horses because we have two spare and I don't want to yoke up Rose and she is not a draft horse and I want the loan of them horses. If you Please.

Suddenly he got this mean look in his eye and he tipped his head way back and looked at me under his hat and sort of laughed again. Books? he says. A wagon of books? Show me, he said as he got off his horse, and so I grabbed him by the hand and pulled him quick over to the wagon and showed him inside.

He looks down at me and goodness, but he seems tall, and he says, Now, Ma'am, I can't loan Army property to a civilian, but I could sell those horses, for something of equal value of course.

I know my face is red and I am trying not to think of his twinkling eyes looking right through my head. What do you want? I said.

Well, he says, he wants a book, a book for each horse, and he gets to pick which ones. I had to think really hard and really fast. To give that man a book was more than I could stand, but if it meant to have all the others, I just had to do it. So up he climbs into the wagon, and says Come on, you can decide the value of the book, if it's worth a horse or not. I don't know what he means but I am up in the wagon with him and I can smell the pages and the ink and the glue of the books.

He picks up a red covered book and holds it up to me and blows off the dust and then reads out the title, A Study of Animal Species of the Northern African Continent.

So I said, What is that about? He opened it and there are drawings of strange animals and monsterous things and it looks like something I truly want to see.

He snapped it shut and said right away, This one's for one horse. Then he picked up another and read out, Annotated Expositional Sermon Texts from the Right Reverend Simon Thomas Brown, and I said Fine, right away. He looked at my face, not at the book, and said, No, this one ain't worth a horse. Then he picked up the magical book with a big word what started with a D which I can't even say, the book with all the spelled out words in it, and he is eyeing me and says, This one.

Oh, no, I said, not that one, and I started to reach for it.

He stuck out his chin and said, This one's worth a horse.

Oh, no, I said again. It's not, really it's not, and I could not stand to see that book in his hands.

Maybe, he said, this one's worth more than one horse.

Well, I said, then you got a horse and a half and you can't do that so you got to find a one horse book.

I get the feeling he is laughing at me under that mustache but I don't care I just want him to rob me of my books and get out fast.

Pretty soon he comes up with a book called The Duchess of Warwick and Her Sorrow by the Sea and I frowned hard. He opened it up and flipped the pages all gilt edges and shiny.

This isn't worth much, there is a page gone, he said. Page eighty-seven is gone.

Oh, Oh, was all I could say. Page eighty-seven! As I thought those words I wondered if he could hear my heart pounding. The Duchess of Warwick was the scarlet velvet lady with the tragic letter clutched to her bosom!

This one, he says, with pure meanness in his heart, I just know. He says This one is a one horse book, as after all, those are big horses and strong enough to pull this wagon of lead. I bet this weighs a quarter ton, he says, and stands up with the Scarlet Velvet Lady book and the Animals of Africa. Sold! he hollers and laughs, and says to me, let's go get your horses, Miss Prine.

The hateful scoundrel.

December 27, 1881

Yesterday the Indians came again. Ernest jumped on my Rose and chased them with a rifle and got Rose shot in the bargain. She is limping but it appears the bullet went in and out her flank and I was stroking her and cleaning her up.

That sergeant in charge of our group said, Back up, honey, to me and pulled out his carbine and aimed it at Rose.

Well, I charged at him and said No, no, and he fired and it went over Rose's head and into a wagon. It was luck that no one was hit, but I won't let him put Rose down. She can get well.

I got that Ernest Prine alone and told him he was a mule headed, low down skunk and he better not lay a rope on my horse again. He just looked at me puffed up and said he was defending his family. Well, I said, that doesn't give you leave to put aside all sense and judgement and go acting like you had the right to my horse. So he called me selfish and said if Papa was here he'd make me give him Rose to apologize. I said right back that Papa would whip his tail for what he done. We parted mad, and I don't care. It ain't often you are given a horse like Rose. It ain't right to steal her, I don't care what for.

I just turned around to walk away, and I saw that Captain Elliot watching us. I hope he didn't hear me fussing at my brother, but if he did he didn't seem to notice.

December 28, 1881

Rose is real sick and for once I am glad for our slow pace. Much work with the horses and poor Savannah cannot walk at all for the sick stomach complaint, so it is nice that we have this extra seat and now she sits by me sometimes and sews baby clothes and croshays little socks and soakers of woolen and mittens and hats. Her baby is going to have more clothes than all us Prines put together.

Harland has been not wearing his coat and has a fever and sniffles so he must stay away from her, and he sneaked away to play with Rudy Willburn and came back burning up feverish and did not eat supper but went right to bed.

December 29, 1881

Just about dusk we stopped by a stream to water, and it was getting dark early because of a new bank of clouds forming. It had stopped raining that morning but looked like it would start heavy any time and sprinkled on and off. Well, I went to the stream to fetch water and was filling up our barrel, and there was some wild blackberry bushes growing there, so I came back again with a pail and began to pick some tender stems and dig for some roots. There are several medicines you can make from blackberry stalk, and besides, if I cut carefully we can carry some to our new home to plant. I followed the little bushes quietly, not wanting to make a commotion. If all those people rushed over here, they'd spoil it all and no one would get any, and maybe they will do us some good. Savannah needs the bark for tea as she is having some bad stomach sickness these days.

Before I knew it I was far away from the wagon, and I reached under a stem and stood up with a start. There I saw a person's hand laying under the bushes. I peered over the bush and I wish I never did that, for what I saw on the other side would take a river to wash it out of my mind. There was a woman's body all naked and bloody. It was cut open at the stomach and the eyes were poked out. Her legs and arms were blistered up and red and black from burned marks and her scalp was almost all gone. It was a white woman and ants were in her face and one foot was trimmed off as if by coyotes or wolves, and there were several arrows in her all over.

As I looked on this horror, all I could think of is that Mama and Savannah mustn't see it. Mama might never come back from yonder in her mind. Savannah might lose the baby. Oh Lord, I thought, if I never do another thing, help me be strong now. So I took my pail of cuttings and put a smile on my face and went right away and found Captain Elliot.

He looked mighty surprised to see me wanting to talk to him, because I have not been at all friendly toward him since he got my books. I had to tell him twice, Captain, there is something I must talk to you about, please come with me. He said Talk here, but I said again, We must go for a walk, please! just as strong as I could for there were other folks around and if anything was stirred up, Mama and Savannah might come to see what it was they were looking at.

I know he thinks I am just a girl but he finally followed me, and when some fellow tried to follow along, I turned to him and said, Please wait for us, the Captain will be right back, in my sternest voice I could manage. The Captain was puzzled for sure, but I took him to the place in the bank and said, It's over there, and I don't want my Mama or my sister to know or to see it so it must be kept quiet.

He pushed apart the bushes and looked for just a second. Then he said to me, I will see that this is taken care of and you can put your mind at ease, Miss Prine, just like I was a lady and I had asked him to saddle a horse or something.

He looked at me real queer, like he was sizing me up or something, but I just said back, Thank you, Captain. He touched the edge of his hat and went back to the soldiers quickly and I seen them later with a shovel beyond the bushes, burying that dead woman.

Then, when we were making supper, Savannah hugged me for bringing her the bark, and wanted to share her tea but I could not.

Captain Elliot came up and took off his hat and said hello to everyone, nodding at my Mama. Is everything all right, folks, he says, and although he doesn't look at me I see his eyes flit this way for a second.

Well, wouldn't you know Mama would pick this time to come back to us a little, and she asked him to have a cup of coffee and some supper. Savannah has not cooked tonight as she can't stand the smell of meat cooking right now, but there is rabbit stew and biscuits, and that Captain just sat right down and had some and my Mama refilled his coffee just like he was company. She doesn't know what a low down man he is, I thought to myself, but I cannot tell her what I know about him so I kept my peace and watched it all and went to do the dishes.

The fire was hissing because little raindrops were hitting the rocks now and then, and he sat there and talked polite like company for some minutes and then said he had to go and he pitched his cold coffee into the darkness and handed me the cup, touched his hat again and was gone. Toobuddy who is named after my first dog Buddy wagged his tail and whimpered when he left like it was his best friend and I told him to hush. Bear just lays there not moving anything he doesn't have to except his eyes, he is older and tired from the trip.

Harland says, Sarah what are you so mad about? but I told him to hush, too.

December 30, 1881

I have done the worst thing I ever thought I'd do and I wonder if this is how a fancy woman feels when she is thinking about her sinful life. I cannot believe I let myself fall into this like a wanton or a harlot. I cannot face Savannah and Mama and the others, and I claim that I have a sick headache, but in truth I just cannot look them in the eye.

Before bedding down last night I checked to see that there was no water running in on the books. The tree bundles could go outside and be watered so I would have a little more room, so I set them all around my wagon, making a little shelter for the dogs underneath, where it would stay pretty dry. In the night the rain continued, thunder and lightning, lightning and thunder cracking like the sky is opening up. After a while it was raining harder and harder. I don't know how late it was but it felt darker than midnight when I finally fell asleep.

I woke up suddenly knowing my wagon and I were on fire. If it was from the lightning or from an Indian arrow I didn't know, but I knew it would burn with me in it. All my books, all my life, everything gone, I was on fire and the smell of smoke was everywhere and I screamed for my life.

Suddenly there was a shape of a man in the open flap, and it was a huge shape, wet and shiny in the lightning flash and smoke coming from it. I picked up a pistol and aimed and the man tore it out of my hands. I saw a soldier's uniform coming for me and I began to scream and he grabbed me and I felt a huge hand on my mouth.

Don't, he says, don't cry. It is only me, and I was stupid, I stopped under your wagon to have a smoke before I changed the watch, his voice says, and in a second I see it is Captain Elliot. He threw his cigar out into the night and held me as I was still struggling against his hands. You'll wake everyone, and your sister is sick, don't scream, please, he says, but I stumbled and the wagon swayed and we fell down on the plankbed.

Then I don't know why but I started to cry, and I felt myself get limp as I cried and cried. I told him I thought I was on fire, and I didn't want to burn to death, and I was so tired of fighting Indians, and traveling, and dying children.

I'm sorry, he says, I didn't think about the smoke, and then he loosened up his hold on me but I couldn't stop sobbing. I didn't even realize it at the time, but as I began to shiver all over and weep like a baby, he wrapped his arms around me and stroked my hair.

As I cried I told him about little Clover and the rattlesnake and about Papa, then I told him about poor Mrs. Lawrence, and then I told him about dear Ulyssa and how I killed those men, and I never thought I could kill a person except I was so stricken at what was happening, and how the Indian man gave me back Rose from the horses, and how we struggled and lost everything. I told him how Mama lost her mind, and how Ernest lost his leg and I had to help hold him down while his blood gushed all over everyone, and how he squeezed my hand so hard it hurt for a week afterward but it wasn't anything because my hand was still there and his leg wasn't. I told how I saw Mr. Hoover get shot in the throat and look down surprised and pulled the arrow out of himself and with it came pieces of his innards before he fell to the ground, and how horrible it all was.

I cried into his chest and he held me while I cried and told me I was brave and strong. And then I cried more and told him I was not brave at all I was a craven coward and begged him not to let me end up like that woman I found. Please, I said, don't let them get me, please.

He kept saying how brave I was, and how he wished he had soldiers as strong, and patting my shoulder real soft. And the next thing I knew, it was morning.

I have slept with a soldier all night, laying on top of him like he was a pile of blankets. Not just any one, either, but that Captain Jack Elliot who has my books and now he has my shame.

He shook me a little bit and said, Miss Sarah, I have to get out of here before folks wake up, and when I saw what had happened my mouth fell open like I was stunned. He put back on his slicker and I didn't even know he had it off, and picked up his hat and shaped it a little from being squashed, then he turned back toward me and picked up my blanket and wrapped it around my shoulders.

I looked down under it and I was only wearing some long drawers and my old camisole, the one that is bursting full of me on the top and had come untied in the bargain, and what a fine sight I was, freezing cold and my hair all around my shoulders, and I started to cry again. I am ruined.

Sh-sh, he says. There's no wrong done in a good cry, and I was beginning to wonder if you ever did. I would never hurt you, he says. And as long as no one knows, no one is ruined. Besides, it would be much more of a shame to be ruined by a rumor than by truth, and then he slipped out of my wagon and away in the foggy morning.

He is a puzzlement, for sure, and I don't think he was laughing at me, but then I remember how coarse he is and I feel ruined.

January 5, 1882

It is Harland's birthday and he is ten years old. He is a big boy and didn't want me to hug him, but he didn't mind at all if I made him a little sweet cake at dinner tonight.

For three days we have seen no sign of Indians, and no further attacks, not even a pat of butter stolen. Perhaps we are past their territory and they no longer intend to make war with us. There is a soldier who took a ball in the arm just like Papa, and I expected him to die only he got well just fine. A man from three wagons back, Mr. Raalle, who has an accent from a far away country called Norway, said that when a wound bleeds good, sometimes that washes dirt out of it and it heals better. I will think of that, since I remember Papa's arm never did bleed and I'm sure that there is always plenty of dirt on the trail.

On top of everything else we have all been taken with the flux and some folks are sick unto death from it. I don't feel terribly bad, but it is embarrassing.

January 6, 1882

Mama asked me to read from the Bible and I said fine but she wanted me to read starting in Joshua 2, and it is the story of Rahab the Harlot and how she saved Joshua and the spies and helped them hide in the walls of her house in Jericho and how forty thousand Children of Israel marched and blew trumpets and knocked down the walls but saved Rahab for her goodness. Well, I just could not stop my face from beaming red and every time I came to the word harlot it stuck in my throat like a bur, and Mama looked at me and said What ails you, Sarah? twice. So I added a lie to my sins and said it is just the flux making me run hot and cold and I went to bed early to wait for the Lord to smite me down and crumble my bones like the stones of Jericho.

January 7, 1882

We all seem to be better. Thank goodness for the blackberry bark. Poor Savannah was stricken first and has become well first, but she still is weak and dizzy often. Sergeant Miller, who is the man who almost killed Rose, says try boiling all your water before you drink or wash your face, it was what his Ma used to do, and the very next day after we started boiling water we began to get well. Some folks are doctoring their water with red chili sauce and some with herbs or tonics. All are trying their own way but this seems to work well.

Also, Rose is much better and seems agreeable to be ridden today. I'm very pleased.

January 8, 1882

I have much to read and have discovered a peculiar box, packed underneath other boxes at the bottom in a corner of the wagon. It had a slick piece of something white and shiny and shaped like a long necked bird on the lid, and a tiny little hook and eyebolt to close it, and when I opened it I found some wonderous things. I was not sure what to make of the things at first, then I opened one little glass bottle, and smelled it to see if it was medicine, and lo and behold, I believe it is perfume. It is strong and sickly sweet, and I looked harder at the other things with a different under-standing. One little jar has red chalky stuff inside and I touched it with my fingers and it stuck on but didn't smell like much. There is a little paper wrapped bundle of sticks which break easy and leave marks on everything.

I have never seen the likes and so have put the things away. The perfume makes me suspicious and afraid I have gotten the wagon of a nasty woman. But, it doesn't seem likely that a harlot would read so many books nor have studies of sermons, nor a Dictionary, which you say as dikshun-nerry. Maybe those things were given to a traveling preacher by a repentant dandywoman, as a sign she had given up her horrid life. At any rate, I can't throw the things out, for someone else in the wagon train will pick it up from curiosity, and words will get back about who threw it out.

Had a dream last night of a good and bad feeling and thought someone's arms were around my shoulders as I slept but woke and found nothing. I wondered if I am a fallen woman and have found that perfume as a sign. But then I think of all Mama's sayings and Bible stories, and I think if I were that kind of woman I would have been glad to find the perfume and the little jar of rouge which I looked up in the Dictionary book and I know is face paint. No, I 'spose I am not that kind, but then why did I like the feeling of dreaming about those arms?

January 10, 1882

Two children, ages nine and eleven, died in one family of the flux. Their Mama is real poorly and will probably join them, but we are not stopping so she will not be buried near them and she is very sad at that. They are the Raalle family, whose Papa I talked to before. We are scared this is cholera but Sergeant Miller said no, he's seen cholera and it is much worse. This is trail fever.

January 11, 1882

No one it seems has any idea about what I did that rainy night. I am glad. At least Captain Elliot has remained gentlemanly and not spread word around. That other fool soldier who thinks he is partners with Doc Holliday came around again and I told him if he didn't leave me alone I was going to throw boiling water on him, and give the stew that made to my dog to eat. Bear got to his feet and growled just as if I had asked him to, and he won't be back, I'm sure. Bear is a black dog big enough to pick his teeth with the likes of that boy.

Every morning for the last week I have found our two pails full of oats and the scraps of a sheaf of hay near my horses. And Rose looks all brushed and shiny. There are comb marks on her thick winter coat. It's like someone is feeding them and tending Rose specially, but I don't know who. I asked Albert did he get around early and tend my stock for me but he said no, and Ernest doesn't get up before me regular. It is a puzzle but it makes my morning easy.

El Paso is in our sights and we will lay over in the town for two days and put up dry goods. Harland was pestering me today and wants to ride Rose, so I told him all right. He rode right alongside my wagon for a while and asked me the silliest questions. All about does Mama miss Papa, and is that why she is so addled, and did I think she loved Papa? Then he wanted to know would she marry again, and if she had someone to take Papa's place maybe would she be right again and happy?

Well, I told him I don't know, maybe if a fellow came along who was real good to her, she might. This made me feel sad, and I never thought about all that before. Sure Mama loved Papa, weren't they always together, taking care of us?

Then he asked me a whole bunch of questions about how a fellow went courting, and what should he do, and what should he say, and what if the lady didn't like him, what should he do then?

Well, I don't know those things but I tried to tell him to just wash his face and hands and comb his hair, be an honest man and a good sport and kind hearted to her feelings, and if she doesn't like him he has got to go slow, and bring her some flowers and such and tip his hat.

He wants to know does a fellow have to be real old, older than the lady, old as Albert, and how old was Mama and how old was

Papa, and I said I didn't know for sure, and he asked again but I can't figure it. He got real quiet and thoughtful, and then after a while he rode off and I didn't see him until we stopped for supper that evening. I 'spose he has found a little girl to spark and there will be no prairie flowers in Texas after this winter.

We are stuck here near El Paso and I am tired of this town and glad we will be pulling out tomorrow. Daytimes are pretty but the nights here are dreadful cold.

All the China folks' names start with Sing which I think is nice and it is like their little bird talk. I have tried to get a handle on the words they say but when I do they laugh and I get embarrassed.

Well, I never saw the like. That rascal Harland has upset the applecart for sure. Tonight he came up before we stopped and said, Mama, can I invite a friend to supper, and will you ask Sarah to make a sweet cake again for company, and she just nodded like she does. Well, he took that for her answer, and made a big fuss about me hurrying and making a cake, which is a task in a campfire oven, and he like to drove Mama to distraction getting her to put on a different dress. Then he went and washed his own face without being told.

I could hardly wait to see the little girl in braids he would bring to our fireside. He kept saying Is it done, yet, is it done? Until we were about to scold him. Well, he runs off into the circle of wagons and pretty soon it is getting dark, and I was never so shocked in my life, here he comes back again pulling by the hand, Captain Jack Elliot.

It didn't take much to see Captain Elliot has combed and trimmed his mustache and scrubbed his face and hands, and he comes up to our group and smiles big at me and nods to me and Mama and the rest. Harland is standing close by him and nudges him with his elbow, and Captain Elliot tips his hat.

Mama, says Harland real loud, this here's Captain Elliot. I was getting a knot in my stomach. Well, Captain Elliot is a staring hard at me and his eyes are twinkling like he's grinning to beat the band under that mustache. Then Harland grunts his throat real loud and out from behind Harland's back comes a handful of drooping wildflowers, most without even a open blossom yet, and then he takes the Captain by the hand and leads him up to Mama. He stuffs those flowers in Captain Elliot's hand and says, Mama! This here's Captain Elliot, come to court you!

Captain Elliot's mouth opened wide and his eyes quit twinkling. Albert said What? real loud, and Savannah dropped the plate of cornbread in the dirt, and Ernest just about burst his sides open laughing so hard he could choke to death.

Mama looked up, kind of surprised like, and tipped her head to the side. Then she says, so genteel almost as if she was a queen, Why, Captain, that is most kind of you, but you see, I am too recently widowed. I am not receiving suitors, and do not expect to in the future.

I thought Ernest was going to die of laughing and he rolled on the ground, then Mama turned to him real serious, and said, Ernest William Prine if you don't get up and stop acting like a lunatic I will cut a switch and wear a hole through your britches this very instant. Sarah, she says, fix the good Captain a plate, and sit down, sir. I was thinking she was in her right mind, but then she says, Now, sir, are you with General Lee's forces? I hear they are moving on through Pennsylvania. How is the fighting? Have you many losses?

I am looking at her and looking at him wearing that blue uniform and I catch eyes with Captain Elliot and see something strange in his face.

So this evening we pretended Captain Elliot was a Captain in the Confederate Army come to suit Mama, who knew she was a widow but didn't see a blue uniform instead of grey, and knew she had children and a grandchild coming but not that she was old.

Harland is sadder than I have seen him since Papa died, and he doesn't understand anything he has done. After some cake, he let me give him a hug, and I told him it will be all right but he should let folks do their own sparking and not meddle, it is like stirring up bees, no good is likely to come of it.

January 16, 1882

We have not had the displeasure of Captain Elliot's presence in two days. Likely we are rid of him and his grinning and I'm sure he thinks we are a family of lunatics.

I am still finding feed every day left for my horses only it is less as it seems to be scarce for all. Albert still will not own up to lightening my load although I know it must be him. Found some track of boots near the horses and I'm going to watch for Albert to lay some steps nearby so I can compare.

We are well into New Mexico Territory, and the end of our trip is in sight, just a few more weeks, and it has occurred to me that of all the things that are important for those Chinese children to know, they must learn to count money. I never was good with sums much, except to add money and take away what was spent. So with all gathered around, and Savannah helping over my shoulder, we are teaching them to say one dollar, two dollars, and eight bits to a dollar, and ten cents and such. Their Mama and Papa are trying hard too because as soon as I drew the pictures in the dirt and put down the few coins I had, they got real interested.

No rain or wind for some days. Savannah is still teaching school, and Mama has been coming out of yonder each Sunday morning for a few hours of Bible stories and praying. Every time she begins and it is not the story of Rahab the Harlot I say a prayer of thanks.

It was a beautiful clear day and Bear and Toobuddy had been chasing rabbits like they do every day, and after supper Bear stretched out by the fire, and Toobuddy laid himself under the pantry at the back only it wasn't our wagon it was the China folks'. Toobuddy is a big red dog and it is about like having a horse in the parlor having him under that pantry, and Mrs. Sing fussed at him to move but he didn't know Chinese and stayed put.

I was about to go get him when she popped him on the head with a broom, and he jumped up quick and startled her good. She bumped the pantry, the wagon gave a shake, and a tall, tall sack of white flour upended on a shelf she had and poured out on his whole body. Now he was a big white dog and he shook and shook, making a cloud of flour.

Mrs. Sing was having a conniption, and all the Sings got into it and pretty soon all of them and Toobuddy were white, white every where. All their black pigtails and colored clothes were white and Toobuddy shook and shook then sneezed and slobbered all over.

Well, I laughed out loud and then Toobuddy heard and came after me. He got real close and couldn't stand it any more and began to shake again. Pretty soon I couldn't see my own hands and I was in a cloud of white too. Mama and Savannah and the boys and me were all laughing to beat the band.

Then the Sings start laughing except Mrs. Sing who had lost a sack of flour, and she came running to me and said real mad like, Three dollar, Missy Sarung! Three dollar flower! I nodded and said I will have to give her a share of our flour, and a happy surprised look came over her face.

She says aloud, I understand! and nods real hard and then she says, Sankyou Missy Sarung! Well, she was talking as good as most people and I could tell she was proud of herself cause she said it to all her children over and over, Three dollar flower, I understand, Sankyou!

January 19, 1882

Mrs. Meyers is fussing around and getting me mighty peeved. She was mad at Albert because even though I have brushed Toobuddy with the curry comb he is still shaking flour and she had out some wet washing on a line and he covered it with flour. Well she knows not to fool with me, and no one will let her near Savannah, and Mama doesn't know what day it is and Ernest and Harland are too young, so she is mad at Albert.

He told her he would try to get that dog cleaned up better and she said something like You and that lunatic mother of yours better keep him away or he'll find himself shot through the head!

I saw Harland's face when that old woman said Mama was a lunatic and he looked dreadful sad. Then I saw him look something else, I don't know what. After a while Mrs. Meyers has re-washed all their clothes and we are having supper and the next thing I hear is Mrs. Meyers a hollering and here comes one of their horses running like crazy and her wet washing line is caught on his collar and dragging through the dirt picking up mud coating it all with brown. Harland is nowhere to be seen.

If she or her fat boys shoots Toobuddy she will be sorry she was born. It is real late and still I hear Mrs. Meyers' scrub board going brritt, brritt and she is fussing to herself and fit to be tied and so I snuck up behind her real quiet like an Indian and leaned up and said in her ear, I killed two white men and five Indians before I was eighteen and I still got my rifle, and if my dog dies for any reason on this trip I don't mind some more target shooting.

January 20, 1882

We have come upon a small Indian camp of some mud and skin houses and they are mostly women and children and old folks, cooking and farming a little plot of corn and squash. Captain Elliot rode out to them with eight other men and they were all very afraid of the soldiers. He tried to tell them we were just passing by, but he doesn't know if they understood or not.

Well, all seemed fine until we were well past them and putting in for the evening, when we heard far off shooting that went on and on. Pretty soon here came five soldiers riding up and waving scalps and hollering as if they are drunk.

Captain Elliot jumped up and ordered those men down and said Dismount! and Throw down your arms, and they all looked real surprised and put down their guns and rifles. He told them they were all under arrest and bound to stand trial, and they began to complain about it as if they were children caught writing bad words in the dirt with a stick. He told some other soldiers to Bind those men and post a guard over them for the night.

Mrs. Meyers was in the crowd behind me and I heard her ugly voice say Good enough end for some dirty blanket Indians.

All I could think of was that they were just little families cooking beans and planting and hunting a deer now and then, and having babies and laying their old folks to rest, not harming anyone, just living. I pictured that one Indian man I stood so close to I could hear his breathing, and those filthy, awful men I killed, and I know Indians aren't no dirtier than any white folks and cleaner than some. Not stupid, either. But I saved my breath. The likes of her isn't going to listen nor be changed in the mind just from hearing sense. Some people sense is wasted on and that's purely a fact.

January 21, 1882

We are staying put. Captain Elliot has rode out to the Indian camp and said that he found everyone slaughtered even newborn babes, and how this was the kind of action that only made the Indian wars worse. He is arresting the men and charging them with the murder of thirty-nine men, women and children, all unarmed and defenseless except for some hunting knives and cook pots.

Later I saw him sitting on his horse again, staring away off, and looking powerfully sad, about as sad as I feel, as I know if all this wagon train were cut down by Indians it would be just the other side of the looking glass.

The Captain has sent a Dispatch of soldiers to bury all the Indians in rows of graves and mark every one of them. This is a kind thing in my mind and I remember how he talked so nice to Mama about the Confederacy and maybe I think he has a heart in him after all.

When he said those orders he looked terrifying and I'm sure not a one of those men would have waited one second before jumping to do what he said. Then he was walking out by himself, slapping his hat against his leg now and then, and he came by our wagon where I was. I asked him would he take a cup of water, and he nodded and drank from my dipper. While he did I said, That was a horrible thing those men did. Then he looked at me real strange, and nodded again, and looked all tight in the face as if it pained him to try to talk. So I didn't push him, I just nodded back and went on with my work.

January 22, 1882

Today is the first day in all this time I have had to feed my stock myself. Albert's boots don't match the prints I seen before at all, and I am certain that it could be some soldier doing the deed. I rode Rose over to where those arrested men were walking in chains and ropes, and hollered out Any of you been feeding my horse? They all just looked at me strange and one of them spat on the ground. It isn't likely it was one of that bunch.

Ernest said this morning he had had a dream about being eaten by a bear and woke several times during the night, and slept with a pistol across his chest. Lo and behold there is bear track all around his spot and Toobuddy is missing but there is no sign of blood or hair like there was a fight. Trees are thicker here and it looks like rain. If that dog is bear killed I will be sorry but if he is Meyers killed I will be mad.

We had some bacon and biscuit for breakfast and broke camp

early. As we were pulling way I called Toobuddy but there is no sign of him. Ernest went to the Meyerses for me and says You seen our red dog? and they said no and got all bug-eyed and scared. They were wandering around in bushes all day long calling out Here Dog! 'til I could have laughed at them, except that I wanted my dog back.

At supper tonight we were all sitting around thoughtful and Mama has talked about Sunday School but the Captain says we will not stop for Sunday, and we are real near the Arizona Territory which is separated from New Mexico north to south. That is our border we are watching for, and he says we should cross it in six or seven days.

Yonder are the Chiricahua and Dragoon Mountains, a pretty looking mountain range that jumps up out of the flatness of west Texas and New Mexico Territory like a surprise. We are much further south than on the way toward Texas and I like this route better, although I hope I never do any traveling of this kind again.

Three wagons of folks have said they like this place and will stay behind in the morning, as there is good rain and water near and flat land without too much rocks for farming.

It is real cold but the rain has held. As the sun went down I felt a snap in the air like it could snow and the clouds are low and dark and it smells of snow too. Ernest says his leg is hurting him mighty bad all of a sudden, and he takes his wooden leg off and hops around tonight, but he just says it hurts worse that way. It is swollen and red and pains him much so he needs to ride tomorrow and not walk all day for a few days.

From the bushes around I hear some whimpering and up to the firelight comes Toobuddy. He is looking mighty weary and worn but doesn't seem to be hurt. He is real hungry and sleeps hard by the fire all night.

I gave Rudy Willburn back his reader as I am finished with it, and he has asked to borrow a book and will take good care to return it before we get home.

Rudy sat with us tonight with his fiddle and played some tunes that were real merry and made us all smile. He said that lady who played the lap harp and spoons was Mrs. Raalle, who we buried aways back. We all feel bad that we didn't get to know her before then but he said their families were friends together back in Louisiana State where they started. They were also friends with those foreigners who all died, and said those folks spoke a little bit of the Raalle's language. He says Mr. Raalle still has a little girl named Melissa, five years old, and Mr. Raalle is real lonesome without his wife and boys.

That sorry soldier who was making eyes at me is one of the men arrested for killing all the Indians. I knew he was no good and when he hangs the devil will be waiting his arrival with a hot poker and a grin.

January 26, 1882

Now as we thought we were finished with Indian fighting, there has been sight of a band of Indians riding with some white men and some Mexican bandits. We are all afraid to be set upon by them as the soldiers are much fewer and Captain Elliot will not untie the arrested men to fight he says.

Then Sergeant Miller speaks up and says, But sir, they should at least have the same chance as all to defend themselves and not be shackled like animals.

Captain Elliot says back they should get the same chance at defense they gave to those babies they butchered. Once again I am real sorry I was standing so close I could hear that. He saw my face but this time he doesn't apologize for saying it and he has a look on his face I can't place, not just mad and not sorry, but I don't know, it is like he is on fire inside.

January 27, 1882

Savannah and Albert both have a fever and are sniffing and headaching. We drove all day and stopped for noon dinner and I said Harland, Please drive my wagon, I am so tired, but he won't.

Mama takes a look at me and there is a light in her eyes suddenly, and she says Harland you drive this wagon, your sister is real sick.

Mostly I just feel tired to the bones, too tired to eat, and sore all over, and real cold.

February 1, 1882

This page is on top of my cigar box because it is my last will and requests. Please bury me deep under the shade of a tree if you can find one and take a one-legged branding iron and burn my name on a marker so it will stay for a while.

Ernest take care of Rose and take her with you to the Army, she will take care of you and she will like being in the Cavalry.

Harland you take these books and read and try to go to school, you are a smart boy.

Albert and Savannah you have a passel of babies and build a fine house and plant all these trees and when you come to pecan picking season, think of me some.

Mama, I love you, you have been a good mama and worked so very hard to teach us all right from wrong and I will kiss Papa and Clover and Harriet for you. I will miss you all and thank you for being my kin.

I repent for all the mean things I ever done and the bad and murderous thoughts I been having about the Meyerses too.

Yours loving and faithful, Sarah.

February 5, 1882

It is said I have the ague and maybe newmoniea. I looked through every n but it is not in my Dictionary book. I hear Mama humming now and then and I am so cold. I thought I was waking up in heaven but here I am still cold and I see there is a mustard plaster on my chest and all that skin under it is red and blistered feeling.

Harland came in and told me he's been driving my wagon with me sleeping in it, and that Mr. Raalle brought the mustard plaster, and that with tending me Mama has come back to herself a little and talks right and does fair well for herself again. Who is doing my share of work, I said, and who hitches these here horses?

And Harland puffs up proud and says he did it all himself.

So I said, It was you combing Rose before, too? And he looked all embarrassed and said he had promised not to tell who it was. Then he jumped out before I could ask again and I started coughing and couldn't talk anyway.

February 9, 1882

When I sleep I toss around and have frightful dreams of Indians jumping at me and cutting me to ribbons, or being eaten by a bear, or standing to watch while my family is killed by a cougar and not being able to get to my rifle. I am almost afraid to sleep but so sick I seem to be called to it all during the day and night only in short spurts, then I wake cold and scared and coughing. It is hard to breathe and it feels like fat old Mrs. Meyers is sitting on my chest.

From here I can watch Rose's head bobbing up and down out the back over the cook's pantry. Mrs. Sing has brought me tea twice a day all these days of sickness. I have a racked cough and cannot talk too much as it sets me to coughing. Soup and tea and coffee is all I want as it helps keep the cold out of my bones. I feel like a little old dirty rag doll and I want to take a bath but Mama won't hear of it.

I hear a cougar aways off. Ernest said there's been track all around and several people have tried to shoot it but no one could say for sure they hit it. No wonder I keep dreaming about a cougar. It is daylight and we are moving but I am still lying on my plank bed which feels as if I have grown roots to it. I am thankful I did not die either from the newmoniea or the mustard plasters. Frost is on the ground and the horses' noses have ice from their breath.

I am told we have come to Arizona Territory and tonight there will be a meeting and Captain Elliot will talk to folks about where each is going. Mama is a different person, she has taken the reins and drove her team some, and fixes supper and talks sense with Albert and Ernest and Savannah about the tree farm we will have. Ernest has shot a deer and he is so proud he could bust. It turns out he has been wearing Mama's spectacles and all this time he thought he was a poor shot he has just got bad eyes.

I begged Albert to take me to the meeting and promised I will bundle up warm and hold the hot rocks to my chest. I wanted to go so bad and put up a fuss that Mama finally said She must be better she is getting ornery, she better go. So I wrapped myself up like a huge walking bedroll. Ernest fixed me a plank on two buckets to sit at near the fire.

Captain Elliot starts with saying we are just one day's journey away from the town of Douglas and some folks claps their hands as that is where they mean to put down. He says from there they will head northwest towards Tombstone and on to Fort Huachuca, then Tucson and Fort Lowell which he says is the Cavalry's destination. I quit listening and start to watching folks all around. They all look plum ragged from the traveling. There are new widows and orphans, and new Mamas and Papas with no babies any longer, and some without eye sight and some with game legs and limp arms from the battles with Indians and hardships of the journey. Mr. Barston's three children look pinched and starved still, but they keep on. Mr. Raalle has this pained look of sadness on his face all the time.

Savannah is rounded out enough to show even though it is only a couple of months, and has hitched up her skirts which looks a bit plump on her. Ernest has grown some and is taller than Albert and it has made him limp real hard as now the wooden leg is too short for his other leg. I bet that is why his stump hurts he is forced to jam it down hard because it is too short, and I must remember to tell him to start over and fix a new tall one. It is as if all this time I've been sick, folks and things been changing, or maybe they changed before, but since I thought I would never see the sun again they look new to me.

February 11, 1882

I do not want to go to Tombstone at all but we are bound to follow Captain Elliot although he says we are not obliged to go into town but to camp outside as he needs to send a telegram ahead to Fort Huachuca. He says it is a Mexican word when I asked him. As we go on I hear a train whistle in the evening and it sounds mournful and lonesome. I wonder what it is like to travel safe and fast in an iron box away from Indians and cougars.

Captain Elliot came by our fire tonight and asked how I was doing.

I asked him did he think trains were a safe way to travel, and he shook his head. It is safer from things like snakes on the ground, he says, but not from the two legged kind. And there has been train robbery and something called derailments which happens when robbers tear up the tracks just to tip it over and kill the folks and rob gold shipments and payrolls and such. Then he said Glad to see you up and about Miss Prine, and left. And although I don't like him I felt like I wanted him to stay and talk longer.

I wonder why he doesn't smoke cigars any more.

February 14, 1882

There is a little valley here with rocky ground on one side and soil on the other. We have got a land patent map from the government office in Douglas and are all talking hard about putting stakes down near this stream. We passed some mining settlements but they were places of rough and coarse folks and hard living and didn't want any part of that. There is a Mexican family living near the road and they know enough of our language to say we are welcome to settle here.

The stream is called Cienega Creek, and runs the length of this valley where there is sycamore and live oak and cottonwood and birch so thick in some places a lizard couldn't squeeze between them. Other places have cactus and scrub brush. There is water plenty, and some hills all around and mountains distant, and so we think it may be a good place for planting our pecan and fruit orchard. Seems we will not head up north to our old place, as we probably don't have enough to buy it back and don't know if it is for sale.

I will write a note to Jimmy Reed and tell him we are back and ask is our place for sale from the folks who bought us out, and to send back word quick before my brothers have every last tree in the ground, and send it to the Tenth Cavalry at Fort Huachuca. That way Ernest will get it and know where we are to let us get the letter. I hope Jimmy has learned to read some but I know Mr. MacIntosh can read fine, so I will say hello to him in the same letter because he will likely be reading it to Jimmy and Miss Ruthanne if they are already married.

Mr. Raalle seems so kind hearted and just as I am thinking I will miss him and little Melissa, he says he will settle nearby, down in the lower flat area there, and try to raise some milk cows and beeves. We are glad to be shed of the Meyerses and hope never to have the likes of them near us again, and just as glad to have Mr. Raalle close by as he seems like a good, even handed neighbor.

It seems we are putting down in this little rocky corner by the stream where the stone will make a footing for a house.

February 15, 1882

The Army is back from Tombstone and today the soldiers are pulling away with the rest of the few wagons who will go on to Tucson and most of them except the Mormons want to stay there. Maybe those sisters will get tired of traveling and stay too, and find them each a husband but I will likely never know.

Captain Elliot asked Ernest again was he bound to join up and Ernest said yes sir, and so he will go along with them but will ride a dead soldier's horse and gear. That is fine with me since as long as I am staying on this earth I would just as soon keep Rose with me.

I told Ernest to be sure to measure up his leg and make himself a new one and he said that was a good idea. It was sadder than ever I knew to say goodbye and fare well to Ernest. He looks so determined and not sad to go, but he promised he will return and will write some.

Captain Elliot came to me with a little package wrapped in brown paper and twine and said since I had saved the Army money by taking care of those horses he felt obliged to return half the buying price. Well, this is pure nonsense I know, but I could tell by the feel of the package it was a book so I took it gladly. No matter which book it was I wanted the other one so bad I could have slapped him.

I waited until he rode off, and then a thought struck my mind that I have not been entirely thankful for the blessings that we do have. I could still catch up with them easy alone on a horse but not with a wagon, so I got on Rose's back and rode gentle after them until I caught up with them. When he saw me he turned right out of the column and rode to meet me.

I still had the book in my hand, wrapped up. Captain Elliot, I forgot to say thank you, I said. He looked real puzzled at that. I straightened up kind of proud and said, Thank you for keeping us safe, and for protecting my mama and Savannah from an awful fright, and, then I couldn't think of just the right words for a bit. So I took a deep breath and said, And, for protecting them from hurtful rumors.

Well, what do you know but he smiled and this time I could tell it, and he lifted his hat and said real grand, At your service, Miss Prine! I put out my hand like I know fellows do to shake hands, and he real quick took off his glove and took hold of it, staring at my hand like there was something written on it. He didn't shake hands at all, he just sort of held on, pressing my fingers real gentle, until his horse shifted its feet and pulled us apart. He started to reach into his coat for something, and he got a soft look around the eyes. He quit smiling and took his hand out of his coat, and nodded, like we were making some quiet agreement or something. Then he saluted me and rode off to catch up with the others. Likely I will never see that man again, but somehow, that doesn't make me feel as good as I thought it would.

I sat on Rose and tore open that wrapping, hoping with all my might that it would be the Scarlet Velvet Lady book so I could find out what happened to her. It wasn't. It was the Animals of Africa. Although I am tickled to have it back, I am sure I would have been happier to let him keep this one. I must mail him a letter some day when I get six bits to rub together and ask to buy The Duchess of Warwick back from him.

For the first time since last July, I don't feel any longer like we are heading into a bad wind and bound for trials and heartache.

February 20, 1882

We have made up a tent from two canvases from the wagons and a blanket in the middle. Albert and Savannah have one room and Mama and Harland and I sleep in the other. I am still weak and they won't let me do much but cooking and cleaning since it is so cold. Everyone has walked the length of the land hereabouts but me, and they all do much talking about where to put stakes or stack rocks for markers and how much land does it look like we should get.

They have dug some holes to see how the soil is and how far down there is water, and so far, there is one hole ten feet deep for a well but it was still dry. One more day of digging and they were down five more feet and hit rock but it was wet. So the next day Albert took off his shirt and shouldered a pickaxe and broke up that rocky ledge, and went down another eight feet, and he was standing in water! He dug as deep as he could and not drown, and it seemed like good water. We covered the hole with a few planks to let it settle before we took some to try. That should keep the dogs from falling in or Harland.

It was decided Albert and Mama should drive right away to Tucson to file our claims, that way there are two heads of the house and we can get two claim patents of six hundred and forty acres each. They expect to be gone three days all told and will leave at sun up. Savannah and I fixed them up with stew and loads of biscuits and beans, and we will stay here and try to make the place homey and wait their word.

February 21, 1882

Harland was out fishing, so we swept out the tent and set up a wash tub inside and heated water up in the big kettle that hangs over the fire tenders. Savannah and I had ourselves a nice long bath and washed our hair. I asked Savannah how she feels to be expecting, and she says mostly it is real nice. It must be nice to be so happy wanting a baby and married. Suddenly, she began to cry, and then just as sudden, she stopped crying but told me she wants her own mama with her when the baby comes and she is happy but scared, too.

We took a stroll down the stream bed out of Harland's hearing. We startled a covey of quail, and they fluttered, making little chick noises as they drifted to the other side of the stream. Sarah, Savannah said to me, will you help me when I have the baby?

Surely I will, I told her. I don't know much what to do, though. Do you know about babies? I said.

It's real natural, she said. She squeezed my arm and said, My Mother always told us girls the main thing to think about is not being afraid, and to remember the precious little one you will have when the travail is over.

Then I felt inclined to ask her some more things, and I said, You know, I heard some women in the wagon train say the very same thing, only they weren't talking about having the baby, they were talking about getting it.

Savannah just looked at me and blushed hard. Then she looked way off into the woods by where we had walked. And she said in a low voice, That's not so bad, Sarah. It's, it is, I find it, rather nice, and she cleared her throat.

Really? I said.

Sh-sh, she said, and made a little smile. You will know when you have a husband. Didn't your mama ever tell you about those things?

No, I said, feeling clumsy. She just says what a girl needs to know the Lord will teach her. Only, I keep waiting, and asking Him about some things which I don't understand, and He isn't in any hurry to shed the light on them.

Oh, Sarah, said Savannah, laughing, only it wasn't mean laughing, it was like she cared about me. You will know some things by heart, if you marry for love. Sometimes I find myself a little frightened, carried away by my own passion, which I have been taught all my life to subdue. But the Lord said that marriage is holy, and the marriage bed undefiled. So there is no wrong in it, like some people think.

Does it hurt? I said real soft.

Savannah sucked in a breath and looked up at the leaves over us. Well, she said, only the first time. But not so bad. Not as bad as skinning your knee on a rock. You've done that haven't you?

More than once, I said. What is it you're supposed to count?

What? she answered me.

I told her Mrs. Lila Duncan in the wagon train said she counted more of something on her ceiling than stars in the sky. Only I never did hear it clear and I wasn't supposed to be listening, so I couldn't ask her to speak right up and repeat it.

Then Savannah laughed again and hugged me. You don't have to count anything, honey. She was just saying that she keeps her mind occupied away from what is happening. But if you love your husband, you don't have to keep your mind busy. It's just a special time. A close time.

What is? said Harland's voice real nearby. He was on the other bank of the stream where he had crossed on a fallen log.

So I told him, Why, the time you skip a rock at your brother real close and splash him good, and I picked up a flat one and skimmed it just right so his pants got wet around the bottoms. Then he threw a big stone in and splashed us both, so we ran away laughing and he chased us a bit, and then he decided he would fish some more.

February 23, 1882

Harland got up and acted peevish this morning and I don't know why. He complained about breakfast and wouldn't eat it, and wouldn't wash his face and ran off mad. Pretty soon he was back and said he wanted to go fishing, but he wanted a horse to ride, not to walk. Well, he whacked one of my big horses, Dan or Terry he doesn't know which he says, for trying to bite him and it kicked him in the leg and bit him too, and he came in bawling. He was really upset and I just can't find out why he is acting so bad, it just isn't like him to be such a bother to us.

I asked him would he help us plan the house we will build and he said No, I don't want to live in your stinky old house anyway, and that made me really mad. But just as I was raising my hand to slap him, he hollered out he wasn't living in any house, because Mama and Albert aren't coming back they were killed by Indians and eaten by bears.

Well, Savannah burst out crying at that and so did Harland! I was standing in the middle of two crying people and didn't know which one to comfort first, so I took them both by the hand and marched us all outside and just kept going and going until we were up on a high place above the creek bend.

As we got there I began to say, Here's where I want to live, you hear? We are going to put a house here and windows out every side and a front porch built up so's we can sit of an evening and see the road in case Ernest comes home from the Cavalry to visit. I held their hands tight and walked a square off, and said, Here's Harland's bed, and here's mine, and here's Mama's, and This is a room here for Albert and Savannah and it must be big for the baby too, then when their house is finished, Mama and I will share the big room and Harland can have his own all to himself if he wants. Here's the stove and be careful! I jerked Harland's arm, You are about to get burned it is really hot and almost red! Then I said Smell real hard and smell Christmas gingerbread men in that stove, and smell peach preserve simmering in the summertime. Harland, I said, shoo those flies off that sweet butter cake and smell that ham and corn fritters! Pretty soon we were all laughing and everyone was cheered some.

Then we got serious and started moving some rocks and making markers in the corners of the house, and Harland used a stick on the ground and cut a line for the rooms and the stove and where the table would go, and Savannah and I did the same and lined out a garden plot and where we would put some pole beans and pumpkins and watermelon and kale and carrots.

Harland said Oh, don't plant nasty old carrots, I hate 'em, but we just laughed. Supper time came and we lit a lantern just as the sun was going down. Suddenly, Bear and Toobuddy jumped up and took off down the road barking loud.

Pretty soon we heard them coming back along with the squeak of wheels, and there was Mama and Albert on the wagon seat, calling out hello!

They have got our patents filed and we have two fine claims, and they have got the wagon loaded with lumber and a keg of nails and some strips of lead flashing for the roof, and Albert bought a new draw splitter for making shingles. It was a good evening and we all talked about our plans until late. It will take a few years of living on the land and then it will be ours.

We have the beginning of a house put up. We have had a visit from a bear and Albert fired a shot at him but he thinks he missed. Even though there is no roof on top we have pitched our tent on the floor boards and it is good to sleep on something besides rocky ground. At the same time we are trying to build a house, it rained for three days and then cleared and feels like spring.

Albert is spending all day on the house and in the field, and making Harland help him dig holes and plant the trees. Some of them have little buds on them from the warm weather. We put the peaches and apples and pears closest to the house, and lined the pecans in rows down the way. Albert said it is a good thing that it rained as he can see the flow on the land and how the trees will best get watered, and how to make a flood bank at one side to drive the water where he wants it.

We are all going to Tucson tomorrow to buy shingle stock and roofing lumber and get Harland some shoes if we can find the Sing family, and best of all, to buy a stove or order one if the dry goods store has to send east for it. I have been elected to write another letter to Jimmy Reed and Miss Ruthanne MacIntosh and let them know where we are settled on a claim in Arizona Territory, so that if they ever are down our way after they marry to stop in, and I drew a picture map of how to find us. I will mail the letter in Tucson and Savannah has written to her folks again too, and finally Harland has made a letter to Rudy and he drew a zebra he copied from the Animal book on it.

March 18, 1882

We went to the dry goods store to get some stores and a bit of yard goods for some curtains. We got a new pick handle and some rifle shells and two tin buckets. The man there who is Mr. Fish said we would need lots more as there was talk of trouble near us and some bad Indians called Apaches. So I took two extra boxes of rifle shot and made sure we had some that met with our rifle barrels.

He kept asking over my head to Albert did he want something else, and finally Albert said, Just give her the bullets she asks for, and that made me feel proud.

Mama said to me, Sarah, get yourself some of that light blue cotton there for a dress, so I asked the price but he wanted twelve cents a yard and that is too much. Then out of the blue, I asked him did he have anything called scarlet velvet.

He looked at me real strange and said, We surely don't carry anything in that color.

So I said, Fine, I just wanted to know what color that meant anyhow.

He looked at me even stranger then, and said, Why you're just a girl, ain't you? and It's red, girl, red! Like I was a fool. Well, I felt like a fool but I wasn't going to let the likes of that man get to me, not after all the things I held up my head for. And I knew I wasn't no woman in a red dress nor a fool either one, so I looked him in the eye real straight and didn't blush at all.

Mama was behind me again, and whispered, Sarah, I got some money put back you didn't know about and you really need a new dress. How you going to catch a husband wearing patched yellow gingham? Get yourself that blue if you want it and wear it to town next time.

I told her I might, but first I asked the man if he had a Godey's book or a Sears and Roebuck new.

Albert and Harland both is getting tired of this lady stuff, but not Savannah, so the men went to discuss Indians with Mr. Fish, and we opened up the Sears and Roebuck for a look at dresses and corsets and such.

Finally, there is a picture of one styled sort of fine, with rows of little buttons. Much too grand to wear around a pecan orchard. The dress costs twenty-nine dollars and is suggested to be worn with their shaper number 4401. Probably I will never have a dress like that, but I would be proud to wear it. And then I see at the bottom it is made of thirteen yards of lavish velvet in plum color with lavender flounces or dark blue with white flounces. Imagine two colors, and Velvet. Imagine having twenty-nine dollars to spend on a dress, too.

Savannah said Well, all that is just too fancy, and people would stop seeing the real beauty of a person which is their spirit and good and simple ways, it was putting on a show. I 'spect she saw my face because she looked real sorry right away, and said, But it is beautiful, although you do not need to wear a dress like that, people will know you are good by your good and simple ways. I tried to smile, and I closed the book. And I took a deep breath and asked Mr. Fish for seven yards of blue and some thread.

It is the first time Savannah ever made me feel bad. I can't tell her I don't want to be good and simple and have simple ways, it would hurt her and she wouldn't understand feeling this way, she is too good. I want to wear scarlet velvet and slippers and lace gloves and ride in a stage instead of wearing calluses on my hands driving a team like a man. It is not her fault. She is right. The Lord looks on the inside, although people look on the outside.

That man is measuring cloth and Mama said loud, Eight yards, make it eight, sir, please. This is a waste of money, I know, but suddenly I feel as if they are feeling sorry for me somehow, and that I should be thankful for wearing a brown skirt and a patched blouse and being simple. I can't wait until we are out of this store, and I can hardly look at this material even though it is for me and it is nice, but I feel low.

We have searched the streets and do not see any sign of a cobbler shop at all. Maybe the Sings have moved on somewhere but we asked around and there is no one who will say they know them. We tried one more time all the way to the far west end of Pennington street which is a bad looking area hard against the old walls of the presidio, but all the Chinese we meet either turn away or try to sell us things, they will not listen to us or act like they know what we mean. Harland is disappointed but we will go back to the dry goods and get him some boots from the catalog.

All together it was a long day and we are camped in our wagon and sleeping on the ground just like before. It is strange to camp with a town so close by, but lonely too, as we are used to camping with a crowd of folks and soldiers. I will be glad to head for home tomorrow and wait for word from Ernest.

March 19, 1882

As we were pulling out this morning we passed by the Army fort and there was a little crowd of Indians near there sort of camping as if they lived there and weren't afraid of the soldiers nor intending to make trouble for them. We came right up against one wall and I could hear a bugle blowing and it sets me to remember all the days of our wagon trip and the soldiers a mustering around the flag every day. It is a kind of lonesome sound, a bugle in the dark before dawn.

Albert stopped the wagon just at the gate which was open, and there were some lines of men saluting in front of one on a horse. The fellow on the horse saluted them back and then caught his eyes this way and squinted at us real hard in the half light and looked sort of familiar. Then Albert chucked the reins and we headed out. The cold hurts my face so I have got my shawl wrapped around up to my nose and I'm curled up out of the wind as much as possible. I wonder if that was that Captain Elliot. All the way home it was too cold to talk, and my mind was busy anyway. I kept thinking about that Duchess of Warwick woman, wearing a red dress and longing for something or someone over the sea. And I thought about her longing for her sweetheart and about how Savannah longed for Albert when he and Mama were gone just a couple of days. Then I thought about kissing a fellow and wondered how it was, and about getting babies, too. Pretty soon I drifted off to sleep.

March 26, 1882

I like the smell of the wooden house in the rain. The hot stove inside and the cold wet outside makes the walls sweat and a little sap is coming down in ribbons. Mama is roasting a fat turkey I shot yesterday, and Savannah put on a pan of cornbread for dressing and she found wild sage just yesterday to season it.

I was laying out our old patterns on the blue cloth for my new dress, but Mama said wait, she wanted to do some thinking. Well, she had some ideas about making a little flounce on it to pretty it up some, and she whispered to me that Savannah likes her clothes plain because she was raised Quaker and we don't have to be afraid of a little ruffle because it can make you feel good to wear a pretty dress. Then she told me a story about a dress she had when she met Papa and a basket supper he took her to and things I never heard about before. I never before pictured her being a young girl and wanting a pretty dress and sitting with young men at a basket supper.

March 27, 1882

I have never been so cold as last night. I pushed my blankets next to Mama and squeezed Harland up next to us both. I kept thinking I was freezing to death, and even the rocks we took from the stove have gotten cold long before morning. I dreamed again about sleeping with arms around me and this time in the dream I knew it wasn't just any old arms but Captain Jack Elliot's. When I woke up I found Harland's hand had dropped over on my head like the Captain's was, and I felt stunned. I kept thinking about this for a long time, but did not reach any decision nor feel whether it was good nor bad. Maybe I ate too much turkey and dressing. I'm sure that's it.

We have an unexpected visitor. It is that Captain Elliot from the Army fort. I thought maybe he came to bring me my book but he says no, and even though I said I'd trade him Dan or Terry back he says no two more times and he didn't bring it with him anyway so it will have to wait. That made me mad.

He sat awhile with Albert at dinner, talking about the trees we have planted and just seemed mighty interested in pecan farming, as if it was the one thing in the world he wanted to know more about. Mama kept saying, Sarah, fetch him some coffee, fetch him some water, how about some buttermilk? to me, as if all I had to do in an afternoon was be handy for some thirsty Army captain. Then she whispers to me, Sarah, comb your hair, there is a switch falling out around your face. So I went to do that and sat on the bed and read a book instead.

Then Savannah came to me and said, I wish your new dress was finished, don't you?

I said there isn't any hurry in it.

So quick as a flash of lightning, Savannah takes a hairpin from her hair and pins up the loose piece in mine. Come on and join us, honey, she said, Captain Elliot will be leaving before dark.

Well, it can't be soon enough for me, so if my talking to him will get that man out of here, then I better go set on the porch with them.

It is late at night now, and every time I close my eyes, I hear Captain Elliot's voice, kind of low and steady, like a song being sung far away. He is always polite to my mama. Must be he didn't take offense at her acting peculiar before. I noticed although he looked polished and pressed, on the heel of one of his boots was a scrape mark like he had taken a spill or gouged it against a rail or something. All the time he was talking, I watched that scratch on his boot. When he laughed, everyone laughed, as if they couldn't help it.

I wonder if he will pay another visit. Not that I want him to, but I wonder if he will.

April 30, 1882

We have been busier than ever before. The new chicks have hatched and all the trees are planted. Albert's arms and back are all muscled out as a blacksmith's and he has worked like three men day and night to do it, and I am proud of our family when I think of them all. It looks as if we have lost about ten of the trees on the trip, but all told that is a good rate of loss. My dress is almost finished as we are going real slow and it seems real fine. I don't know when we are going to town again, but I will wear it then.

Mr. Raalle came to visit today and stayed for supper. He said he has built a small one-room house for himself and Melissa, and finally got a well in, although he said using the stream was just fine. Mama told him how streams in the Territory are mostly only good in the winter, and he would be glad this summer he had a well, when the stream was dry as dust. Likely we will have to dig deeper come August anyway.

Little Melissa looked healthy enough but raggedy, and it is clear that Mr. Raalle is doing his level best but she has no mother to comb her hair nor keep her clothes mended and clean. Mama fussed over her a bit and said what a fine girl she was, and would she like to help make some biscuits for supper, so she did and was very happy to have all the motherly attention.

Savannah let me feel the baby kick yesterday and while we were smiling at the feel of it then she hugged me and that little fellow kicked me in the stomach! What a wonderful thing to have a baby. I hope she is not so scared any more.

We have gotten a letter from the Lawrences. They are getting started on their cattle ranch, and have built a house of the limestone there. They have had a tornado, but no damage done. There is no word from Ernest. We hope he is well. I am writing him another letter to Fort Huachuca and one also to Captain Elliot about the purchase of my Duchess of Warwick book.

Mr. Raalle told us he heard in Tucson that Mike Meyers got shot in the head in Tombstone. He challenged some gambler, and although it was against the law to wear a gun in town, the man had a Colt in his belt and plugged Mike without a second thought. Well, I wonder who is shooting that fancy rifle now?

May 9, 1882

We have had a short spell of heat and then cool again and the days are beautiful but the wind blows without stopping. Flowers are blooming everywhere across the land and every day the trees seem to have more and more leaves and flowers too. Mama has continued to stay with us and does not seem to slip away or stare off any more. I asked her did she know she had been a little peculiar since we buried Papa, and she said, Well, yes. But, she said, Sarah you had a hand on everything and all was going well, so I just slipped away. Then when I thought I would lose you, I saw I would have to come back and take hold of things again.

This makes me feel real strange. If I hadn't gotten so sick would she have stayed touched? And why did she think I had things in hand, didn't she know I was just driving horses and sleeping with a cocked rifle and haunted day and night with fear and work?

I have been reading and reading many books. I know if I ever get word who they might belong to I should give them back so I am trying to read as much as possible in case that happens soon, but I would be sad to have to do that. I must never forget to be grateful for the gift of these books.

The dogs are going crazy, someone is coming up the road.

May 10, 1882

Well, I was never so surprised to see anyone as Jimmy Reed coming up the road last evening. He trotted up to the house on a big beautiful quarterhorse and hopped off quick, shaking hands all around, and then grinned and looked down real red faced and shook hands formal with Savannah. I guess she is still pretty to fellows even though she is in a delicate condition.

Not only was he coming he said, but he was staying as well. He was driving horses and a heifer and a white-faced bull, too. Jimmy has told us that living in the MacIntosh's bunkhouse was a trial and he sorely missed Mama's good cooking, and that Miss Ruthanne has her cap set on the ranch foreman, and did not even once look his way the whole time he lived there.

We understood when he left that they were already promised, but it seems if there was a promise it is forgotten, and his working there was a waste of time. Jimmy took his pay in stock and said he earned extra by working hard and breaking mustangs and such. So now he has a herd almost fifty and needs a good place to run them.

This is a pecan farm, we told him, not a ranch, as without Papa we decided not to run horses, but Jimmy said he wants his own spread anyway, and he has seen some good country on the way.

Jimmy Reed is taller and filled out some from when we last saw him. If the food was that bad, it doesn't seem to disagree with him, as he is tall as Albert and strong looking and his hair has gotten darker. He sits a horse like he is part of it, and that's a good sign, Papa used to say. He got his stock put in our little pen for the night and we all stayed up late and talked a long time and then he asked if he could throw down on our floor.

It would be a sight better than the rocks he's been sleeping on, and no scorpions or rain likely to get on him, he said.

I feel funny sleeping with him in the room like this, and in the dark he says to me, What's that you're doing, Sarah? I told him I write a journal of our travel and life and I will put the candle out soon, so he said Good night, and began to snore right away just like he always did when he was a kid.

I remember that sound and now it seems it has been missing all this time but since we were in strange country I didn't know it.

May 14, 1882

Jimmy has staked himself a section of land near to the Mexican's spread, their name is Maldonado, and it has some wild and rocky country, but plenty of stream to water his stock. He filed his claim right away. He is borrowing our canvases and made a tent for now. He is building fences and a corral, first things first. Sometimes he eats supper with us, just coming in as if he was family. Sometimes he stays at his place.

Mr. Raalle came over to pass the time and brought us butter and cream and buttermilk from his cows. He said he is learning from the Maldonados about how to make those adobe bricks and dry them in the sun. He is going to make bricks all summer in the heat and build himself a house. He said it was good to use the land and to learn from those who knew what the land had to offer. I think a cactus fence like the Maldonados have might be a good thing to keep coyotes and bobcats and such from the henhouse, but Albert says it is a bother and he has a fine henhouse already.

May 22, 1882

Harland seems to spend lots of time at the Maldonados' house as they have seven children. They just play and play hard all the time. I went over there to get him one day for supper and took a bowl of sourdough starter to them. They seemed ever so nice but we did not speak their language at all. Except that rascal Harland has surprised us all and when we asked questions or they talked to us he would say She wants to know if you have a garden, or He says there are lots of baby chicks here this year. It seems he has picked up some Mexican talk from playing with the boys and it makes it nicer to have some talk with them rather than just nodding and smiling.

Mrs. Maldonado led me out to the chicken coop and scooped up some pullets, five of them, and gave them to me and so I asked Harland how do I say thank you and he said it. Pretty soon we had stayed too long and the smell coming from the stove is awful good. We will have to make friends with them and get Mrs. Maldonado to show me how to make it, and get Harland to teach me some words so I can be polite.

I have started to read a book named The Happy Bride. It is all about how a girl should act and what men expect from the girl they want to marry and such. It is a wonderful book and I plan to study it hard and put it to practice. The first thing I must do is become more religious. I will have to learn to be "a righteous example of piety and purity, virtuous to a fault, kind and sharing," if I am to be the Happy Bride in the book. "Bible study is the first importance in being a wife." No wonder Savannah is so happy, I am sure she is one of God's angels here on earth. More than anything else, I think I want to be like her. I will have a lot of work to do to be pious and pure of heart.

As for that rainstorm and a certain soldier, I will just turn from my wicked ways and be sure never to place myself in a situation like that again. If I was, I would turn him away with a strong command rather than bawl like an orphan calf and fall asleep like I was safe with him. This book says "a young lady is never safe when in close physical proximity to a gentleman, and although he would pursue her, he thinks all the more of her if she rebuffs him heartily." So I have thought of a hearty rebuff that I will tell that Captain Elliot if ever I see him again, or any man who presumes to be in close physical proximity.

The book doesn't say what to do if you have slept in your underwear on top of a soldier in a wagon during a rainstorm. I will study this book so the first chance I get not to be an old maid I will be ready.

May 29, 1882

Jimmy has gotten somewhat of a house built although it is just one little room with a stove. He is going to drive to Tucson tomorrow and sell a couple of horses if he can to raise money for tools and fence wire and such.

Mama said why don't I go with him and sell some of our first vegetables, so I am taking a bath tonight after supper and will wear my new blue dress, and Mama's good straw hat. I told Mama I thought we should have someone with us, since Jimmy isn't really my brother and all, but she said she didn't want to go and wants to stay near Savannah since she is getting close to her time, so we will have to take Harland, and he is real excited.

June 2, 1882

We were about to leave that morning real early before sunup but couldn't get Harland out of bed, and when we did, he is running a fever and covered with red spots. Mama was real upset and said she will try to clean the house real good because it looks like measles, and it is good for us to go and get away, and Albert and Savannah will move to Jimmy's house for some days. Mama said for us to stay an extra day or two in Tucson and not to worry.

I remember having measles and it was a whole month to get over it. That was before Harland was born, and I was little but I remember being awful sick. Likely he got it from the Maldonado children or will have given it to them, and she said she will put him down comfortable and walk over and warn them they are in for a spell of sickness with seven children all in a row.

It was mid morning before we pulled away, and borrowed Albert's wagon. At first I thought I shouldn't be sitting on this seat next to him, but then I got to thinking he is just good old Jimmy who I have known for years. As we drove we talked about all that had happened since we left, and I told him the story of our journey to San Angelo and back, only leaving out a couple of parts.

He said he was real interested in Rose and she looked to be a fine horse, and I said she was for sure. He has a beautiful chestnut stallion he said, and he would like to know if he could breed her and then I would have two, since Rose is old enough now. He is breeding all his mares, and most of them are in foal right now.

This is a good plan, I said, but I remembered how the book said I must be pure and innocent, so I said I would leave it all up to him. Well, he asked why, and I said it is not like when we were children, I am a young lady and don't have to do with such things as that, it is man's work.

Pretty soon we stopped for dinner, and I showed him all the

arrow holes in Albert's wagon. He asked me was I still a pretty good shot, and I said yes, pretty good.

We camped near a store at the south edge of town. I slept in the wagon bed and Jimmy slept underneath. All night long I could hear him snoring soft like.

All the horses gleamed in the morning light like they were scrubbed new, and I knew Jimmy liked to take care of those horses just like Papa. Pretty soon here he comes with a pail of water and says, Sarah do you drink coffee?

We had a little breakfast and coffee and he said to me I looked different. I asked him how, but he couldn't say, he just said Kind of sparkly.

So I said, It is my new dress Mama made, and he said maybe so. Then he was off to trade his horses, but he said it was not a lady's place at a horse corral, there might be rough characters there. I said I would take all the vegetables to the stores instead, and we parted company. I am glad he thinks I am a lady, and I have to be careful how I seem to other folks and hope there is a single fellow in town who will notice my new dress, but I must not notice that he notices, if he does.

Jimmy had a really good day, and has put two hundred dollars in his pockets. Some of that he will leave behind for a fancy metal cistern for holding rain water at his house that he has ordered. He said he doesn't like credit, and paid his bill at the store in advance, he likes cash on the barrelhead.

Jimmy said he was finding out who bought and sold horses, and when he needed to hire a good wrangler, who to ask for later on. I declare, he doesn't seem that old, but he acts like he has been doing this all his life. I just didn't realize that Albert and him were paying attention to the horse business with Papa. Ernest was who I always talked to, and who always had time to talk. Maybe Ernest had time to talk because he wasn't tending to business. Anyway, he is gone to be a soldier and Mama just now is understanding that and is not pleased with him at all.

Just for fun, Jimmy said, since we have to stay a couple of days, we will eat at a restaurant and sleep in a hotel on the last night we are here, but he said not the Cosmopolitan, as he heard it was a dirty place, and we drove past it and looked and he was right. Then we drove to the Carillo Gardens, which is a pretty park they have made, with shade trees and a pond with brown and white ducks swimming by. It was a lovely place and we stayed all afternoon in the cool shade of some trees, and had a picnic lunch there that Jimmy went and bought. A Mexican lady came by selling little sweet cakes, and I bought some, three for a nickel, and we split the extra one. When I brushed the crumbs off my dress, a little duck came right up and picked the grass clean in a minute!

We did indeed eat a steak dinner at a little restaurant called Levin's and it was pretty good but the pie doesn't hold a candle to what we make at home. Later on that place got too jumpy for me with wild dancing and although there were lots of young men there to choose from, I decided there was a train load of avarice in the room and didn't feel good about being there so we left.

July 4, 1882

A letter came from Ernest at last, early today, by way of a long-legged Cavalryman named Elliot. We planned on the Raalles to come by for supper so I had ironed my blue dress to be ready, but I was wearing an old one. Captain Elliot rode up and just at that minute, Savannah came to me with a fresh bucket of milk and stepped a little sideways and slopped that milk all over me. Then she says, Oh, my, I'm so sorry, Sarah. I'll do it up for you.

But I said it was all right, I figured to wear the other work dress that was out on the line.

And she said, Oh dear, you can't, because you see a wind came up and whipped that dress right out of the clothespins, and it is covered with mud so you'll have to wear the new one. Then she says, I'll do up these others for you because I feel so bad about it.

But she didn't sound sorry one bit, and as I was putting on the new dress, I heard her a singing out loud like I would never do if I had just taken on extra washing and ironing. She has got a twinkling look in her eye today.

Mama said, Must be the baby making her just a bit flighty. As she said that she pushed me in the house to change and offered Captain Elliot the rocker on the porch.

When I came back, he said he rode out here because we have been waiting to know about our kin. Ernest's letter didn't say much at all, though:

> *Dear Folks, I am doing fine and stay busy. I was expecting to fight Indians but there is a shortage of men who can shoe a horse, and since Papa taught me which side of the horse the nails go in, I have been made the post blacksmith. I have whittled up another wooden leg, and the doctor is saving my old one in case someone else can use it. If there is an Indian campaign I will go along to shoe horses and fix wheel rims and such. Hope all is well. Yours truly, Private Ernest Prine, U.S. Cavalry.*

Mr. Raalle came by for dinner because it is the Fourth of July, and brought fried chicken he had made. Little Melissa seems to be growing out of her clothes, and Mama offered to make her up some last when she saw him, so he has brought some yard goods, too, and many thanks in advance. Mama measured up Melissa and hugged her, and they both seemed to be having a fine time. We had some watermelons just barely ripe enough to pick, and squash, and a recipe I got from Mrs. Maldonado called pollo y maiz. There was no way around having to ask Captain Elliot to stay for supper, and he did stay, without even politely refusing.

Later we saw a little dust on the road, and Harland said, Look's like Jimmy's coming over. After a bit Jimmy rode up on his fine stallion and said hello to every one. When he shook hands after being introduced to Captain Elliot, you would have thought there was dry lightning in the air, why you could nearly see sparks fly between them. Jimmy got all tight in the jaw and red in the throat like I've never seen him before, and Captain Elliot's eyes made that grey flashing like when he was ready to fight. I swear I don't know what gets into men. It is like putting two roosters in the same coop and feathers are bound to fly. I know my brothers could scrap over nothing and come up bloody, then help each other dust off, and it appears those two could go at it without a word said between them. They've just met, for goodness' sake. It wouldn't be much of a fight, though. I think Jimmy is pretty scrappy but I have seen Captain Elliot strike like he was ten men.

Suddenly, Captain Elliot said it was getting late, and he had a long ride ahead, so he begged our leave and saddled right up.

Mama stood up and said, Will you take some of that pie for the ride? We've got plenty. Harland, fill the Captain's canteen. Sarah, go fetch the Captain some of that pie.

Yes, Ma'am, I said. I didn't hear what he answered, but I didn't want to argue with my mama. I went into the kitchen, and turned around and there he was behind me, strapping on his gun belt and fixing his uniform straight. When I got the pie wrapped carefully in brown paper, I turned to hand it to him.

That rascal grabbed my hand, pie and all, and leaned down quick and kissed my lips! Then he straightened up and took the smashed pie, and said Thank you, Miss Prine. And he left. Just like that.

I felt like my shoes were glued to the floor, and a hot, heavy feeling ran through me, and all I could do was put my hands against my mouth and feel my fingers tremble. After a while, Mama called me, and I answered that I was washing up the pie plate, but that was a lie. I went in the bedroom and took Mama's little looking glass up and studied my face. It didn't look like the face of a girl who kissed men on the lips. Actually, I didn't do any of the kissing, and it was no more a little kiss than Mama would give on my cheek, but I sure forgot all my hearty rebuffs, caught off guard like that.

It appears we will enjoy fireworks from heaven tonight, as it got dark early and the lightning started overhead in long sheets through the heavy clouds. Then a dust cloud came up, and after it a hard rain. The first raindrops came down on the tail of the dust ball, falling like mud drops on everything and turning the world brown. Then I thought about Captain Elliot riding in that storm. Maybe he will have sense enough to hunker down somewhere and wait it out. Serves him right, I suppose.

While we watched from the windows, Jimmy said he is pretty

sure Rose is in foal. He brought his mouth harp tonight, and wanted to sit by me. It is sure easier to sit next to Jimmy than Jack Elliot. It doesn't feel all jittery and nervous, just easy. I wondered if Jimmy wanted to kiss me. I wondered if he would try.

July 5, 1882

All the men slept at one wall and the ladies in Albert and Savannah's room. When I got up to start a fire for coffee and feed the animals, Jimmy was up already and out. The land smelled good and clean and wet and cool. Jimmy and I did the feeding and brought up water from the well. He even drew up some extra water for washing later. When I asked him why, he said he saw some trees overblown by the wind and my brothers will be out working and muddy, and there will be washing later. I smiled at him and said he was pretty smart, then he laughed a little at me and said I always sure looked sparkly in the morning. That made me blush, I know, but I liked hearing it.

Jimmy said my horse Terry needed shoes and it was too bad Ernest wasn't around, but he could do it for me so I said fine, I'd trade him something, and did he need some sewing? Well, he said he's just going to think about it, and wouldn't be in a hurry to collect. I wondered if he wanted a kiss right then, but he didn't say any more. By that time we were in the house with the water, and Albert looked up at us real queer, and said What have you two been up to?

Well, I said, Albert Prine, we've been fetching water and what else would you think? But he just looked back and forth at Jimmy and me as if we were strangers for sure.

I don't know what was ailing Albert, and he never would say. Then it seemed to me that maybe I haven't been careful enough to seem as purely above reproach as The Happy Bride book said. But Jimmy has been around for years and we have all worked side by side all that time. Why would he think it is different now? It was just work, there was no sign he even thought about kissing me at all. It must be he is a real gentleman.

July 8, 1882

The Maldonado children all passed through the measles just like Harland except for the littlest one, they call Yoyo, which is short for Yolanda. She seems to be failing and has not kept anything down for sixteen days today. Mama was over there yesterday with Harland by her side to make sure of the language, but when she came home she said she sure didn't know what to do for Yoyo. Yoyo breathes all right, but has spots in her mouth and everywhere, and vomits day and night no matter what they do or give her and she is thin as a little lizard.

July 10, 1882

Today is Yolanda's fourth birthday and we laid her in her tiny grave with flowers and a rag doll her mama made. She looks like a dried up, pretend child, not real at all. I have never seen a child so starved and sick. All are sad but relieved that her suffering is ended.

Papa Maldonado started making her a coffin yesterday, and it is carved with little birds on it flying towards heaven with a little angel behind them. Only her mama cannot leave her and rocks and moans by the grave which has a little fence around it to save her from coyotes and such. Mama stayed with her at the grave, and the Maldonados and Raalles are here in the house and some of their other friends that I don't know.

After a couple of hours the children begin playing. They just cannot be sad too long, it is not in them, as children mourn in little bits here and there like patchwork in their lives.

Mrs. Maldonado at last began walking back to the house. The Maldonados have the biggest mesquite tree I have ever seen, and just as they came to the garden gate under it, down to her feet flew a little dove like she had called it there. She made a cry like she had a pain, and pointed, and everyone got quiet for a second. Then the little dove flew up, up, over the house and out of sight fast. Mrs. Maldonado fainted away. Then there was so much fussing I felt like I was in the way. So I walked out to their stock fence where it was quiet.

Just as I imagined, the troughs were empty and their brindled cow looked at me pained and lowed. I went and filled her trough and while she was drinking like she was scorched, I milked her before she would bust a teat and took the milk back in the house. Then I found her some grain and a sheaf of hay, and as I was about to close up the gate, there was Jimmy standing right behind me. I just wanted to be helpful, I said.

Well, he lowered the bar for me and said he understood, and he was leaving, and would I like to ride home on his buckboard with him? So I did.

On the way home he said he knew how I could pay him for the horse shoeing and he asked me could he hold my hand. So he did. I didn't mind. Nobody has held my hand since I was a little bitty girl. There is a real comfort in it. Jimmy's hands were hard and leathery, just like Papa's were. He's not any taller than I am, but he's strong and his hands seem so big. It made me warm inside.

July 12, 1882

Harland has drawn a big picture of a grand house and I told him it was fine and we put it on the wall with some little nails. He is real proud. He reads pretty well and draws a good picture, and talks Mexican like he was a native. Our neighbors call him Arlando.

Savannah came in from pulling weeds this afternoon and said she had a pulled feeling in her back, and needs to rest. She looked peaked, so I began filling the washtub for her to take a cool soak.

When Savannah stood up from her cool bath she suddenly called out Sarah! and a big splash of water ran off her into the tub and she grabbed her sides. I hurried quick and dried her off, and she began to cry a little. Oh Sarah, she said, I am scared the baby is coming. So I helped her into her nightdress and ran to fetch Mama.

Mama was right there by the chicken coop, and said, yes, that water was a sign, and sent Harland to tell Albert and then on to fetch Mrs. Maldonado, as she knows how to have lots of children.

Later, I tried not to think of Mrs. Barston, but Savannah started to struggle, and I began to worry and shake all over. That awful pained sound coming from Savannah was like a knife that cut into me, and she cried out Mother, help me! I am dying! But then, she gave one more long, terrible push and a moan, and there in Mama's hands on a white towel was a wiggly, wet baby boy.

Mrs. Maldonado began to cry happy tears, and Mama, and me too, and I hugged Savannah and ran to tell Albert.

It was strange to run out into the evening, as I had no idea the time had passed and the late clouds were rolling in and smelled like rain coming again. Albert was so white in the face he looked like a ghost, and holding tight to the fence post like it was the only thing keeping him standing up. He saw me coming and I thought he would perish on the spot. Come in the house, Papa Albert, I called. You have a baby boy!

He sort of stumbled away from the post and I had to laugh at him. Then he grabbed my shoulders and said, Is Savannah alive? All is well. And Clover Jeremiah Prine is a sturdy boy with a loud voice.

I took Bear and Toobuddy and a rifle, and since I don't want to cinch Rose because she is expecting too, I went bareback on her over to Jimmy's to tell him the news.

July 13, 1882

After Jimmy got done scolding me for coming to his place alone after dark, he was happy about the baby. But he kept up for a long time about Apaches and cowboys and other outlaws, and didn't I know how to be scared and careful, and all.

Well, I know real well how to be scared, I have had a lot of practice. But Rose knows the way to his house fine, and I could see the light from his window after I turned a corner, and that wasn't such a long way at all.

Then, the rain started to fall. And a strong wind began howling around the house like it would pull it down. Then I really got afraid. Not of the storm, nor of the darkness outside, but the storm was too bad to go out in and I had not been smart to come with it on the way, and I was stranded there. If I went home and Rose spooked at some lightning and broke a leg I'd lose her and her foal. And if I stay, Jimmy will think I am a wanton woman, or low.

Suddenly it comes to mind what Captain Elliot had said, that it was worse to be ruined by a rumor than by the truth. Sometimes the truth is real simple but what folks make of it in the telling is a mess like a rat's nest. The truth is here I am again in a rainstorm with a man.

I couldn't go and I couldn't stay. My family might not understand. Or they might say it's only good old Jimmy, never mind. When he first came south with his herd and slept on our floor, it didn't matter at all. Now it seemed to matter, big as a mountain. Jimmy, I said, will you make me some coffee? I feel chilled a bit.

So he did and while he fiddled with the coffee grinder and all, I thought hard what should I do short of changing my name to Rahab.

Did you put Rose in the shed? he asked me.

Yes, I did, I told him, and the dogs are under the house. Jimmy has a good horse shed, he takes care of his animals. Pretty soon the coffee started to smell good, and Jimmy began cooking some bacon. I sat there thinking and coming up empty, like fishing without bait, I was in a real quandary.

What is the matter, said Jimmy to me, are you sick?

But I couldn't think of what to say so I shrugged.

Jimmy was stirring some flour into a bowl. Do you like pancakes? he says. It's one thing I can make but it ain't much supper for company, but if you don't mind, there's a keg of sorghum on that shelf over your head, Sarah. And he began to pour pancakes on the griddle.

I felt like I moved through mud, and I watched him flip the little cakes and smelled the coffee and bacon, and I tried to think but my head just quit on me.

Suddenly, it didn't matter what I thought because I heard Bear growling under the house and as he did a loud knock came on the door. A man's voice hollered Hello, The House, and bang! the door pushed open, with a fellow in a dripping slicker standing there. He was no taller than me, but big in the shoulders and stocky in the middle, carrying something heavy and slopping mud and water all over the floor. He took off his hat and nodded to us and says his name is Moses Smith, and asked could he wait out the storm in Jimmy's barn, and held out his hand to Jimmy. Jimmy answered back his name, and Mr. Smith nodded to me and said Evening Mrs. Reed, real simple. I didn't feel like telling this man he had me wrong, because he gave me a skitterish feeling like there was a snake under a board you were standing on.

I knew Jimmy pretty well and I guessed he wouldn't put up no stranger in his barn full of foaling mares and a prize stallion, and just like that he said, Sit here a spell, Mr. Smith.

Mr. Smith takes off his slicker and leans it on a peg against the door, and slings down off of his shoulders two sets of saddle bags that hit the floor real loud and hard like they are loaded with lead. He pulls up a chair and says, That smells good, Mrs. Reed, and smacks his lips. He is wearing a suit coat and a slick red vest. It looks to be fancy, expensive duds but dirty and torn, like he has worn them through their best days awhile back. Under his vest I see two crossed leather belts of loaded shot with pistols hanging from them tied down to his legs. The only people who wear guns strapped down like that, need to use them in a hurry and often.

Jimmy, I said, You'll have to get another plate down.

He mostly ate like a hog, and I was really afraid. I kept thinking I had left my rifle in the shed with Rose where it would do me no good. We kept up with him thinking that we were married, and he asked could he bed down in a store room, but Jimmy said he only had one room. I figure he sized the man up pretty quick, too.

Mr. Smith said, Would you put up my horse, Mr. Reed? and smiled real ugly at me when he said it. In that second I pictured him following Jimmy out to the shed and killing him and my fate would be worse than that.

No, I can't do that, was all Jimmy said, without any explaining. What is that heavy stuff you're carrying? Jimmy asked him right out.

Mr. Smith laughed with his mouth full of pancakes and slurped at his coffee, and said, No, that's real light, son, real light. Then he laughed some more.

Time went past more slow than I could imagine, and I did up the dishes while Jimmy talked about politics and the new Territorial Governor. That fellow Smith didn't need much of a lead to tell a piece and went on and on with tales that seemed to be much too tall for one man to have lived. Jimmy stayed calm and acted like he enjoyed listening, but I see in his eyes from across the room that he is biding his time, letting him have his yarn, as it wouldn't do to disagree with that man.

Pretty soon, he declares he is ready to sleep, and then he snickers real dirty sounding, and says he'll face the wall over yonder and leave us privacy. He scoots his heavy bags for a pillow and stretches out wet and dirty on the bare floor. Right in front of the door.

Jimmy came to me and said real soft, Sarah, you have to stay. If you leave he could follow you if I can't stop him.

I told him back, What's to keep him from killing you in your sleep anyway? And Jimmy pressed his hand against his shirt and I see he has something heavy in it. He whispered that he kept extra tools near the kitchen stove sometimes. So, he got out two blankets and spread them as far away from Moses Smith as he could, and I laid next to the wall in my dress and shoes and all, and Jimmy laid next to me.

He whispered to me was I scared, and I said some, then he took my hand in the darkness and into it slipped something cold and sharp. He had put a knife in my hand big as a Bowie knife. He whispered again real slowly like he was making the picture in my head for me, Just think of skinning a deer. It is just like that. A deer. Then he unbuttoned his shirt and set his hand on a gun hidden on his chest.

We laid there together, not talking, hardly moving, stiff and scared, until the sun began to come up. Laying there on the floor next to Jimmy I felt less afraid of Moses Smith, and a little afraid of Jimmy. He was so close I could smell his clothes. His hand was on mine and I wondered if he was meaning that to be a comfort, but I couldn't ask. I was too scared to sleep, but not too scared to think about laying close up on the floor with Jimmy. I watched him breathing. I saw his face in the dim light of the low lamp. His whiskers sparkled like a little halo around his chin. Moses Smith snorted and rooted around like a hog. Jimmy grunted when he did. He looked at me and I caught eyes with him and nodded. I could see two little stars out the window from the angle I was at. After a while they went away. And a while after that the window got pale and sort of gold colored.

First Light! Jimmy calls out. Time to tend the horses, Mrs. Reed! And we hopped up, springing off the blanket like two lizards off a hot rock. The air was thick and heavy from the rain, and instead of feeling fresh, the world felt weighed down.

We scuffled around quickly making a real big fuss over starting up the coffee, and I put that big knife into my apron pocket with the handle sticking out, then Jimmy hollered to Mr. Smith, who had not moved an inch, Mr. Smith, we have to tend the stock, excuse us, we have to get out the door. Well, Mr. Moses Smith reached under himself and pulled out a big forty-four Colt and waved it around the room. Jimmy pushed me behind himself quick.

Smith opened his eyes and looked around, probably trying to get his bearings, and said, Oh, sorry folks. Pretty soon he moved out of our way as we were not backing away. The smell in the heavy warm air was making me scared, because it was the smell of him.

Quick as a fox we stepped aside as he moved and pulled open the door, and I took off toward the barn, but Jimmy grabbed my arm, and said between his teeth, Don't run. When we were sheltered from Mr. Smith's eyes by the shed door, I turned around to stare at the house and see if he was moving around in there.

Our coffee is probably turned to tar by now, I said to him, after about an hour.

Jimmy said Maybe that'll get rid of a varmint we got. As we were shaking oat dust off our hands and sleeves, there was Mr. Smith leaning over the fence and looking in with a grin at all those horses and at us.

Nice herd, Mr. Reed, he says. Are you interested in selling any?

Jimmy said back, No, we're expecting to increase the herd by next year, then I'll be selling. None of the mares are ready yet, and the stallions don't go anywhere, he said.

Smith nodded and grinned and said, They don't, aye? like he meant to change Jimmy's mind one way or another. Then he mounted his horse, and started off slow. At the corner of the corral he turned around and said, Oh, by the way, folks, that was a bad storm. Appears to have blown away all trace of your clothes, Mizz Reed, and any sign that you actually live here. Then he laughed in a way that I imagine is heard in saloons, but I never heard anyone laugh so that it made me feel as ashamed as that before.

We stood like two trees rooted to the ground, and watched him disappear around the bend, then I walked back to the barn and sat on a bale and stared at the horses in front of me, all sleek and fat and loved, and I cried.

July 19, 1882

We are making a little trip once a week to the stage station to check for mail, and it is real handy to have it so close at hand. I have gotten a letter from Captain Elliot, addressed directly to me and not to the rest of the family, so I took the liberty of reading it myself first on the way home.

Dear Miss Prine, I write to inform you that due to the increased number of recruits, Cavalry horses are going at a premium now. Therefore the value of the book you inquired about, The Duchess of Warwick, having been traded for a high quality draft horse that would be of good use to the Army, has increased. If you still desire the return of the book, it will be necessary to deliver the selfsame horse, in prime condition, or make a cash offer exceeding the present value of the horse, which is sixty dollars. Cordially yours, Captain J. E. Elliot, 10th Cavalry HQ, Fort Lowell, Tucson

What a lot of nonsense, and the most pompous bunch of stuffed up words I have ever heard and from that man! Most Army horses I have seen are a sad lot, and anyway those were the foreigners' horses, I didn't trade a good book for any swaybacked old ten-dollar Army plug.

I am going to write that man back and let him know that he agreed the book was worth a horse even, and that he has got to stick by his word. If that is a sixty-dollar horse then he has already got a sixty-dollar book. I declare but it is going to be a piece of work for me to remain pious and generous and kind to a fault!

July 28, 1882

A couple of men came through here and stopped to water and said thank you folks. They were in a hurry and didn't rest their horses long enough, I could tell, but living here it is best not to ask too many questions of men in a hurry.

Jimmy asked me to come to his house and make suggestions about how it ought to look. Harland is going with me as he has drawn many pictures of houses now, and he is going to draw one in the dirt for Jimmy. Jimmy offered us drinks of rain water from his cistern and we admired how he had it rigged up to a spigot in the house so you just have to turn a handle and have water right away.

I asked him did he want some adobe like I was making for a cool room, but he said he wanted a wood house. He is digging a cellar close, so there will be a cool place to store things. It was hard to make him say just how did he want the house, mostly he kept on asking how would I want it if it were mine, so I had to tell him, and he marked off things on the ground. I like working with Jimmy. We get along fine and don't ever seem to disagree, just ask each other's opinion. It is nice to know someone you don't have to prove a question to all the time. Even my brothers aren't as easy to get along with. He likes a hard day's work and isn't afraid of it, and that's a fine quality in a man.

Then Harland went to the corral to look at the horses. Jimmy waited until Harland was behind the shed door, and then said to me, Sarah, you are a good hand with things.

So I said, Well, unless it's buttonholes, I hate sewing buttonholes.

Then he laughed sort of nervous, and said, You got a head on your shoulders and ain't afraid to work hard, that's what I mean.

I nodded. Seems he was trying to hand me a compliment.

Then he said he'd been thinking he needed to start a life here, with a family, and it was nice having the Prines so close, but it wasn't a family like he wanted.

So I said, I'm sure you miss your folks and all.

Then he said, Sarah, would you be my family? Here?

Right away I thought of the Happy Bride book, but I wasn't sure if this was a marriage proposal, and should I say something like No, Indeed Sir? Jimmy, I said, exactly what are you asking me?

And then he said, just like this, I'd like us to marry. Would you think about it and not say no right away at least? After all, there's time while I get the house built up bigger first, before I'd ask you to live here.

Finally, I told him I would indeed think about it and I would give him my answer in a week.

I decided on the way home that I will make up my mind before I tell my folks. Harland kept saying, Sarah what ails you? and You look silly, Sarah, what are you thinking about?

My mind was going a mile a minute, thinking about being married at last. I will have a home all my own and maybe some children. I truly never thought this day would come, that I would be promised to be married. In the Happy Bride, it says the best thing a girl can be is a good wife and mother. It is a girl's highest calling. I hope I am ready.

August 4, 1882

At last, we have all had a night's sleep, the baby only woke two times. Mama said soon enough he'll sleep the night through, and we'll all rest.

This morning I told my family why we haven't seen Jimmy all week, as he has been giving me plenty of space to think about something big. They seemed mighty surprised, all except Albert, who looked at me kind of vexed. Then I put my rifle under my arm and called Toobuddy, and went for a slow walk down to Jimmy's place to have a talk with him.

Jimmy is a good man, and I've seen him grow up and I know he is not too good looking, but he is real clever, just look at that indoor running water spigot. He knows horses, and is making a good living already. And I see how Savannah and Albert are like one person, kind hearted always to each other's feelings, and how he fusses over her and cares for her every little whim like she was a treasure to him.

And then I thought about that night we spent afraid of that Moses Smith fellow. And how when he saw Smith's gun, Jimmy jumped in front of me. And I knew my answer.

He was cutting wood behind the tiny house. When I saw him, he had his shirt off and was measuring and making such a racket he didn't see me coming. So I stood there, quiet, until Toobuddy made a whimper and Jimmy turned around.

You came back, was all he said. Like that alone was surprise enough. Then suddenly he grabbed his shirt off a stack of fresh pine lumber and started wiping sweat and trying to put it on at the same time. It made a little ripping sound as I walked up to him.

So I said, Jimmy, be careful there. You know I hate to mend buttonholes.

August 9, 1882

I feel like I have turned into another person, like someone else walks around in my shoes, and I don't know who I was before, nor who I am now. But the truth is, I am going to become Mrs. James Eldon Reed sometime in October, and Jimmy has written to Tucson for word of when there will be a judge available or a preacher in town.

That afternoon at Jimmy's house there was no one around, and he gave me my first kiss. He was really edgy about doing it, but I didn't budge. It was plain and simple, and didn't make me all crazy feeling like that other one I got from that ornery soldier. Since we're engaged, it is all right. I'm sure Captain Elliot's kiss made me feel strange because he was not being a gentleman. I wanted to tell Jimmy to kiss me some more, but I remembered how pure I'm supposed to be, and although I have given up hope of being too pious, I will have to wait for more kisses until later.

I wrote Ernest about the news and about baby Clover being born, and he has written back already, in a hurry mostly because they are sending him to the Dakotas to join in the Indian wars there, which was just what I was afraid of. Besides, there is plenty of Indian trouble here, but the paper says the Governor is not letting the Army help with outlaws, only Indians. They have named the renegade Apaches outlaws, so they say there is not really a Indian war here to fight. That is all pretty stupid to me, as trouble is trouble no matter what name you tag on it, but the Army is chock full of rules, Ernest says, some of them with no sense attached.

He said thank you to me for writing Captain Elliot, as the Captain grinned for a week and was in an amazingly good humor after hearing from me last time. In my head I think he should have got his eyes scalded from reading what I wrote, but there is no explaining that Captain Elliot to anyone. Then Ernest told that man that I was marrying Jimmy Reed, and so there is a little folded up paper inside Ernest's letter from the Captain to me.

I figured it might be a kind note of congratulations, which The Happy Bride says I will get many of that sort from friends and acquaintances, but it says only this:

> *Dear Miss Prine, I sincerely regret to inform you that The Duchess of Warwick and Her Sorrows By the Sea is no longer for sale. —Fondly, Captain John Edward Harrison Elliot, U.S. Army, 10th Cav.*

Low down dirty ornery rotten skunk of a cussed mule-headed soldier! What's he want with my book anyway? And what kind of a way is that to write a congratulations? I am so mad I could walk clear to that fort and take him on single handed.

August 16, 1882

Jimmy is building us a house, and every day I walk over of an evening and listen to him tell about it. He asks me where to put this and that, and do I like a porch all the way around, foursquare, like he does. It is too big, I think, but he said, Well, maybe there will be children to fill it.

He has gotten done with most of the heaviest parts with the help of my brothers and Mr. Maldonado. The Maldonados are always there to help you and are good friends. Mrs. Maldonado showed me how to cut ocotillo sticks for a fence without getting cut to ribbons by tying up pieces with a string so when it is cut it snaps away from you.

Tomorrow, Mama and Jimmy are going to Tucson with the whole Maldonado family, and they will not let me go no matter what I say. Albert is to check on Jimmy's horses for horse thieves, but I have to stay home.

When I got peeved, they all accused me of being touchy and sulking. Let them go, I say. It is hotter in Tucson than here, and heaven knows it is hot enough here to bake bread without an oven. There is no reason I cannot go, they are just being selfish.

Savannah said Stay here and let's make a new batch of lye soap, she has a special recipe that is real fine. So in this wretched heat I am going to go outside and start a big fire and boil a kettle of fat and ashes. This will be hotter than Tucson, and a sight less fun than traveling with all of them and singing songs on the way and such. I wish the Lord would just knock me over with kindness and goodness and simple purity, because I don't seem to be getting the knack of it on my own.

August 20, 1882

There is a Presbyterian preacher in Tucson who will come out to marry us the third week of October, and Jimmy has arranged it. I don't know what a Presbyterian is, and I told him couldn't he get the Methodist preacher to come, and why don't we go to the church for it? but Jimmy didn't answer. It was what he has arranged, and that's that.

Then I figured out the reason myself is that it would take at least two days to go to town to wed, and all would want to be there, and he will not leave his horses all that time in this wilderness.

He has made a huge foursquare porch, roofed all around with the biggest roof I have ever seen. Jimmy said it is exactly like the MacIntoshes', and they had a good house. The first room he had with the cistern will be the kitchen, and he has built better shelves and a cooking table, and made me stand and pretend I was kneading dough to get the height just right for me. The porch is much bigger than the house, he said, because when we want to add a room, all we have to do is put up walls. The roof is suspended by the posts all around, and will cover space for four or five more rooms easily.

He made steps up to the front porch, seven real wide, shallow ones. When I asked him why so many small steps, when four would have done the job, he said, Well, children have short legs, and he grinned. Luckily I was standing really close to him when he said it, because the idea of it made him want to kiss me again and I was glad to be handy.

August 23, 1882

I have started sewing, making new things for my new life. I have to get busy and copy over all Mama's receipts for baking and cooking. She says some are Jimmy's favorites. And I have to copy down my patterns so I am using my newspapers glued together. Harland said that is sissy stuff until I said, Well, it takes a skillful artist to make a precise drawing, then he got interested and even fussed at me for not gluing the papers straight enough for precise work.

Albert shook his head and said, Sarah you read too many books and say words like you are putting on airs to us. Then Savannah told him to hush he would wake the baby.

Seems to me they are not happy about something and touchy this morning, but I have things to do, so they will have to mend their own fence today.

August 30, 1882

When I went to see how the house is coming Jimmy wouldn't let me inside because he said the varnish gas is still bad. There are windows in every wall, and real glass in all of them, with shutters to pull up when it storms to keep out the gale. He is changed a little, kind of gruff today, just real busy trying to finish the house, I suppose.

There has been a cooler spell, and although we know summer is not over, the heat is gentle today and things are growing everywhere, not looking so scorched as they did in June. I am making a rag rug with scraps the Maldonados gave me from all their children's old worn out clothes. I told them what a happy rug it would be as it carries all the children's laughter with it, and Mrs. Maldonado cried and hugged me and made me eat two huge tamales.

I wrote another letter to Captain Elliot, this time much nicer and more sweet, trying to convince him that I do want that book back but we should come to a reasonable agreement about the payment. I suppose I could take Terry or Dan back to him, but I'd rather not.

September 12, 1882

Jimmy is building furniture. It is rugged and not refined, but solid and will last a long time. Meanwhile, I am piecing a quilt, making it really big for us both, and I have gotten started on a tick mattress that will fit inside the bed frame Jimmy has built. When we get a roost full of chickens I plan to start saving feathers to make a bed.

There has been shooting and a stage coach robbing. Some lawmen and a posse are after them and stopped here to water up. They said there is a cave nearby where the outlaws are hiding, and to keep our doors locked and our stock penned. Well, we don't own a lock, but we know what to do with horse thieves.

My letter to Captain Elliot came back from the fort, unopened. It was found in the dirt where the stage coach robbery had been, along with several others. I will send it again.

Jimmy said I should forget it, it is just a stupid book, but it is not, and I can't.

October 2, 1882

I received a letter today from a Major I. A. Thomas at Fort Huachuca, with my letter enclosed. It seems Captain Elliot's enlistment was up, and he retired from the Army, saying he was going home to Texas to be a Texas Ranger and has taken up residence near Austin.

Major Thomas then wrote: *it is sometimes wiser to let these things be, and not to pursue a lost cause.* He surely couldn't know what I want from that man is to pay to have my book returned. I wonder if he thinks the letters I have written were friendly in nature and not business? If so, then the Army is surely made up of a mighty foolish lot of men, with a few exceptions like Ernest.

October 9, 1882

Our wedding is going to be held on our own front porch, on the side away from the sun which has no rooms yet and so is large enough for many people to be in the shade. It is hot again, and I have been at work for two days on a new dress. Jimmy went to town and came home with some handsome yardgoods for me in dark blue.

Savannah has made a stitched and cut out collar that looks almost like lace, and gave it to me today, and it will look wonderful on the dress. This will be my wedding dress, so I am taking my time. I am making rolled trim cords of the scraps of light blue from my other town dress, and tucking that in the edges of seams, and two rows of tiny buttons down the front. It is the grandest dress I have ever seen, and will have a sweeping gather in the back with a bow on it like the Sears and Roebuck dress, but I will not have a shaper to wear it with. Then I am making two skirts and blouses, both of which can be let out later if needed for babies.

If anyone had asked me when we were struggling on the road to San Angelo would I be settling down next year with Jimmy Reed and a herd and a big house of my own, I would have plum laughed my head off.

Albert has built a big stone wall around their well, and rigged a block and tackle up to run the bucket up and down with. Jimmy asked him about it and Albert was rude to him, and I don't know why.

But Jimmy said, Aw, it's just old Albert's way of saying he doesn't want to lose his little sister. Maybe that is why he is so cross lately, he can hardly sit across the table from me.

I asked Mama, isn't there anything else about marriage I need to know? I can make a cake, and butcher a hog or chickens, and plant a garden, and drive a team. But it seems like there is something she should be saying about other things about men.

Mama just looked off at the hills, and said, Be sure to bathe regular and make him, too, if you can. And pray every day.

I went to find Savannah, but she was so busy cooking and tending the baby that it didn't seem like I could get a word in edgewise. Every time I started to talk, she would say, Pass me that flour bowl, would you Sarah? or Take this for me? Hand me that, please, no the other one. There's the baby fussing, just a minute Sarah, would you set that down there? until I just gave up. I never have seen her in such a stir, as if she was more stirred up inside than out. There are lots of questions I want to ask about marriage, but no one to ask them, so I will have to be patient and wait and wonder on my own.

October 20, 1882

Yesterday was our wedding day. In the morning, Jimmy told me to come see the inside at last. Lo and behold, he has bought me a wedding present, and there in the kitchen is the biggest finest stove, all white with steel handles and lifters coiled up so they don't get too hot to touch, and hanging on a rack by little rings are three iron skillets and four big pots, in the corner is a big washtub, and standing over it is a real wringer set up for washing clothes better than with a rub board alone. There are shelves on the walls, a big table, and a line of knives stuck in little slots at the edge of it. These are things he bought when they all made me stay at home that time, he said, real proud of himself for hiding them all this time.

Never in my life did I expect to see such a fine kitchen, much less have it be mine. I had to touch everything and lift everything, and feel it all, and look inside the stove from every little door and opening. The other pot belly stove is in the sitting room, for warmth in there. This is a rich house, I said, and it makes me want to cook something. It also made me want to kiss him some, but I didn't say that, I just smiled.

I had made him four white shirts and two pairs of wool pants for a wedding present, but it doesn't seem like much compared to this.

All the Maldonados came, and brought us a cat to get at the mice around, and seven glazed pottery plates, and a wagon load of food. I could have eaten myself sick on corn tamales and roasted chilies and chicken paella. Albert and Mama brought us two big calf skins to use for anything we want, and a kerosene lamp, and a pen full of chickens, and a little machine like Mrs. Maldonado uses to make tortillas, a wooden thing with a hinge to make the little corn cakes flat and thin.

The preacher was a tall, thin man who came with his wife and stayed all day at our house before the ceremony. He and his wife turned up their noses at all the good Mexican cooking we had. Mama has brought a pot of squash and corn and roasted a piece of beef, and it had cilantro and chili in it too, like the Maldonados make, so the parsons went home hungry. The only thing they could manage to get down was Savannah's butter cake, and luckily she had made four of them, because I think the preacher and his wife ate a whole one themselves. They got in their buggy and left long before sundown, as they were afraid to travel after dark.

Well, I have found out the other things about marriage. And it wasn't at all like I thought, either. Mostly Jimmy was real embarrassed and quiet, and couldn't look me in the eye. I kissed him and said, Jimmy, I love you, honey, do you love me?

He said to me, Are you mad at me?

And I told him No, not a bit. But I wished he'd have said he loved me, too. It seems that now we're married and alone and after what just happened, he could feel free to speak his mind, too. But he rolled over. Goodnight, I said, and he didn't say anything.

I listened to that old familiar snoring for a while, then I went to sleep myself.

This morning, he was gone from the bed before I woke up. Out to tend the horses. So I got up and dressed quickly in my new skirt and blouse and apron and went to start the coffee. There was a fresh stack of wood and a box of kindling next to the stove waiting.

We have roasted a turkey, not a goose as I promised Harland and Savannah last spring, but Christmas dinner at Mama's house is a fine one, with the weather so pleasant and mild that we set up tables out front and spread out such a bounty it was a wonder.

Whatever had been bothering Albert toward me seems to have lifted, and he is his old self. We all miss Ernest dearly and sat together and wrote him a long letter with words from every one. Pretty soon everyone talked so fast I couldn't write to keep up, but we laughed and had a wonderful time.

Jimmy said just to show Ernest how big Baby Clover is, he wanted to paint his little feet in ink and stamp them on the letter. Well, everyone else thought it was a grand idea except for Baby Clover, and he began to cry with everyone fooling with his feet and stamping him up and down.

When they were done his Mama made a frown and went in the house to wash his feet off, and came back with him under a blanket, nursing. Then she said, Albert, I want you to know your son has a tooth! Ouch! And everyone laughed.

I have prayed and prayed, and it seems I may be expecting. I don't know whether to tell Jimmy yet or wait until I am more sure. I finally asked Mama how to know. And she grinned at me real hard.

All is cold and clean and the horses have put on winter coats. Rose is too big to ride, and I spent all this morning with her, talking to her and smiling at our shared babies. I put my hand on her and felt her colt wiggling. Then I patted my own belly and said I Love You for the first time to my baby. I think tonight after supper I will tell Jimmy. This will surely set him thinking. I have tried every way I can think of to get him to say I love you to me. Now he will. It is a fine thing to have a baby. He will be right proud and happy, I am sure.

January 12, 1883

Jimmy said he will buy more lumber on the next trip to town and start a nursery room. I told him that was a fine idea, and we will need a cradle and cloth for diapers, and he just grinned like a goose all day.

With a little dry weather I have been stacking up my adobe blocks and making a little outbuilding. Mostly I just wanted to see how it was done and there's no lesson like one you learn with your own hands. Ruben Maldonado has helped me moving adobe. Jimmy said this adobe building is nonsense, but I feel it is worth a try, and if this one falls down, it will be a lesson from the mistakes.

Coyotes have been after my chickens, and got one today. They dug right under my ocotillo fence. So today I am digging a trench all around the chicken pen and filling it with cholla burs which we collect with a piece of string and a forked stick. Then I bent some loops of wire and hammered them into the ground, just like pinning batting down to a quilt, and pinned those burs in place.

January 14, 1883

Jimmy says it is dangerous to the baby. He lays there tossing, and sometimes goes and sleeps on the floor in the kitchen. It doesn't seem like it has to be but there is no convincing him and since he knows horse breeding, I thought, maybe he is right. I told him I'd like to sleep together anyway, and just hold hands and be close, but he says that makes him nervous.

I got most of the roof on my little adobe shed. Good time, too, as it looks like it will come a rain. No coyotes have been able to get into the chicken coop, but I hear them sniffing around. It is hard to keep Bear from going after them. One at a time they would be no match for him but they are traveling in packs and I'm not sure he could take them all at once, and I doubt Toobuddy would be much help.

I have named my kitty Speckles as she is spotted with colors like a crazy quilt. She brought me her first mouse this morning. Bear decided he wanted a piece of that mouse too, but she told him No in no uncertain terms and his nose has a big deep scratch to prove it.

Jimmy had to go to Tucson for some business today. Went over to Mama's this morning, and Albert and Savannah have finally moved into their own little house, so Bear and I walked over and said hello and admired Baby Clover. Then I told them all my news about expecting. Savannah cried. Everyone seemed overjoyed except Albert acted strange again, and had a hard time to smile. I have known him too long and something is in his craw but he isn't telling. Well, that's just too bad, as Jimmy and I are real happy, and building a fine ranch, and I'm not letting a cranky brother spoil it.

January 26, 1883

In the middle of the rainy night one of the mares has delivered a wobbly little chestnut colt with beautiful white boots on all four legs. Jimmy is just so happy he could bust. This morning he has asked me to make a written record of all the horses, and name them all, and note the sire of all the new foals that will come, like a chart. So since it is still raining hard, I will be working on a ranch record which he says is really important for breeding in the future. He says my papa only had a few head and let them pretty much go wild, but he plans to do some special breeding and wants a line of first quality horses to sell, especially with the next generation in about five years. This will be a business, I can see, not just a living. So these records are very important and I am going to enjoy naming all the pretty horses. I named the yellow colored one Honey after Rose's mama.

I am feeling fine and have no sign of stomach upset at all. Also no sign of rounding out, but that will come soon enough, Savannah says.

February 19, 1883

Savannah has told us she and Albert are expecting again. Soon there will be Prines all over this valley!

We have had a spell of beautiful weather, although now it is cold again. I put all my books into my adobe shed, and it is fine. So far it is a good shed and watertight enough to float away in a flood like a boat.

Jimmy went to town for four days and said I couldn't go, but the Maldonado boys stayed here and slept on the kitchen floor. I tried to make them tortillas and chilies and red gravy like their Mama makes for breakfast, but I could tell they weren't too good and the boys only ate them to be polite.

Then there was nothing to do, so I read a new book I have not read before. It is called Elemental Botanical Theory. It was difficult and is one I will put some thought into. Then I got to thinking about my missing book and a certain ornery soldier who has it, and I got out page eighty-seven from my cigar box and read it over.

I wonder what use Captain Elliot would have for a story about a woman in straights as that? It seems more like he would be the type to read Elemental Botanicals than about ladies wearing scarlet velvet in trials and tribulations. Maybe I will write to the Texas Rangers and see if they can locate him, and perhaps I can sell Rose's foal for money to buy it back. Seems like by now the book is not worth an Army horse, and I think if I had traded with the U.S. Army for that book, and he has taken it with him, why then he has stolen from the Army. Then I think this is purely foolish, as what would the U.S. Army need with a story book?

Then to fill my mind with pious and good thoughts I finally got out The Expositional Sermon Texts, and began the first one. Every time I came to a new paragraph, I wished Captain Elliot had this book instead of the one he has.

March 21, 1883

Mama came back from a trip to Tucson with Mr. Raalle and Harland. She said Harland has had a talk with the school teacher, Miss Wakefield, and she gave him the loan of an arithmetic primer, and told him to do all the problems he could do on some paper and bring them in next time, and she will find time to help him. She was a stern looking lady, with thin and pinched lips, he said.

She is probably just stern because you have to be with a room full of ornery children or they will get the best of you quick. Maybe she wanted him to know this is serious business, too. So Harland came over today and we sat and looked at the numbers and tried our best to work them. Most of the first ones I can do, but I kept quiet and let him work it out so he can learn. After the second lesson, though, I am really lost with it. Then he said she also wanted him to write a theme and draw a picture, so he borrowed my Animals of Africa book again and read all about giraffes, and said he is going to write about a wrangler who roped a giraffe and went on a wild ride. That sounds like a good story, I said, I will be glad to hear a fun story like that so you must read it to me when it is finished.

I finally am a little plumper, but not as much as Savannah. She told me I work too hard, and I should be careful of myself, and that Albert said Jimmy wouldn't let one of his mares put in the day I work, as it would be too much for them. She said, You know Sarah, Albert knows horses too, and he treats her like a queen, and I know these things for a fact.

I am going to try to slow down and not work like a field hand all day. I surely don't want anything to go wrong. There is just so much to do, I don't feel like resting but I will try.

April 2, 1883

Found Rose in labor, lying on the hay and struggling with her foaling. All night long I stayed with her, listening to coyotes howling and petting her head. About dawn she started pushing hard, and Jimmy pulled her baby for her. A beautiful dark brown colt. She licked him and nuzzled him and loved him and made him stand right up. I felt real proud and happy for her. She wouldn't let me get close to him to touch him, though, so we went to the house and cleaned up and started our day. Went to bed with the sun tonight, very tired.

July 17, 1883

It has been so hot we decided not to work this afternoon, but sit and rest. Yonder from the south clouds are building up, and I hear thunder already. If the wind changes and cools, we will know rain will come and cool our thirsty ranch. All the horses just meander around from one shade to another, wishing they were cool. The people here do, too. Our cistern is about empty, so we are being careful with water.

I feel lonely today, looking at all our ranch while sitting on this porch. I feel far apart from everyone. Don't know why. There is a stack of mending here to do, and if I get that done I have some embroidery here.

August 25, 1883

I have been feeling poorly all day. Just ache all over. It is hot enough to kill some of our chickens and we are all praying for rain.

August 29, 1883

April Alice Reed. My baby girl, born August 28, 1883 at 11:30 at night, my daughter, my little lamby. If it was possible for me to have chosen to die rather than go through that childbirth, I am sure many times during it I would have gladly died. How anyone would go on to have another baby, I am sure I do not know. I cannot sit up to write anymore.

September 3, 1883

I am finally able to sit up to write now. On August 26, I started feeling the baby coming right after breakfast. I walked and walked. Jimmy wouldn't let me walk to Mama's house, but rode over to get her. All the walking I did to help the baby come along, I could have walked to her house and back by way of Texas. Later I tried to go to bed, but when I lay down the feelings got worse. I began to get scared as the pains came on stronger.

I thought I could be brave, but I screamed and screamed. Savannah tried to hold my hand but I think I crushed her hands because she pulled away with a yell.

Mama said I must relax more, and Savannah said, try to work with it. But there is no working with something that feels as if your legs are being torn off by the roots, and your insides are being cut with axe blades. They kept saying, Sarah, just let it go, you are fighting against it too much. And I hurt so bad that I told them both to stop talking. There was nothing I could do but fight against my dying. For two days I laid in that bed, soaking with sweat, tired and hungry and scared to death, until finally I gave out and couldn't scream any more.

It was only when I had no more fight in me that the baby was born. So I understand what they were trying to say, but I don't know how any woman could give up and make herself surrender everything to what feels like being torn in half by teams of horses. I quit begging them to kill me when I thought I was really dying, so I laid there and waited for it to happen like Mrs. Barston. I wanted it to happen, to get the pain over with, and nothing else mattered except that. I don't remember having the baby, just hearing Mama saying, She's pushing! She's pushing! After that all was pain and darkness until Mama handed me a tiny pink baby girl. I could hear her crying loudly, and feel her in my arms, but I couldn't open my eyes to see her.

When it was finished, there was not a single part of me that did not feel worn and exhausted and sore. My eyelids are sore. My fingers are weak. I cannot hold the baby in my own hands, she feels like she weighs about a hundred pounds in a little block like a sack of flour. Lord, tell me this is the last one I will ever have, and I will be forever grateful. If I had had any idea, I would have never married as long as I lived. Even Savannah said she had been worried, that it took so very long, and so much laboring. Hers was not as bad as mine was, she says. Then she brought me the baby and helped me to try to nurse her. Savannah, I said, do you reckon I'll die yet before I get over this?

No, no, she said. Don't even think such a thing. You just rest and let us tend you and you get well.

I can sit enough to hold the baby and nurse and to write a little. Her name is April Alice. She is a little dark haired thing, all red faced when she cries, which she does a lot. She is perfect and I love her fiercely, like a mama grizzly, I suspect. Every time I sleep I have terrible dreams, and still many pains and cramps. In my head I feel like I want to get up, but just trying to tend to my personal needs is almost more than I can do, and it is embarrassing to ask for help to the outhouse like I was a child. So I sink back into the bed, half thankful for it and half hating it. Dear Savannah. Dear Mama. Precious baby. Sleep baby, please just sleep now.

October 20, 1883

I wonder if every new mother feels as if there is nothing left of herself. Every minute of my day and every last thing I do is tied to this little someone else. I am scared to death I will do something wrong, and she will die or grow up meager or sickly. And I got to thinking about all kinds of things like, how will I know how to teach her not to be selfish? And, how will I teach her to be honest? And how will I know if she has a sickness when she is too little to say what hurts? I am driving my mother to distraction asking her questions.

November 11, 1883

Savannah delivered another baby boy today. His name is Joshua David. It was just like before for her, she struggled for about five hours and then it was over. She was calm as a dove, and made me feel ashamed of how frightened I had been with mine. There is no outrunning fear, though, it comes on you and you have to face it. Childbirth is not an enemy you can fight or conquer or outrun, it takes you and tears you apart from the inside out and you have to just submit to it. I never understood why a girl would choose to be an old maid, but now I do.

November 14, 1883

I went to see Savannah and little Joshua today, and brushed and braided Savannah's hair for her. I only stayed about an hour because I was so exhausted, and when I got home, Jimmy said, When are you going to tend to your own house and get some washing done? Then he said, If you got enough strength to drive a buckboard over there you got enough to iron me a clean shirt.

Then he went off to do some work and I tried to do some wash, and cried all afternoon. I got the wash hung up by night fall while April screamed at the top of her lungs the whole time. Most of the wash is diapers, and I only have a few left. And now I see it is starting to rain and supper isn't made yet and Jimmy is still cantankerous, but the baby is sleeping and I wish I could, too, but I must cook something.

December 18, 1883

What a wonderful Christmas present to see Ernest William Prine coming up the road. He was wearing a uniform with corporal stripes on the arms, and looking all filled out and like a man we hardly recognize. He stopped on the way home and had his picture made, and has given us each a little one to remember him by.

We sat around Albert's and Savannah's big stone fireplace and talked until late. Jimmy went home early to tend stock, but I spent the night. I nursed little April and listened to Ernest tell stories of his life, and he rolled up his sleeve and showed us where an arrow had gone clear through his arm.

He will be staying a week, then has to start back. He is bound for Fort Bliss in El Paso, Texas now. We all have much to tell him and show him. I have missed Ernest dearly, and begged him to stay with us at least one night, and he said he will.

December 25, 1883

Christmas dinner today was hectic and scattered and everyone seemed almost glad to be done with it. Between my baby crying four or five hours in spite of anything I tried, and Savannah's new one and little Clover wanting attention, I burned the pies nearly black and forgot to put salt in the crust to boot. If it wasn't for Mama and Harland helping nothing would have been done at all. Jimmy stayed in the barn working on the horses but kept coming in every few minutes asking if supper was ready yet, until I could tell Mama was about to light into him. Every time little April fell asleep in my arms I tried to lay her down. She would start crying again and no one could soothe her for another hour or more. I am fit to be tied.

I see Savannah and Albert both tending their tiny ones and they seem so calm. But even Savannah couldn't calm my April, she just shook her head and didn't know what to say.

February 13, 1884

A new year is upon us. Little April sleeps more now and I am feeling as if I have gotten over the childbirth. Mama said it took so long because I didn't get any rest. She has come a few times and carried April home, and I just stretched out on the bed and slept hard for three or four hours, and that helped more than anything.

Jimmy went to town. It is cold and frosty, but not rainy. I kind of like the way the cold air smells and the way everything sounds early in the morning in the winter. Saw a flock of geese flying in a V today. You don't see geese often here. They made a strange noise, calling to each other. I thought about trying to shoot one for supper, but then I decided to just watch them fly away.

April 1, 1884

Jimmy has gone to the stage station to get mail. I have not written this journal so long because I am busy with my sweet baby. I love her but she cries so much and is so peevish. She seems to have colic often, and I have tried every remedy known, but to no use. She is finally sleeping through at least seven hours at night, so I am not always so wrung out. It is hard to get much done, trying to tend her all day. I don't know how Savannah does it with two, but hers both sleep more, maybe that's how.

Jimmy works hard all day and doesn't understand how I get so little done, but he isn't the one trying to do it all with a colicky baby on his shoulder night and day. Every time I sit still for more than five minutes I fall asleep.

Some men came and bought two horses for eighty dollars each. Jimmy has bought steel water troughs and a rocking chair for me and two chests of drawers and some tools and seed. Our house is the only white painted house in the Territory, as people have remarked about it to us. I am proud we have a fine ranch.

May 1, 1884

Have felt a deep sadness all this week. Not sure why. Our ranch is prosperous and some mares are expecting again but I told him not Rose, she can wait a year. We had a big argument over how he wanted to get all the use he could from his brood mares, and I said, Well, Rose is mine and has been given to me twice, and isn't yours to USE and I don't want her pregnant and that is my decision.

Jimmy was mad and said it would serve me right if Dan or Terry got her and then the pony would be worthless.

Jimmy works hard all day every day but seems lately he is always short tempered with me. Maybe I should have let him breed Rose if it made all that difference to him. He seems to have a lot of business in Tucson, too, but doesn't prefer me to go along, although sometimes I'd like to.

Some Easterners drove out from the stage line and came by just to admire the place, and it filled me with a mean feeling, like they took pleasure from our hard work and they didn't deserve it. I'm about to give up being righteous and generous to a fault, and I feel like a draft horse that has pulled all day.

Took some scraps for quilts over to Mama's. Harland was doing lessons, Savannah's babies were both there sleeping side by side on a quilt on Mama's bed. Mama gave me coffee with milk in it and said it would perk me up, so I went out under the peach trees to sip on it. The trees that we brought from Texas are bending down with fruit that is not ripe yet, and beautiful, and all seems peaceful here, although not as orderly and white painted and fancy as our ranch, it is calm and welcoming here and cool in the shade of the fruit orchard.

Sitting there on a rush chair I saw Savannah walk from her house across the way over to where Albert was digging an irrigating trench, bringing him a pail of something to drink. They talked a bit, then they smiled hard at each other, and Albert bent down and kissed her like a man shouldn't do in public. He kissed her long and hard, and she wrapped her arms around him, and nuzzled her whole body against him, and smiled, and he held her tight to him and I could see them both sigh together like they were one person.

Again I wondered what it must be like to be Savannah, and be loved like that, and maybe in time will that happen to me and Jimmy? Must be her good and simple ways, and Bible study. I haven't been kissed at all since months before the baby came, much less kissed like they were doing.

I thanked Mama for the coffee and left. And I just can't quit this sad feeling, lonesome and achey.

When I got home, Jimmy hollered, Sarah, you been wasting time, iron me some shirts, I'm going to town.

July 22, 1884

It seems Jimmy does more hollering at me than talking, and today I had my fill when he started complaining about his eggs being too cold. I turned around and lit into him like a wet hen. I told him he could just hold his tone of voice and act like he was married to me instead of like I was a field hand he'd hired, and that if he didn't like it that was too bad. I have had enough of being fussed at when I am doing my level best and never once have shirked a chore as long as I was able. I told him he didn't even act like he loved me at all, and for a married man he was about as nice to have around as a cholla cactus and a lot more noise. He just stood there like I'd hit him on the head with a stick, and then went to the barn and then came in later and said he figured he'd been pretty ornery. He said I was right, and he hadn't realized he was making me so mad. Well, what did he think, that I would just take all his hollering forever?

I wonder if he'll gentle down a little, now. He even helped me put April to bed tonight.

July 27, 1884

Today I stood for hours and hours under a big palo verde tree in the afternoon rain, and let the wind blow around me and wished the lightning would strike me down. My shoes were soaked through with mud from Jimmy's grave, and I stared at the mud trying to figure. It made no sense, but I let the rain soak me through and I cried. And it wasn't for Jimmy it was for me.

Most of what we think happened is from Ruben Maldonado tracking the signs of brush and dirt and broken branches later. Jimmy had been out rounding up some horses he let run in the east section of our land when his big old chestnut stallion stepped in a hole and lost his balance. There was cougar track nearby too, and maybe it scared the stallion. He threw Jimmy hard and we think he landed on a jagged tree stump because that's where the trail of blood began. That alone would have been bad enough but his foot caught in the stirrup and he must have hollered real loud and the stallion took off running for home. He pulled Jimmy through the worst of our land until he was over the rocky ledge where he lost his footing and jostled enough to shake Jimmy's foot out.

Standing in the garden I saw the horse come back looking wild eyed and rank, and put him in the corral without taking off the saddle.

I got on Rose's back and hitched up my skirt in the waistband and hugged her with my legs. It wasn't hard to follow the horses' clumsy tracks, as I saw the direction he came from and the rocky ledge wasn't far from the house. But it was real hard to look at Jimmy's face, all cut and torn.

He moaned when I tried to move him. I rode back to the house and got a big blanket for him to lay on. I made a rope around her neck and made Rose pull Jimmy real gently back to the house. Baby April was crying inside. There was nothing I could do but let her cry, and I dropped off the rope and rode hell bent for Albert.

My family and our neighbors did all they could do for him. But his back was broken, some ribs were gone, and blood dribbled out his mouth without stopping for three days. Instead of making water he made blood pee too, and he had no feeling in his feet or legs at all, but he knew he was bad. I know he was in pain and it was hard for him to breathe and I stayed by his side without sleeping trying to comfort him.

Finally, on the fourth day everyone was so tired and knew the end was close. I sat staring at his broken body in our soft bed thinking but not thinking, the same thoughts running through my mind over and over. My beautiful life with Jimmy would soon be over and it had barely begun. Our sunrise was night. The next name entered in our little family Bible would be the last one.

I thought it was as sad as I could be at the time.

Savannah made me take a bath, and it felt good to be cleaned up although I felt hollowed out inside. I went back to the chair which had been my home all those days and sat nearby. Albert alone was by his side, standing over Jimmy, looking somber. Everyone else had gone out to the parlor and was eating some supper and talking soft about where to dig his grave.

Then Jimmy stirred and said to Albert, Tell her I love her, will you?

I began to let tears run down my face.

Albert said, You go ahead and tell her, Jimmy, she can hear you.

But Jimmy said, No, you have to write her and tell her I love her, please.

Albert said, Write her?

Then Jimmy said, Tell Miss Ruthanne I loved her always, and he let out a long breath and died.

December 1, 1884

If it wasn't for the good neighbors we have in the Maldonados, I would have given up by now. I rise early and work the day through with my baby on my hip and go to bed with the sun and sleep hard the night through. I am tireder than I knew was possible. Sometimes one of the girls comes over and helps with April, and Estrellita is real good with her so that I can get a lot done. I am sure that the Lord's way is right, but it is tedious and sorrowful.

I thought maybe I should see a doctor as there feels like this hard rock in my chest all the time. Mrs. Maldonado said, Aye, chikita, te corazón destrozado. They think I mourn for Jimmy and sometimes I do for the work he could do in a day.

I dyed my new clothes black, but only the outside ones. All my petticoats are white and pretty still. There is no sense mourning to the bone for a man who thought of me as a brood mare to get use from.

I thought about Mrs. Hoover today, and I wished I had an inheritance and a house in Boston away from dust and Indians and snakes and trials. I wish my papa was here to help.

Wrote Ernest a letter and asked him to quit the Army and come live with me and make this ranch work for me, but it has been five weeks and no word yet from him.

January 6, 1885

Dear Sarah, got your letter. I hope you all are missing me as I am missing you. Tell Mama and everyone I am faithful to love them all and have been in a bad fix but made it through at last and kept my scalp. Truly Yours, E. Prine.

He didn't mention coming home to help as I asked in my letter or anything. Seems it ain't important, I 'spose.

Harland comes over and helps me some, and is a real hand, as he is a strapping big boy. He reads better than I do now and said he has passed the fifth grade test. And Miss Wakefield married Mr. Fish at the general store. He thinks it is funny and calls her Mrs. Trout.

February 9, 1885

Made April a little dress out of a scrap of gingham with a little sunbonnet to match. I wonder how I will raise her and what will become of her. I plan to help her learn to read, as I have learned myself with help from my Papa. I truly wish he was here to help my baby learn letters. What a rocky trail we have been over.

Jimmy's big old bull he called Beaumont got out of the fence today and hooked poor old Bear with a horn before I got him shooed back inside. I was really scared, and thought what if the bull killed me and no one knew, who would find my baby? Bear is real sore and won't eat. I made him a couple of blankets to lay on, on the porch near the kitchen door. I don't find any blood on him, but he looks bad.

After I got all the chores done tonight I made coffee and sat in my rocker with April on my lap until she fell asleep. I wouldn't be fit to keep company with a grizzly bear lately. My hands are raw and cracked open from being wet all the time and working in the cold, my hair had a tangle I couldn't get out so I cut it loose and now there is a short place on one side, and I caught sight of my face reflected in the window while I was washing up from supper and I looked meaner than a scorpion.

I went to Mama's and Albert's to ask if they knew anything to help Bear. Savannah was hanging out her wash when I walked up and she asked me how I was. So I told her.

I said, Mostly I'm so blessed tired I could scream. I hate that Jimmy Reed. I hate that ranch and those God-forsaken horses and I hate chickens and weeds. I hate the cold in the winter and the blazing heat in the summer and the dust and the rain and the wind that never stops this time of year. I hate sweeping and sewing and ironing clothes. I hate washing diapers and I hated being a wife and of all these things I hate being a widow most. I wish I'd never laid eyes on that skunk Jimmy. I wish to goodness he'd never come here. I only thought I wanted to be a wife. I just wanted to be happy. There's nothing happy in this.

Savannah's mouth opened when I said all that and she just looked at me shocked. She said, Sarah, honey, you just need to pray for strength and courage. The Lord . . .

The Lord won't do a blessed thing, I said. I am stuck with this mess and I'm going to work myself to death in another month of this.

Oh, Sarah, don't say that, she said.

It's true, Savannah, I said. I am plum fed up with all the work I have to do and it is all because of a worthless man, and any other man ever comes around me better be carrying a pistol with one more bullet than I've got or I'll have the last word. Then I saw her face looked like she might cry. She was only asking about my health after all and I was purely rude and full of the devil today. I didn't mean to yell at you, I said, and I'm sorry. Even while I was saying I'm sorry I was still hollering. Then my baby started to cry.

I left Savannah on her porch looking red-faced and teary and marched myself home.

All day I fretted and worried and kicked the fence and bothered the horses until they were all skitterish. Then at sundown I rode Rose back to Savannah's house and told her I was sorry again. She said she already forgave me, but I don't know why she would. I don't deserve it, hollering at her that way.

After all that fussing I still had too much to do, but I didn't feel so purely mad, just worn out. Albert said to me before I left their house that he was coming over tomorrow to lend a hand for a few hours.

No, I told him. You have too much work of your own to do here.

But he said there was no arguing, and then he laughed and said he'd arm wrestle me if I wanted but I might as well knuckle under as there was no changing his mind. Then they made me eat supper with them and spend the night snugged up on a pallet of warm quilts near the fire with April. Lord please forgive me for being so low down. There is only good in this house and the people in it.

February 22, 1885

Bear followed me to Albert's today, just like always. He seems fine now and I am surely thankful and have prayed for him just like he was a person. Mama said that is foolish, as the Lord always watches over his animals, but I told her I needed Bear a lot more than the Lord did, and with all the angels in Heaven, surely there is no need for guarding against snakes and outlaws there. I prayed for Bear to get well and he did, so it must be the Lord agreed. She couldn't argue with that, but said I was probably reading too much and my thoughts were getting turned a bit sideways.

March 1, 1885

Toobuddy is way too old for all the silly games he plays like a puppy, but he doesn't know it, which is why I ignored him acting foolish at first and why now as I am writing this, there is another man probably dying in my bed. This afternoon I was washing up linens, when here comes that dog acting stranger than ever. He hunkered down on the ground and made the cryingest sound. Then he'd run around and around in a circle real tight, and jump up and do this all over again.

Bear went to him and sniffed him and acted suspicious, and barked a couple of times. Then Toobuddy charged up on the porch and nearly knocked me off my stool. I was mad because he jumped in the air and landed with one foot in the rinse water and got it dirty.

Get away, I hollered, you dirty dog! Then Bear started to bark and bark, and sniffed him again and barked more. Something was up, I knew, but I speak better Chinese than I do dog, so I finished hanging up my wash while I wondered what to do.

Finally, I decided I'd take a walk with them and see where that silly dog goes. Most likely he has run across a skunk or something. I checked on little April, and she was just down for her nap and fast asleep. Bear, I said, stay home, stay home. He went and sat by the front door, so I knew April would be safe enough even if she got scared that I was gone.

I picked up my rifle and put Jimmy's long knife in my apron pocket, and went out to the yard, and immediately Toobuddy took off across the hill. I tried to follow but he was fast out of sight, then suddenly he would appear again and make that odd crying sound and go off running. Well, the faster I followed the faster he went, and as I stood up on the top of the hill west of our house, I saw him turning around at the base of the arroyo below and heading back for me. I knew if I went down the hill I'd never hear April cry, but I was pretty sure she would sleep, so I decided to head on down and take a look.

I thought I smelled a bear for a second, so I held my rifle ready and remembered to check the trees. As I went down the hill the smell got worse, but it changed from that bear smell to something else, the smell of a dead animal rotting. I began to think that stupid dog had led me to a deer carcass, when I heard a moan that sounded like a man.

I hurried through the brush, watching all around as it was thick and the smell was just awful and I was afraid of surprising a wounded animal. There at the foot of the sandy cliff, like he had ridden off hard without stopping, was a carcass all right, a big yellow horse, bloated up and rotting, with a saddle and bridle still on, and it looked picked at like the buzzards had been there already. I checked the trees around me and saw four of them big black ugly things sitting there, watching, looking like posted sentries of Hell.

Then I heard the moan again, and I walked carefully around the horse. A man was pinned underneath it, still alive. He was covered with mud and blood on his head and filthy dirty, and kept waving his hat weakly.

Mister! I called to him and he jumped.

Help, help me please, he said. I can't get it off and the buzzards will eat me alive.

I said right away, I will do what I can.

I started to leave when he called out, Have you got water?

I'll bring some, I promised, and get you out of there. Stay put, it ain't far, I said, then I hurried fast all the way home without stopping to breathe, so that when I got there I was winded.

I hitched Dan and Terry up to my little wagon. Then I went into my bedroom and pulled the old mattress from under the bed and put it in the back and got two horse blankets to put on it, because that fellow was so filthy. I filled buckets with water from the well, picked up a canteen and filled it, and got my rag bag of old, clean diapers and as big a rope as I could carry, then I woke up April. I took her to the outhouse quick and then to the wagon and plopped her between my knees and started off over the hills. Toobuddy had stayed with the man, and now Bear followed us and jumped into the back of the wagon to ride.

It was a terrible time to get through the brush with the rig instead of on foot, and we got so stove up at one point I had to get out and push them back and go round another way, but finally we got to the place where the man was pinned under that horse. I unhitched my team and put them up near the carcass, but they didn't want to stay and I nearly got dragged away when they felt they were off the wagon as there was no brake to help hold them still.

I handed him the canteen and told him to drink slow, but he wasn't going slow, he drank so hard I felt pity for anyone that thirsty. Then I looped the rope around the dead horse's head, and then through the shank of the yoke, and tied the other end to the saddle stirrup that was sticking up all cockeyed like the rider had tumbled with the horse.

Then I started them going, and the man yelled. I called to him, If you holler you'll scare them and they'll bolt. Something started ticking in my head like a clock. I didn't know what it was, but just this nervous edgy ticking, and I shook the reins, terrified that I was killing him by this. He was quiet, then, and dragging that horse made the smell just thick in the air so I thought for a moment I would choke.

April stayed in the wagon bed and watched, and called out, Nasty, Mama, stinky nasty!

When I got the horse moved I untied the rope from the stirrup but cut it off where it had touched the rotting head, then I tied up the team at a tree but didn't hitch them so they can't bolt with April in the wagon. I got the buckets and rags and a blanket and went to him. He smelled even worse, and looked to be pinned under there a couple of days, as he had wet himself and more, and his face was completely hidden in blood and mud, his hair smelled like rotted blood real bad. He laid there for a second, and I thought he had died, then only his lips moved.

I can't feel my legs, he said, real weak and thin sounding. Maybe it's just from lying here but I'm afraid my back's broken.

That ticking in my head got louder and louder. April started to cry to get down, and I fussed at her to stay put and be good for me. I soaked rags in water and laid them on his bloody head. I've seen a broken back, I said, maybe your back's not broken or you wouldn't have felt any pain and hollered out. I'll have to get you home before I can get you to a doctor. As I washed his face carefully, I could see he had a big open gash in his hair. When some of the dried blood came loose it started bleeding again, real heavy. April was fussing.

Then he groaned with pain, and waved his hat toward the horse carcass and said, Please save my saddle bag. Don't leave it, please.

It occurred to me this could be a very bad man I was tending, and I might be sorry. The horses whinnied and a buzzard flew down real bold and sat on a rock over us. I shooed at him with a diaper and kept on cleaning. The man took another drink and then took the diaper from me, and started wiping his own face and seemed a bit revived. Well, sir, I said to him, you have to get out of these clothes and get cleaned off, and I brought a blanket to wrap you in. I pulled off his boots and started to unbutton his shirt while he laid there.

He said, I can do this, you shouldn't, miss. He was looking down at himself and the mess. Then he asked me if I had come alone.

No, I told him, my baby is in the wagon, but Albert has gone to Tucson so there is no one to help close by. Just at that moment he took my arm suddenly and I cringed at his dirty hand on me.

His eyes blinked several times and he said Miss Prine? Mrs. Reed, I mean? The ticking in my head stopped and I felt like a chime sounded.

Captain Elliot! I could hardly say the words. This man was in farmer's clothes and was so dirty I would never have guessed. And he was hurt bad. Well, Captain, I said, I am a widow now and I have seen a good many nasty britches, but you do this if you can and I will get a blanket for you to lay on and clean off. I handed him the knife and he began to cut off his pants.

He shook his feet, and then groaned. My legs, he said, my legs hurt. It must have been all that weight of the horse crushing his legs, and now they were coming back and pained bad. He lay there for a minute, in so much pain I didn't know what to do.

I tried not to look at him, and went to get the other bucket, and said with my head turned that if he could get himself onto the blanket and clean up a little, I'd rinse him off and wrap him up in a clean one and take him to the house for a bath and some doctoring.

He said he had been there two days until this morning when Toobuddy found him. I remembered that dog always did cotton to Captain Elliot, no wonder he acted so crazy. I turned when he rolled on the blanket, and saw April trying to climb off the wagon, dangling above the ground, and ran to catch her. He did what cleaning he could like I said, but still couldn't get his legs under him to walk.

I knew I couldn't lift him so I backed the wagon to him, and braked it, and had him hold to the team's reins while I went around to the front of them and we pulled him up onto the mattress. There he lay still as death the whole time I hitched the team, and I think he must have fainted away, but he was breathing, so I dumped the water and picked up April and headed for the house.

I took him around back where my wash tub was still full and soapy, and since it was a far sight cleaner than he was, I figured it was a good first dip at least. He had to fold up like a cricket to get in, but said his legs wanted to work a bit, and I checked his back for other cuts. He was mighty bruised, but it appears all the dried blood on him came from his head. After a bath with kerosene and still another of soap and water, he finally smelled like something other than death, but still he couldn't move around very well.

Wrapped in a quilt, he leaned hard on me all the way into the house, and I put him in my bed. With rags under his head instead of my feather pillows, I tried to tend his head. He was real patient and I think he went to sleep, and twitched a bit now and then. I got out my sewing scissors and cut his hair and finally got at the wound and it was pretty bad, a big cut from over his left ear across the top and down his forehead almost two inches, and there was a big lump underneath. I remembered hearing about a fellow who cracked his head bad and broke his skull and died, and I wondered if Captain Elliot would die in my bed like Jimmy did. I dabbed it with some mercurochrome and he still didn't move, and that was when I was sure he was about dead already. I fixed him up with a big bandage, pulling the skin tight together and wrapping it around and around, then I lifted his head and took away the rags and gave him a pillow. I can make another pillow, I thought, and if he is going to die in my bed he may as well be comfortable.

While I have been doctoring, April has become an artist. She got into the blueing bottle and fingerpainted the white pine floor in the parlor and made little smears and lines and hand prints everywhere. I was too tired to be mad at her and too drained to fuss. I just picked her up and took off her dress and underwear and washed her up and dressed her again. I still had stock to feed and dinner to make, so I stoked the fire and cut up some vegetables for soup, and took April with me to the barn.

Later, I got Captain Elliot to wake enough to eat some soup and about three biscuits, then he fell fast asleep again. It looks like my parlor will have little blue handprints forever to remember this day, and April thinks her blue fingers are fancy. I will sleep with her tonight. I am so tired.

March 3, 1885

For two days I nursed Captain Elliot and slept with April. It wasn't much trouble, mostly he just slept hard like he was nearly dead, and ate, and slept more. One time he cried out Git buzzards! and waved his hands, but it was a dream and he was embarrassed. None of my family nor neighbors have been by and I am thankful for that, as it is just easier sometimes not to explain things.

There are no man's clothes here at all except for a couple of shirts that I had made Jimmy which I wear over my blouse when it is cold, so yesterday I went to Savannah and got a pair of Albert's pants for him to borrow and told them and Mama all about what had happened. They said they will come by tomorrow which is this afternoon.

This morning I found Captain Elliot out on the porch in my rocker. He was wearing Albert's faded work pants, and had put on Jimmy's shirt which didn't fit at all. As he was having breakfast with us he said he'd seen Jimmy's headstone under the palo verde tree, and he was sorry for me.

I didn't want him or anyone else to be sorry for me, so I only said, You'd better rest a while.

After noon, he sat for a bit and watched me put April down for a nap, and I started to knead some bread dough, then he said, Mrs. Reed, would it burden you to ask for the use of your husband's razor? I'll understand if you don't want to.

But I didn't care at all, when I thought about it. There wasn't any sentiment in a man's razor. And there wasn't much sentiment in me, either.

Pretty soon he came from behind the house looking all clean shaven and that was the first time I really recognized his face. He had changed the bandage too, and said it was healed up real clean without much of a scar, and he said I was a pretty good doctor and a barber too. I laughed a little at that, but it is too soon to have healed much.

He had to get back to Tucson, he said. He has been hired by the Army as a private Soldier, a Lieutenant with the Sixth Cavalry at Fort Lowell as a Special Advisor in Indian Affairs.

That sounds pretty impressive, I said.

It's not, he returned. It's just a job I know lots about.

Then he told me how he had been following track of some renegade Apaches with some stolen cattle and horses, and they had discovered him and turned on him and ran him until his horse lost footing in the soft sandy cliff and broke its neck on top of him. He told me how he never did want to fight Indians any more, but because of the massacre done by the fool soldiers under his command while we were coming from Texas, there was a man named Geronimo and a band of other Indians sworn to kill every white in the Territory for revenge. And so many good people were murdered somehow he felt he carried a burden for the beginning of the whole act and had to protect the white folks.

I just looked at him quiet, then, and put my dough in the pans and washed my hands, taking my time and thinking. Odd, how sitting there in an old plaid shirt and Albert's brown pants, all clean and calm, he didn't look like a soldier, just a man. It was only when he moved around or when he sat on a horse and thought, that you could see it in him, like a chestnut blood line. It's the stance, the head, the gait, Jimmy used to say.

Why did you leave the Army at all, then? I asked him.

He didn't talk for a minute. It was a difference of opinion in the arrest of those five soldiers, he said. He knew he couldn't sleep at night with them released and excused, just like they had spilled punch at a Sunday picnic, so when his enlistment was up, he packed his bag and left. Suddenly he jumped up with a start, and almost scared me. Where's my saddlebag? he said.

It was hanging on a peg under the eaves of the smokehouse, where some of the smell will be soaked away, and he was powerfully worried about it until he had it in his hands. He didn't tell me any reason for it, but just smiled at me kind of soft and gentle like. Then, he needed to borrow a horse and saddle, he said, and would return it in a couple of days, so I said fine, and then he said with a soft voice, I'm in your debt, Mrs. Reed.

The sound of that made me blush like a little girl, and I turned and went quick to the corral.

I let him use the big mare I named Honey because she is gentle, and Jimmy's best saddle. She doesn't like to be cinched and puffs up her belly so the strap will hang loose and the rider will slide off sideways, but Captain Elliot tricked her and blew on her nose and made her let out her air, so he made a quick job of it. Then I remembered the trade I had gotten into with that man and thought maybe I should have given him Terry or Dan to ride, and that would be the end of it.

I said to him, That there's a fine brood mare, please be careful. His eyes got that mean sparkle in them and then I recognized him sure, for that smart grin he has like he's got the best of me. He acted like he was going to say something, and opened his mouth, then changed his mind.

He leaned down for a second, and said, I'll be back with her fast, but you shouldn't be staying here alone with those Apaches around.

I told him, I'm not alone, I have my dogs to warn me, and the Maldonado boys come over two times a week.

He was gone before my family got here. They all came together, with food, like it was an old friend they were visiting. Albert wanted to hear about Geronimo, but I didn't know much, except that Captain Elliot the Lieutenant said he was nearby.

April woke up and showed them her blue fingers. We fixed supper early and ate my fresh bread, and I told them all about what had passed the last three days, and about how Toobuddy tried to follow him away but I made him stay.

Captain Elliot rode up with a small group of soldiers, in a sharp pressed uniform and on a tall black horse, leading my mare. He stayed long enough for the men to draw water from my well, said Hello sweetie, to April, and handed me a bundle with Albert's clothes tied up, they looked like they had come from a fancy pay laundry. It sounded odd to hear them call him Lieutenant, and I wondered why he took the cut in rank for this job. It must mean something to him, I suppose. He told me that Geronimo had been tracked down to the town of Willcox and into the Chiricahua mountains, maybe as far as Mexico, so not to worry about him especially. Then he wheeled his horse around and was gone.

April stretched out in my arms and waved bye-bye until he was gone over the hills. I felt a frown on my face, watching him leave, but I wasn't sure why. Then I laughed. Looking at the south end of a northbound horse would make anyone frown. I felt cheerful the rest of the day.

Decided to make soap today with Savannah's fine recipe. I had it about ready, when I got a hare-brained thought, and I went to the adobe book shed and pulled the feed sacks out of the back. With a stick I pulled up the piece of board, and there was my little wooden box. I took it to the house, and opened the jar of rouge and scooped out a little spoonful of the red stuff and dropped it in the boiling kettle of creamy lye soap. Then I opened the perfume bottle and poured about half of it into the soap. It bubbled up and blistered across the surface like horehound syrup on boiling sugar.

I stirred it all in, and the soap turned pink and the smell of that perfume came out strong. When I ladled it into the molds, it seemed to stay pink. The perfume had pretty much boiled away, but just a faint smell like a tiny flower came through. That was just what I had wanted. I determined to wrap up some and take them as a gift to Savannah and Mama, and April and I got out paper and the blueing bottle and painted pictures, let it dry, and wrapped up the pink soaps with the blue paper pictures and tied them with twine.

March 23, 1885

Rode Rose and took Savannah and Mama some of the soaps and a three egg cake, just for fun. Savannah said the soap was the nicest she had ever seen, and smelled so good she would be ashamed to use it. But I told her I didn't think there was any shame in a flower smelling pretty, and cleaning up with a pretty soap shouldn't be a shame either. Mama said she agreed, and that it would be a pleasure to have a bath with it. They were very amazed, and asked again and again how did I make pink soap, and I just grinned and wouldn't tell them at all.

The Maldonado boys are working today at my ranch so I decided to take the afternoon off from home, and stayed with my family until late. It is so good for a spell not to have to lift my hands to hard work. I have eaten of Mama's good cooking this afternoon like there is no tomorrow. And now the left over corn-bread she has put in a bowl with milk on it and I am finishing that. There have been many days of beautiful spring weather, cool and clear, and with all the hard work from sun up past sun down, I am looking mighty spare, she said, so eat up, this will put some meat on your bones. It was like being a little girl again, having my Mama fuss over me.

March 25, 1885

I boiled up some fat and this time strained it extra fine, and made more soap with pink and perfume. When it was cool, I cut each piece in half so it was small. I wrote on almost every sheet of paper I had, a little picture of a flower and Mrs. Reed's Fine Ladies' Soap and tied a twine around each one.

I took April some changes of clothes, and Bear, and hitched my wagon up, and placed a big basket load of little soaps in the center. Then I put on my best dress, which was my blue wedding dress now died black, and my best hat, not just a sunbonnet, and drove us all to town. It was strange to be on the road alone, but I didn't mind it and I sang songs to April some and told her stories and she slept some.

I went to Fish's store and I told him he could have the bushel basket of them for two at seven cents, and see how they sell. Then I would bring another batch if he liked them but they would cost a nickel a piece. Mr. Fish was amazed at me, and opened a package and sniffed it then wrapped it up, then said it was no deal. But as I got clear of the door and he saw I was headed for Goldwater and Heath's across Main street with little April hanging onto my skirt and moving as fast as I could with her and Bear following, he came after me and said maybe he had changed his mind.

I left there with seven dollars and his old Sears and Roebuck catalog.

I went to the telegraph office myself to place an order for more rouge and perfume, which I could never order at the general store where folks would see. This way it would come to me at the stage station near our house, and wrapped up like any ordinary package it would not cause loose talk. Then I went to the Ronstadt's livery and found the leather man, who sold me some fine tallow. I still had three dollars left, so I took April to the park where we shared our lunch with the ducks, and looked through the Sears and Roebuck and thought about things.

I was tempted to buy some fancy soap molds, but what if Mr. Fish doesn't want more? So I priced a few other things, and decided I would put my soap money in a jar and save up for myself some ladies' niceties that were never before considered as useful as white paint and new saddles had been.

April 8, 1885

Came to town with another batch of soap, my last if the stage doesn't get the goods I ordered soon. When I went to Mr. Fish's, he about jumped off his stool, and said, come with me, Mrs. Reed. I never did see a more greedy look in a man's eyes. He offered me five cents a bar if I would promise not to go to any other store with my soaps.

I just smiled, and said, Five cents would be fine for this load. We'll see what happens in the future, I said. Maybe I am a better soap trader than horse trader, at that.

I took ten dollars from Mr. Fish for those soaps, and I went to the livery and bought more fat and asked the man to make me up a leather stamper with my soap's name and some little flowers. I paid him half in advance and said I will pick it up that afternoon. He will do the work for two dollars and six bits, and make it extra nice, which is good, I said. Then I bought fine white paper for the wrappers and a skein of bright blue crochet thread for ties instead of twine.

I had just left the little dry goods shop with my packages and April's hand in mine, feeling fine, when I thought I would check at the depot for any mail that may not have gotten put on the stage yet. Some kind of wild ruckus broke out down the street and I heard yelling and a gunshot, then more guns, and I pulled April behind me and shoved my way into the closest doorway.

I never did hear what happened down there, but Tucson is a rough old cob of a town, and people that live there just have to be ready to duck or draw. In my deep pocket, my kitchen pistol was banging against my leg, and I thought, I am a hard woman, for sure, and not genteel like Savannah, not as I wanted to become at all. Maybe when times simmer down I will be able to walk around without a sidearm in my pocket and a rifle under my wagon seat like an outlaw.

I am glad I went to the depot, for my package was there! The address had smudged and so it waited for me at the depot all this time. As I was picking it up and signing the receipt, April toddled off to the doorway and proceeded to upend my package of thread and papers and they started to blow about the room, so I rushed after them, trying hard not to smudge them on the dirty floor.

I grabbed April upon my hip and stood up at last, and accidentally bumped right into a man who was bent over picking up a piece of white paper for me. He turned around and immediately his hat was in his hand and he smiled.

Well! Captain Elliot said out loud, You sometimes find the nicest surprises at the depot!

We were in a little scurrying crowd of people, and I felt embarrassed, but they weren't noticing us, they were doing their own business there. He took my elbow like a lady and led me over to the door and out to the front porch.

Mrs. Reed, he said, what a fortunate meeting. Is your family close by? We could all have lunch together.

I told him, No, I came to town with April and Bear.

The sparkle in his eyes turned to a snapping fire for a second, and he asked me, You drove to town alone?

It's business, I said. I couldn't ask Albert to take a day off just to carry me around. He got a look on his face like when Mama is going to scold one of us, but he just shook his head and didn't talk for a second.

Well, he said, then would you do me the honor of a dinner at Levin's?

I didn't want folks to look at us or see a widow having dinner with a soldier. I said to him, I promised April to see the ducks, and I brought a picnic.

At that, April hollered, Duckies! Duckies! and clapped her hands.

Captain Elliot reached for her and said, Can I hold you for Mama, Missy? and she held out her hands and practically jumped off me into his arms. Then he held out his elbow for me to take, and said, If you are finished with your business, may I see you to your picnic, Ma'am?

I know my face was red, and I couldn't talk, my throat was choked. He had just invited himself! So only to be polite and not cause a stir I put my hand on his arm and he carried my package, and I walked with him down the street to our wagon.

Never in my days would I have expected to have a picnic with Captain Elliot on the grass at Carillo Gardens and watch April chase ducklings whose mamas quacked at her all afternoon. He leaned on one elbow and ate my fried chicken and then bought us lemonades and buñuelos and fed half of his to a goose just to watch April squeal and giggle at it. Then she fell asleep, lying on his lap while I was re-packing our basket and we were quiet as the afternoon warmed. Suddenly I looked at him and he was shaking all over, laughing inside.

What is so funny? I whispered.

He looked at me with that mean look and pointed at April asleep on his lap and said, Does this run in the family?

Well, I was furious, and just had to leave and walk around to keep from waking up April. I suppose he just laid there and watched me go, but I walked clear around the pond before I could settle down. Ornery, no account. Mama was right it is never any good to mess with soldiers, they are a sorry bunch and I was real peeved I had bothered to waste my time with the likes of that man all afternoon when I could have been shopping with my soap money. And I still had blueing to buy and a hotel room to take and I wanted to leave this park and now.

I went back to get my things, and sat on the grass and began to pick up the rest of the picnic.

He was lying stretched out long with his hat over his eyes and one hand on April's little head, and he said, without looking up, Where'd you go?

Well, I was mad, and still am.

He grinned real big and said, You weren't mad, you're embarrassed. If you were mad you'd have taken your stuff and your baby and left. I tried to tell him he was wrong, and he just kept grinning. He said, You think I don't feel like a plucked chicken in front of you, after you pulling me out from under that horse and all?

That's different. I know it is. It's not like he could lose his reputation for being rescued from an accident.

Then he lifts his hat a little and peers at me from under it. Seems to me, he says, we're both the rescuing kind. He put his hat back down and said, Anyway, that's not such a bad trait in a person, and you'll never lose your reputation from anything I say about you, I guarantee.

I didn't say anything, I just sat there, pondering it all.

He starts grinning again and says, Besides, it was the best night's sleep I've ever had!

And I threw the tablecloth on his head and he commenced to shaking all over, laughing silently.

After a bit, I had things packed in the wagon, and he gently set April down, still sleeping, on the bunched up tablecloth and got up to his knees and leaned on his heels and faced me. Let's see, he said, How does it go? Wash your face and hands, and be a good sport and tip your hat? What else is required of a gentleman friend? Oh, yes, bring flowers and be kind to her Mama? He was smiling so sweetly and not grinning like he was laughing, and I couldn't help it, I felt my face turn red and hot.

So I said, Captain Elliot, I am recently a widow and am not receiving suitors and do not expect to in the future. Something caught in my throat and felt like I was choking. I said, I have a child to raise and a ranch to run, and I've got to make some money to pay my hands and make it 'til the fall when I can sell some horses. In my head I was thinking I don't know how I'll do it because they won't let a woman in the trading corral, and Albert will have to, but it will be the first harvest time he'll have, and besides, it was the first time I thought that I owed the Maldonado boys for their help and I had been selfish.

His face got serious. Mrs. Reed, you take a lot of chances, and you stand up to them all. Why not take a chance on me? You can see I'm widely admired by both dogs and children, he says, real grand, And I ask you, is that not a fair recommendation?

I shook my head. A soldier is not what I want to hook up with anyway, least of all a smart alecky one like this, and I need to get to a hotel, and get home, and make some more soap to sell. I meant it, I told him, I'm not interested in suitors, not anyone. Not ever.

And I felt burning tears flood into my eyes and turned my head from his hard gaze.

Captain Elliot would not leave well enough alone, and although any real gentleman could have seen I had had quite enough of his company, as further proof of his poor character that man saw nothing of the sort.

Kneeling there in the grass at the park, I started to tear up, feeling stiffened and shamed, and wanting to sniff back tears like a baby. And he took liberties and touched my arm and made me look him square in the face. For a while we kneeled and faced each other as still as two posts in a fence line, until April woke up and came over to me. Just as she did a tear drop that had been blurring my sight rolled onto my face.

She said, Mama got owey? in her baby voice, then stood on her little toes and kissed my cheek, and said, Give you sugar, all better! Then the tear filling my other eye spilled out. She poked out one little pink finger and picked the tear off my cheek, examining it on the tip of her finger as it sparkled. She held it toward Captain Elliot and said, Mama got owey?

He was drilling a hole in my head with his eyes, but he said to April, Yes, honey. Mama's got owey. Straight through the heart, I'd reckon.

She tugged on his uniform and said, Give Mama sugar! like it was a command. I couldn't believe it, I was betrayed by my own baby daughter. Then he got that strange look on his face I recognized by this time, and his mustache tipped up on one side.

It might be safer for me, he said, and easier, to give old Mr. Geronimo a sugar, right now, Little Bitty. But you give her sugar, plenty. So he picked April up and held her to me and she about choked me hugging my neck and kissing me again and again.

He climbed up in my wagon without an invitation, and drove us to this hotel on Congress. I was too upset to tell him no. While we drove he told me some long story about a General Crook and trying to get back from some campaign before July Fourth and did I want to go to dinner at Levin's Gardens and hear the Sixth Army Band and see some fireworks?

I was too confused to think, and I believe I nodded to him that I would meet him, but now that I am more in my mind, I am sure that I will not be here then, and have no need to spend money for a fancy dinner. Besides, I didn't say anything, I just nodded, and that doesn't mean anything as I was addled for a few minutes like Mama and she used to nod all the time and it didn't mean anything.

I remember reading about such an unwanted situation in the Happy Bride book, so I will send him a letter and say that if he thinks I have an intention of meeting him in town, he has mistaken my courtesy for friendship, and that a lady does not make such an arrangement, and to please disregard it, or something like that.

That man makes me feel like I have my bonnet on backwards.

April 16, 1885

I started a letter to refuse Captain Elliot's invitation, but have not had the time to finish it. I will have to see if someone is going to the station soon to take it. Mice or rats have got nearly all the oats, and Jimmy would have a fit if he knew his horses had to go without oats for a few weeks until I can buy them. It seems I forgot all about practical things while in Tucson last.

Harland said maybe you can order them from the Sears and Roebuck, so he is over here looking hard through all the pages.

I caught him studying the ladies' bloomers and corsets, and asked him was he planning on ordering a few, and he turned the page and began to concentrate on farm implements instead.

I had a long talk yesterday with the Maldonado family about all the work they have done for me and they were at first offended that I would pay them. I figured up I would already owe them each for three months at least, and in most ranches, that's about a hundred dollars apiece. Even with my soap business there is no earthly way I will see that kind of cash, so it was agreed that they could each have a pick of a horse for past labor, and that they will come only two days, not three, at least until I can sell some stock. Then after the summer is over I will still give them that calf, who is turning into a sturdy looking heifer already. This is not nearly enough, but I must do what I can.

They went home leading the two they had chosen, one light-footed mare and a stallion, but I know they purposely did not pick the best horses here. And they did not even glance at Rose, for which

I am selfishly thankful. Their Papa felt close to Jimmy because they both loved and knew horses, and I'm sure those boys could have made a better pick, but they are generous to the last. If I could be sure it would only be for breeding, I would have insisted they take the big chestnut stallion that Jimmy rode to his death. He is a beautiful blood line, but I am scared to death one of them would also be killed by him. He has stayed skitterish since Jimmy died.

April 17, 1885

Woke up with a cold. April had been fretting and sniffling yesterday, too. This morning I got a real surprise. Ruben Maldonado, who I now know is only eighteen years old and I am already twenty, rode up and asked me if we could talk a while.

Well, I had a headache and a sick feeling behind the eyes from this cold, but I could see he was very serious, so I said, Of course. That sweet boy asked me to marry him. I still can hardly believe it. He said he works for me for free and gladly, though not because he is generous, but because he is in love. It was the saddest and sweetest thing to see that great big boy say these things to me with such a red face.

He is a hard worker and genuine and kind, and I know he will make a good husband. But I have no feelings like that toward him at all, no more than I would for my own brother. I should have understood when Jimmy asked me too, some of those same feelings. Maybe we could make a good life together. Ruben is a nice person. But I want to love someone, too.

I was sure scared of being alone but I know now that I didn't love Jimmy, and I don't love Ruben, and being alone isn't so bad compared. But then I remember Albert kissing Savannah and her all wrapped up in him, and I never in my life have had nor gave such a kiss, and I truly want to have a feeling like they do, like they are hungry for each other.

Ruben's face was sad and I knew I had broken his heart, and I cried when he left. It's hard to explain, but I feel like I would always be his big sister.

Jimmy has left me this place to run which is too much for me alone, but it is a good ranch and it will only be two more years until I own the whole thing, and then I could sell it and move back to Mama's, or maybe even go to a big city away from all the killing and trials here.

I am not so mad at Jimmy any more. I suspect Jimmy would never have loved again like he loved Ruthanne. Maybe she refused him and broke his heart like I broke Ruben's. We were surely happy enough at first, and maybe we could have made a pretty good life and a fine ranch, and children to fill up this big old house. And maybe we would have just worked ourselves into an early grave and left five or six children with too much to handle here.

April 18, 1885

Ruben and Rudolfo came and worked just like they always have. There is no sign on Ruben's face that his heart is broken, except that when they ask me something or talk, his eyes look a little to the side, not right at mine.

Mama and Savannah came over yesterday afternoon. Ruben had ridden to their ranch and told them about April's sickness. Mama brought some cough elixir and horehound syrup, and we gave April a spoon of each, although it was a struggle as she made it clear she was not happy to have the medicine.

Now, it seems April will sleep. It is cool tonight, and I have placed steaming pans of water around her bed so much that it smells like rain inside the house. It is nice to have just the women to talk with, and no men to hear. We made some soup and cornbread and talked until late, and they will stay the night and leave after sun up tomorrow.

I told Mama and Savannah about Ruben's proposal. That got us to talking about marriage and we laughed and cried some, and missed Papa, and it felt good to belong to each other again. I don't feel as lonely today as I have in months. At least I know there are other women around me. I think my Mama and Savannah must be special people in the Lord's eyes, as they have gone about doing generous and loving things without even a second thought. For me, it seems like the only thing that comes natural is aggravation and hard work.

But Savannah hugged me and said, Don't you change one little bit, we'd never be here if it wasn't . . . and then she started to cry, and so did Mama and I just had to join them. I know Mama and her were crying for love, and for all their dear feelings for our families. They don't know I was crying because they are wrong, because I am not good like them, nor sweet tempered and loving. I was crying because I felt like they didn't see the real me inside, and if they had they wouldn't shed a single tear at all over me.

Sometimes I feel like a tree on a hill, at the place where all the wind blows and the hail hits the hardest. All the people I love are down the side aways, sheltered under a great rock, and I am out of the fold, standing alone in the sun and the snow. I feel like I am not part of the rest somehow, although they welcome me and are kind. I see my family as they sit together and it is like they have a certain way between them that is beyond me. I wonder if other folks ever feel included yet alone. Maybe I am getting addled living out here on this ranch.

As Mama was ready to leave, she told me she almost forgot she had a letter from Ernest and he said to her to let me know he had thought hard about my wanting him to come run my ranch, but just couldn't do it, but sent his love and since I was now a widow, he enclosed money he had saved up just for me. Then she gave me a ten-dollar gold piece he had folded into the letter.

Mama, I said, you take that money and get some flour and coffee or some extra nice things and maybe a piece of yard goods and make a dress for yourself. I don't need it.

Mama said, Well, Ernest would be real disappointed if you don't take it.

But I said, Not as disappointed as I was that I can't count on him. I don't need his money as much as I need his head and hands and muscles.

Savannah said, Don't judge him too harsh, he is young and is just trying to help, so I nodded and said I would only think of him kindly, and let Mama put the money into my hand. It does no good to try to explain to someone as good as Savannah just how mean and selfish I am sometimes. I will put the money under the candle holder on the shelf for a rainy day.

Then Mama pulled the letter out of her pocket and handed it to Savannah, and said, Make sure I don't forget anything. She said, Ernest also asked if any of us had seen Captain Elliot who was headed back to the Territory.

I know she saw something funny in my face, and I blushed. Well, I said, I've seen a little more of him than I expected.

At that Savannah squeaked out a laugh like a tickled mouse, and covered her face in embarrassment. I was only thinking of running into him at the depot but when I saw the look in her eyes, well, we all laughed hard.

Mama said, I declare, you girls are naughty! I will have to turn you over my checkered apron and paddle you both! To go on, Mama said sternly but smiling, Ernest says he holds Captain Elliot in high regard and has wondrous tales of his bravery to tell when next he sees us. So if we happen to make his acquaintance again, we should all welcome him grandly, if only for the love of Ernest and the respect of his men.

We laughed more and more, and it is the first time I pictured myself hauling Ernest's hero, naked with a wet diaper on his head, in the wagon, and nursing him without a second thought. Savannah just couldn't quit giggling. She is not nearly as shy and blushing as she was before. I thought how funny of her to be so righteous and so Quaker and so good natured, and just a bit naughty, too. No wonder Albert thinks she sets the sun.

April 30, 1885

Made a batch of soap and tried some different ingredients in each fourth. I boiled some flower petals into a extract and added that to one, some pine sap in another, some other flowers, and then some apple leaves. All of these didn't work at all and one made the soap runny and it wouldn't set up.

It seems it is a day of unusual chores, and I felt restless and in need of more changes. So I dragged the shelves Jimmy had made for the pantry over by the parlor window, since they were never full anyway with just little April and me, and began to fill them with books. Then I put my rocker from the bedroom on the other side of the window and a rug in front of the chair. I put up Harland's picture of a grand house that he drew long ago, and a little colored picture card that Jimmy had brought home from the church meeting he went to in Tucson. That was the same time he brought me our family Bible, which I have on the top shelf. The card is a painting of the Lord Jesus with a lamb in his arms cuddled up close.

Now it is a fine room, and it is mine. I will spend some happy times there. From where the rocker sits I can see out the window to the road if anyone is coming by, and I can see little blue fingers on the wall and floor. Some folks would scrub and bleach them out, but I think I will only have one baby, and she is bigger now already, so those tiny hands will always remind me of how precious and tiny she looked.

May 2, 1885

Wrote Ernest a letter and one to the Lawrence family in San Angelo, and mailed them at the stage station today. The man there said there might be a delay in the mail because of some serious Indian trouble with Apaches, as the Army has lost some men who were guarding the mail shipments and there will be no replacements for awhile.

I went home and got April ready with some extra clothes and went to visit Mama and Harland and Albert and Savannah. I want to sell some horses off, I told Albert. There are too many for me to take care of. Or, I will trade him horses for a share in the pecan farm.

Well, he said I already have a share in the pecans, and he wanted to own Jimmy's big stallion himself, but I told him no unless only for breeding, for that he could have him. I'd never sleep at night knowing Albert was riding that chestnut. We discussed this and Albert never did quite see my side clearly, and insisted Jimmy must have just made a bad judgement, not that the horse was to blame.

You know, he said, Jimmy had made some other bad judgements before. So I asked him what did he mean, and is that why he was always so peevish toward Jimmy? Albert was about to answer when here came Savannah with milk-lassies for everyone, and he said no more about it.

We talked about making a trip to Tucson tomorrow or the next day, and I told them the Apache trouble the stage manager warned of. I hope Ernest is not fighting Indians but shoeing horses still. Albert is going to take five horses off my hands and sell them in Tucson if he can get a good price. He knows what Jimmy would want, he said.

May 4, 1885

It has been two terrible and dreadful days since I could write because as I gathered up my baby and some plates of gingerbread and sacks of fruit and quilt scraps Mama gave me, I looked toward the east where my house stands and saw a big commotion of dust in the air.

Albert got real serious looking and said, It's too much dust, it looks like a stampede. And then he said, Or someone stealing your horses. Right away he went in the house and got his rifles and Savannah began loading them while he saddled a horse.

I said to him, Saddle up another one, I am going too, and he looked at me kind of curious while I ran to the wagon and pulled out my rifle. We will lay low and be careful and if we are too outnumbered to fight we will just be thankful I was not there to be killed for the horses and stay quiet.

Here came Harland toting a saddle with a determined look on his face, but Mama said, No, Harland, you can't go, and he was mad.

I took him by the shoulder and put my kitchen pistol in his

hands and said, We need a man here to watch over Mama and Savannah and the babies. Then I said, Always watch what is behind your aim when you shoot. If you miss your shot, don't take down one of us, and he grinned at me and said, I know that already!

Then I took a last look at my sweet April and hugged her tight and kissed her little face and hands and handed her to Savannah who was grim faced. As we rode off my bonnet blew off and I realized it was the first time I had sat a horse in a while. My rifle was in my hand and the reins in the other, and April's little face kept appearing in front of my eyes and I knew I was more afraid than ever before, and glad that no matter what, April would be in Savannah's care.

We cleared the hill near my spread and saw the dust was still aways off. It might be coming from the Maldonados' place further off, or beyond that is the Raalles'. There was something going on for sure, and I felt sweat running down between my shoulders. On we rode, pulling up short at the entrance to the Maldonados to creep between the stand of live oak trees before we could be seen.

There were Indians at their barn, shooting rifles, and other Indians on horseback riding near the house with bows and arrows, but it seemed they were done firing for the time being. From the house now and then came one or two lone gunshots. Beyond the hills black smoke began rising, first in little puffs, then bigger and bigger until we see flames rising over the hilltop. The Indians began screaming louder and louder when they saw it, and Albert and I began to whisper just what is our best defense, and wondering hard what is burning yonder.

There seemed to be at least a dozen Indians there, and two dead in the yard, and another man dead by the corral that might be a Mexican by the clothes. Albert and I have four rifles between us, and we are not sure we can do more than draw their fire and get ourselves killed for the trouble.

Another shot comes from the front window, and one of the Indians was hit in the back and fell to the ground. That started the others to hollering just awful and raining shots in at the window, then up from the south came a new Indian with a burning torch and threw it on the front porch.

All the Indians gathered there to watch the Maldonados either come out fighting or burn to death, for the flames went to the vigas on the roof like lightning. As they were bunched up together, it was our only chance, and we began to fire at them very carefully. We had sent five of them to the devil before they understood there was fire coming from behind.

Inside, people were crying out and someone threw a chair through a side window and smoke shot out like a cannon. The Indians began to turn and fire at us, and Albert got hit in the head but not killed, just skinned right near his left ear. He was bleeding bad, but kept loading and shooting.

I worked as fast as I could take sight. Sweat was burning my eyes and I couldn't see. In a minute, two more hit the dust, and the Indians began to draw away, fired at from both sides and still not seeing us hidden in here. As they got out toward the far fence, they split up, heading different ways, on foot out to the desert. We would have let them go but they were headed toward our places, and we mounted up, loading up, and headed after them.

They had disappeared like a rabbit down a hole. For miles around, there was not a movement, not a sound, not even so much as a lizard crawling or a bird overhead.

When the Maldonados came out of their house they ran and ran around the yard just crazy. We got off the horses and Rudolfo walked slowly to the body on the ground. It was his brother Ruben, and his big old shoulders shook hard as he cried and picked up Ruben like he was a little child and held him close. Mr. Maldonado had an arrow sticking out of his leg above the knee, and he needed a doctor, but he was yelling for his wife, and couldn't find her anywhere. Finally we found her in the back near the chicken coop. She had been out there tending her chickens when they first came. Then we saw that she was shot in the head, and in her own hand was a pistol with only one bullet gone.

Mr. Maldonado was beside himself and roamed around the yard, crying to God, walking with that arrow in his leg dancing in front of him as he moved, like he welcomed the pain. Their other children were all crying, just sitting on the ground hugging each other. The roof fell in on the house then, although the adobe walls stood fast, and all of us were covered with dirt and ash, breathing the black smoke from the house until we were black too.

Albert said to him, We will come back, we have to go check on our places, but I don't think he understood, as Mr. Maldonado was still holding his hands up to the sky and crying out in Mexican when we rode away. At my place all looked peaceful, but Bear sniffed the air and he knew something was wrong. We decided I would ride to warn Harland and Savannah to hide in the cellar.

When I got to Mama's, all were determined to help our neighbors, not to hide and wait, so together we hitched two wagons. They brought one wagon with shovels and drinking water, and Savannah came with the babies in another, as we figured the Indians would not return to where they thought all were destroyed. They came quick, all the babies were crying because they were disturbed, and they followed me back to the Maldonados'.

Then I went on to catch up with Albert. We made the crest of a hill, and laid eyes on the worst sight yet. There by the Raalle's clearing was seven Cavalry men standing and firing in all directions, and at least eight more, laying dead or dying nearby in the dirt. At least twenty Indians surrounded them, dashing toward them on their horses as if the soldiers' bullets couldn't harm them.

Behind that scene sweet old Mr. Raalle lay tied hand and foot spread eagled from the branches of a tree and looking like a Indian pincushion. The Raalles' house was already a stand of black boards and singed adobe, but fire had spread and the smoke rose from a hay stack and the chicken coop and outhouse. I whispered to Albert that those soldiers are surely counting their shots now.

To our thankful hearts, we heard hooves behind us, and Rudolfo rode up with a repeater rifle of his own and two full bandoliers on his shoulders. The three of us crept closer and closer, and at Albert's word, all at once began to fire on them. Instead of returning fire, the Indians rode quick to the top of a rise further east, held each one's weapon in the air, and whooped at us.

It was a word of defiance, I know. It was like the time when we were children and Ernest had wrestled me to the ground and made me say uncle, and then I ran off and stood on top of the corncrib and said I took it back and I would never say uncle to him for all my days. Some of the soldiers fired last shots, some quickly got on horses and went after them, and I saw them ride over the next hill and counted eighteen Indians that got clear away.

Behind us, here came Mama, Harland, and Savannah and the Maldonados, all carrying pitchforks and sickles and anything they could carry that would made a dent in a man, with the littlest children in the rear and holding tight to the babies. They were a little pathetic bunch of determined looking soldiers. In front of us, the battle suddenly turned. The Indians on horseback had led the soldiers in a grand circle, and came charging over the hills right at us all.

I had fired my last shot, and cried out to Rudolfo to throw me some shells, but he was cut off by a fast riding Indian. Albert was bleeding so bad from his head he looked like a moving dead man, but still was loading and firing, though too far from me as he moved back to protect the children. Even Harland has squeezed off some shots.

Someone yelled out, Sarah! And as I turned and looked, barreling toward me with a spear in his hand raised over his head is an Indian man with hellfire in his eyes. I slipped off that saddle fast but as weak-kneed as ever I have been, and the spear nicked the pommel and stuck in the dirt behind me. The Indian wheeled his horse around and pulled out a rifle, stopped and aimed it at my head. I fired at him, but there was no bullets. I pulled the trigger again and again, and he began to laugh and point the rifle at me, coming a step closer each time I pulled the useless trigger.

The empty clicking of my rifle sounded so loud, like a cannon near my ear, but still he stayed on the horse, smiling hard and aiming. Finally, he cocked the action, and I tried to scoot behind the horse, but it jerked and ran. There was so much dust and smoke, I could hardly see anything beyond that rifle barrel and I knew I was dead.

Oh, my baby April, I said, over and over. The Indian raised the rifle to sight it in on my head, and I dropped my useless aim on him. Just as I thought I would hear a bang and die, he flew off the horse, dragged down in a crazy confusion of dust and blue cloth.

A soldier had him by the throat and I saw a hand go up with a knife. The Indian's rifle went off wild into the air, and then he laid limp on the ground. I ran.

Again, the soldiers had the Indians on the run, there being only about six or so left alive, they mounted up and this time after just a few minutes, the soldiers returned weary and exhausted, but with no one left to chase.

Savannah was cuddling the swarm of children who seemed to be all sobbing at once. Mama was tying an apron around Albert's head. He was talking to a soldier, and I saw them shake hands, and suddenly I recognized that soldier just from the way he stood and moved.

I was sitting in the dust near Rudolfo, shaking bad like a pot that is boiling over, and Rudolfo looked just terrible hard and pained, staring at it all. Then he turned to me and said very softly, Ruben loved you, Señora Reed.

I told him I knew, and then I hugged him, and I don't know what came over me to tell such a lie, but I said, I loved Ruben, too.

Rudolfo looked cheered for a moment and then started to cry. It was the saddest thing, that big, man-sized boy strapped with guns and ammunition crying in the dust. I decided it would not matter to him that I only loved Ruben like a brother, but it mattered a lot that his brother died with a little happiness first.

Smoke was rising now from the last standing building on the place. Mr. Raalle had planted pretty hedges all around that turned out to be a fire path from each outbuilding to the next. As the dry wooden shed started up in flames, horrible child like screams came from inside it. The whole crowd of us ran to it, but stopped, it was already a huge fire and flames shot into the sky.

Then suddenly, there was Captain Elliot, sparks all around him, tearing at the door, kicking the embers, he went right through the wall and came out with Melissa Raalle in his arms, the both of them smoking and singed and little hot red cinders clinging to their clothes as if they could burst into flames together like a human torch. Melissa's hair was matted and burned up, and part of the back of her dress fell away, showing a bad scorch place on her back.

Mama was there, and Melissa shrieked Mama! and held out her

arms, and the two of them fell to the ground, Mama rocking her back and forth like a baby, and Melissa wailing and shrieking without stopping for many minutes.

It was a long time before anyone could move. At last, one by one, soldiers started to get a drink from the Raalle's well, and to sit and get their breath. I just stood there, feeling that if I moved I would faint, but as long as I stayed rooted there, I could stand. All seemed to get quiet. There was no sound except for the crackling of the cooling coals left of the Raalle's home.

April came to me calling Mama, Mama, but when she saw me all dirty and black, she ran back to Savannah, afraid of me.

Lieutenant, said Albert's voice behind me, We have lots of folks here to bury. Could you spare your men a while to help us with a Christian burial before you leave? We'd take the soldiers, too.

Jack Elliot looked at him, and said, I'm not in command, here, Albert. The commanding officer is lying over there. Then he turned to the others. Will you men help bury these folks?

And they all nodded, looking around themselves at the horrible scene. One of them picked up a shovel right away, it had been leaning against the adobe wall and was not burnt.

Wait, I said. This is a homestead. If Mr. Raalle doesn't live on it, he doesn't own it. She's just a child, she can't live here alone. And if you bury him here Melissa may never see his grave again. Put him up at my place, next to Jimmy. And you men can clean up and I'll feed you, and you can put down for the night there.

Captain Elliot said, Well, men, You'd better listen to the Colonel, there, and I saw him look at me real strange again.

So Mr. Raalle is buried next to Jimmy and four soldiers from Fort Grant. It is too far to carry them back all that way, since that fort is not near Tucson. And Ruben Maldonado is next to his Mama and Yoyo's grave with three other soldiers near. His Papa begged the soldiers to dig his hole too, as he thinks he will die of the arrow in his leg. Somehow he had got it out before we got back, but he still thinks he will die of it.

One of the soldiers is well enough to travel back to the fort. All those men ate a big supper late at night when they got done with the burying, and I told them I would stay in the house while they cleaned up out back, and gave them all lanterns and plenty of the soaps that I couldn't sell anyway, and thought how lucky it was that I had made all that and couldn't sell it, so I had it on hand.

It is an awful thing to look on such sad circumstance and not be able to shed a tear. It is not because I do not feel for these folks, but maybe I feel too much. Part of me is glad, in a low down, mean way, that it is not Albert's or Mama's graves we are digging. Glad that it is some soldiers I don't know and neighbors and friends but not family. Lord, I must be the cussedest woman there is to think that. Finally, I felt so guilty for thinking those things that I cried. Then I began to feel the heartaches of our friends and neighbors and I cried for them, too, as we said prayers over each and every grave.

Then I heard Savannah praying on her front porch, and she was saying Thank you, Father, that our home and family was spared, and I suspect she may feel the same way I did, and maybe it wasn't so awful then.

May 5, 1885

Captain Elliot said I should stop calling him that as he is not in the regular Army and now holds the rank of Lieutenant anyway. I told him when he said he was off to fight Indians I thought he meant far away, but we agreed that the soldiers were our only chance for we might all have been dead. He said the leader of these Indians was Ulzana, part of Geronimo's tribe or gang, and now maybe Geronimo would stay in Mexico.

One of the soldiers left early this morning to ride to Tucson to tell General Crook about their battle and how badly it went for all concerned. The others will leave after breakfast and having some fresh bandages and water for all. Then we were on the back porch while Captain Elliot was washing his hands and face as we talked and I saw for the first time that his hands were blistered and burnt pretty bad.

He said it didn't hurt, but I scolded him and made him let me bandage up all his fingers, as they looked down to the bone in places, and he could end up with gangrene or something and die. I wrapped all his fingers carefully.

When I was done he said Thank you, Sarah.

So I kind of smiled and said did he think saving all our lives gave him leave to be familiar with me?

He looked around us and saw no one near, and said to me, No, but this might. And then that Jack Elliot took my face between his mittened up hands and kissed me plum on the mouth. My heart jumped about three beats.

Captain Elliot! I tried to whisper in a angry voice. I never!

And he just grinned like he does, and said, I know.

Then he had me by the shoulders, and said, It's just too dangerous, I wish you didn't live out here alone, you should move back with your family for a while. Or come to town.

Well, I said, I hate Tucson, it is dirty and ornery.

And he said back, It just needs a few women that are clean but ornery to straighten it up.

And then he kissed me again, different that time. Real hard and took my whole mouth and wouldn't stop even when I tried to push him away. He just kept on and kept on, and crushed me against him until I thought the life would go out of me for the feeling of lightheadedness and flush I felt. My heart was trembling inside and my legs felt watery and I couldn't stop breathing so fast and whimpering a little. His hands moved up and down my back and his whole body pressed against me. Then it stopped being hard and forced and became real tender and soft and kind of hungry feeling. He was kissing me so that I felt myself get weak, and I held onto him from faintness. When he finally let me go, I had to grab the wall to keep standing.

Then that man just grinned at me, and laughed a bit and said, I thought so! and went and saddled his horse.

May 15, 1885

Mr. Maldonado has got well in spite of himself, and he and Rudolfo and Estrellita have gone back to working as usual.

Albert's head is scabbed up and painful and now that side of his face kind of hangs down a bit and his smile is crooked. But Savannah said to him it is the most precious smile in all the world, crooked or not, and she kissed him right in front of the children and all of us.

Every few minutes, a burning hot feeling on my lips and the memory of hard pressing of hands kneading against my back makes me feel a certain other kiss all over again. It was not like the first one he gave me a long time ago, and surely nothing like any kiss Jimmy ever gave me. One time I think, he was mocking me and telling me I am a wanton woman, and then the next I think, he was scared for me and maybe it was him that killed that Indian that had me squared in his sights, and he loved me so much he just had to kiss me. Just like Savannah kissed Albert.

I must think about something else for a while. But then I remember his warm arms and his big strong legs touching mine and how hard and wide his chest was and how hot his kiss was, and I go outside and feed the chickens. They are getting mighty fat.

May 16, 1885

We go to get mail together, armed like a band of outlaws. Today I was expecting a package of rouge and perfume for soap, but instead I got a folded up paper package in a real neat little printed hand I didn't recognize. I opened it up and it was ten different little packets of flower seeds. There was no bill inside, but no note either, and I kept looking at the address, and it was surely meant for me, but no way to know who it was from.

The stage manager said, Appears you have a secret admirer, Ma'am, and smiled. Mama and Savannah looked at me strange but I just said I don't know who, it must be a mistake.

Melissa is healing up but will likely always carry a scar about as big as my hand on her shoulder and back from the fire. I'm sure she will carry scars on her heart for her dead family too. She will live with Mama and has already made a place for herself as Harland's little sister. He is very kind to her and protects her at every turn, as if he is glad to have someone look up to him again, since Clover died he has been the youngest. He has returned to his studies. I told him I still wish for him to go to a college somewhere, and maybe there will be one nearby someday.

Rudolfo has married a neighbor girl who speaks no English. Her name is Celia and she is only fifteen, and just came and moved in with Mr. Maldonado and the children, and Rudolfo's sister Estrellita is only a year younger.

We have gotten a newspaper from Tucson by way of the station manager. People in town are mad at the Army for letting the Apaches still carry out their misdeeds, it says, so General Crook and some soldiers went out after Geronimo on the 18th.

I wonder if Jack Elliot is riding with them. We keep our eyes on the horizon and our guns loaded.

June 18, 1885

We have come to Tucson with Rudolfo and his new tiny wife, Celia, and Melissa, Mama and Harland, and Savannah with the babies. Albert stayed home to work and look out for the horses. I have a heap of respect for my brother and I am proud to know his company.

We are here for trading and I brought two baskets of soaps. One basketful is piney and wrapped in plain paper which Harland and I wrote on: Mrs. Reed's Gentlemen's and Fine Laundry soap, and the others are the Ladies' soaps all pink and perfumed. Mama was surely surprised at how much money I got for it all, and I bought a hat from Mr. Fish, my first ever purely store boughten hat. Mama sold vegetables and eggs and some small sacks of pecans, the first from the trees, and peaches, and she got almost fifty dollars herself, but turned that money into plenty of dry goods, coffee and flour and tools and such.

The word is all over town that General Crook and his men have rounded up the last Apaches. For that news we are all thankful. Maybe the killing will stop. Surely the Indian folks must want it to stop too. It seems to me that any time there are men making a war, somewhere there are women and children at home waiting and worrying.

There is a commotion going on down by Levin's Gardens and restaurant. The Sixth Army Band is tuning up to start music, and they sound just awful. All those horns blaring away at each other like squalling geese, it is amazing how that noise could transform itself into music that all goes together in the right places. Every now and then they play a bit of a tune and then go back to blaring at each other.

Harland yanked my skirt and said, What are you staring at, Sarah? Who are you looking for?

I said, Just for Rudolfo and Celia.

And he said, They are behind us where they were a minute ago, you are looking the wrong way.

Then for the next hour or so, he kept accusing me of looking for someone in the crowds of people, but he is wrong, I am not. Finally, I told him to hush and quit tormenting me, couldn't he see I had things on my mind? I am looking for us all a place to sit and eat, and to listen to the band. And for thieves who might steal our goods in the wagons. Besides, there are blue uniforms all around, and I thought I might recognize some of the soldiers we had fought along side of.

Then Harland pulled my arm and said, Hey, look, there's Lieutenant Elliot.

Let me go, I said as he pointed. I was afraid he would draw Captain Elliot's attention to us. Harland, I said, I didn't see him and I don't care to. I felt every nerve in my body stand on end when I caught sight of him, afraid he would come over and say something to me, but he only turned the other way, talking with some soldiers. That he didn't see me was a relief at least.

Sarah, said Savannah, what ails you?

The heat, I said back, it is the heat, I'm afraid I will faint here in the street.

My goodness, she said, Just look at you, perspiring like that! Come in this shop quickly, and we'll cool you down. So they were all fanning me and making me drink glasses of cool water for a while. Then we heard sounds of the band starting to play, and Harland wanted to go and was very impatient.

As the sun set and the air cooled, we sat under a shade booth covered over with a tarpaulin which didn't shade us a bit, and listened to the band play. They were pretty good, but one horn player fainted from the heat, and they all sweated hard and looked like melted candies standing in a store window in the sun. Then General Crook gave a long and interesting speech, but April was fussing and wouldn't sleep, so I didn't hear it all. There were blue uniforms all around us, and some men with bandages on them, streaked with red. Finally, the sky filled with noise and bright sparkles as the fireworks went off. The wind blew the ashes from the explosions over onto us, and with it came the scent of black powder and burning fire. Melissa started to cry and hid in Mama's arms. All around us the crowd cheered for the fireworks, and my family sat there motionless, stiff and silent. We smelled the powder and ashes and heard the crashing sounds and squealing from the people around. It chilled me to the bones.

June 19, 1885

Today being Sunday and the first time Harland or I have ever been near a real church house, we spent the morning in the Methodist church. Mama said later that the preacher was as good as any Baptist preacher she ever heard, and she was truly inspired. Savannah agreed with her, and said wasn't it good to be in the house of the Lord, but she was used to more quiet and reverent preaching, and was not accustomed to so much condemnation and fear. Well, I was glad to be in the house of the Lord at first and hoped that some goodness will rub off on me from being near all that piety, but I felt my insides squirm when he began to preach about hell and the fate that awaits all those guilty of killing and savagery and drunkenness and lies and cheating and adultery. Drunkenness has never been a problem with me, and I don't know what adultery means, but lies and killing I have done.

By the time he got to hollering repentance and grace and salvation and about how this is my last chance as God will not always strive with men, I was feeling about as low as a snake on the ground. Outside, where the colored folks had gathered to listen in, some woman with a high voice suddenly hollered Save Me Jesus! and about scared me to death so that I jumped up off my seat.

Then that preacher pointed at me and said, Come up here and repent Sister! You are called by the Holy Spirit to repent, and he is pricking your soul with your sins. All eyes were on me, the whole place turned and stared. In front of everyone, he yelled, Place your hands on the Bible and repent of your sins, sister. I supposed he wanted me to tell them out loud to everyone, and there were a lot of shocked faces in the seats around me, but some of the faces just seemed real interested, not repentant. I thought I was about to choke to death.

So I said, I killed some people.

And the preacher hollered, Lord forgive her! Who did you kill?

And I replied, Two bad white men and some Indians I don't know how many, at least ten.

Suddenly he quit looking so full of the Holy Ghost and said You killed ten Indians?

I had to clear my throat to make a sound he could hear, but I said, Well, I 'spose I'm a pretty good shot. Then the whole place broke out laughing, and I felt real strange. When they got quiet, I said, And I told a lie. But then I caught sight of Rudolfo's face, and how he looked at me with a sad kind of understanding in his eyes, and I remembered sweet Ruben and how much those two brothers loved each other. I was feeling very guilty and was going to admit that I lied about loving Ruben, but instead I said, Well, when my husband passed I only dyed my dresses black, not my petticoats, and that is a lie of mourning, so I'm sorry for it.

Then suddenly behind me there was a line of people all sobbing or sad looking, repenting and putting their hands on the Bible and swearing repentance and begging for grace and a second try. The colored folks outside were having a time, praising the Lord at the top of their lungs and shouting down the Holy Ghost that like to scared horses in three counties. Then there was some glorious singing like the roof would raise off, and it was truly a joyful noise unto the Lord as there was not a true musical note voiced among the entire congregation.

After church the children were all fussing and hungry and impatient. I felt kind of sick to my stomach and couldn't eat dinner. Maybe that is the Holy Ghost working on my innards, but it feels more like a case of the scours.

June 25, 1885

It is purely hot. I told Albert it was the Devil giving us a little taste to remind us to be careful, and he laughed and asked me were my petticoats still white. Well, I have to admit they are, but now that I have repented for it, it doesn't bother me too much. The Maldonado family has rebuilt now and gone back to their chores, and yet all seem to move slowly and painfully, as if the starch has gone out of them all. Rudolfo comes only one day a week now.

Mama said to me she misses Mr. Raalle most dearly, and she had begun to look forward to his visits as he was a good man. I wonder if she had grown sweet on him, as she seemed terribly pained that he died in so dreadful a way.

Harland has finished his lessons from Mrs. Fish, and is eager to return them to get more. He is teaching Melissa letters and numbers and how to add and subtract, and she does pretty well. She has started an embroidery sampler too.

Savannah and Albert are expecting again. Now she said it just as matter of fact, like it was not a surprise. Well, she is a good Mama and I am happy for them both to have a fine, big family.

Sometimes at night I lie in bed and just feel hollowed out. Part of the inside of me aches to have the kind of family that Albert and Savannah have, and to know someone in a tender way the way they do. It is real clear to me that they are precious in each other's eyes. I think the only person that ever looked at me the way Albert does Savannah is Jack Elliot. What a fine set up that is! He is a sight harder to make heads or tails of than Albert. Captain Elliot has this recklessness about him, and a way of holding on that you don't know he is holding on, and a way of laughing that is like he takes pleasure in the act of laughing itself. He is better to have around in a scrap than a trained wildcat, though.

Now and then, I lie awake thinking I might like to have someone courting me. But it would have to be someone who is a square shooter and who has a train load of courage. And it would have to be someone who doesn't have to talk down to folks to feel good, or to tell a person they are worthless if they just made a mistake. And he'd have to be not too thin. Why, I remember hugging Ernest was like wrapping your arms around a fence post, and I love Ernest, but I want a man who can hold me down in a wind. Maybe he'd have to be pretty stubborn. I don't have any use for a man that isn't stubborn. Likely a stubborn fellow will stay with you through thick and thin, and a spineless one will take off, or let his heart wander. Goodness, what am I saying? It's not like I'd really want to hook up with Captain Elliot at all. Surely there's got to be some-one besides that ornery rascal who might want to court me.

June 28, 1885

I looked up on the hillside this morning and saw a rider coming this way. He pulled up at my well and began drawing a bucket up. I was standing out in the garden behind a tall row of beans and tomato vines, but I knew him before he turned around. Jack Elliot.

He took a long drink and went up to the door and knocked, then stuck his head inside and called Mrs. Reed? then peered around the place. I bent over and kept picking bugs off the plants. April was playing in the dirt nearby. My two dogs ran to him and frisked around, happy to see a familiar face, then started yelping too.

Mrs. Reed? he called again, and I had to stand up and face him or become a fool.

I called out hello, and he took off his hat. I could see he had something in his hands then, a little brown package, and a terrible strong smell of perfume was coming from it.

He said he'd picked it up in town, and brought it with him, but it must have been cracked in the box, because as he rode it began to smell stronger and stronger. He cocked his head and looked at me real odd, and said, Mrs. Reed, do you have a secret?

I tried to tell him it was nothing and just a special order, but the look on his face showed me he knew perfume when he smelled it.

Finally, he handed me the smelly package and said What is it, really?

So I explained to him that I made soaps and why I bought perfume, and how I couldn't pick it up in town but at the station where no one would know. We laughed about it when he said at least he smelled better than one other time we had met.

Funny how when he laughs, he seems so nice and warm hearted, kind of like a feisty horse that you really love, full of energy and spirit but not meanness. It is only when he grins and gives me that look of mischief in his eyes that I know who he really is.

He said he came to make sure April and I were all right. And then he said he could see my garden needed water, and went to fill the bucket again. So I showed him how Jimmy had rigged up a system with a tub and a drain pipe so we could pour the well water directly into the tin tub, where it ran down a pipe and all the way to the garden, and there was a gate valve on that end, where I could fill a watering can again and again. When that was done, he went to look at my new crop of foals, and admired each one, and talked about maybe buying a horse from me.

At about that time, here came Harland up the road riding one of the huge draft horses. He called out to Captain Elliot and said everything was all set.

What does he mean? I said.

It turned out Captain Elliot had arranged to spend the night at Albert's, and was here to pay a call on me.

Well, I told him, I am still not receiving callers.

Then he grinned and said he was not here on a social call it was strictly business, and he was here to do my bidding, mending fences or whatever needed doing. And, he said, he worked at a very reasonable rate but wouldn't tell me what it was.

I could see I was stuck with the man, so I pointed to the wood pile and the axe, and he went and took off his uniform shirt and started splitting wood. I went around back and took in my underwear quick off the line although it wasn't completely dry, and hung out some sheets and April's clothes and dish towels and such. Then I went inside and tidied up the breakfast dishes which I had left, and started sweeping. It may have been a long time passed, or a little, I don't know, but as I got to the doorway with a little pile of dust, there he was standing in my way, and startled me.

You look like you're trying to do tomorrow's sweeping today, he said.

So I said, Well, the dust just never stops here, and the wind blows it inside. Move your feet. And I swept it out beyond him. Now, if you are a hired hand, I'm not paying you to stand here and direct my sweeping, I said.

He grinned and saluted me like I was an officer, and said Yes, Ma'am! All day long he worked hard, just like Albert or Jimmy would have done. He wasn't as fine a touch as Jimmy with the furniture and he spilled white paint on the porch trying to put another coat on the front of the house, but he worked hard and didn't bother me. Except that just his being here bothered me a lot.

I could hear him whistling and humming and talking to either the dogs or the cats, as they were all under his feet but he didn't scold them he just let them be and shooed them for safety. He didn't eat at dinner, but by supper time, he accepted some steak and biscuits and fresh tomatoes, and corn relish I had put up, and peach pie. Then he tipped his hat and said he would be back early in the morning, and got on his horse and rode off toward Albert's.

June 29, 1885

Just at sun up, he came riding back. He took weeds out from under the porch and killed a big rattlesnake under there. He trimmed back a vine that was tangled around the garden fence, and straightened up all the posts and tightened the wire that held the cactus sticks. And he admired the little rows of seedlings popping up, which were the flower seeds I had received by mistake. Then he mucked out the whole stable and built a brace to push my leaning chicken coop back to upright, and then painted the chicken coop with the last of the house paint.

I was checking two loaves of brown bread in the oven, and straightened up to look out the window when I saw him down on his haunches, tickling one of my three kitties and smiling. Then he went to the pump by the back porch and used the soap I keep there and washed up. He ate a big slab of ham and almost half a loaf of hot bread right out of the oven, and I had to tell him to slow down, he would get sick from eating such hot bread. But he said in the Army he never had such bread, and hot or not, it was good.

He stirred up things by moving and straightening things I can't even lift, so there seemed to be mice running everywhere, and my kitties were all over the place, chasing them or carrying them in their mouths. It became a contest, the cats and dogs both trying to gobble every mouse they could get, even if they had to take them away from each other, so there were a few noisy scuffles between them.

By mid afternoon, he built me a fire to make some more soap, and even helped me strain the fat. Then he went to the corral to tighten up some fence, he said, but I didn't watch him as I had to stir the soap. He came back just as I was pouring it into the molds, and admired the pink stuff, and I explained that I still had some perfume left over, and the one that broke was for my next batch.

The sun was low in the sky, and in an hour it would be supper time again, and so I expected he would stay like yesterday and I was cooking up a big dinner. But he came back with his horse, and dressed up, with his hat on, ready to leave.

He nodded to me and said, I came to tell you, I have worked for you two days.

Yes, I said, you did a good job.

Then he said, I didn't do it for free, Mrs. Reed.

Well, I said, what do you want? I was counting up the hours he spent in my head and thinking I could give him maybe ten dollars, if he was going to push me for it.

But the look on his face was something other than I expected, and then he grinned that half grin of his and his eyes sparkled. You know what I want, he said, and stood real close to me, so that I could feel his body even though he wasn't touching me. My lips felt hot as if they remembered the feeling of his lips against them. It was hard to breathe and my throat was so dry that when I spoke, my voice made a funny sound.

If you think I'm going to let you kiss me again, in such an indecent way, well, you'd better not try it, Captain Elliot, I said.

Then he got real serious and said, Not only would you let me kiss you Mrs. Reed, you want me to. However, as nice a payment as that might be, I had much more in mind.

I know my eyes opened wide and I was shocked. I felt like I had the wind knocked out of me.

Oh, don't look at me like that, he said, putting his hat back on his head. You know that's not what I meant. I asked you to meet me in town for the Fourth of July and you never said no, but I have a suspicion you'd never show up if you didn't feel obliged to. So now you owe me. He mounted his horse. A date in Tucson. By noon on the fourth. I'll meet you at the depot, and plan to stay at least a couple of days. And don't come alone with your baby, it's too dangerous. And you'd better show up or I'll be back, until you owe me your whole ranch. Then you'll be the subject of more talk around town than a sin like white petticoats and being an Indian soldier!

June 30, 1885

I have to admit, with a couple of days of a man's hand my ranch looks bright and shiny, and the house is freshly painted, and the cats are full and sassy, lying in the shade licking themselves. After Captain Elliot left I saw that he had lied, and when he said he was tightening up the corral fence, what he was really doing was digging a hole. He had planted a little bush by my front steps and there was a brown piece of paper stuck on the thorns of it. Picking it off, I got stuck and a drop of blood from my finger soaked into the paper. Written there in the same little tight capital letters that came on the seed packages was this:

THIS WILD ROSE BUSH WILL LIVE MANY YEARS.
PRUNE IT ONLY IN THE DEAD OF WINTER.
WATER EVERY OTHER DAY AND
COVER IT WITH A BLANKET FROM FREEZES.

What possessed him to do all this work and give me a gift like that, just for a date in town? A rose bush. I wonder what the flowers look like? I never have seen a real rose bush, and I didn't know they lived years and years. I will have to ask Mama about roses. I got right up and hammered some stakes in the ground around it and wrapped wire about them to keep the rabbits and things from eating it. I don't feel so mad at him, but purely puzzled.

July 1, 1885

Last night I had a dream that Captain Jack Elliot was here lying beside me in this bed. I was so sure it was real I could feel his skin and hear him breathing, and I reached over with my hand and there was no one there. I felt sad. Then I was mad at myself and got myself up on my knees and asked the Lord to forgive my wanton heart. And when I slept again I dreamed of being kissed like he did on my back porch, and there was nothing like it in all my days. That time I didn't wake up but felt him wrapped around me like he was before, and somehow smiling that funny grin and kissing me at the same time. Then I slept in real late this morning, and didn't wake up until April came and crawled up on my bed. I looked over around for a sign of him being there in the night, and there were none. And I felt some relieved but more empty than a leaky bucket.

Albert rode over here today to see how things looked, and he said real carelessly, Well, looks like you have had some work done on the place.

Albert Prine, I said, you have showed a scoundrel side of yourself by helping that man to trick me.

He nodded at me and grinned. It wasn't any trick, he said. Jack wanted to help you out and said you'd agreed to pay him. What'd he charge you?

I said, I have to drive all the way to Tucson just to eat dinner and supper with him, and sit the whole afternoon in his presence and be tormented!

Oh, he said, still grinning, That's mighty odd.

That's not all, I said, it's going to cost you too, since I am promised not to come alone with April, but must be escorted safely by you. I figured that would singe his tail feathers good, as he hates to take time off especially just to be an escort, not even on farm business.

But all he said was, Fine, we'll take Harland and drive half a dozen of your horses to market, and he and I'll be busy selling horses while you keep company. The Fourth of July will be a big day and lots of people will be in town. Come spend the night at Mama's on the third, and leave April there and we will leave before first light and be there by noon, he said.

How, Mister Albert Frederick Prine, did you know it was the Fourth of July?

July 4, 1885

We left Albert's place early, and even with the string of year-lings along we got to town before noon. Albert would not let me ride a horse but insisted I drive the wagon. Harland has his schoolwork all neatly held in a satchel just like the town boys use, and he said it was a gift from Jack Elliot.

Well, I told him, that man doesn't give a gift without a string attached, and he said What does that mean? But I couldn't explain it, I just know it for truth.

Albert knows something about all this but he is not telling, and I am not real happy with him.

True to his word, Captain Elliot was waiting at the depot in a rented, shiny black buggy, which he helped me into almost imme-diately and put my bag in the back. Then he said hello and talked a bit to Albert and Harland, and said he has arranged for three sol-diers to camp at our places, one at each, to guard while we are in town. That is probably a good thing, although all has been quiet for weeks now.

I had gotten my mind all prepared for putting up with his shenanigans, but he seemed polite and courteous, and only teased me when other people couldn't hear, for which I am thankful. We strolled and looked into shops I have never been inside, and I discovered there is quite a bit more to Tucson than I had thought—more than Jimmy showed me. Also, there is now an ice factory in town and it was so wonderful to have a cold, cold drink in the warm afternoon.

We went to the ice shop and he bought a cherry phosphate with two soda straws to share it. I never had such a fancy, tingly thing to drink and I was afraid it was liquor but he said no, just sugar and cherry juice. He pretended to drink some but mostly he let me have it all, and while I drank it he pretended to be looking out the windows but I saw his eyes flit back at me now and then.

I figured he was real proud of himself for renting a buggy, so I told him it was nice, and just to make conversation I said maybe someday I'd like to have one. It sure was a smoother ride than my old wagon. Anyway, I began to be in a better mood. But, if he thinks he is going to kiss me again for a lunch and a buggy ride, I will never, ever let him.

Then he took me to a place in Carillo Gardens where there were little canoes to ride, and made me sit down and he rowed around the tiny lake. We admired the water lilies growing in the shady places, and the ducks and geese, and there were even two important swans he said were brought from California just to be admired in the pond.

Then I understood he had said imported, which means brought in from somewhere else, not important, and I thought it was funny and said, Well, they look pretty important, too.

He said, I like to see you smile, which made me embarrassed, so I tried to talk about something else. I hope no one looks this way and thinks Captain Elliot is my fellow.

Before we knew it, we had talked away the whole afternoon about this and that. The carrying on out in the streets was getting crazy by then, men were shooting guns and boys were lighting firecrackers, scaring dogs and horses, and it seemed like you took life and limb in hand just to ride back in the buggy through town.

We had a real elegant dinner in a place with carpets on the floors and table cloths and silver candlesticks on the tables, and a real stiff man asked us what we wanted and sniffed at me when I couldn't decide. It was some pretty fancy cooking. Little carrots in a ring decorated the meat which they called Prime Rib but it was just a piece of roast beef. There was cake with thick frosting for desert.

When the man came back with the bill, I waited until he left, then asked Captain Elliot how much it is. I figured if he expected me to pay him back in Tucson, then I had brought my money, and this was a grand and fancy dinner, so this must be what he wanted.

He put his hand on mine when I reached into my bag, and said Sh-sh, real softly. Never, never, he said, pay for a man's dinner. Your contribution is simply being company.

I was purely puzzled.

The restaurant started to clear out, and the noise and carrying on in the street was louder. The band was playing again, real music this time, and up on the side of the hill by downtown the fireworks began. He took my arm and we walked down to where we could see the sky fill up with the sparkling things and hear the booming.

Pretty soon, he asked me, How come you jump every time they go off?

So I said, Well, I don't like the smell of black powder, it just makes me remember. And then I choked up like a little girl and couldn't finish.

He put his hand on my back and said, Come with me, Mrs. Reed. And right away we whisked away from the fireworks and back to the buggy, where he pointed it away from the downtown area and snapped the whip and we drove out to some open road. It was calm there, and cool, and the breeze kept the smell far from us.

You're still shaking, he said.

No I'm not, I told him.

He just made a tired face at me and nodded, saying Okay, you're not.

We were silent for a long time, and finally, he was looking at the stars, real thoughtful like, and said to me, You know, I've never thought about it before, but fireworks always bothered me too. I remember the smell of gunpowder and the sound of cannons when the Union Army took our town. I remember people running, and the smell. Then he took a deep breath, and said, They burned our house over our heads. My mother had just had a baby, and I was six years old. She begged them not to set it on fire. She gave me my little brother to carry while she took my two sisters' hands, but I couldn't get out, a burning timber fell in between us. Then she came back for us and handed me out a window just as the ceiling fell in on her and the baby.

His voice sounded like ashes, dry and hot and withered, like he still felt the heat from that fire. Then he said, My Pa was in Georgia starving for the Confederacy, and got home two months later. No, he said, I don't much care for fireworks.

Well, I didn't know what to do. I felt myself being sucked into a dark well full of his painful memories, which seemed just as bad as my own. Then, like I was someone else watching us from over head, I saw myself put a hand on his arm and squeeze it. He laid his hand on mine and we just held hands together, as if we were keeping each other in the world and if we let go, one or the other would just slip away from sadness. I felt the hard muscles in his arm, and the calluses on his hand. I caught myself looking hard at his hand on mine in curiosity, at the little hairs on his knuckles, and at the dark weathered skin and blue lines that stood up across the bones. In the cool and quiet night, we both stared at the stars, like they whispered words of comforting to us. There was a kind of strength in it, in being together, that was stronger than being alone.

After a long time I said to him, Did you know some of the stars have names?

He looked at me and smiled with that warm look he gets now and then. Yes, he said, but I don't know their names, do you?

No, I said, but lets name them ourselves. We'll name them after everyone we love that is already in heaven, and every night when we see their star, we'll have a good memory of them instead of a sad one. See how beautiful it is up there?

Then he looked at me so hard that it sort of scared me, so I kept talking but with my face turned away from his.

We picked out stars in figures we could find again, and named them after his Mama and his little brother, and my Papa and my little brother, and Ruben Maldonado, and Mrs. Lawrence, then he picked one for his friend he lost five years ago, but he wouldn't say a name for that one. On our way back to town I realized I didn't pick one for Jimmy, but he didn't ask me about it, so I decided not to mention it. I'll pick him out one later at home.

Albert and Harland were already put down in the wagon, but Captain Elliot had rented me a hotel room, on the second floor, where I didn't have to worry about someone looking in from the outside, he said. He walked me to get the key, and then took my arm again up the stairs and unlocked the room and handed me the key. He struck a match and lit the kerosene lamp and it brightened up a bit.

This is real nice. I have never stayed anywhere completely alone, I said, looking around.

He sighed real hard, like he was still looking inside himself somehow, and closed his eyes. Then he said, Well, it's not so bad, and you can sleep as late as you want. The hotel clerk will order you a bath if you want in the morning too, and bring you breakfast, all you have to do is ask.

He went toward the door, and I followed him close, ready to lock it because I felt a bit nervous. He turned around. Miss Sarah, he said, taking my hand again, Thank you for a fine afternoon. Then he kissed my hand.

Captain Elliot, I started to say.

Please, he said, call me Jack.

Well, Jack, I said, I had a very nice time.

He smiled. Will you go for a drive with me in the morning?

That will be fine, I said. I felt caught in his eyes.

Suddenly his lips were on mine. Instead of being forced or quick, it was just a sweet, little kiss, and it made something inside me burn hot like I stepped over a fire. He stopped for a second, then kissed me again, pulling me against him, scaring me with the storm I felt in my insides as he pressed me tight.

Wait, I thought, I was going to tell you not to try to kiss me, but you didn't give me a chance. I couldn't get the words out, it was too late. Then, too soon, he stepped away from me, grinned his funny half smile and tipped his hat and slipped out the door.

Good night, I whispered into the dark hall, and although I didn't mean to, the word came out like a prayer.

July 5, 1885

Even though I tried to stay awake last night and ponder all that happened, I seem to have fallen asleep when my head felt the pillow. I was up this morning with the sun. By the time I was bathed and dressed, it was still very early and there was no sign of Captain Elliot, so I went into the dining room alone and had some coffee and pancakes.

The coffee was weak and the pancakes were undercooked, so when the waiter came to refill my coffee I had to say, I'm sorry, I'm just not hungry, but he acted like he didn't care a hoot. Town people are strange. I was half done when I felt someone standing near me.

Captain Elliot. Immediately I felt myself flush hot and remembered how he had taken me off guard because I was so tired last night. He will not get away with that again.

Well, he said, you promised me a ride. He didn't say much, but sort of guided me out to the buggy, and climbed in beside me.

We started off down the road, and we saw a lady on the walkway with a dear parasol over her head. I asked him, Captain Elliot, would you please take me to a store where I can buy one of those parasols for shade?

He looked at me like it was for the first time, and said, Your wish is my command, Ma'am, and turned the buggy around.

He pulled up in front of a ladies' millinery where they had the nerve to display a corset in their front window. Are you sure this is the place? I asked him.

But he said, Well, if it isn't, then they will know where to go, most likely.

In ten minutes I had myself the most beautiful parasol for a dollar and eighty-one cents, and the lady said since it was lavender, it was all right to take it while in mourning, so I was very happy. When we got back to the buggy I set my hat back a little on my head and opened the parasol, and the little ruffles sashayed around in the breeze when we moved. It was beautiful.

We drove way out of town to the Silverbell Mine, and from a hilltop there Tucson looked mighty small. Contrary to yesterday, he hardly said a word the whole way. We walked around a bit, and had some water from a canteen he had brought, then he gave the horses a scoop of water in some odd leather bags like I'd never seen before.

Then we drove back to town and south to where someone was building a beautiful new house all of bricks. He showed me where the town was growing and we rolled among houses that were a grand sight beyond the adobe and wood ones around the presidio walls.

Then he seemed to loosen up again, and told me things about his family, and where he grew up in Mississippi and then in parts of Texas. He told me Savannah reminded him of his oldest sister Penelope, and how he admired her, and we agreed that they were first caliber women. All morning we talked and talked, when we finally got back to the hotel for some dinner we were both tired.

We had a small lunch and lemonades, and there was a picture on the restaurant wall of a rocky cliff and a little boat on the ocean, and it reminded me of the scarlet velvet lady book I so wanted returned. I suddenly asked him, Whatever happened to the book I traded to you? Is it lost? I still want to buy it back, even if it is damaged or torn, I don't care.

His eyes got narrow, and I got a sense in my head that he began to tell me a lie, and he said, Well, it did get damaged, during a battle a ball struck it and killed my horse right from under me, and it wouldn't be possible to read it so . . . He just let the word drift away.

What I wanted to know was why it got shot with a horse under it in a battle, why wasn't it on a shelf somewhere in a room? but suddenly he asked me if I minded giving him leave for a couple of hours, and that he needed to check in at the Fort. However, he said, nothing would stop him from coming back to see me before supper time.

I was disappointed. I will never know what happened to the Duchess nor why she was filled with sorrows, nor who was on the little ship. I took one last look at the picture on the wall, and he saw me look at it, but didn't say anything and only rode me back to the hotel and left.

While he was gone, I went to my room and took off my dress so I could be cool and tried to take a nap. But all I could think about was Captain Elliot. Then I realized what was happening. I didn't feel near so hollowed out, being around him. I wished he could have stayed here a while and talked some more. And I thought about all we had done and said over and over, trying to remember it just right, and recall every word he'd said. When I finally dozed off, I dreamed about his arms around me and his kisses taking my strength away. Suddenly, I thought he was in the room, but I cleared my head and heard him knocking lightly on the door and calling my name.

I had to say through the door that I would meet him downstairs in a few minutes, to give me time to fix my hair again and get dressed. I stopped to say a prayer to get all that out of my mind, and I thought it worked at first. When I met him, he was with Albert and Harland, and they were all three dressed up and looking clean, and smiling at me. I felt like my thoughts were tangled up inside more than ever.

We had supper and Albert handed me almost four hundred dollars from selling those horses. Afterwards, Captain Elliot said he must get back to the Fort, and my room was still rented for another night, so we will leave early in the morning to get a jump on the afternoon heat. He thanked me for riding with him around town, but I felt like I hadn't done a thing but rest for two days, so I don't know why I deserved thanks. No one thanks me at home for working like a mule.

Riding my wagon home with Albert driving was plum tiresome. What a bumpy old thing it is, too, and Albert, I said, why don't you see if you can miss some of them ruts you are so fond of, and give me a few bones left whole when we get there?

He just said back, Well, Miss High and Mighty, take the reins yourself if you want. But I didn't. I had some thinking to do.

July 9, 1885

I went this morning to spend time with Mama and Savannah. We put our heads together and made some pies for dinner and plenty of good things. While we worked, we talked and talked. I don't know how three women in a wilderness with the same kin folk can have so much to discuss, but we seem to manage it. In the afternoon it was warm, so when the little ones were napping, we sat in the shade. I was surprised when Savannah asked me right out what did I think of Captain Elliot, and she seemed real eager to hear.

Well, I said, you seem to be real set on him calling on me for a purpose.

No, Sarah, she said. I just thought after your calling in Tucson you might have softened in your opinion of him a bit.

I didn't know just what to say. Mama looked at me and said, Your brothers and him did a trick, fixing that all up together for you. Can't tell if he's courting or not, taking two boys along. You girls want to help me piece some quilt blocks? They're cut and matched. Care to?

We both nodded. I always like to sit and piece quilts, I like how all the little pieces that weren't meant to go together end up making a pretty pattern. My Mama has a real hand at quilts, and the one she keeps on her bed took a ribbon at a fair once. She prizes her quilts and has no patience with me if I get careless in the stitches or any threads come loose.

When Mama went inside to get the quilt pieces she had bundled, I leaned over close to Savannah's ear and said, I think that Captain Elliot is smitten with me.

She laughed quietly behind her hand and said, I think so too. Did he act like a gentleman? Did he take you places for dancing or anything like that?

No, I said. But I don't know how to dance anyway. We ate at a fancy restaurant. And we rode in the buggy. And he just talked some and was quiet some.

One thing I know, whispered Savannah, is that if he was quiet, and you were quiet, and neither of you minded it, then you are in love.

What? I never heard of such a thing, I said. Why should being quiet mean you're in love?

Because, she said. That means you aren't nervous with each other, or affected, or likely to be hiding intentions behind too much conversation. A friendly silence can speak between two who will walk together a long way, she said.

Is that in the Bible? I asked.

No. My Pa said it, more than once. He liked to be quiet, and sit by the fire with Mama and watch her read or sew, or the both of them would just watch the fire die down before turning in. Then Savannah's face turned very red, and tears filled her eyes. He must be so lonely, she said. Oh, Mother.

I hugged her tight. Your Pa sounds like a thoughtful person, I said. A good person.

I miss my mother so terribly, she said, and sobbed a couple of times. Then Mama came back out, loaded up with a bundle of scraps tied with string, her little box of thimbles and needles, and a pitcher of buttermilk in the other hand. She looked upset right away.

She was thinking of her mother, I said softly.

So Mama put her arms around her, and Savannah hugged us each, and then smiled after a while. She's looking on me from beside the throne of God, Savannah said.

Yes, honey, said Mama. And she patted Savannah's head and kissed her hair.

We began to piece the quilt blocks, and put several of them together. And the talk turned away from Jack Elliot and did not go back to him. Inside myself I was glad it had taken a different route. And yet, I thought of him between each and every word we said. I felt like he was there amongst us. Hovering around our shade and our stitches was his name and his face and his funny one sided grin.

This morning Rudolfo rode over to tell me he and Celia are expecting. I am very happy for them. He said Celia is really sick, so I told him to see if he could get some blackberry tea for her from town, and I wrote a letter to Fish's for him in English requesting the tea. It's too bad none of the wild blackberry cuttings I brought from Texas ever took.

Somehow it didn't surprise me to see a blue uniform watering his horse at my well this afternoon. Captain Elliot has brought me two packages. One is soap fixings I ordered, and the other is a present for me, he said, from him. It was a book called Treasure Island. He said it was a fine story and full of excitement and pirates and it was his favorite book. Then he pulled out a present for April too.

She opened it like a little glutton, and whooped at the pretty things. It was a whole set of little colored wooden blocks. Each block had three letters of the alphabet, and a carved in picture of an animal, and a word she can learn to read. All different colors, too, she began to hold them up to us and ask Red? Blue? and we would say, Yes, or No, that's yellow, that's green. She said yellow in funny baby talk, but the rest she said real well, and she was just beside herself over the blocks. It wouldn't be polite not to ask him to stay for supper, so I did, and he stayed. It was a warm evening, and after we ate we sat on the porch fanning and not talking much, watching April make tumbling down stacks of blocks.

Finally, I said, Are you planning to sleep at Albert's again? He said he was. He came to see if I needed chores done tomorrow, but Albert had asked him to help him a bit, so he wouldn't be by until the afternoon.

July 20, 1885

Noon was still aways off, and April and I decided to have a cool bath on the back porch. Toobuddy had followed Captain Elliot back to Albert's, so I sat Bear by the front near the rose bush, and pointed my finger at him. If you see any ornery looking man coming this way, I told him, you bark loud, Bear. And if he doesn't stop coming, don't hesitate to take off his leg.

I thought it was early and we'd have plenty of time before Captain Elliot came, so I filled the wash tub with cool water and we were splashing and having a nice time, both of us like little bathing girls, when I heard a horse whinny. I looked up through my wet hair, and there, right in front of me was a man on horseback.

It was that Moses Smith fellow from long ago. Well, looky here, he said. If it ain't the Mizzez Reed and a little rat?

Get away from here, I said. Haven't you got any decency?

He just got off his horse and laughed and said, Well, I ain't been accused of it lately. He was just peering at me and looking scary. I was looking for my towels and they were too far away to reach without getting out of the tub. He walked up onto the porch and I was too scared to move but trying to cover myself with my arms. I come for some of your cooking, Mizz Reed, he said. But I see that I can have something else instead.

No you can't, I said. My, my husband will kill you for saying that, and my baby is here. Bear, Bear! I hollered at the top of my lungs, but Bear didn't come.

Smith just sneered and I saw he was missing teeth from rot. Your husband is worm fodder, Mizz Reed, I seen his stone in the yard. Then he shook his head at April, And rats, he said, is for drowning. I grabbed April and stood up quick, both of us all wet and slippery, and tried to get to the door with her but he was too fast. He took April from me by one arm, dangling her in the air, and she started to cry.

Don't hurt her, I cried out. Please don't hurt her.

So he said, Let's just say you'd better keep quiet, I don't want to hear a bunch of noise from you. Get in that house.

No! I yelled, but he held April over the tub head down and lowered her into the water. Stop! Stop, I said, and he took her out and dropped her with a thump on the porch. She shrieked. The sound tore my heart apart.

Get in that house! he ordered. Like a whip he pulled a hunting knife from his belt.

April cried and coughed, in a terrible panic. He followed me inside but left April screaming on the porch, and he shut the door.

I pulled the table cloth up to cover up with and he laughed and kept coming at me and put the knife back in a scabbard. I began to run around the room, but he just kept laughing, and I could hear April was still crying so hard that it broke my heart, and finally he got hold of my table cloth and yanked it out of my hands. I swung my fist at him and hit him, but he just grabbed my hand and twisted and pulled on it so I thought he would pull it off.

He shoved me hard against the wall, and crunched himself up against me, breathing horrible breath, and smelling like a old bear rug. He was short but real strong, and I tried to tell him, My family is coming over, and my neighbors, they're due here any time.

Shut up, was all he said, and held both my hands in one of his big dirty hands, and with the other hand he began loosening his pants.

Don't do this, I said. Please don't hurt me. I'll give you all my money. I'll give you a horse.

I thought I told you to shut up! he hollered then he slapped my face so hard I thought my neck was broke and for a second I thought sure my eye had been crushed, it swelled right up. He looked at me and grinned. I'll take your money and your horses too, he said, and slapped me a second time, so hard it twisted me around and away from him a little. I thought I could run, but I was dizzy, and he grabbed my hair and pulled me back, dragging me to the floor.

Then I began to fight him with all that was in me, but he just held on and seemed to enjoy it. Finally, he leaned over on top of me and I couldn't lift my hands under his weight. I could feel him pushing his knees between mine, and I felt eaten alive with panic.

No, no! I screamed, and again he slapped my face, but this time I almost didn't feel it. When he raised his hand to hit me I did the same and slapped him back and it surprised him enough that he missed what he was doing with his knees and was straddling my legs, so I used my right knee and kicked with all my might between his legs. He bellowed out with pain and just got sort of stiff and I kicked him again, which got him off me and I ran toward the kitchen table.

He grabbed one of my ankles, still holding his privates and moaning, but he had me tight like a trap, and I dragged him with me some, trying to get to the hidden pistol. Then he was behind me, standing up, and got to me just as I touched the pistol.

He picked up a knife off the work table, and said, You're going to pay for that, and he laid that knife against my breast. At that very second I pushed the pistol into his middle and pulled the trigger. I always kept the first chamber empty for safety. He looked down at it for a second and laughed like a sort of bark. Empty! he said.

Suddenly the front door flew in almost torn from the hinges and Jack Elliot was on Moses Smith like a wildcat. Smith was fast for such a heavy man, and took Jack's punches without a wince. One time it looked like Jack was up against the wall, and just as Smith raised his bloodied knuckles again, I aimed the pistol and shot, striking him in the arm. Jack twisted away from him and got him down to the floor, and beat his head again and again on the floorboards, making the house shake like thunder.

Jack, I said, you're going to kill him!

That's what I had in mind, he said. Smith lay silent on the floor. Jack said to me, Keep that gun aimed at him and if he moves a hair blow his brains out. He ran to his horse and brought in a rope which he tied quick around Smith's neck and dragged him like a dead corpse outside. I reached for my table cloth while he did.

Smith woke up then, and began fighting more, but Jack got the best of him, and when he hit him one more time, and swung him hard with the rope collar he was still wearing, Smith's head fell against the iron pump near the well, and he didn't move while Jack tied him hand and foot.

I stood like a statue, frozen to the spot. There by the front steps, sweet old Bear lay dead. Toobuddy laid down by Bear's old body and whimpered and looked sad. Jack went in the house and pulled a quilt off my bed and wrapped me up in it, and I held on tightly.

April! I yelled. Where is she! Then he went all through the house much faster than me, until he found April, naked and terrified and crying, under a bushel soap basket on the back porch. He wrapped her up too, and brought her to me, and led me into the house and sat us down.

All that time he never did talk, but dipped a cloth in cool water and pressed it to my eye, and murmured Sh-sh to April, and patted her head as she began to quieten down.

Then he got another wet clean cloth and gently pulled the quilt away from me. I looked at him with dread in my heart, but there was nothing but kindness in his eyes as he tenderly put that cloth against my breast where it was bleeding. I watched him do it with surprise because I didn't even know I was cut. He lifted it and dabbed gently, and finally he said, I don't think it's bad, just the very surface. Then he put the cloth back and pulled the quilt up onto my shoulders.

Jack? I said, and I wanted to say more but nothing would come out of my mouth. April was so frightened and exhausted, she sobbed a few times and fell right to sleep, bundled in my arms, so he took her gently and laid her on her bed. When he came back, he knelt by my chair, still without saying anything, and took the cloth and refolded it so it would be cool and put it back on my face.

Jack, I said again, if you hadn't gotten here, he would have done it, I was almost out of fight.

Then I don't really know why, except that I wanted to so much, I leaned over and took his neck and kissed him. I slipped out of the chair and into his arms and he held me close and kissed me long and hard, and I kissed him back. Then I leaned my face into his neck and just held onto him for dear life.

Don't leave me, Jack, I said.

Not ever, he whispered back.

July 21, 1885

Jack made me go stay at Mama's house. He took Moses Smith to town and handed him over to the Sheriff. I was so bruised and beaten I stayed in bed one whole day. Mama was glad Jack had come there just in time, and she held my hand and cried a while when she thought I was asleep.

I feel like I was hurt inside more than I was outside, and walk the floor at night and sleep fitfully. I also feel like I should tell Mama that I kissed Jack and it wasn't any innocent sweet little kiss like Jimmy used to give. But I don't think Mama would understand and she has never been fond of soldiers although she doesn't mind Captain Elliot too much. All day I look toward the road, hoping to see him riding up. But all day he has not come back.

I know it is too quick to get to Tucson and back in one day, but I look anyway.

July 22, 1885

I am tired and restless. I have a sense that Moses Smith will be lurking behind every rock or tree or corner of the house. I got Rose and rode aways up the hills, and took both my kitchen pistol and my rifle, and plenty of shot. When we reached the place I wanted to stop, I got down but felt purely spooked by the woods around, so I went further up 'til there was a clearing. But there I jumped at every prairie dog or bird call, and like to shot my own foot off with a shaky hand before I realized I was riding with my finger on the trigger. Albert will have to fix this here stirrup as now that there is a hole in it, it is bound to break.

Lord, I was more scared than about any time in my life. Every time I think I have been just as scared and horrified as a body can be, I find there is new terror I am to become acquainted with. What is the use of that, God? How can we get anything done being that scared? And why is there such a person as Moses Smith left alive to walk the earth with the likes of decent God-fearing folks?

I wish Jack Elliot was here. It seems the only time I can take a full breath is when he is nearby. It's my own hard-headed ways, I suppose. I just hate to give in to things and admit I need help. But he is the only person I ever knew who didn't act like he was offering it. He is just there, doing what needs to be done, as if it was the only thing to do. Most people who help you, when they aren't your kin, do it with a kind of disregard and look real hopeful to see your gratefulness and cowtowing to them for the rest of your days. He isn't like that a bit. I suspect if he was to be around more often, I wouldn't mind too much. I suspect I might be kindly disposed to his kind of help, after all.

July 30, 1885

April was fussy before but now she distresses me night and day and will not let me out of her sight. She cries and is fretful and nervous and won't have anything to do with anyone but me. I can't even get to the outhouse without her, she stands at the door outside and cries terribly and throws herself against the door again and again until I come out.

I keep telling myself to stop watching for Captain Elliot to ride over the hills, as there has been not one word of him since that terrible day. But all day I still watch.

Good old Bear is buried on the hill next to Jimmy. He was a fine dog. Albert said a dog doesn't belong in a people graveyard, but it is my graveyard and my people and my dog, so I guess I can put them together.

Finally this evening Jack came back. He said Moses Smith's real name was William Gunther and he was wanted for train robbery and murder and horse thieving in Bisbee. When the Bisbee Sheriff got him, they held a trial the next day and Moses Smith hung from a high gallows yesterday at noon. That is one hanging I think I would like to have seen. Seems if you have a stake in it, watching a hanging doesn't seem as hard as I used to think.

I can't help it but my heart beats fast when I see him coming over the hill. Jack Elliot is an ornery soldier, but there are so many times now that he has come between me and destruction of different sorts, that I feel close to him without even talking.

After supper he came to me and said, Let's take a stroll under the trees, and he had a peculiar look around the eyes, almost like fear, although it is hard to say as I have never known him to be afraid of anything. We walked in the orchard this evening as it is cooler there, and he ate some peaches and declared he liked them, although I know they were too long on the tree. April would not go to him as she used to do so easily, but hid her face when he reached for her. He stopped me and looked real serious for a second, and said Are you well?

Sure, I said, I'm pretty sturdy. He just smiled and went back to talking.

He was talking about my ranch and saying things about cattle and horses and the different efforts it takes to run each, but I kept losing track of his words. I was studying his face and seeing the sun-squint lines around his eyes. There was a little nick of blood on his chin like he must have stopped to shave near the stream before riding up. His hat was in his hands and in the speckled light through the leaves, I saw there were some silver hairs in his brown hair. Finally, he was looking at me and I thought he must have asked me a question, and I wasn't even listening.

Captain Elliot, I said, how old are you?

He wrinkled up his forehead and said, Thirty. What has that got to do with cows?

I don't know, I said, and I purely didn't. Were we talking about cows?

No, he said. Actually, we were talking about cows we could buy if you'd see it to sell all the horses except a couple. And if you'd be interested in a partnership.

What? What kind of partnership? I said. Now I was really puzzled.

So he took a deep breath and started again, like he had just said all the words before. Well, Miss Sarah, he said, I was thinking I have some real fond feelings for you, and for your baby too. And I never planned to do this but I can see that I am bound to keep running out to this ranch and I cannot sleep at night for worrying about your safety. So I thought I will ask you to marry me.

Well, I have to admit I have spent a few hours in the last few days pondering what I would do if he came up with a suggestion like that, as his attentions have lately seemed to grow more earnest and showed all the signs mentioned in the Happy Bride. Sometimes I imagined I would laugh and spurn him and send him running, scalded with harsh words, and most times I imagined what it would be like to wake up next to him of a morning.

Walking here in the broken evening light, I secretly suspected he would say something like that, but suddenly I didn't like the sound of it at all. It was too much like what Jimmy said, you're a good cook, and I'm a hand with horses, so together let's build a ranch, and I didn't want to be just a partnership, I want to be a wife like Savannah.

So I said to him, Well, you better think again, you are not asking the right question. He was purely puzzled, I could tell. April started to squirm, so I set her down but she held onto my skirts.

He said again, I am asking you to please marry me, please? He was stressing the pleases like that would make the difference. I just walked away.

Why should I? I asked, just because you rescued me again?

Well, no, he hollered, kind of mad.

Well then, why? I said back, just as mad.

Why? Why? What do you mean why? He was getting real upset, and it was the first time I have ever seen his feathers ruffled, no matter what.

Exactly that, I said, Why?

Because, he started, and got all red in the face and then he said these words, Because I love you more than I knew was possible and I need you. And I want to care for you all the rest of our lives and I want to marry you.

Well, I said, feeling like a cat with a cornered mouse, that's a pretty good reason, but you are still not asking the right question.

I stuck my nose in the air and walked away from him, with April stumbling along behind. He was struck dumb for some minutes, and I knew for the first time, I had got the best of Jack Elliot. He always thinks he has me figured, or that he is in charge just because he is a man and is big and handsome and all.

He came up after me and said, Well, Sarah, I think the world of you and admire you a great deal.

Well, I said, any man who knows me could admire me but I don't want to be married to someone just because he thinks I'd make a good wife. I know I make a good wife, I work hard and clean house and sew and cook a fine cobbler. That's not the question, either.

Well, he shocked me good, for he threw down his hat and said, Damnation, Sarah, you can take the starch right out of a man. What is it you want? What will it take to make you want to marry me?

And so I turned around and smiled a tiny smile. That, I said, was the right question. Then suddenly I couldn't believe what was coming out of my mouth, as if I had practiced a speech, but I hadn't at all. All it will take Jack Elliot, is for you to swear that you hold no secret longings for some other woman, and that when you say you love me you mean it.

Then he grabbed me in his arms and kissed me hard, and we stood in the shade a long time, kissing each other in a most indecent way, which I have grown to like quite a bit.

July 31, 1885

Savannah and I cleared the table and did dishes while the men talked. Later we sat on the porch and watched the south hills, as the sky was full of distant clouds and lightning flashes. Melissa Raalle came skipping over and called out, Auntie Savannah! Mama wants me to borrow some molasses if you have any. So Savannah went into the house to fetch it, and left me with the men and the babies on the porch. Melissa grinned and giggled into her hand.

Albert smiled at her and said, Have you got a secret, Melissa? She nodded yes. Are you going to tell it? he asked her. She shook her head no. Melissa always has a secret, he said to Jack, and both men tried to look very interested in her secret, which made her blush and giggle, entirely pleased with all the attention she was getting.

After a bit she said, I'll tell Uncle Albert! and she climbed up on his lap and put her hand on his ear and said loud enough for all of us to hear, I saw Mr. Jack and Miss Sarah hiding in the trees and they were kissing!

Albert looked at me, kind of shocked and foolish, and said Sarah!

Jack looked at me the same way, and said Sarah! Then he said to Albert behind his hand, but loud enough for me to hear, I can tell you I was there, and it was a scandalous act! Then both of those hooligans started to laugh, and Albert whispered something back to Melissa which sent her into peals of giggles.

Well, you three can just sit there and laugh yourselves silly! I said, and walked into the house to find Savannah.

She was coming towards the door with a jar of molasses she was wiping with a wet rag, and said, Sarah, what is the matter?

Men are low and vulgar. They must be born that way, I said, As any time you get two in the same room they either fight each other or join up and nuisance someone else. Those two are teasing me. Savannah just smiled and nodded, and set the jar down. Then she took my hands and led me to her fireside chairs and we sat facing each other. She just kept looking at me, suspicious and smiling, until I said, Savannah, what is it?

Did he ask you yet? She said.

I sucked in my breath. You knew? You knew before he did it?

She nodded. He told us last time he was here he wanted to marry you. She lowered her voice to a whisper and hugged me. Oh, Sarah, I'm so happy for you!

Well, don't you want to know what I answered?

Then she looked puzzled and a bit stunned. You mean you told him no?

Why shouldn't I tell him no? I said. Suddenly, I was feeling strained and odd, and I said, I'm not in any hurry to get married again.

Savannah looked more shocked. But Sarah, she said, I've seen how you look at him, how you blush when his name is mentioned, I've heard how your voice gets soft when you say his name. And then that time in town when Harland saw him but he didn't see us, and we all saw you nearly faint because of it. I thought you were sweet on him, she whispered more like a statement than a question.

What could she mean? It was only the heat made me faint that day. Savannah, I said, What do you think of Jack Elliot? Is he a scoundrel? Is he a liar? I can't think anymore, he has my mind addled something awful. Do you think he loves me?

Savannah just smiled. Oh, Sarah, she said, all he talks about is you. He writes us letters and asks after your health, he wants to know everything about you and how to make you happy.

Well, I said, He doesn't write me letters. What kind of way is that to show a girl you love her? Do you believe him? Would he say all that to trick me into marrying him, like, like Jimmy did?

Savannah's face got somber and all the smiling swept from her eyes. She opened her mouth to speak, then stopped, then tried again and said, Jimmy wasn't such a good man, Sarah. I'm sorry to say this but Albert told me some shameful things about him.

I said, You know, Savannah, I thought he would make a good husband, but I know he didn't love me much at all. I was just handy, and useful to him. Whatever you know about him that had Albert so mad all that time, I wish you would tell me so I can stop worrying about it.

Savannah dropped my hands and looked hard into the fireplace, all black and dark, but clean as a whistle, without an ash or cinder to show when the last fire was there. Sarah, she started, then her voice made a funny gasp, He used to go to town.

I know that, I said, He went on business, and brought home ranch goods.

Well, that's not all, she said, When he went to town, he went to see. Oh, Sarah, he lied to you and pretended to be a good husband, but he went to Maiden Lane all the time, and after you were married he went more than he did before. He had done it for years, that is why Albert didn't want him for a brother in law. Even though they grew up together, Albert had no respect for a man who would behave like that while he was married.

I stared into the black fireplace too. That explained a lot of those trips to town, when Jimmy would get mad every time and not want me with him. I asked her, Is there anything else?

Savannah took a deep breath, and said, Mr. MacIntosh wrote us and asked if we had seen Jimmy, and that he had paid him with some horses, but only with ten. All the others he had with him, Jimmy had taken in the night from a far pasture. But we couldn't tell you, because we didn't know it until after you had betrothed each other. It was too late. We wrote Mr. MacIntosh about it, and he must be very rich because he wrote back to us that you should keep the horses then, as it was the most valuable thing you'd get from the marriage because, she stammered, because he said Jimmy Reed was no bargain. She took my hand again.

All I could say was, Oh, no.

Melissa's voice called in through the open window, Auntie Savannah? Do you have some 'lasses?

Yes, honey, called Savannah, and handed her the jar through the window.

Then I heard Albert's voice say, What are you women doing in there?

Just talking like you are, she said back. We'll be out directly, and it's getting dark, there could be snakes, so why don't you walk Melissa home while we put the children to bed?

I heard Jack's voice say, Melissa, want a horsey ride? Albert, you carry that molasses so I don't turn into a stack of hotcakes. Climb up here, now give me your feet, okay, hold on!

Go, horsey, giddup! yelled Melissa. And there was a loud clumping of boots as he galloped off the porch with her laughing all the way.

I saw a leaf blow in through an open window, and knew the storm was getting closer. As I shut it, a gust filled with sand shook the glass in its frame. April was already sleepy, and fussed while I put her nightshirt on, but for once in her life, she went to bed quickly and without much commotion. Savannah was changing the little boys' clothes, and I took a cup of water and drank it while I watched her fuss with them. Joshua David was pretty easy, but when little Clover got his clothes off he ran around the room naked and whooping.

Savannah just rolled her eyes at me and sighed, Every night it is the same thing. I think you are right, Sarah, they are born this way.

Is Jack that kind of man? I asked her. I was still thinking about Jimmy and feeling scalded to the core.

She turned and looked at me, then a smile spread across her face. No, I don't think so, she said. And, Albert was at first so worried about him paying attention to you, after that horse incident and all, that he wrote to the commanding officer at the fort and asked after his character. Every soldier there thinks highly of him, except for a couple that he disciplined, and his commander says that he is of strong, good, moral character.

In my head I realized I was right, they are all in cahoots against me.

Sarah, she said, Do you love him?

I couldn't look her in the eyes again, and had to take a deep breath. I 'spose I don't know what love is, I said. He keeps me riled up inside, and I dream about him, and I wonder about him, and I watch for him over every hill when he's not here. He can make me so mad sometimes I can't see straight. But when I hear his voice, my heart jumps funny. And he has kissed me.

Savannah held her hands to her mouth, shocked. Sarah! Really? Clover, if you don't lie down and hush, I'll have to tell Papa you were bad, now stop that. She put his covers back and Clover kicked them off again. She led me into the parlor and said, lowering her voice, Did you kiss him back?

I nodded.

Oh, Sarah, before you are married? Oh my!

Suddenly I felt very guilty. It was that day the Indians attacked, I said. We were all so upset, and sad, and afraid, and when he got ready to leave, I bandaged his hands, and he just took my face and kissed me. How could I dare tell her about the other times?

Savannah's face got studious and she looked about the room, and went to light two lamps. Of course, she said, and sighed with relief. Of course, it was a terribly emotional time. You were both overcome. You both needed someone to reach out to, and I have

Albert's hand to hold to keep me going but you have no one. Of course, you needed each other during such a terrible time. I'm sure it wasn't meant to be, well, anything else. And he is always so worried about you, surely he was just thankful you were unharmed.

I wondered what her reaction would be if she knew all the rest of the kisses. Then, I said, then I kissed him tonight when he proposed.

Oh, she said. Well, that's different. Betrothed is allowed, and probably hard to stop since you had kissed once before out of fear for your lives.

I nodded, righteously on the outside and afraid on the inside that she could see it in my face that I wasn't sorry too much. Oh, Savannah, I thought, how righteous you are, and how wanton I really am, and you don't understand.

Do you love him? She asked me again.

I nodded, yes.

Well, then, she said, Betrothed is okay, just a tiny kiss or two, before the marriage. Have you set a date?

No, I said. I thought maybe in December. Maybe Ernest could come for Christmas, and that would be a good time. What do you think, Savannah?

She shrugged. I'd never pass up a chance to be as happy as Albert and I are. I loved him from the first minute I saw him.

Then all I could think of was the first time I saw Jack Elliot he was just a stranger, and kind of frightening, and he had married my brother to this sweet girl and had messed up the Bible verses doing it.

Just then, the men came in the door, bringing with them a gust of cool air and dust that smelled like rain coming. We all sat and Savannah made coffee, and it was good and strong, and we began to talk together like I never had before with my brother and his wife, and somehow that made me feel even more connected to Jack Elliot. Just like my conversation with Savannah had never happened, suddenly I was back in his spell, and each time his eyes caught mine there was a fiery sparkle in them that made me want to blush, and I remembered kissing him and wanting to marry him. Is that love?

Then he got so bold as to discuss our marriage plans with them, and I just listened to the sound of his voice, like it wasn't happening to me. What Savannah had said about the horses was weighed on my mind, so when there was a time of quiet and refilling the cups, I said, Captain Elliot, I have decided when we are married you can do what you want with those horses, sell them all if you want, except for Rose and a couple we might need to work and pull the wagon. I'd rather run cattle like you said, and that's fine with me. He looked at me and crooked his mustache, and his eyes twinkled bright in the lamplight.

It got late as we talked then, the wind howled around the little house, making noises in all the corners, making us thankful for the shelter of the heavy rock walls, and after a while we saw the lights go down in Mama's house, except for one in the front window for me. Savannah said, Just let April sleep here, I hate to wake a sleeping baby. You men better walk her to Mama's house for safety. Both of you.

Captain Elliot started to say, I'll walk her, Albert, you needn't bother, but Savannah insisted. There's always safety in numbers Albert, now hurry along, she said, shooing us off the porch. I knew she thought she was protecting me from any more fervent advances. But, how I wished she wouldn't.

I picked up my last letter from Jack. It was very formal, starting with

> *My Dear Mrs. Reed,*
> *I have been given orders to search for some Indians who made a ruckus at the San Carlos Agency and left the reservation, and I might be gone for several weeks. I believe it is important that we should come to an agreement on a date in the future to meet, and suggest that a church would be a good place, and of course we will be properly chaperoned by a minister and your family. Then and there might be a good time to state our future intentions in the matter we discussed previously, and so, to form a binding agreement on the subject.*

What a dust cloud of words he writes! I had to smile as I got some clean paper and began a letter back to him.

I told him how I wanted to get Ernest home for the wedding and that December might be a good time to do it, and asked him if he could arrange to hire someone to stay at the ranch so I don't have to put Albert to such trouble for a whole month while we're gone.

August 28, 1885

Today is April's birthday, she is two. I will be twenty-two soon. My, that seems old. I had all my family over for dinner, and we shared our meal on the porch on the coolest side of the house. I told them I have finished reading Treasure Island and Harland said it sounded mighty fine, and could he borrow it, so I will let him, but he must be careful with it. He promised he would, and I know he will lay awake at night, dreaming he is Jim Hawkins and imagining he is fighting pirates in his room.

The rose bush is blooming, covered all over with white roses with a beautiful smell. I want to see Jack again. My eyes are tired from looking down the road.

September 14, 1885

There is a letter from Jack, and something for Albert and Savannah. Jack says in his letter that he is still out on a mission, and does not know when he will return, but he sent a letter to Ernest's commanding officer, urging him to grant Ernest some leave at Christmas. He will come as soon as he can, he said.

The letter begins with *My dearest Mrs. R.*, and ends with *In Devotion to You, J.E.* I read those few words over and over, listening in my head to his voice saying them. I can't seem to imagine how all this has come to pass that now I am to marry that man.

October 1, 1885

Jack sent another letter and said to me he wanted very much to take me to meet his father, who is still alive and living on a ranch near Austin, Texas. Since it wouldn't do to go there before we are married, he asked Mama if she thought it would harm April's health to travel for a month so he could take us all three on a Wedding Trip, and we will stop in and see his Papa and do some other sight seeing from a train. Imagine taking a baby on a wedding trip! But he said, we are a family, and he wouldn't dream of not having her along to show his Papa.

A train trip is something I have always wanted to take, so I am excited, and I planned to use some money and have some nice clothes to take along. I want to look like a lady, not a wagon train settler this time, so I am going to town and I will come home with some corsets and new cloth to begin sewing up a storm.

October 6, 1885

My whole house was a flurry of patterns and bits of cloth in different colors, and we were talking and having coffee and sewing and laughing when out of the blue there was a knock on the door, and Jack was standing there. Come in, I said, and he reached for me to put his arms around me, but I pulled away. Come in and say hello to Savannah and Mama and Melissa. They are here helping me sew some traveling clothes.

He just smiled, and said, So glad to see you all, and shook my hand instead. I squeezed his fingers so he knew I was truly glad to see him, too. He reached into his blouse front and pulled out a piece of paper. I have something here you might like to see, he said, handing it to Mama.

He didn't know she can't read, so I said, Well, the light's pretty bad, let me read it for you, Mama. Ernest's orders, he's got leave for December, from the eighteenth to the thirtieth! We were all plum excited to look forward to him coming home. Just a few weeks away. Oh, my, I said, that means we have a wedding to get ready for in the same few weeks.

Jack grinned, Look's like that's in full swing too, he said, looking around. Did you get my letters, Sarah?

Yes, I said, I got two. And I'll be glad to go see your Papa with you, that will be fine, don't you want to invite him to come here for the wedding?

He shook his head. Cattle ranch, you know, you just can't leave, and he's stubborn, won't trust it to anyone else. But I wrote you three letters. Well, but that's why I'm here, I wrote him we were coming and so I have some business I wanted to discuss. I know he always needs good horses. What would you say to selling him some, and we could travel with them, ship them, when we go?

I looked at Savannah. She pretended to be concentrating on a buttonhole. So I said to him, Well, I think that's a pretty good plan. I'll try to have them ready and shoed and all. Do you want to pick out a few head now so I know which ones to work on?

No, he said, you don't have to do anything to them. I have taken six weeks leave for that time, and I'll be here to get them ready. I just don't want to take any that are your favorites or anything. I can see you all are busy, but if you'd allow me to just wander through them and look them over, maybe we'll choose them tomorrow. I mean, Miss Savannah, if I still have leave to stay the night at your place? She nodded. Ladies? he said, nodding and lifting his hat back to his head.

It seemed like he had just filled up the room with himself, and now the door shut and it was so empty. I tried to keep sewing, and think about the horses he was picking out. I stuck my thumb with the needle so many times I made a blood stain on my new dress and had to run dip the sleeve I was working on into some water. Putting the dress on the table, I said, Well, I just have to see which horses he is looking at, to be sure he doesn't pick wrong.

Mama looked up at me and smiled like a cat with a mouse between its paws. Well, Sarah, don't you think he might get the wrong ones? You don't want to lose Rose, you'd better go see what he's doing. Now out with you! And don't run!

I found him in the barn looking at the big stallion. He's a pretty valuable horse, I said.

Jack looked up quick, startled that I was behind him without making a sound. Lord, Sarah, he said, Ever thought of becoming an Apache Scout? You walk like an Indian.

I told him I hadn't meant to sneak up on him, and asked him had he really come here just to look at horses?

No, he said. It was just a believable excuse, I really rode here just to kiss you.

Well, I said, some people say too much kissing before a marriage leads to unfortunate consequences.

He folded me up in his arms, and said, How much is too much kissing? Then he kissed me. Is that too much?

No, I said.

So he kissed me again. How about now?

Not at all, I said again.

Then he kissed me like he had done before. Is that too much? he whispered.

I think it's getting close, I said.

Okay, he said, then I'll settle for a hug, and he squeezed me to him where I listened through his shirt to his heart beating faster and faster. After a bit he said, Even this is dangerous. Let's look at your horses.

So we walked among them and petted them, and I told him which ones were the parents of which, and that I had a list I kept, and he looked at things like the shoes and feet, and the teeth and the set of the eyes. And we talked no more of kisses and dangerous hugs, but I thought about them plenty.

October 8, 1885

I apologized to everyone, even Toobuddy, for being in such a bad mood yesterday. It is not because Jack left like they said, it was just my time of month so they shouldn't say it's because I love him. Do I love him? Is this love? He is not comfortable and familiar feeling like Jimmy was. He is not peaceful to have around, nor calm. He is like a thunderstorm, big and noisy and sometimes frightening. And always, there is a sense of something about him. He's a good shot and a dangerous fighter, and brave even when the Indians surround him or the walls are burning down. But walls don't burn every day.

He's just a man, though he takes over a room without knowing it when he's there. It must be that soldiering, and being in command of soldiers, that makes a man seem to do that. He is too tall. He is too handsome. I have seen women in Tucson cast their eyes at him while we drove through town. What kind of man is that for a husband?

He's only good with horses when it comes to riding them and keeping them going, but doesn't know about breeding lines nor feeds and grooming like my Papa and brothers and Jimmy. He doesn't go to church regular, and is right there in town, so there's no excuse, and he has never once asked me if I studied the Bible. And he likes to torment me, and laughs when I get upset when he does.

No, of course not. I do not love Jack Elliot. He is low and coarse and a soldier, and not the kind of man I want to spend my life with.

November 1, 1885

I got a letter from Jack today. *My Dearest*, it began, without even saying my name, as if I would recognize that it was addressed to me alone. It talked about his schedule and how he had bought train tickets, and had something important he needed to discuss with me. And it ended with *In deepest devotion*, and it made me sigh to read those few tender words. I love Jack Elliot. Oh my soul, I do love him so.

November 29, 1885

I have not had a letter in so long. Maybe he will just come again to see the horses. But he doesn't come and doesn't come, and I am growing to believe it was a dream. How could I have thought I loved a man like that?

December 4, 1885

A package arrived at the station from Jack. Inside was a letter, and a gift for April, and one for me. The letter says he will be here on December 15th, and has arranged for the wedding to take place on the 20th, and we will stay in town until the 22nd, when we will leave early in the morning for Texas. He asked me to arrange for someone to bring April to the station so we can have the two days alone and then take her with us.

April has gotten a pretty little hat with a ribbon around it and a little silk flower on the back, which she insists goes in front so she can see it in the looking glass, and she just won't listen to me. My gift is a beautiful pair of lace ladies' gloves. They must be only for church or traveling, as they would not hold up to even the lightest of tasks. They are beautiful and I will treasure them. How thoughtful he can be! How could I have doubted myself?

December 19, 1885

Jack is here. Ernest is too. We have a houseful of excitement and so much going on with horses to ship and all, leaving tomorrow before sunup for Tucson.

I feel all in a flurry and I wish I could just say No, this is all a mistake, stop everything. The whole house is a mess, and everyone seems more excited than I, and they just carry on so, that I can't get a word in edgewise. Ernest has bathed and tended the horses I am sending to Jack's Papa, and he was just in here asking me for horseshoe nails, like I would keep them in the kitchen. Mama is finishing some sewing for me but wants me to find the yellow thread I was using, and she fussed around in my sewing bag. I don't know where that spool went, I told her just use anything that will hold.

Yesterday Ernest talked a blue streak and wanted to see my land and we did but all the while I was thinking about everything else I needed to do. Jack and Albert are talking horses from morning to night, and suddenly they both decided this would be as good a time as any to frame up a new room on Albert's house. With all the boys helping they have put up a room in no time—all but the last clapboards are finished—but it is just one more commotion on top of all the wedding fuss, and of course, Harland mashed his thumb blue with a hammer, and Savannah's babies cried all day from the noise, and Mama and Melissa cooked up a feast for all of us three times a day, but their house is too small so they did it in my kitchen. On top of everything there is all that dishwashing and wood chopping, and glory, but I am tired.

Finally, I shooed them all away this afternoon and I took a long bath and made some coffee and sat in my chair and thought about everything. It seems as if I can only think if I write my journal, it just connects the part of my head that is busy doing things with the part that is busy thinking about everything else. I know all these people are so busy because they love each other and me. We are a noisy crowd of love.

December 20, 1885

Dear Sarah,

I know you like to keep everything written down in your journal, and if it were possible for you to see yourself, you would certainly want a record of this day. You looked so lovely today, all proud and erect in your fine new dress. Pale, though, but I'm sure you were apprehensive as I was when I became a bride, though it just added to your appeal, as you seemed innocent as a young girl and most becoming. What a show the Army put on for your wedding! I have never seen so much shiny brass and dark blue uniforms and all those drawn sabers flashing in the cold bright sunlight, well, it was a sight to behold. That beautiful coach with the matched team wearing tassels and polished silver that you drove away in was just the most elegant thing I have ever seen, too.

Did you know that Jack asked me personally if Albert and I wanted to take our vows again, alongside you, because he felt he had done a botched job of it when we married? But I told him he hadn't botched it at all, as you can see we are very happily married together and have a fine family coming along, so he must have done it just right.

What a striking figure Lt. Elliot makes, such an imposing man in his uniform, but he seems to be so gentle when you get to know him. He bears an unusual combination of fine traits, and it is no wonder that you love him so. Even the preacher seemed intimidated by his presence and all the power created by rows of soldiers at attention surrounding the altar. Did you see Harland's face when Jack saluted his men so crisply and stern looking, and then winked at Harland?

*Well, darling, have a wonderful time on your trip, and don't
worry, we will take care of everything here for you and bring
April to the depot ready to go day after tomorrow. May the
Lord bless you and keep you, The Lord lift His countenance
upon you and give you peace.*

Your loving Sister, Savannah

December 20, 1885

What have I done, Lord? I have gone and said I will love and
honor and obey that man for the rest of my days and I don't even
know who he is. There was Albert with Jack's hand on his shoulder, laughing after the ceremony, and he kissed Mama on the
cheek and Savannah too, carrying my baby in his arms, smiling
and talking like he was the happiest man on earth.

Then he brought me here to this fancy hotel room, the best
they've got, and said, You just get ready for bed, I've got something
to do. And he didn't seem happy or like he wanted to kiss me or anything. He seemed so intent and dark inside that I was frightened.
Oh, if there was some way to slip out of this room and disappear
and just erase my name off that marriage license! All my doubts
were right and I have made a huge blunder. And now I am sitting
here waiting for him to come back and do unspeakable things and I
am so terrified I can't bring myself to move from this chair.

This is a terrible mistake, and I repent a thousand times and I
will never never say or think another bad or selfish thing Lord, if
you will just get me out of this. I promise I will be as good as
Savannah, and better, and never complain any more about anything, and I will be so meek and mild and good and gentle, even
Savannah will have to admire it. And I will learn a hundred Bible
verses by memory, maybe two hundred. There will be no end to
my good nature and there has to be a way out of this. Maybe
Lord, you could just open up the earth and gobble him down, and
he will disappear and everything will go back to normal. The

whole town will laugh at me, worse than after that day in church, but I don't care. Maybe he has gone to visit some street woman down on Maiden Lane like Jimmy did. On our wedding day too.

Oh, Lord, what have I done?

December 21, 1885

Jack stayed gone so long last evening, that I finally got into my nightdress, and feeling full of dread and loathing, got into bed to await my fate and pray with all my might for the earth to open up right in the middle of Congress Street as he walked up to this hotel. It would be in the paper tomorrow, Man Swallowed Alive by Act of God on Congress Street, All Rescue Efforts Failed, Grieving Widow Mourns on Wedding Day. I heard the key in the lock and the door hinges squeal, and closed my eyes tight, pretending to be asleep.

I heard him set something down, and his voice said, You look like you are waiting your execution! I opened my eyes and he was standing over me with his hands on his hips, and I couldn't say any words at all. Get up, he said, and come sit down. We have some things to discuss.

I was feeling embarrassed sitting down with him in my nighty. He opened the little brown sack and took out two glasses. Then he brought out a little bottle. What is that? I asked.

Whiskey, he said. He poured some into both glasses, just a sip, and then filled them with water from a canteen. Here, he said, handing me a glass and taking the other one. He had a strange look on his face that scared me even more. I sniffed the glass and didn't like the smell, and all I could think of was, what kind of shame was he leading me to now? Then he sort of pointed his glass at me and said, This is the last drink I will ever have, and I want to have it with you. Sip it slow. It will help your nerves. And mine, too.

I'm not nervous, I said to him, but he just smirked at me.

He said, If I said boo to you, you'd jump out that window and run barefoot to California. Don't tell me you're not nervous, it's time for some honesty. Now try it, please.

So I took a little sip. It is surely the devil's own brew, burning and hot and nasty tasting, and it made my eyes water and I shuddered real hard like when I was little and Mama dosed me with castor oil.

Amazing isn't it? he said, why people will go out of their way and lose everything that's important to them for something that tastes like it would cut grease. Just take a sip, and listen to what I have to say. You don't have to drink it all. With that, he took half of his and gulped it down, and cleared his throat. These are married things, all right, between a husband and wife? Secret, even from your Mama.

I nodded at him, getting really scared, and I prepared myself to hear a horrible tale of wicked women and loathsome deeds.

Well, he said, I was married before. But not with a preacher, not in a church. She was an Indian and no preacher would marry us, or her people either, so we just married each other. He looked like he was trying to cut a hole into his glass with his eyes.

I took another sip of the whiskey. Where is she now? I said.

I don't know, he said, and gulped down the rest of the whiskey in his glass. Her brothers and some men from her tribe found us and beat the hell out of me and dragged her away and disappeared. I hunted for her for a year, but they left no trail at all. Maybe I was just young and stupid and couldn't find it. She was pregnant though, and I know how they felt about half breed babies, just like most white people do. When I told you I had a friend that died and wouldn't tell you the name, well, it was on Christmas day six years ago now, that I decided she was dead, and I quit looking for her.

I said, I imagine that broke your heart. Then I got to thinking again about how Jimmy never did love me, only Ruthanne, and because of that, I never meant much to him. So I felt real heavy in my heart, and I said, And so, you're telling me you still love her?

No, he said with a twisted sound in his voice, looking frustrated. That's not what I'm saying at all. It isn't the kind of thing a man wants known all around, but you deserve to know something like that. Neither of us are the same as we were six years ago are we? I did love her. And I'll always remember her, but I love you now, and for different reasons. More grown up reasons. I was young and irresponsible, and I wish I had been more thoughtful of what would happen to her instead of selfish. I caused her more grief than a woman should know, and maybe caused her death. I don't ever want to do anything that could cause you bad times ahead, but I'm just a man. And sometimes kind of selfish. And I don't want you to think because that preacher made you say honor and obey that I expect that. I don't want you to turn into a good little wife, I want to be married to you just like you are, spitfire and all.

Well, I said, that's a real fine compliment, Captain Elliot.

He smiled at me and then he laughed softly to himself. I think you are getting relaxed, he said. He took the glass from me and set it aside, and held my hands in his. And he stared at me until I had to turn my eyes away. I have a wedding gift for you, he said. My sister sent it to me, it used to be my mother's, and I hope you'd wear it now and then. He handed me a little envelope of paper, and inside it was a beautiful little brooch with a tiny clock hanging from it. All around the little clock was a sparkly little cut glass ring.

Here, he said, the diamonds were loose but I had them fixed. That's what took me so long, the jewelsmith was closed and I had to go to his house and make him open the store to get it for you. The watch keeps pretty good time, he said, and you just turn this here if it is slow, to make the hands catch up.

These here are diamonds? I asked. What is this white thing? There was a round ball of creamy white from which the little diamond watch hung.

It's a pearl, he said. A pretty good one, I reckon, the jewelsmith tried to buy it off the watch and replace it with some other stone he had, but I wanted it to look like I remembered it.

Oh, I gasped out, oh my, this is beautiful! Oh, Jack, thank you so much. All my life I have wanted a pearl to wear. I would be proud to wear it always.

Well, he said, not when you are wrangling cattle, it wouldn't be socially proper to wear diamonds to a roundup.

I have a gift for you, too, I said. I was ashamed of myself for plotting how I'd get my money back when the earth swallowed

Jack Elliot down. I stood up and hurried to the bureau, but I hadn't even unpacked, and I noticed that he made a face when he saw me go instead to my bags.

Weren't you planning to stay? he said.

I told him, We won't be here long enough to get all that out and then re-pack tomorrow, but here it is, I had your name put on it, but if you don't like it, well, here. I handed him the watch and chain that was engraved now with his name.

Oh, look at that! he said, and popped open the cover. Why this is just fine! And it's already running. Seems, Mrs. Elliot, that we both have time on our minds. Isn't that something? he said, opening the cover and reading it and closing it, and opening it again. It's real fine. Thank you kindly. He put the watch in his hand and made the chain into a little coil around it. Take one more sip, he said. There's one last thing we have to discuss.

My head was starting to spin when my eyes moved around. It doesn't taste so bad, now, I said.

He nodded and gave me that half a smile. I reckon not, he said, good thing this is the last drink for both of us. He was eyeing me again. Now, he said, I want to talk about children. I want you to know that I love April like she was mine, and that's no problem. And I want to have all the children you want, but not so many that you wear yourself into the ground like some women.

I nodded, but I didn't understand. Jack, I said, I had a real bad time having April. Real bad. I want to have other children too, but you should know that it wasn't easy for me. Savannah has a much easier time, I said. Oh, I shouldn't have said that! Oh, I'm sorry! Please don't tell her I said that to you!

Sh-sh, he said. It's okay. The liquor makes you talk, that's all. It's another good reason to stay away from it. I'm sorry you had a tough time. I'd hate to think of you going through that again.

I nodded at him and said, If you'd stay close by, Jack, I'll be okay. I'm not afraid.

He squinted a bit of a smile. I know, he said. At least you don't look like you are marching to a gallows any more. Then he held out his hand towards me and said, Come here, my love, and tell me you love me true.

Well, I am sort of used to having you around, I said. Once again, just for a second, I saw that look on his face like I'd poked a nerve.

I've grown somewhat accustomed to you, too, he said. You're cold, you're shaking all over, he said, putting his hand on my shoulder. Why don't you get back under the covers and stay warm?

I didn't know what to say, so I just nodded it would feel so good to put my freezing feet back under the blankets.

He stood by the bed and began to undress slowly, and I climbed up on the feather mattress, embarrassed to watch, but I listened to the boots, the belt, the clothes as they hit the wood chair, then I felt the bed sway down.

Just a minute, I said, aren't you going to wear anything to bed?

He just grinned even bigger, showing his teeth, and said Mustache! and pulled up the blankets.

No one should write down, even in her private journal, the things that happen on her wedding night, but I never want to forget the first time I knew John Edward Harrison Elliot. He told me he loved me more than life itself, telling me he had longed for this moment forever and forever, and he asked me did I like this or that, which I couldn't even choose because the answer was always yes.

Jack kissed me until my lips were swollen and my throat was dry as cotton, and kissed the scar on my breast, whispering A little sugar, to make the owey all better. Then he kissed again, And one for the heart, where the wounds are deepest. He whispered to me, a hundred little soft loving words I could hardly hear in between a constant raining of kisses, and then he took my breath away; it was never like this before. The feather bed felt like it was a cloud up in the sky, and we slept a while and then woke and loved again, and slept, and loved again with the sun fully up.

He made it seem like the most important thing in the world to him, and before last night I never knew why some women would actually desire to do those things with a man, but now I truly do. Always with Jimmy it was just a matter to be finished and hope it took, like breeding a mare.

The sun was touching my eyes and I woke knowing it had to be nearly noon. The lamp had burned out in the night. Jack, I whispered, turning to see his sleeping face on the pillow beside me. Jack, I don't want the earth to open up and swallow you down any more.

He opened his eyes then and looked at me real strange and wrinkled up his brow. I reckon that's good, he said. Was that a possibility in your mind?

Well, I said, I was really scared last night when you were gone so long.

Thought I wouldn't come back? he said, gleefully wrapping me up in his arms and scooping up blankets with me in a bundle. Or, did you think I would? He gave me that piercing look and I know he is right inside my head looking at my thoughts, then he nodded and stuck out his lips and said, Well, are you sorry I came back?

I suppose not, I said.

You suppose? Suppose! What does it take to convince you?

I just grinned at him.

Sarah! how shameless! he said, acting like he was shocked, but I know he wasn't at all. Well, he said, Wife, you'll have to be convinced later. I'm worn out and hungry. Even the Army feeds its prisoners.

Well, Husband, I said, then we should get dressed and eat.

And so we began our wedding trip, and we will stay one more night in this hotel and leave tomorrow at 7:15 on the train for Texas.

The huge train jerked and puffed and the whistle blew. They would all be there without me for Christmas. Ernest will be gone before I get back. Goodbye, I said into the glass.

Mama waved and her mouth was saying Merry Christmas. Savannah was just a flash in the conductor's red lamplight. Suddenly I knew how she must have felt to say goodbye to her family in Texas to come here with us. I hung onto the window, feeling the frozen metal edges around the sliding glass, staring into the cold past the vapor and sparks, back toward the light from the depot. Hot, salty tears seeped from my eyes and dripped from my chin.

I sat across from Jack on the strange, upright seats, and he gave me a look that was for once not a smirk but one of real sympathy, and he handed me his handkerchief. They'll be here when we get back, he said.

Not Ernest. Right away, my thoughts turned to my brother and the long talks we had had just before my wedding. While he made quick work of checking and repairing all the horses' hooves, he said he was proud to have me married to Captain Elliot. He said his job as blacksmith was pleasing to him, and it put him to doing something valuable that didn't take such a keen eye for distance. I tried to get him to tell me things about Jack, but he just went on and on with stories about their army life. I suppose men don't look on the same things in a person that a woman wants to know. Ernest seemed to have no suspicion at all that a man could be a bad husband even if he didn't cheat at cards, or could be cruel or thoughtless to his wife even if he was a straight shooter about his business affairs. He acted like I was being peevish for no reason.

Just before we all drove to town for the wedding, Ernest gave me a gift for my wedding. He must have saved up a long, long time, for he gave us a solid silver bowl, and six real silver spoons and knives and forks for the table. He told me to polish them with potash, and said it will taste better than eating off tin forks. Then he gave Jack a real stiff salute and handed him a package, and inside it was a fine, smooth, pair of tall black cavalry boots for dress. He said he had the bootmaker take a pattern from Jack's old ones while he was gone one time. Then, it seemed like Ernest had done what he came for, and he quit talking so much to me, and made himself part of the rest of the group as if he slipped away in the crowd. I asked Mama to keep my silver things safe until we get back, but Jack is wearing his boots now. When Ernest said goodbye to me, he hugged me long and hard, and there came a cold, faraway look in his eyes, and it was like I could see into yonder in that look, like I knew it was the last time I would see him.

The train was stuffy and cold, and even though the car had a little hot box at one end, it made me long for fresh air and warmth all at once. Jack had brought April a little slate and chalks and an eraser to amuse herself while we rode, and he left me alone for a while, talking to her and watching her draw scribbled rings, and exclaiming proudly at each picture when she announced what it was.

We ate breakfast later in a dining car, and there was pretty linen tablecloths and a colored man in a handsome white uniform that asked us what we wanted. April was good as could be, and talked a blue streak about the scenery out the window, and the napkin under her chin, and anything else that popped into her head. And when we stood to leave, she held up her hands to Jack instead of to me.

Well, I said, she's a big girl, she should walk.

He looked at me and then said to her, Walk next time, ride now, and picked her up anyway. She's my girl, aren't you? And April put her arms around his neck while we returned to our seats.

It is so strange to have this happy feeling inside and be pleased that she likes him, and still so uncomfortable, like I am riding in a dream with a strange man. When he is gone, I feel more normal, but when he is nearby, I feel captured by him, and overcome with curiosity about him and everything in his whole life. But he is not the kind to sit and expound on himself, and I realized it took a glass of whiskey for him to tell me just one important fact from his past. Maybe it is not so good that he has given up all drinking, just to be married to me. There is too much I want to know.

A man in a train uniform came to us and gave me a note, saying it was from two ladies in the car on the other side of the diner. It said they had seen me at breakfast, and wanted to make my acquaintance, and would I come to tea in an hour?

Go ahead, Jack said, it will make the time pass quicker.

So I told the man Fine, if Jack would stay with April and watch her, and if she doesn't throw a fit over me leaving, I will come.

Very good, said the man, real formal like, I shall tell Mrs. Faulkner and Mrs. Blankenship that you will join them presently. And may I present your name, Ma'am?

Yes, I told him, Mrs. Sarah, and then I caught myself and I know I blushed, and Jack stared at me hard, Mrs. Jack Elliot, I said. The porter left us, and Jack left his seat and sat by my side. He took my hand then, and seemed to be admiring the wedding ring in the sunlight coming in the window, but he didn't say anything, and when I looked at his face he looked out the window fast, as if I had caught him at something.

April climbed in my lap, and I suppose because she had been up early, she drowsed and fell asleep, so it was no trouble to set her on his lap when the porter returned. And taking the man's stiffly bent elbow, I went to meet the ladies. They seemed like very fine, high class women, and they were both dressed so elegant, and sat gracefully in their seats and ordered the porter to bring tea and cakes, just like they were used to ordering people around.

We had all said hello very politely, and they asked me if I'd rather have tea or coffee. Well, I said I preferred coffee, but if tea was more convenient, that would be fine.

They kind of sniffed, and one of them said, Coffee! Must be fresh from the Territories.

Well, yes, Ma'am, I said, I lived there all my life.

Then they asked me about my husband, and what he does, and I told them he was an officer in the Army and an Indian fighter, and they exclaimed and raised their hands to their mouths and were so interested and asked dozens of questions. They asked wasn't I worried about him all the time, and I said, well, we only just married, and if there was Indian trouble around I would be much less worried knowing he was close by.

Well, they just practically twittered like little birds at that, and made eyes at each other and then this other much older lady sitting across the aisle said to me, Where do you live? So I told her about my ranch and tried not to seem proud, although they all said it must be vast and how nice to have all those acres and family with other holdings as they called it.

Yes, I said, and we have good neighbors too, and I told them about our friends and they seemed fairly shocked that we lived near Mexican people, but I said, For a fact, they are fine folks and good and generous. I'm proud to know them. They just smiled at each other and winked their eyes, and offered me cake.

Then they began to tell me about their families, as if they had a list written down to recount, and all the fine things they do and the fine houses they live in with a thousand acres around them. I wanted to be polite, and I listened and admired all the things they said. Then Mrs. Faulkner said her son went to West Point and her youngest daughter Persephone had married an Army officer who went to West Point, and did Captain Elliot go to West Point, and did I know she was such a beautiful girl and had already given her a grandchild, and did I know that Persephone was an ancient Roman name for the goddess of beauty?

It was a tangled knot of questions all at once, and I tried to remember them all. So I said, I am sure you are happy for your daughter, and I will ask the Captain if he went there since I didn't know if she meant the west point of the Rio Grande or some other river, and then I said, Actually, Persephone is a Greek name for the daughter of Zeus and she was not a goddess she was a prisoner of Hades.

They just all clapped their hands over their mouths kind of

shocked, and I could see Mrs. Faulkner had got riled up as her jaw got tight and her lips pinched together. The old lady, Mrs. Dunn, she said her name was, sort of chuckled, and said Where did you get your education, deary? How ingenious of you, how quaintly unsophisticated! Then she announced she was tired, and thanked me for coming but it was time to rest before luncheon.

I was being invited to leave!

Just at that minute, everything got quiet, and suddenly I saw Jack with April holding his hand coming down the aisle looking for me.

He took off his hat to the ladies, and said to me, Pardon us, but the Colonel here was disturbed at your absence, Mrs. Elliot, and ordered me to dispatch and find you immediately. April buried herself in my skirts, and I could feel her trembling.

Oh, oh, they exclaimed over April, How darling! they all said, blushing and fanning themselves at my husband as he bowed and smiled at them. I thought he looked pretty silly, and had a look in his eyes like he was making fun of them, but they just tee-heed about him and said, What a nice man to take care of the baby.

Then Mrs. Blankenship, who is a mousy grey little woman, said, But my dear, I thought you were just married?

My first husband was killed right after she was born, I said. Thank you for the coffee.

And I rose and left them without another word, although I could hear Jack saying goodbye to them or some other such nonsense and they were all twittering again.

Captain Elliot, I whispered, I wish I had my dictionary with me. And then I said to him, what does it mean, quaintly unsophisticated?

I don't know, he said, and we sat for a while quietly.

I think they were insulting me, I said.

He just shrugged, and said, Foolish old biddy hens, I was going to tell them April was mine and we married yesterday, and see the look on their faces. You spoiled it.

Jack! that's awful. But he smiled that smile he has, and I felt quietly pleased.

December 25, 1885

Christmas morning. The day started dark and cloudy and cold, and it seems to be snowing now and then, the flakes brush past the window and do not settle. April slept bundled in her own bunk last night, and I woke early, wrapped in Jack's strong arms, comfortable. As he lay with me we watched out the little window and saw the snow skittering across the glass, and he said to me, I'm glad you're here, I dreamed last night that I woke up and I had dreamed all of it, and I was back in the barracks alone.

We are anxious to be done with traveling, but Jack has talked more today, and we are good company for each other, and never seemed to tire of something to discuss.

I felt happy until today at dinner someone in the Dining car reminded me it is Christmas day, and started to hum a Christmas carol, and someone else joined in, until the whole car was singing Hark the Herald Angels Sing. Jack and April listened, but I just stared hard out the window. It feels like there is a hard knot in my chest. This is the first Christmas I have ever been away from my family, and nothing here is familiar, and I am gone away with a stranger and my baby, and I felt like I wanted to go back to bed and cry.

Sing, Papa, she said to Jack, and he looked up startled and opened up his eyes wide. Then I saw a look of warmth spread across his face like she had said the sweetest words he had ever heard.

He smiled at her and said, Well, I can't sing right now, Mama has an owey and needs a sugar. April obediently kissed my cheek. Why don't you tell her about Christmas? he said. I have to ask about the horses and take care of something, and I'll be right back. Stay here and wait for me, okay? So I nodded. He kissed April's head as he left.

April sat and listened like she was much older than two, as I told her about Mary and Joseph, traveling far away from their homes and being cold and lonely and scared. And my voice choked up, and I brushed away tears quick so she couldn't see them. So I rushed the story ahead to the Baby's birth, and the angels singing, and the kings from the east.

Jack came back looking worried. One of the foals is down. Hard to tell if it's sick or just cold, right now, he said.

Is there anything we can do? I asked him.

He shook his head. Christmas carols continued all around us, covering our conversation.

Jack said, Do you know what good little girls get on Christmas? No? Good girls get presents from Saint Nick. Look here what I found back on your bed. He brought out a little wooden box, and April took it timidly. Open it, he coaxed.

She reached into the shredded wood stuffing and brought out a beautiful little doll with a china head and hands and feet, all dressed in a little dress, with real, soft hair on its head in tiny curls. Oh! she said, Oh! Look, Mama, a Mrs. Lady! She picked up the doll and hugged it tight.

You are a rascal, I said to him. My lips hurt from holding back my tears, so that I had to wait a moment. Then I whispered, I love you.

The train pulled into the Austin station at 4:45, held up some by a snow storm that made the engineer slow down far out of town. By the time we arrived, however, the snow had turned to rain, and all looked dismal and gray.

There was no sign around of anyone looking for us, so we found a place out of the stream of people to sit on our trunks and huddle warmly together. April held her dolly proudly to her, feeling important to be the protector of so beautiful a thing. Mrs. Lady is 'fraid, she said to me.

Well, I said, we will keep her safe won't we?

Through the people then, I saw Jack leading the string of horses through the downpour, and I counted them, still five, so the little one had made it alive. He was talking to a man, and shaking his hand, slapping shoulders and all the way men do when they are glad to meet each other. Then they disappeared around the side of the building.

Here came those three ladies, the ones who thought they wanted to meet me and then made fun of me. I sat very straight and proud, and tried not to look at them, but they were coming this way, and I could hardly avoid them.

Oh, Mrs. Elliot! called Mrs. Faulkner, We just wanted you to know what a lovely time we had meeting you and your lovely family.

Just lovely, echoed Mrs. Blankenship.

Do pay a call while you are in town, dearie, said old Mrs. Dunn, Here is my card. Ask anyone in town, we are in the big white house. Merry Christmas!

I was about to tell her I would rather walk barefooted to Boston than visit her for Christmas, but April held up her baby and said, Christmas! Papa gave me Mrs. Lady!

The ladies all looked at each other and twittered again, and left with their noses in the air, and I heard Mrs. Dunn say, You know he came from, and, Oh, we've just made it for the other train! Then I couldn't hear any more.

They went to where another train was coming in from the east, and I watched them for a bit. They were across the platform and in a little crowd of people who all seemed to hang on every word they said. They were talking loud so folks would hear how important they were, about Mrs. Faulkner's son who was arriving on this train all the way from West Point Academy, and how he was high in his class, and an honor student or some such. Well, here came a young looking soldier, so thin his uniform swung around him, up to them, and politely said Hello, and Now, mother, this is not the place for such things, when Mrs. Faulkner tried to hug him and kiss him on the depot steps.

Just then he caught sight of Jack in his uniform, and that boy snapped to attention stiffer than I have ever seen, and cracked his elbow up in a salute and looked like a tin soldier toy I saw in a store window in town.

Jack saluted him back, and said At ease, son, to him.

Yes, sir! the boy said, and made a funny posture with his feet apart, but he still looked stiff enough to knock over with a blade of grass. Then I heard Jack talk to him, and the boy said how he was in his last year, and Jack nodded, and introduced himself, and an odd look came on that boy's face. Lieutenant John Edward Elliot? he said, Sir, pleased to make your acquaintance, sir. Honored, I mean, sir.

Jack shook his hand then and asked was Colonel Hargrave still teaching mathematics?

No, sir, said the boy. Lieutenant Elliot, sir, I have requested to be assigned to your post, when I graduate, Sir.

Mrs. Faulkner had stood there watching all this, and her eyes ran over me while her son was busy saluting and praising my husband, so I just smiled politely at her.

Jack said, Well, Cadet Faulkner, go have Christmas with your mother, I'm sure she's cold out here. They exchanged salutes again, and the Cadet walked away.

Mrs. Faulkner had sidled up to me and said Good day, Mrs. Elliot?

I just looked at her, and I saw in her eyes that she was wanting some kind of approval for her boy because of his career ahead, and she suddenly just looked like an old lady, not fancy and rich and frightening. An old lady whose son admired my husband, and who herself would be as helpless in the Territories as a newborn calf and not nearly as useful. Good day, I said back. It is a funny thing how much more proud people can be of themselves if they never step back and take a good look in a glass.

In just a few minutes more, there was a man joined us and introduced himself as Jack's Papa, shaking my hand and talking a blue streak, and I was amazed at how little the two men looked alike. Charles Elliot, or Chess, as he proclaimed everyone called him, was straight talking and to the point, a man not as tall as his son, and obviously used to hard work in the sun by the lines deeply grooved in his face.

He loaded us into a beautiful four-seated buggy pulled by four horses all the same size and weight, and we rode for at least an hour, maybe more, through open, rolling hills dotted here and there with dark shapes of trees. I wished it was a clear day so I could see it all. It gave me a nervous spell to think there are all those trees to hide behind and we were driving directly through any kind of ambush that might await us, but Chess seemed not to care a bit.

We finally came to a stop, nearly frozen and wet despite the hood of the buggy. From outside in the rain I had no idea whether we were entering a castle or a cave, but in the house, warm with fires and brightly lit in every corner with lamps, I felt I had come inside a dreamland. It was a grand house, and its rooms rambled on and on, and the large parlor where we came in was lined with rich looking wood and hung with paintings, and there was real carpets on the floors with fringe on them.

A Christmas tree stood in the center and lent its smell to the place, but the smell of pine did not cover the other smells that came to me. Ham and turkey and goose, and dressings and bread, and spiced pies of apple and mince and sweet potato. I found I was dreadfully hungry, and when we were sent to a room outfitted for us, we all changed clothes quickly.

April was to have her own room, a beautiful place with a little bed with lace coverlets, like a princess. I have never in my days even imagined such a room, and it was wondrous but my first thought was it will spoil her rotten, and now she will never be satisfied with her plain things. It was more beautiful than the hotel we had stayed in. I put our wet things by the fire hung over the backs of chairs, but I was still exploring the room when Jack said, Mrs. Elliot? Are you aware you are holding up Christmas dinner?

I said over my shoulder, Jack, where's my pistol? I can't find it.

It's on top of that wardrobe, out of the reach of Little Bitty. I promise you won't need it during supper, come on.

December 26, 1885

Chess is a friendly man, and not given to long periods of silent thought like his son Jack. Last night when I got to the table he held out a chair for me, and his eyes fell on the brooch Jack gave me, and I saw something faraway flicker across his face. It made me feel odd inside, like I wasn't worthy of the brooch, but still proud it had been given to me.

All the food was wondrous and just as good as it was plenty. He had laid a table like he was expecting an Army, though, and there was just the three of us, plus he had also invited an old gentleman friend of his, a Mr. Arlington who struggled to eat it with false teeth. They talked about old times and told stories of the war that I know Harland would love to hear. The men all talked at once, sometimes forgetting I was there, laughing about things and now and then saying something I didn't understand and chuckling over it. Jack acted mad when his Papa said the Army was full of lace panties nowadays, and he actually raised his voice to his father in a way that would have got my brothers a whipping no matter how old they were.

But Chess just looked at me curiously and asked me, What do you think of that?

I wasn't sure if he meant his comment or Jack's, so I thought a bit, and said, Well, sir, no one in the Territories wears lace panties that I know of, and he and Mr. Arlington just about split their sides laughing. I was real embarrassed, and I stood up to leave the table, but Jack had his hand on my arm.

Don't let him bother you, he said. He's just trying to see how far he can go before you call him out.

Well, I said, sitting again, the acorn never falls far from the tree, does it?

I thought I had made Chess angry when I offered to help with the dishes to the lady who had served it all. He called her Lupy and said she was his cook and housekeeper, but he didn't even offer her to sit with us and eat, she just served and cleared, served and cleared. I thought this was mighty unfair, and when I talked to her she didn't answer at first, so I tried in Mexican, and lo and behold, she just talked a blue streak.

Her name is Lupe, but she didn't mind the gringo boss, she said, as he is a good man and kind to her and her family, and her husband is a cattle hand and they have a good life. She insisted I shouldn't do dishes, as I was a guest. So I said to her, I hope I am not a guest, I am family. And I just got up after dinner and helped out.

Finally, she shooed me out of the kitchen, saying, they would be waiting on me to have Christmas, and she was going home. As I came from the kitchen I stopped at the door to roll my sleeves back into place, and I heard the men talking and it was about me.

Jack's voice came through like he was answering a question that had been put to him, Well, I'd rather be back to back with her than in a troop of soldiers, when push comes to shove. That made me feel good for sure.

Mr. Arlington said, There's no real ladies any more, just fluffy priss and hard stuff.

Jack sounded angry then, and said, You wouldn't know a real woman if she ran over you with a flatbed, old man!

Mr. Arlington and Chess both laughed, and Chess' voice said, Look at him, Bobby! He's fit to take you on, crutch and all. You poked him in a nerve that time. He's bad all right!

Mr. Arlington said, Yep, he's bad. Sickern' I ever saw over a pretty little . . .

I didn't want to hear any more and I burst through the door making a loud bang.

They all three stood, nodding to me, and Chess said loudly, sweeping his arm toward me, And here she is, my new daughter! But I could tell there was something mocking in his voice, and he was making me feel edgy, and I could see it in Jack's eyes too. Like there was some reason to keep my eyes open and my powder dry. Did you get Lupy straightened out? Chess asked.

No, sir, I said. I was getting real fed up with his mocking tone. Lupe is doing the best she can considering the characters in this room.

Ah-hah! he said. Look at her eyes. The flint emerges! You are wrong Bobby, here at last, is a real lady! and he took my hand and kissed it softly, and said, Welcome to the family, Miss Sarah. Let's have Christmas!

Chess had gifts for all, even Lupe, but she had left for home and would have to get her lace shawl later. He gave Jack a beautiful saddle, shiny with polished leather, and I admired it along with him. April got a most wonderful little dress and coat, and although it was too big for her, I said I will take it up a bit, and then when she grows I'll let it out. It was just too beautiful, and I am only sorry that someday she will outgrow it.

Chess just looked at me funny and said, Well, pass it down to the next one, honey, if it's a girl, of course. Then he grinned real hard at me and I finally saw some of Jack's looks in his face, in that smile and those straight white teeth.

Then he handed me a large box, and a small one. Open the little one first, he said. Jack tells me you're a hand with a gun, but you're fond of a long barrel?

Well, I said, my hand on the lid of the box, I take all the caliber I can get, and I like a repeater with a smooth pull.

Chess grinned again, Well, honey, maybe you can use this in your lighter moments, say for church or the opera. So I opened the box and inside was a little tiny pistol with two barrels like I had never seen before, and wavy white handles, and a silvery barrel and sights. It's only two shots, he said, but likely in church that's enough to get your point across, and then he and Jack and Mr. Arlington just laughed and laughed.

Pearl handles, said Jack, just the touch for the well-attired lady about town.

Jack! I'm no lady about town!

Put your feathers down, Jack said, That just means in social circles. Open the last one. It's from me.

But you already gave me so much, I said. Well, then I opened the box and inside there was a paper wrapping, and under the paper was a bundle of cloth. It was an amazing color of dark red, with shining little fur that stood right up, and felt soft as a horse's nose.

I stared kind of addle-headed into the box, and he said, Well, take it out, Sarah, see if you like it.

Oh, I like it, I said, I like it fine. But I couldn't bring myself to lift it out of the box. I felt the cloth and whispered, What is it?

He looked odd at me, and came over and said again, Take it out and stand up and try it on, and he took my hand and raised me up, and lifted the thing from the box. Here, he said, It's a cloak, nice and warm for the winter. We don't get much winter but what we get is damned cold. Look, velvet on one side and black linen damask on the other, if you want it plain for some different dress. He draped the beautiful thing around my shoulders and arranged it, and fastened a big shiny soft cloth thing in the front. Sarah, do you like it? he asked. It's real velvet, do you like it? Look in the glass there.

I stared hard at my reflection, and I touched the cloth and lifted it and looked at it close, feeling the softness.

Mr. Arlington was saying behind me, What kind of man gives his wife a scarlet cloak for Christmas?

Chess answered him back, Oh, it ain't a bad color, that's a fancy red. It's what the snooty busy bodies in the Art Society call dove's blood or some such nonsense.

Jack was standing at my side, watching me like a hawk. I tried to talk to him, but I moved my mouth and no sound came out.

It was a scarlet velvet thing. A cloak, he had said. Warm and soft and beautiful and amazing to see and made of scarlet velvet that feels like a horse's nose. And there was no way he could have known I wanted something like that, for I didn't know myself, it was just a long ago dream from a word on a lost page of a book now gone. Oh, Jack, I tried to say, tears ran down my face, and he began to look disappointed. Oh, Jack! I finally whispered out, and I threw my arms around his neck and hugged him close.

He seemed stunned, and said, Well, don't cry, if you don't like it.

Oh, leave her be, said Chess. Women love to cry over presents and letters and such. Of course she likes it, don't you know anything by now boy?

I had to leave the room and go get my handkerchief, and as I walked, sniffing, I felt the heaviness of the cloak, and the way it swirled around me when I walked, and the soft, brushing sound the cloth seemed to hold in itself, like it whispered to me. I dug into my brown bag, and pulled out my Christmas gift for Jack. It was a sad old leather thing compared to what had been given to me.

And then Jack called out, Bring Pop's gift in, when you come back, so I found the box of fancy cigars he had brought for his father, and I was holding both presents in my hands when I returned.

Jack, I said, I'm sorry, it isn't much. I hadn't felt stingy when I ordered the saddlebag, but it just seemed paltry now. I thought your old one was getting ragged, I said.

Jack took the bags from me and said, These are first rate, Mrs.

Elliot. He leaned down then and kissed me real quick and sweet on the cheek. Oh, look, he said, somebody's tuckered right out. There was April, leaning against the bottom of the Christmas tree, and looking precious in her new dress, fast asleep.

December 27, 1885

I am pregnant. I know I am. No one would believe me if I told them, and certainly only God could prove or disprove my claim. But last night the baby happened, and I am so sure I will count the days from today and prove myself right. There will be a baby the end of September, but I will tell no one yet. Oh, Jack, you will be a father, and this morning at breakfast I felt like I was glowing with secret pride for you, but I will not tell you either.

I wasn't going to write any more, but it turned out to be such an eventful day. Since it was the first day without rain, even though the sky was still gray and heavy we toured Chess' ranch. It is a big spread, and he has over a thousand head of beautiful cattle on hundreds and hundreds of acres. The house is so big, it is amazing, but it is small compared to the barn and the other buildings for storing equipment and such.

Chess told Jack, You know, you could come here and live with me. I sure wouldn't mind you filling up the house with children, it's too quiet all the time. But Jack just said he couldn't do that, and he wouldn't say why.

I wished he would tell me why, as that is a generous and kind thing for his father, but then I thought how I would never see my Mama and Albert and Savannah and Harland again, and when Chess asked me to convince Jack to stay in Texas, I said, No, our home is Arizona Territory. There's too much blood spilt on that land to leave it. It costs to live there, and we've both paid a price.

I enjoy hearing Chess tell of his life and the lives of people Jack knows, for even though it is all strange to me, he has a way of telling it that is comforting and good. Jack told me in secret that his Papa was as rough and ornery as any outlaw, but if he is, it doesn't show, and to me he seems refined and gentle.

Maybe Texas is just more civilized, I thought, but Chess said, No, just older. When Arizona gets older, he said, she'll learn to put up her hair and let down her skirts and not be so wild. Then he said, That reminds me. Did Jack tell you about him being run out of the church?

I just looked stunned.

Jack laughed, and said real quiet, Thanks, Pop.

Chess started to laugh and laugh, and then he lit one of his cigars and offered Jack one, but Jack refused it. Well, Chess said, You know, Miss Sarah, when Jack was eleven years old, all the boys and girls in the Sunday School were going to do a recitation. There was going to be a big Jubilee for Missionary Day or some such, and they all were to memorize Bible verses to say. It got to be a real contest, with one saying "I can recite ten verses," and the next saying "I can do twenty."

I noticed Jack shaking his head and smiling that funny half smile of his, and he said You're going to tell it aren't you? to Chess.

Well, Chess said, Jacky there was never a dull boy, and didn't brag one bit, but studied and memorized and studied some more. Each night I'd find him up with a lamp, reading that Bible.

I smiled and thought, Mama will be so glad to hear this story.

Chess caught my eyes and made that mischief-loaded grin that looks like Jack's.

When the day came, there was a visiting missionary from China or somewhere, and pastors from three churches with Bibles open, ready to test the Sunday School. Girls went first, and the crowd applauded each one. Jacky kept changing places to be the last boy in line. When they finally got to Jack, they asked him how many verses he had ready, and he said, not just verses. So the missionary said, "A chapter?" And he said, "not just chapters, either," he said right out loud he had memorized an entire book of the Bible. Then Chess started to laugh, I can still see that missionary lady's face, and the way her mouth hung open before she fainted dead away on the platform!

Jack, I said, what did you say?

A whole book just like I said, he said to me.

Chess was laughing like he was going to choke, but he sputtered out, They never had any rules about it.

That's right, said Jack. No one said you shouldn't recite the Song of Solomon.

He got all the way, Chess gasped out, laughing, All the way to the two breasts feeding in the lilies, and then he couldn't even talk any more.

Now Jack was laughing too.

I stood up. This is too much, I said. Jack Elliot, there is nothing like that in the Bible.

Yes, there is too, he said, and he stood up and began to wave his arms as he spoke in a dramatic reciting way. Behold thou art fair, my love, thy two breasts like young roes that are twins which feed among the lilies. How much better is thy love than wine! Thy lips, O my love, drop with honeycomb, honey and milk are under thy tongue.

John Edward! I almost shouted. You should be ashamed!

What for? he said.

April, it's time for bed, I told her.

She immediately started to cry. No, Mama.

Yes, I said, you have heard too much of this vulgar talk already. Jack Elliot, shame on you. Now come on, April, you are going to bed, and I will tell you a story and you will say your prayers and pray extra hard for your father's soul. So I went to April's room and stayed there until she went to sleep, too mad and too embarrassed at both those men to return. I wasn't through with my bath when Jack let himself into the room.

I told him I would be done quick, but he said, real soft and warm, No, you won't. He rolled up his sleeves. Then he began to recite words to me, words that sounded like the Bible but were full of love and longing and some beautiful girl hunting for her precious love, and the young man combing the village hunting for her too. As he talked, he picked up the sponge and ran it over my arms and shoulders, squeezing out the water and watching it drip down.

O my love, my fair one, he said, Arise and come away, and he lifted me up where I shivered and dripped in the cold air. He took a towel and dried me, not letting me take it, and said, As a rose among thorns, so is my love among all the daughters of the earth.

Then he started to unbutton his shirt, so I helped him.

He picked me up in his arms and swung me into bed, kissing me long and sweetly, and he whispered into my mouth, I am come into the garden, my sister, my spouse, I have gathered myrrh with spice, I have eaten my honeycomb, and he kissed me more and more. He kept mumbling words, and I heard him say, Open to me my beloved, my dove, for my head is filled with dew.

By that time, I no longer thought of him as a scoundrel.

I don't know how but April has lost a shoe, and declares she can't move without it, and she is sitting in a big chair in the dining room, wailing at the top of her lungs. I am confused whether to ignore her and let her think her crying gets her nowhere, or to paddle her behind and let her think her spoiled attitude will bring her grief.

These are the kinds of things I always wish I could ask my Mama. It does no good to ask Jack's Papa as he adores April and when she was naughty he just laughed. She is never far from him when he is in the house, and is so willful I am embarrassed some-times. It is probably a good thing that we will not live here in this beautiful house, as I surely do not want to raise up a houseful of spoiled, nasty children, and Chess seems to think, although I love him dearly, that it is his right to spoil Jack's children if he pleases.

He spoils me too, and I have hardly done a lick of work this whole time except for some dish washing with Lupe. My hands are all soft in the palms for the first time I know of, and I am bound for some blisters when I get home, but Jack says it is nice, it is how a lady's hands should feel. I think then that a lady is just someone rich enough to have someone carry her around, and not to have to split firewood and drive a wagon nor scrub and clean and haul water. But I just kept my thoughts to myself, as I know he would try to argue about it but I have learned that there are some arguments you can't have with Jack because he doesn't understand what I am saying no matter what.

I have something nice to take home, we have gone into town to a place I think it is called Photoengraveurs, and had a picture made of ourselves. We are all posed and stiff looking, leaning up against the iron positioners. I have got one of these to give to Mama. I hope she is pleased.

January 12, 1886

All are saddened today at our leaving. We hugged and kissed Chess more than once, and rode to the depot and said goodbye again. The train pulled in with a cloud of steam and noisy wheels, and we of course had to wait for the passengers getting off before we got on.

January 15, 1886

Jack is drowsing with his head leaned back against the seat, and whenever I get a chance to look at him without his eyes piercing mine back, I study his face. I still see a stranger sitting there. One I am getting used to, but not one I feel familiar with. There is much about him that pleases me and takes my breath away with kind attentions, and there is something in him that I feel I will never touch, a secret man inside, the one that I saw on horseback guiding the wagon train.

He woke when April patted his arm and said Papa, hold me.

Jack, I said, she is awfully spoiled.

I know, he said, but holding her isn't the reason. And now is not a good time to un-spoil her, for the sake of the other passengers.

I nodded at him, he is right. We will have to ease her back into our usual life, and it will be better when we get home because that will be familiar surroundings. He said to me, with a hopeful look, In the spring, Pop is going to drive a small herd of cattle to us. Maybe just two or three hundred head.

What? I said. That's a small herd? We don't have land to run that many. There's no grass there like in Texas.

I know, he said, we'll have to buy more land, and run up some fence on part of it, too, for a big corral. It will take a while, might be summertime before we see them, but he said he'd rather stake us now than wait 'til he dies. He's too ornery to die anyway, so it's a good thing. If he comes himself, he might stay a while.

That's fine with me, I said, if he will just stop making April think it is funny when she is bad and throws a tantrum.

He took her in his arms, and then reached into his blouse and handed me an envelope. Here, he said. I had to get this from Pop because I had sent it to him to keep for me.

It was thick paper and written out in a long, lacy, rolling hand, with a golden stamp in one corner.

It's a share in a silver mine, he said. One tenth. If I hadn't been drunk I'd have had a half, but it's yours now. You saw it that day, the Silverbell? Well, I won the share on a bet, I don't work it or anything. And it pays anywhere from fifty to a hundred dollars a month, which won't make you rich but it is enough to hire a man permanently and pay for some things so you don't have to work so hard all the time. Here's the bank book, too. There's enough for you to take on some more acreage.

But Jack, I said, aren't you going to be there?

He just looked at me odd, and said, Sure, sometimes, but I'm not leaving the Army.

I didn't know what to say. Maybe I am spoiled too, but I felt like throwing myself down on the seat and crying. That is fine to hire a man, but Jack won't even live with me? What kind of way is that to be married? What will I do alone with some strange man on the place, what if he is a bad man?

Jack said, What's the matter? Did you think I was going to brand cows every day?

Well, no, I said, you only brand once a summer when the calves are big enough. But I didn't think I'd have to do it alone. You said you didn't want me to live there alone. I knew I was about to cry, then, and turned my face from him. You said you'd never leave me, I said into the window glass.

I'm not leaving you, Sarah, was all he said, and we rode silently a long time, listening to each other breathe and not talking. April slept in his lap.

I know what it was. That Faulkner boy saluted him and made him remember how he liked being called sir by the other men. Nothing I do or say can compete with the admiration of a bunch of ragged soldiers. Even the Indians respect him, I have heard tell. But he will take a wife and leave her to fend for herself while he goes around riding and shouting commands. Well, that's a fine thing. I am married again but I am still alone. Only now I have had a few weeks to find out what it is like not to be alone, and so that only makes it feel worse.

Sarah, Jack said, what's wrong?

I just kept looking out the window and said, Nothing.

That made him mad. I don't care.

January 16, 1886

We were only a hundred miles or so from Tucson, in a bleak area without any trees. Overhead the sun shone brightly and reminded us we were far away from the rainy Texas Christmas. I was looking out the window thinking that we must be passing my brother Clover's little grave somewhere nearby. Those days were long ago, but I leaned against the rumbling wall of the train car, and remembered all those times and I wondered if Ulyssa had married yet, or if she would, and if I would know Alice and Louisianna if I saw them. They must be near grown.

I was so far away in my head that it wasn't until the train stopped out there in the middle of the desert that I looked around to see what was happening. There were riders on horses outside the doors of almost every car, and I heard shots and saw one of the riders fire into the air.

Jack stood up in front of me, and I saw just like that he had turned into that other man, the one who commanded men and burst into burning buildings. He grabbed April and looked deep in her face, and said Hide, Little Bitty, don't move a muscle and don't make a single sound no matter what.

April's little face filled with terror, but she closed her mouth and didn't start to cry, and I watched him settle her under my seat and take my cloak and fold it and lay it in on top of her. I took off my brooch, and looked around quickly, and pushed it between the back and the seat of the bench where the cushion hid it.

Sarah, hollered Jack, and he had come from the sleeping car and tossed me my big pistol just as a man burst in through the door waving a twelve gauge shotgun and with a rag tied over his nose. He pulled the trigger and a huge hole opened in the roof of the car. People all around shrieked with fear. Without taking another breath, Jack drew the gun he always wore and shot him. Passengers screamed again, and Jack went to the doorway, waiting for another robber to enter.

Two more men did come in, and Jack squeezed himself near the other door, below the seat. One of the men with a red hand-kerchief over his face pulled it down and looked around at all the scared people.

Who killed Pete? he hollered. There didn't have to be any killing, all we wanted was your money!

He held a pistol to a man's head and the woman sitting beside him screamed out, The shot came from back there, and pointed in our direction, then she started wailing.

Shut up or I'll plug him anyway, said the man. So she just whimpered and sobbed, and one robber stood by the door while the man with his face exposed walked down the aisle. Who shot him? he asked again. No one made a sound. He stopped right in front of me. I had the pistol hid in the folds of my skirt, and set my finger on the trigger real light. The man studied my face a bit, and said to me, You aren't even scared. What's the matter, are you blind? All these people are scared to death and you just sit there.

I said to him, I've seen your kind before.

He licked his lips and grinned. You know who pulled the trigger on Pete, don't you? Was it you? Did you shoot him? But you know who did, don't you? Who was it? I could make you tell me.

No, I said. I don't think you could. I could feel my little April trembling against my ankle.

The red kerchief man looked at his partner and waved his gun a bit, and the other man said, Everybody off, Now! I could see from the corner of my eye through the window that lines of passengers were standing outside and people all through the car scooted out quickly. Red kerchief leaned in towards me. Everybody off except you, that is. You're going to tell me who killed Pete. The robber at the far end followed the passengers out.

Someone outside was struggling with one of the robbers who was trying to take something away to steal, and the robber shot the man down right away, and then shot him again through the chest. I couldn't see Jack anymore, and didn't try to look his way, as that would give him away to the man in front of me.

I looked the man square in the eyes. You have no need to rob me, I said. I have nothing to take.

There's a gold ring there, he said. I could even let you keep it, of course, if we could make a bargain. It's pretty shiny too, looks real, where's your husband? Would he mind if we made a bargain? One that would keep you alive?

I heard Jack's voice say, He'd mind like hell, and Jack's revolver barrel was right against the man's neck, and when he cocked the hammer it sounded louder than thunder. Stand up slow, Jack said. Hand her that pistol. The man weakly obeyed, and moved away from me. Just then his partner burst back through the door looking excited, and pulled his mask down, then his eyes fell on us and he stopped smiling.

I stood up and aimed my pistol at him, pulling the trigger once to chamber a bullet.

Hah! he said at the hollow click it made, and raised up and aimed at me.

No! yelled the red kerchief man.

I didn't stop to think, I pulled the trigger again, and hit him in the ear. He let out a howl and dropped his gun, holding his ear with his hand, blood running through his fingers like soap on a washboard.

One of the robbers outside the train hollered in, What's going on in there Corey?

I aimed at him again and said, Your nose is next.

Jack nudged his pistol into the neck of old red kerchief, and said Answer him, and say the right things.

Fine! called Corey, Just fine, the kid is acting like a fool and shot his own ear off.

Well, I thought, there we were holding prisoners on the inside of a train while all the folks who had sat beside us were prisoners outside and being robbed, and a trunk of some kind was brought out of the caboose and smashed against a rock until it broke open. We saw the men fill their saddle bags with gold, and some women fainted. Some of the robbers talked to each other, and they went and shot one of the engineers then, and starting at the front of the train they began to search each car. They must have realized they were missing a few of their men.

Jack pushed the men into a corner, and said to me, Cover them. Then he said to them with a downright evil look on his face, Move. Just move a little. That's all it will take, you can see she's not afraid of sending you to the devil. Then behind me I heard the sharp swishing sound of his saber being drawn, and he picked up the pistols from the men and stuck them in his belt, and waited by the door for the searching robbers. Three of them came in, guns drawn but not aimed at us. Jack yelled at them, Drop the weapons, now! They saw him and began firing at him, and I saw him shoot two of them fast, but miss the third one who hid behind a seat.

Well, Jack just leaned down with his gun and fired under all the seats in a row, and the man yelled out, I'm hit! and then let out with a string of cursing like I never heard in all my days and hope I never hear again.

Get up, Jack said to him.

I can't, he hollered, I'm hit. I'm dyin'.

And then the man fired a shot at Jack and I saw him spin around quick. He dropped his sword and shot the man again, and again he let out a string of cursing.

You're not dying, not yet, said Jack, get up! You're under arrest but you aren't dead. Yet. The robber struggled to his feet, and I could see he was bleeding from his shoulder and one leg. Jack said, You tell them to leave those passengers be, and put them all on the train, the dead ones too, and leave their things you stole and clear out, or you'll <u>be</u> dead.

One of the men in front of me shifted around where he was sitting and I pulled back the hammer. I began to think, what if one of these bullets has strayed and hit my April, and she never let out a sound and died under that seat?

I suddenly wanted to hurt these men, to make them scared as I was, so I said to the red kerchief man called Corey, Hair trigger on this here pistol, and you make me nervous. Sweat ran down the man's head and he was shaking. If my April is hurt I will kill him anyway, I thought. I was filled with a terrible hate, a terrible meanness. I hated these men so much I was afraid of myself more than I was afraid of them. I could stand right here and look them in the eyes and shoot a man dead without blinking.

Do it, Will! called the sweating man in front of me, Do what he said, Will, do it! She's crazy, Will, do it!

So the man named Will called out the window. There's a Army soldier in here, says we're all under arrest. And Clay and Billy and Pete are all shot dead. He's got a crazy woman with a gun guarding Corey and the kid. He wants you to give them all back their stuff and clear out.

The robbers talked among themselves again for a minute. Hey, Soldier! one of them yelled. What we got us is a Mexican standoff. We got these here passengers, so you let our boys go and carry out the dead, and we won't hurt anyone else and let you get on your way.

Jack said, No deal. Return the passengers to the train right now.

Hey boys, Will shouted. He's got a gun to my head, you better talk to him. Then one of the robbers rode up to a man in a conductor's uniform, and whipped out a pistol and shot the poor man down. I saw Jack's face go pale, and he flinched. Then I heard a gun fire again, real close, and Will began to scream like a child and holler curses. Let them people go! he cursed again. I'm crippled up bad, he yelled out the window. He's a shooting off little pieces of me.

Jack said through his teeth, Next one's your knee.

No! yelled Will, Come on, boys, talk to the man.

One of the robbers hollered back, Will, you're a coward! Hey soldier, you keep him. We don't want him anyway!

I had an idea quick. Jack, I said, Tell them he's got a big sack of gold here he was holding out on them. Five hundred dollars' worth at least. Jack grinned at me.

It ain't true! screamed Will.

This man, Jack hollered, dragging Will toward the door and showing him to the robbers, then bringing him back inside so they couldn't shoot him for us, This man has a sack of fifty dollar gold pieces he took off a banker in here. He wasn't going to tell you but they dropped all over the floor. And the other two, Corey and the kid, I saw them put them in their pockets. There's a thousand dollars in that sack! I was guarding the banker carrying it. I reckon you want to talk to these fellows all right, and I'll give them to you. You just put those people back on the train.

It's a lie! Will shrieked.

Jack's gun sounded again, and Will began to scream. My other foot! He shot my other foot!

The robber outside rode closer to our train car. We think we'd like to talk to those men. What do you want, Soldier?

Ride off, said Jack. Up to that ridge, and you give us time to load up the people and get the engines running. Then when she starts to roll, we'll drop off your men, and you can have 'em.

Okay, hombre, said the man. It's a deal.

From where I was, I could see Jack fish into his own back pocket for a minute, and he took out a gold coin and slipped it into the pocket of Will's bloody pants.

The passengers crowded into the other cars, staying away from ours. The poor dead and hurt ones were brought on too, and the train lurched as the engines fired up. At last it started to roll, and Jack dragged Will back to the door.

I looked at my two prisoners and said, Come on, get up, but they sat like statues.

Don't shoot us lady, said Corey.

Move, I said.

Hey, tell her not to shoot us, Soldier. We did what you said. We didn't do anything. I didn't even want to rob this old train, they made me.

Shut up, said the one they call Kid.

Jack looked back and made a face. Mrs. Elliot, he said, Don't shoot them, unless you have to.

April! I called out. Are you all right?

Yes, Mama, came a little voice.

Okay, I said, then I turned to them, I probably won't shoot you then. Get off this train, you sack of filth. All three of the men jumped, Will screamed in pain when he landed, and Jack dragged the bodies to the door and rolled them off. There was blood everywhere, and I finally felt like I took my first breath in an hour.

Sarah, Jack said to me, That was a damned stupid thing I did, and got another good man killed.

No, I told him, you never know how they will react.

You know, he said, most Indians have got more honor in them than those kind. I just nodded. Indians at least won't turn on their own, nor cry like babies. Sarah, Jack said again, his voice real soft, you did good. Now get me a doctor. And he sat down on the seat near him and rolled to the floor.

I handed April to a kind lady who comforted her and smiled at me with a look of sympathy. And I stayed by Jack's side, and took his shirt off him and found the place in his side where he was shot. It must have been when he dropped the sword, but I never knew it. Blood had run inside his shirt and clear down his pants into his boot. I undressed him as gently as I could.

One of the old men passengers said he wasn't a doctor but had helped the Army surgeon in the war, and said, Confederate side, if that matters to you Ma'am.

No, I said, I don't care which side. He looked at Jack carefully and felt the hole with his finger. The bullet had gone clean through, he said, and there was no smell like it was a gut shot.

I think Ma'am, that he'll be just fine in a couple of weeks. In the war, we'd have just patched him up and given him a toddy and sent him back to the front tomorrow.

Well, I thought, and you lost the war, too, but I didn't say it to him.

Jack, I whispered, are you hurting? He nodded, hardly daring to move, and I recognized how that felt to have that kind of pain. Do you want something? A man here has whiskey to help the pain.

No, he said.

I don't mind, Jack, You don't have to suffer so, I said. What can I do for you?

He opened his eyes at that and made a face at me. Don't treat me like a child and give me back my pants. Then he winced in pain again.

Jack, I said, that man there says he thinks you'll live just fine.

He looked around to see if people were watching us. I hate to pass out like that, damn. Lost too much blood I reckon.

I was feeding his feet into his pants legs. Anybody would pass out being shot like that. Here, can you do these buttons?

Yes, he said. When the day comes I can't button my own pants I want you to shoot me. But do a better job than you did on that fellow. Shooting his ear, Sarah, I'd say that was a real poor shot.

I know, I said. I suppose I was nervous.

He winked at me, and said, Now quit fluttering over me and give me a shirt. Where's my Little Bitty?

Safe, I said. You must be all right, you're giving orders again. I'll bring her to see you when we get all the mess cleaned up. She has already seen enough blood in two short years of living. I helped him into his shirt, and felt him suck in a hard breath when he moved. Then he leaned back and shut his eyes, and his breath started to come evenly again.

Jack, I said, Don't you leave me.

He smiled faintly, with his eyes still shut. Not ever, he said.

January 19, 1886

We pulled in almost three hours late, and when we got there, the depot was just buzzing with people curious as to why it was so late. All my family was glad to see us, and most amazed when we got off the train, seeing me in my cloak and April in her fancy duds, and Jack hunched over and walking slow, holding his side.

Some of the folks on the train thought Jack was a hero. Some of them were angry, saying he let the robbers get away with murder and gold in their pockets. Although it never occurred to them that they had cowed to the outlaws, each and every one. And of course, none of them even mentioned that I had stood beside him through the whole thing, but some things don't count if you're a woman, and that's a fact.

Jack got madder than I have ever seen him, when I told Albert to drive us to Saint Mary's Hospital. Well, I said, there's this fine hospital just sitting there, and no reason they can't get a doctor to look at you for a day or two.

So he said, They won't let you in there if you aren't a Catholic.

Yes, they will, I said, because you aren't coming there as a Catholic or a Methodist or a Confederate or a ornery Cavalry soldier! You are coming there as a man with a hole in him where one don't belong, and they have got a doctor that knows more than that fellow on the train and can at least sew you up. Now keep still, you're aggravating me!

Jack just pulled in his lip and I saw fire glint in his eye, then he lifted his hand and flinched in pain but saluted me weakly. Yes, Ma'am, General Elliot.

Now, I said, that's better. Besides, I thought I was a Colonel.

He closed his eyes and leaned back, looking tired and hurt, but he murmured softly, Battlefield promotion. And he didn't say any more until he got inside and talked to the doctor. They sewed him up fine, and treated him extra well, except he did complain that all they served him was stewed oatmeal to eat.

Mama took April home with her and I stayed to be near Jack. The hospital has let me sleep in the other bed in his room and offered me to eat there too. It isn't good but it's filling and bland, for sick folks. I lie here at night and watch Jack sleeping, and help him if he needs to get up. He has a fever, but not too bad.

I began thinking about the train robbery, and how odd I felt, knowing how I could have killed those men in cold blood. Defending myself or someone I know is different than defending my child. I got to thinking that even if I didn't have a gun, I would tear them apart with my bare hands to save my baby April. I wonder if all mothers feel this way. Suddenly I knew why it is so dangerous to mess with a bear with cubs or any wild animal with babies. I am part and parcel with them when it comes to that. Lord, there is a mountain lion side of me I never knew before.

January 21, 1886

He was glad to get out of there in only two days, and did his best not to complain about the ruts in the road on the way home. He groaned one time, but I didn't apologize to him, I think he'd rather take his pain without too much sympathy. And I was right, all the insides of my hands are open blisters now.

Home at last, and my little ranch house looks mighty plain, but it is home to me and I am glad to see it. Jack is resting on the front porch. The man he hired did a fair job of the place, and Jack asked him to stay on, and promised him to build him a room with a stove. I told him he could have the adobe shed I built, if he wanted it, as it was nice and cool and just needed a stove in the winter and a cot could be built easy enough, so he is agreeable to that. His name is Mason Sherrill, but he says I can call him Mason.

January 26, 1886

True to his word, as soon as Jack was up and around, he was gone back to the fort. I am pregnant and living here on this ranch with a baby girl and a man I don't know, and my husband has got his worthless and holey hide back to where it can be saluted all he wants. He loved me last night so sweet, I thought surely he had changed his mind, and he swore how he will miss me but he left anyway. Taking up marriage is a good excuse for taking up cursing, I think.

February 4, 1886

Jack will be home tomorrow. I have so much to do, there is a cobbler in the oven for him, and I hope he likes apple as well as peach. Mama gave me a sack of pecans and I have made a pie too, and beat and aired our mattress so it smells fresh. Savannah and Albert and their children are coming tomorrow evening to share supper. I am ironing all my dresses and then I will wash my hair.

February 5, 1886

Jack must have left by midnight last night, for he was here with the morning sun, and he swept in here while April was still asleep and carried me to the bedroom. Jack Elliot, I said to him, I have chores to do.

Aw, he growled, this is a chore to you?

While we had breakfast later, he sat with April on his knee, and she ate potatoes and eggs off his plate, now and then offering him bites.

Sarah, he said, I need to ask you something.

Ask, I said without looking up, as I was trying to get some egg off the bottom of the skillet.

Sarah, haven't you had your time yet?

I set the skillet down on the table. I'm not expecting that for several months.

He looked at me real hard, like he does sometimes, only this time I met his eyes and didn't look away. Then I saw the most amazing thing I have ever seen. His eyes welled up with tears, and he stood up quick and set April in the chair, and went to the window and looked out. Jack? I said, you're not angry are you?

He turned around and held me tight, and kissed the top of my head, but he didn't say a word. His heart was racing, and his breath was fast, too. And he went outside and picked up the axe, and although Mason has cut me a cord of wood, Jack split and stacked two more cords, swinging that axe like a crazy man.

A cold wind was coming, and Jack came inside sweating and chilled, so I made him drink some coffee and change clothes and warm up. When I brought him the cup he wrapped his arm around my hips and hugged me to him, and put his face against my belly, like a sweet caress, and I could feel his breath through the cloth of my skirt, and then he smiled at me.

I brushed back his hair, and he said, Have you known for a long time?

I knew the night it happened, I told him.

He just looked at me, and I thought I'd hear an argument, but he said, Well, I reckon a lady wouldn't tell until she knew for certain.

It's better that way, I said.

We had supper with Albert and Savannah, and little Clover was naughty and wouldn't be still, so Albert took him in the other room and fussed at him.

Savannah admired my gravy and said how smooth it was, and then all of us enjoyed the pie and cobblers and coffee. Savannah is very full of child now, and looks like she is ready to birth to me, but she said, no it's still a month and a half away. Her back hurts terribly, she said, though, and she will look forward to having this one, as it has been harder to carry than the first two.

Jack was just sitting there beaming like a lightning bug. Oh, Jack, I said, and laughed at him, You're going to explode if you don't say it. So he told them we were expecting a child too, and there was a lot of talk about when, and I told them September twenty-sixth, and they laughed, thinking I was joking.

February 6, 1886

We rode this morning, slowly and gently, over the hills following Cienega Creek far past the Raalle's old place, which has just gone to ruin now. There are weeds everywhere and the only way you can tell there used to be a home there is that some cinders remain where the buildings were, and a couple of bushes have grown back that don't match the natural plants. We talked about the family we will have. Jack thinks children are a blessing but he practically scolded me and made me promise not to work too hard nor lift anything really heavy. He said to keep in mind that I am by nature hard headed and too independent for my own good, and I had our children to think about and their future and he didn't want them to grow up without a mother. Once again I saw a frightened look in his eyes. It is a rare sight in a man like Jack, and it appears the things that would frighten most men don't mean much to him, and the things most men wouldn't think about scare him plenty.

So I said, Well, how am I supposed to carry on without a husband to do those heavy things?

All he said was, That's why you have Mason.

That's why I have you, I said back.

He just looked away at the horizon and urged his horse further up the ridge. We got a long way from the house, and at the highest point on a ridge, we could see in all directions for miles and miles.

After a few minutes of looking at the land about, he says without turning my direction, I don't plan to quit the army.

Why? I said.

He didn't say another word. He just looked way over the hills. I suspect he is fighting more than Indians and cowboys and such somewhere inside himself. That's why he can't quit. He's got something burning inside and just has to keep on fighting it until one of them wins.

Finally, I got off my horse and let her wander, and stretched my back. Then I looked at my feet and saw something patterned in the dirt, and I scuffed it up. It was just an old broken piece of Indian pot. It looked a thousand years old, broken on that hill and forgotten for years. I tossed it back to the ground. I'm not asking you to quit, Jack, I said. I married you lock, stock and barrel.

Then he was beside me, and he put one hand on my shoulder, and we stood there a long time without talking, and then just like that we both mounted up and drifted over the hills back toward home.

Yesterday morning Jack headed back toward the fort, and around noon it started to rain. This morning it is still raining, sometimes slowing just a bit, but it has not stopped. Low places are full, and doing chores in the mud was tedious, and I feel so sick, my head just spins around.

Mason was real kind to me and I think he suspects my trouble, and said if I'd kindly allow, he'd toast some bread on the stove and that used to help his wife's stomach. I'm real uneasy having a strange man in my kitchen, but I put my little pistol in my pocket and said, Please come in, I would appreciate it very much. It has only been two days of baby sickness for me, but I want this over with right now, I can't go on and get things done feeling like this.

He was right, the toasted bread settled my insides some. He asked me if I wanted butter on it, and looked at my face, and said, I 'spose not, Ma'am. Then he went back to the little adobe room of his and left me here listening to the rain. It is hard to fix April something to eat, but she is little and doesn't mind having toasted bread for supper, and I am purely grateful just now that I don't have to cook more than that.

February 9, 1886

Rain comes and comes. There are no low places with puddles any longer, all have become streams. The well is filled with mud,

although we don't want for water as the cistern is overflowing
too. The stream that used to flow down by the road looks like a
great, brown, angry river. It makes a roaring that I hear under the
pattering of the rain. Trees sweep by in it, brush and branches torn
loose from somewhere, and I thought I saw a man floating by, but
rushed out to help and it was just a big saguaro cactus. Still, it
looked so dead, and I began to feel touchy and nervous with all
this rain. We are surely not used to this much rain in the Territories.

All my land, as far as I can see, is running water. Mason and I
spent the morning trying to build up the corral to keep the
horses' feet from rotting, they are standing in six inches of water
and old manure. We finally had to give up, and instead drove
them and the cow out of the barn and up a hill. They will be
much colder but their feet will keep. I don't know what to do
with Beaumont, if I let him loose he is liable to kill someone or
run off, so we turned over the trough, and laid it around with
boards and made an island for him to stand on. Of course, he
wouldn't go up it, but Mason said if the water rises more, likely
the bull will take the hill by himself. The chickens are fine roost-
ing on their poles, but unable to eat as they normally do, pecking
and scratching in the dust, so we tried to make pie pans into hanging feeders with twine tied into holes he punched with a nail. I
was sorry to see my pie pans go, but do not want to lose all those
chickens.

Frogs began to climb onto the porch, first one or two, then
dozens of them. I sweep and sweep, flinging them far out into the
water, but they swim back. I am wishing now that Jimmy had not
made such shallow steps, as they are just right for a desperate frog
to get on the porch.

Well, just as I thought the frogs were the nastiest thing and
swept the last one off again, here came sliding up out of the water
a great big bull snake. I tried to sweep him off but he coiled up on
my broom, and held on tight when I shook it. I had no choice but
to get my pistol and shoot it in the head, and still the dead snake
held on. I got a fire iron and pried him off, and a hunk of my
broom straw came off where it was shot.

April was on the porch in a chair watching all this, and pretty quiet, holding her Mrs. Lady to keep her safe from the water, she said. But suddenly, she called out, Mama, Snake getting Mrs. Lady! I turned around and saw the biggest rattlesnake I have ever seen moving up the leg of her chair. Its head was big as my fist.

April, I said, that is a bad snake. You must pretend to be a statue. Be a stone statue, and don't move. If you move honey, he will try to bite you.

April held her finger to her lips, and said, Sh-sh, Mama.

Don't move, I whispered, Honey, don't move. I reached in my pocket again for my pistol, then I put it down and ran to the bedroom for my rifle. I was always a much better shot with it.

When I got back, I stood at a far enough range the snake wouldn't charge at my movements. The rattler's head was hidden, but its body curled and writhed up the arm of the chair. Then there it was, its head appeared right over April's left shoulder. Its tongue flicked hard at her. April, I said, raising my rifle, you must make Mrs. Lady be very still. Don't even breathe. Don't wiggle one little bit. I aimed, and tears started to blur up my sight, I couldn't make out the tip of the barrel, much less the snake's head. It opened its horrible mouth, like a yawn, and licked closer and closer to her hair.

Mama, she whimpered, Mama shoot me?

No, I said, Mama's going to shoot the snake, but don't move, sweetie, don't move.

I held my breath. The snake's long body swirled up in a coil on top of the back of the chair and a length of it slipped between the cushion and the backing.

Mason came trudging through the water and stopped short, and I heard him say, Oh, Lord, real softly.

I wiped my eyes.

Mama? April started to cry. In a moment I thought she would panic, and if she moved she would surely be struck by the snake. It raised its head over hers, tongue flicking faster and faster now, and the rattle started shaking. April's little face turned red and her lips curled up, tears rolled down her face, but she held still like a statue. Mama?

I raised the rifle again and drew a bead on the snake, now it looked so small and moving around, coiling around my baby. I sniffed hard and held my breath, and stiffened my whole body, and pulled the trigger.

April let out a scream and her body quivered hard, and I grabbed my heart, knowing I had shot my child. Mama, mama, izza snake gone? She was holding the edge of the chair with all her might. Mama? April's mouth moved silently. Snake gone?

I looked again. It was truly gone. At least its lifeless head hung down over the back of the chair, although the body still held tight to the rungs. April, I said, Run to me, baby, the snake is dead! She flew into my arms, and I held her, trembling, listening to the noisy frogs on the porch. Oh, my brave girl!

Mason skinned the snake and pinned it to a board, careful to save the rattlers at the end. He didn't say much about it, except, Glad your little one is all right, Ma'am. I went back to sweeping frogs, determined to keep them out of my house.

Toobuddy is covered with mud and dripping, he runs and plays in the water, then slings his wet furry body up the steps and likes to sit right by the door. I popped him on the head for trying to eat a frog, as I know they are poison and he will die if he does. I don't know where the kitties are, hopefully safe in the rafters of the barn.

Mason said then, Ma'am, my room is awashing away.

I hadn't even thought of him, poor thing. Bring your bunk up here, quick, I said, anything you need to save, I'll help you. So we went through the mud again and I brought April in one arm and carried his guitar and a rolled up blanket under my other one. By the time he got his bunk set on the porch, we were all three cold and soaked to the skin, and April is upset because Mrs. Lady is wet.

As I was changing in my room, I thought about Jack trying to get home, and wondering if he tries to cross the stream, he could be swept away. We set Mrs. Lady on the table, and straightened her hair. Mason had changed into his only dry clothes outside, which had been rolled into that blanket I carried. I couldn't let him just sit out there in the cold, so I told him to come in and I will fix supper.

He rolled up an old sheet and stuffed it under the door to keep out the frogs, and brought his guitar, and sat by the fire. As I heated the stove and cut up the meat for stew, I realized I had not felt nearly as sick today. Maybe it was all the fussing around, and the fright, maybe it just took it all out of me.

When the biscuits were in the oven, I sat for a minute to rest my feet while they cooked. I asked Mason if he played that guitar or just carried it for someone, and he kind of smiled and said he picked a bit, so I said, Well, would you pick a tune for us?

So he did, he played and sang, songs I have not heard mostly, one called Clementine, and one about the Red River, and I said I have crossed the Rio Grande twice when I was a girl, but not the Red. Then he said his voice wasn't so good, but I could hear the tune in it, and it was a nice voice for a ranch hand.

We passed a pleasant enough evening, and Mason seems like a nice man, and doesn't give me reason to suspect he has a bad streak in him at all. He is about as old as my Papa would be now I think, and he likes to hear me talk about books I have read, and said he never learned to read. Then he asked me if he could trouble me to read to him, and I said surely, and we talked about which book to start with, and so I began to read Treasure Island aloud.

The rain fell. Frogs croaked outside the door, and I finally put Toobuddy into the back storeroom to keep him from eating them. I ate only a few bites of stew, but the biscuits set well so I felt pretty fair. He listened hard to the story of Treasure Island like it was an amazing thing to him to hear a story like that, and after more than two chapters said he knew I was tired, but he'd like to hear more tomorrow. Well, I couldn't let the man sleep outside in the frogs and the cold, and however many more snakes could be on the porch by now. So I said, You better bunk here by the fire, and he made him a place on the floor, and we turned out the lamps.

Just before I turned in, Mason said to me, Ma'am? Don't you worry about your man. He's got sense enough not to cross that water like it is. I laid awake and thought about Mama and Harland and Melissa, and I know they are on a rocky place up high, so they are probably fine. Albert and Savannah too, are higher than most places around. But the Maldonados are lower and further down the stream bed, where the water is likely running all the harder.

Jack will not be here. He can't get through.

February 11, 1886

Mason went to feed this morning, shivering and wearing his wet clothes from yesterday so he would have a dry set for the house. I made him coffee and pancakes and bacon, and he said it warmed him through the bones. The water seems down, and I saw clear sky through some clouds, but later at the afternoon the clouds thickened up again and rain fell more heavy than before.

We sat by the fire and I mended some clothes. April built a square with her blocks and sat Mrs. Lady in it, proclaiming her safe from everything bad, snakes and rains and frogs and bad men.

Doesn't she ever want to come out and see the world? I said.

No, said April.

I think she does, I said, I think she wants to be mostly safe, but to see outside too, and not be shut up in there all day.

She can have a window, said April, and removed one block.

If I was her, I said, I'd want a door too.

No. Bad men come in the door. Don't want door.

Mason smiled at me then, She'll want a door soon enough, he said. Seems like they just grow up so fast now days. We talked about his family, grown and gone, and his wife who died of cancer. He was a lonely man.

I read more of Treasure Island to him, and it pleased him a great deal. It seems to me there are so many lonely people in this world, and so little of life is kind and good. In a way, I am thankful for this flood, since without it, I might never have talked to him much, and Mason is a nice fellow. Another day passed before us, and it was night and dark, when the rain finally stopped falling.

February 12, 1886

We have tried to inspect all the place for damage. My garden is nearly washed away, just full of rubble and stones, and one side of the fence down. Beaumont is standing on his island bellowing for food. The horses are cold and shivering, and Rose looked at me with her big sweet eyes and I felt mighty guilty leaving her in the cold and rain, but her feet were not going to rot.

The stream is flowing, thick and muddy but fast, and tumbling things along with it. I saw a pig float by, and it scared me because it looked like a person's pink-skinned body at first. From where we can go to the south it looks like the neighbors are in about the same shape, just nearly washed away, but I see the roof on a house, and I hope they are fine but we are trapped here on my land and can't tell for sure.

I helped Mason all I could, and sure as I thought, if I stay busy I don't feel quite as sick, but food still doesn't look or smell good at all. And things I used to like don't taste right. I used to love eggs but now I don't think I could eat an egg and keep it down for all the tea in China.

I heard a sound and thought it was one of the cats, but when I went outside I saw in the distance my Mama waving an apron high over her head and calling my name. She was across the muddy water, and jumped when she saw me. Then she hollered, Baby is coming! Savannah's baby! Something's wrong, Sarah!

I'm coming! I called to her.

No, she shouted back, Too dangerous. Just want you to pray! Have to go now, and she turned and hurried away.

Mason, I said, I have to get to Savannah's house.

But, he said, You heard what she said. Your Mama just wanted you to know about it and say a prayer, she don't want you to come.

I took a deep breath, Well, Mason, Nobody on this earth is closer to God than Savannah, and if He has to listen to <u>me</u> praying to get to her, we are all in a world of trouble. I think she needs someone nearby, not just off somewhere praying.

He just nodded, and said, Maybe, Mrs. Elliot, it ain't that. Then he closed his mouth a second and said, Let's see what we can do.

All up and down the stream, the banks we knew were gone and the tumbling rocks and branches made fierce ripples in the brown water. Mason studied and studied.

Maybe, I said, I could jump it on a horse. Rose jumps real fine.

No, Ma'am! He said, and got all stiff in the neck. No, Ma'am, I won't have it. I won't be a part of you jumping a horse in your condition. No, no, no! There'll be no more of that, you ain't going to do it. No, Ma'am.

Well, all right, I said, What then?

He studied it more. It's lower here, but wider. If I lassoed that tree yonder, and we'll pull 'er tight, and see if she holds at the roots, then you could ride a horse, and hold that rope, run through the bit. He got the rope, and I saddled up Rose and brought her down to the rope he had cast. He tied it tightly around a palo verde, because they have long roots, he said, and I mounted up and he handed April to me. Then he took her reins and fed one over, and started to lead us into the water.

Mason, I said, Don't you walk across, it's too dangerous.

He just looked at me and said, You know, Ma'am, it does a man good to pray now and again, and he kept walking into the water.

It got deeper and deeper, and Rose swayed, half swept away, trying to swim with her feet, Mason struggling to keep her footed on the ground. He was over waist deep and the water came up to Rose's belly at the lowest place. It seemed like we were in the rushing water forever, and then suddenly we were on the other side, and Rose bounded up, fighting the slick mud, but safe and sound.

When we got to Albert's house, I could hear Savannah crying from the yard. Albert looked up and didn't seem surprised to see me a bit. It started last night, he said, around midnight. The baby should have come by now. She's having a bad time.

Mason stayed with Albert and they took April to Mama's to be with Harland and Melissa and the little boys, and I went and found Mama brushing Savannah's hair and talking to her, making a long braid.

Then another pain took her, and she cried again. Sarah, she said to me, It hurts so bad this time, so bad!

What shall I do? I said to her, what can I bring you? But her only answer was another cry of pain.

We stayed and comforted her, and finally around two o'clock, she said, I have to push.

Then the pains started worse and worse, and Mama and I got ready to take the baby as it started to be born. Mama said, Oh dear, Savannah, this baby's turned bottom first. Suddenly there was a frightening rush of blood and water, and the baby was born.

A little girl! I said. Very small, I thought, too small. Savannah cried out again. Mama wrapped the baby and cut the cord.

It's over, dear, Mama said, It's over now.

No! yelled Savannah, and pushed harder and harder.

Mama, I said, Mama there's another one! This time a baby's head came first, and the little thing started to cry tiny baby mews with only its head born.

Savannah said, I can't push any more, I can't. She started to cry in heartbreaking sobs.

Push, Savannah, I said. Then I started to say a prayer in my head, while with my mouth I said, Come on, you can! Push again, it's almost through! She tried and tried, but nothing happened. The baby mewed. Finally she put her own hands on her stomach and pushed with her hands, and the baby was born. Another tiny little girl. Twins. Precious and perfect, but so very small. Savannah collapsed like a little rag doll in the bed.

Mama and I cleaned the babies and put them by her sides. Albert and Mason were sitting on the porch, nervously trying to keep talking about the rain and flood. Mama crooked her finger, and Albert just jumped off his chair, and ran to Savannah.

Twins! Oh, my goodness, he said, Thank the Lord. Twins.

Girls, said Savannah. She has named them Rachel and Rebeccah, and has put a little thread around Rachel's foot because they look so much alike. Albert bent over her and kissed her head. I left them alone and went and sat on the porch.

February 14, 1886

I was never more surprised than to find my brother Albert banging on my door in the small of the morning. Sarah, he says, will you come with me quick? Savannah is real sick.

What shall I bring? I said to him.

Traveling clothes, he said. I'm taking Savannah to the hospital. Mama is on her way over here to tend April if you'll agree to come with us. I know Savannah'd want you near.

My heart started pounding. Oh, Albert, I said, don't you even ask. I'm nearly dressed, just don't wake April. Neither of us said another word to each other. I got up behind him on his bare-backed horse, holding a couple of big quilts to help bundle Savannah in. There on Albert's porch were Mama and Melissa and Harland, ready to walk to my house. They were holding Savannah's children and comforting the ones that were wakeful. As soon as they saw us on the road they started toward us, for my house. I could see their breath in the cold morning air lit by the lanterns they carried.

When she got next to me, Mama said she thinks Savannah is failing, she is getting weaker instead of stronger. Mama said, Sarah don't look so afraid in front of her, if she sees you looking at her like that, she'll be sure she's dying. I went with Albert to hitch his horses, he is taking the four-in-hand to make better time. All at once he sat on a bale of hay and put his face in his hands and shook all over.

I put my arm around his shoulders and he said, Oh, God, I will never ask for another thing my entire life. Just don't take my Savannah away. Don't take her, Lord, I can't live without her, and then he said, Take me, please, take me. Let me die, only save her, God.

Suddenly he got up and moved quicker than ever. I tried to say She'll get well, while we worked, but as soon as I said the words I was filled with dread and worry. Oh Lord, I thought, please save her. Just do this one thing and leave Savannah here. Albert and I are taking her to the hospital. When we went to get her and put her in the wagon, she just cried pitifully and said, Somebody please love my babies when I'm, and then she fell deep asleep and we couldn't wake her.

It was dark and cold, and I shook like I never have before. Albert carried her to the wagon as gentle as if she was made of eggshells. Even under the light of a dim lamp, she has black rings around her eyes and looks so pale, paler than I have ever seen anyone since my brother Clover died of the snake bite.

February 15, 1886

We reached St. Mary's Hospital by 10:30. The road was terrible. It didn't rain but we were caught in mud twice, and four times we had to ford washes running hard with rocks and broken trees that scared the horses. Albert and I were soaked through and covered with mud. They have sent a telegram for a specialist in Prescott. If he is willing to ride hard he might get here in two days.

February 16, 1886

I am sitting in a little room they have in this hospital for folks to wait for news of their loved ones. The sky is low and gray and ugly and this room is dark with only a single, small globe lamp. It is early morning and no one is here but me. Albert is talking with the doctors. The special doctor from Prescott still hasn't arrived. They won't let me go to Savannah and that is the hardest thing I can bear. I feel as if God is tearing my sister from me and these heartless people will not even let me say goodbye. They say it is best for her.

How will she know we loved her if no one is there to see her through heaven's gates? I cannot imagine anything more cruel than to make Savannah pass to her reward all alone in a strange place. Albert tells me every time he comes in that he needs me to be here with him. I want to see Savannah. I have been through this with my brother, my Papa, my first husband, and a host of strangers dying, and now I cannot be with my best and truest friend on this earth.

Albert came to the waiting room looking like the most broken man I've ever seen. He sat by me and told me they are not giving her much hope, that doctor still has not come, and they have packed her in ice to try to stop her bleeding and the ice hurts her so that she begs him to take it away. I stood up and ran toward the door, and I was going to run to Savannah, to find her, somewhere in this place, and make her feel better.

No, Albert said. He stood in my way and took hold of my shoulders. You can't. If you go to her she will know she is dying.

Albert, I said, she isn't a fool. She knows.

No, he said again. She mustn't give up hope.

And then I cried, and Albert and I just held onto each other. Albert, I said finally, she asked me to love your children. I thought I'd get killed by Indians or some horse or something. I've been counting on her to be there.

Oh, no, Sarah. Don't say that, he said to me, and shook his head. Then we didn't talk at all, just sat and stared at the floor or out the window at the gray sky. After a while, a nurse came in and said the special doctor had ridden night and day, and just arrived. He asked Albert to come to him.

Sometime in the afternoon, a nun brought in a pot of coffee and some bread and butter sandwiches. I couldn't stand the smell and started to get sick and had to leave the room. Outside in the cold it was dismal but the air felt good in my lungs. I walked, trying to get control of my insides, wishing Jack was here. I don't know what I wanted him to do, except that if he was here I know things would work out fine. Lands, how will I take care of April and this baby and Savannah's little Clover and Joshua and twin baby girls? How will anything go on without her? Who will write Mr. Lawrence in Texas? Probably me. And I will have to write Ernest, too. I must put down this terrible thing on paper and relive it every time.

When I went back inside the room was empty still, and I tried to start a letter to Mr. Lawrence. Maybe he will pray for her and she will hang on for his sake.

I was glad to see Albert come in again. Two nurses were with him and a short man with a thick gray beard. They told me he was Doctor Springer from Prescott. He said very plainly that Savannah has nearly bled to death. Then he said he has a brand new, special treatment to give Savannah extra blood from other people, but he checked Albert's and it is the wrong kind, so would I mind checking to see if they could give her mine? I put my hand to my throat, and imagined butchering a steer and the way it's bled out.

All of it? I said. I'd give it except I have a baby girl and one on the way.

The doctor looked real concerned for a minute, and wrinkled up his forehead. We will only take about a cupful or two, he said. Not enough to hurt the baby, and only a few drops at first to see if it will match.

I'm sure we're the same, I told him, Sisters under the skin closer than some by nature.

I will not write that I was not afraid. They stuck a needle and a tube in my arm, not my throat as I thought they would. Albert sat in a chair between us. Savannah looked as gray as if she was already gone. All the ice was gone and they were warming her with hot blankets. As I was lying near Savannah and they pumped my blood into her, I thought I could see her turning pinker by the minute. It went real slow. For two hours I laid there, and finally the doctor said that was all, but they had found one of the Sisters, Sister Magdelena, whose blood also matched Savannah's. They started as soon as we swapped places on the narrow beds. They gave me a blanket and I was so tired from all the worry, I slept until dawn.

When dawn came, Savannah called Albert's name softly and I woke right up. Sister Magdelena had stayed with us, and she made signs and said, Thank you, Virgin Mother. Then Savannah said her feet were cold, so Sister Magdelena brought more hot blankets and Albert and I found an old fashioned metal warmer to put next to her feet. I am ever thankful for Doctor Springer. He stayed up with Savannah all night, and this morning said he was going to rest in an office but he would be just down the hall. He said they will probably give her more blood this afternoon, from someone else. He smiled at me real nice and said I should rest today.

February 24, 1886

Albert brought Savannah home today. She has turned around and will stay with us. Mama said the angels in heaven will be lonesome a while longer. I couldn't say anything about it. Every time I opened my mouth, I nearly choked. I sat in her room and read to her a spell, and brought her the babies to nurse, and helped her with her private needs. She is weak as a newborn kitten, but she smiles and says thank you to everything I do. The sun is shining today through clouds scattered like patchwork blocks across the sky. Albert is a new man, although he looks real old and tired. Oh Lord, is all I can say. My heart is overflowing.

February 28, 1886

Jack came today, and we shared stories about the flood and what had happened in town, the birth of Savannah's little girls and her troubles. Mason is living in the parlor because the adobe shed I had built is so washed away that one side is falling in. I am so thankful I had not left my books out there as they would be all ruined.

He took April on his shoulders and we walked up and down the creek, amazing ourselves at the washed away look of everything and the brush caught high in the trees at the water line from the flood. Jack, I said, there's something been on my mind I want to say to you.

So he sidestepped some silty mud and April laughed at the bouncing. I'm here, he says.

I followed them, and said, You told me you want me to be careful not to let the children grow up without a mother. Well, don't you ask them to grow up without a father, either.

What do you mean? he says.

You know what I mean, I told him.

It isn't the same. A child needs a mother lots more than a father, he says.

That comes easy from you, seein' as you still got yours, I said.

He quit hopping around with April and looked down at his sloppy boots. I'm sorry, Sarah. I didn't mean that. But it isn't the same.

You don't know that. Maybe a boy needs a father to teach him man things. This here might be a boy, you know. I can be a mother to him but I can't be a father. And April doesn't need to lose any more people either. There was so many things I wanted to say, and none of them would come out. I didn't know how to put to words that I didn't ever want to wait, not knowing if he was alive or dead, and I didn't want to have to be brave for the children's sake.

Run, Papa! squealed April. Run like a horse!

So Jack ran a little, and she jiggled up and down on his shoulders like a jug of syrup.

All I'm saying, I said as he ran around me, is think of us before you jump headlong into something.

Jack turned his head up at April. We've got to do what Mama says, don't we, Little Bitty?

April nodded.

Let's give her a salute, he says, and he snaps to attention and says Yes Ma'am, General Elliot!

March 2, 1886

Jack worked hard yesterday and all day today, side by side with Mason, fixing and cleaning mud from every place. Rudolfo and Celia have a new baby and all of them spent two nights on their roof in the cold rain, and they have mud in the house on everything. Rudolfo says he is going to build a trench clear around their house, so if it ever happens again, the water will not get so close.

We will be back tomorrow to help our neighbors clean out the mud, and all of us have to dig out our wells when the water level goes down more. Jack went to the stage station with the wagon, hoping to pick up the parts for the windmill he ordered, but it had not arrived. He will be staying a few more days, too, and I am so happy for that.

Having him here almost a week is so nice. Every night, without fail, I sleep snug in his arms, wrapped up warmer than I ever thought I could be in the winter.

March 10, 1886

Yesterday morning Jack told me goodbye, and kissed April. I looked him in the eyes, knowing I saw something more than just a goodbye. When will you be back? It's not soon, is it?

No, he said, it might be a long time. Geronimo and twenty or so other Apaches are hiding in Mexico, and it's a bad trip, and the weather's terrible.

Why don't they just leave him alone? I said. Leave him in Mexico.

Jack shook his head and said, Can't. He's stirring up more tribes to rebel and raid. He was sent to a reservation but broke away and escaped, and there's a warrant for him now. He's supposed to surrender, but he didn't show up, and we have to go get him. I might be a month or more, maybe two. If there's messengers sent, he said, which there usually is, I'll get word to you. If that windmill comes, just have Mason lay it up near the well. When I get back we'll build it up.

Toobuddy followed Jack to the end of the yard. Take him with you, I said, I don't mind.

Jack looked at the dog and pointed at the house, and said, Get home, boy! No, Sarah, it's too far, and he'd get in the way or get worn out or something. We'll be moving right along.

I watched him ride away, and a terrible feeling of dread hung over my head.

Later Harland brought me a letter they picked up with their mail, and said Albert and Mama both got one just like it too, from the Lawrences, probably about Savannah's sickness.

Dear Sarah,

How sorry we are to tell you the news. Poor Ulyssa has taken the tuberculosis. She is going there to the Territories for the lung asylum in Tucson. Her doctor said it is the only hope, but she is terribly sick. Also, because she is so very sick, you must not visit her or see her at all until her doctors allow. You are so devoted about letter writing that she has said your letters sustain her and she feels she is a part of your lives out there. I'm sure it will be a double comfort if you can write her. Don't be alarmed if she doesn't write back, it may be some time before she is well enough to. If she does write to you, press her letters with a hot flat iron heated like you would scorch a shirt, before opening it, to crush the disease out of it. Otherwise, we are all well, and although we have suffered some from being quarantined, it will be lifted next month as long as no one else shows signs of the consumption. Alice wants me to tell you she has learned to ride a horse. Take care. I will write more later.

Your friend and sister, Louisianna Lawrence

I am so sad for Ulyssa, and I just can't imagine why it is that some people's cup of life seems to be full of bitter water all the time. Savannah is heartbroken, and came to my house today, leaving her babies with Mama. She sat on my front porch and cried a long, long spell. She has not seen her loved ones since she left them in San Angelo, and now Ulyssa will be just a day's ride away and she still can't see her. I held her like a little child and rocked. She cried and held on to me and we sat on the porch until the sun went down. I asked God what did He mean by it all. It would be nice if Savannah could visit them in Texas, but I'm sure she is not strong enough to travel all that way. Finally she went home to nurse her little ones.

Tonight when I tried to sleep I laid there, cold, in the dark, and felt a tiny, tiny wiggle inside me, and I think it is the baby. So I lit a lamp and got up to write this piece for a spell. I wanted to cry, but I felt too lonesome to cry, sort of like if there's no one to hear my tears, there's no use to shed them. My chest hurts inside when he's not here. Damn that Army, and Geronimo, and duty and honor and saluting and folderol. Come home, Jack. Just come home.

April 18, 1886

The pieces of my windmill lie in the rain and sun and wind, near a well which my hired man, tired and overworked, has dug out again for me, as another storm filled it with mud. Mason is building a water tank with cement and rock. The garden is in and leafing. Rose came to season and I think one of the draft horses got her, because they are always close by her.

Beaumont got out and decided to eat my rose bush, and I knocked him in the head with a two by four, and chased him away from it, picking up the petals from the last rose he had crushed. Then I hit him again for good measure.

Savannah's babies are bigger and stronger now. She is almost back to her old self, although she is tired all the time. Albert has bought lumber and cement and nails, and when it is dry enough, he works on building another room on their house. There has been no word from Jack all these weeks.

This baby I'm carrying moves all the time now. And I have plumped up, more than with April, and I'm not sick anymore at all. In fact I feel pretty good. I have finished reading Treasure Island to Mason, and he liked it fine. I would give anything to know Jack is safe and coming home soon.

April 22, 1886

A few days ago, a line of riders came this way early in the morning, all wearing blue uniforms. They said Jack was still south, traveling with General Crook and hunting Geronimo. I offered them food, but they refused it and only watered up then pressed on toward town.

This morning another rider in a uniform stopped on the sandy cliff across the road from my house, and looked this way a long time before he edged his horse down the steep side. I felt it was Jack even before I knew it with my eyes. My heart was filled when I saw him, but filled with anger and hurt and love and fear and longing all at once.

When I had him in my arms I pounded my fists against his chest, and tears ran down my face, and I kissed him hard. He was purely confused, I'm sure.

April 30, 1886

Jack is gone again, heading south instead of north toward town. He stopped at the stage station to forward a letter to the post, but returned to his duty and Geronimo. I told him I'd wear a feather in my hair and leather moccasins if he would stay home and hunt for me instead, and not give him near as much trouble finding me. But Jack just laughed, and said, Sarah Elliot, you are a treasure for sure. And he rode off.

I told Mama he said that and then she didn't feel sorry for me one bit, but quoted the Bible saying, Where a man's treasure is, there is his heart also.

Right now, I said, I'd rather have his hide close by too.

May 5, 1886

A short letter came to the station from Jack just two days ago. He says they have ventured far to the east, and will enter Tucson from the north where it is far away from the ranch. Then he said to be prepared for some Army folderol and ceremony, and not to expect to see him before the tenth, but be sure and come to the fort at one o'clock on the tenth.

Well, I don't understand why this is, and I can't shake that feeling of something being wrong. One o'clock, the tenth of May. So I took the letter to all my family, and showed Mr. Sherrill, and we will plan a trip to town. I told Albert this was just like Jack to plan something and just expect the world to stop for his plans, but

Albert just smiled and said that's how the army is, he figured. And Savannah hasn't been to town for months except for being sick, and he is determined to get her some new shoes and yardgoods, so she will be glad to go.

We left yesterday afternoon and took a slow pace to town for the sake of the new babies. Harland drove my wagon with me, Mama, April, and Clover and Joshua. Albert drove with Savannah and a canvas on the back so the baby girls are out of the sun and she can nurse in private.

We made camp by the south end of town, and I dressed in my best things today, although I had to let out my dress and put a long shawl over the back where it won't close. We went by the asylum first and left messages and a box of things for Ulyssa, and then found a place to get Savannah some shoes.

Finally, it got close to twelve o'clock, so we finished our shopping and ate a bite, and drove to the fort where we all went inside. I asked the first man I could take hold of where I could find Captain Elliot, and he looked at me kind of odd, but said, well, up there on the podium, Ma'am, but you'll have to sit in the audience until it's over. I didn't have a chance to ask him until what's over, because a man in a uniform just covered with gold braid and shiny buttons stood up and held out his hands.

It was General Crook, I remembered him from the speech in town, and Jack was behind him. We found some seats as quick as we could, each of us holding a child on our knees. One of the twins began to fuss, and Savannah opened up her blouse and hushed that baby with a breast.

I could tell Jack was walking with a limp, but I don't think anyone else noticed it. Then the General said some fancy words and it was hard to hear because he was facing Jack the whole time, and then he hung a medal on his chest, and called it The Congressional Medal of Honor, for bravery and exceptional action in the line of duty or some such. I wish there was some way I could recall all those big words and write them. Then there was another speech, and two other soldiers got medals too, and a woman dressed in a black dress and veil received a medal for her dead husband.

Next, there came some other talking, and the General read a long letter he called a commendation, and told Jack to stand again, and pronounced that he was no longer a Lieutenant, even though he is a private soldier, but has the rank of Captain. I have always thought of him as Captain Elliot though I know he has been a lieu-tenant for these last few years, but that is why the soldier at the gate looked odd, it was a secret from them until just now.

April stood on my knees when she saw him, and the crowd had just gotten quiet when she hollered That's my Papa Jack! at the top of her lungs. I saw Jack break into a grin, and he tried to hide it while he saluted the General real smart, then turned to me and April, and gave us just a little salute off the tip of his hat too.

Pretty soon Savannah's other baby started to cry, and she cov-ered her chest with two babies and we fixed a shawl over her. The speeches were over, and some soldiers marched by in a formation, one of them playing a drum as they stepped. Then it was all over, and people stood up and began to wander around, talking to each other.

Captain Elliot, I said, touching his sleeve. Would you sit here by me for just a minute? Jack looked at me and tipped his hat to the folks he was talking to.

Yes, Mrs. Elliot? he said. Then he whispered so softly I wasn't sure I heard it, You are a sight for sore eyes. I can't wait to get you in my arms.

I just cleared my throat and tried to keep my face from glowing red. Well, Captain Elliot, I said, would it trouble you in the midst of all this military goings on, to shed the light on just what has occurred here today? What is that medal for? They aren't handing them out like penny candy, so you must have done something.

He looked away, kind of tired. Then he said real quiet, Ever notice how if you do something hare-brained and you fail, you're an idiot, but if you succeed, you're a hero?

I studied him and thought to myself then that I spend all my days trying not to do anything hare-brained in the first place.

Jack was home again today, and the weather is powerfully hot. We had an argument over nothing really, but he made me really mad, and so we are sitting on the porch in the heat, watching the sun go down, and it is the first time I know of he has been so cross that we just can't talk.

He finally told me that he is going on another long campaign, and he said he was terribly sorry for acting so cross. The General says this time no one is going home until Geronimo is back on the reservation, or dead, or in prison. He will have a week off, then he has to go, and doesn't know when he will be back. It may be all summer long, it may be after the baby comes. He is just tied in knots, he says.

Well, I think to myself, that he is a private soldier, he could just quit, or say No, I'm sitting this one out, but that doesn't occur to him to say, so I'm not sure I will make the suggestion. At any rate, he is in a better humor and I am thankful for that. I'd rather be around Jack in a bad mood than most other men when they're trying to pay me a compliment.

Just as I thought the day's excitement was over, a strange and wondrous noise came to us over the hills. It was a cattle drive headed this way, and Jack saddled up quick and rode out to them, and stayed gone a long time. It was his Papa. Chess came himself, driving with about twenty men and two hundred and fifty head of fine cattle. So much to do.

May 26, 1886

He rode out of here early in the morning. I wanted to cry but instead I just told him he was the orneriest cuss I knew, leaving a pregnant wife with all those cowboys and a herd like that.

Well, Chess heard my words, and said, Miss Sarah, I had fully planned to stay a while, to help out and such, if you'd allow. So now I have two men sleeping in my parlor, and twenty more sleeping on the porch, and I can't go to the outhouse without some man seeing, which I do so often with the baby pressing hard against my insides.

I waited until Jack rode away, and laid myself on my bed and just sobbed. Chess came to my door, and said, Don't worry, he'll be back, he always comes back.

I hate him, I cried. He doesn't love me. He shouldn't leave me. I hate him. Chess put his hand on my shoulder and I took hold of it. Oh, Chess, I love him so much it hurts! It's not fair, men get to go off and chase around the country and get medals for doing stupid things and women get to sit home and worry.

Then I was done crying. Crying over that man is a waste of water. And I still have to go to the outhouse again.

May 29, 1886

Chess made me tell him all about the story Jack told of his winning that medal, and he seemed real proud, and didn't once say what a fool stunt it was to ride that horse off a cliff over the top of them Indians' heads and save that Federal Marshal and the two Army officers, one a major and one a captain. I think those men should have not got themselves into such a fix, but all he said was, Jack's a hoot, ain't he?

April is happy as a fat cat to have her Grandpa living with us. I had to scold her, and then I scolded him too, for just laughing at her naughtiness. I told him I wasn't going to have such a bad girl, and that he should realize that she needed more than just love and petting, she needs a firm hand and a good backbone, or she'll be an unhappy lady when she's grown.

Chess said he saw the right in my words, and he will try.

July 1, 1886

A letter has come from Jack. They are standing off in the Chiricahua mountains, but see no sign of Geronimo surrendering. He must have plenty of squirrel, deer and water up there, but, he says, an Indian warrior can last through starvation and thirst like no white man ever thought about. Then he closes with *Give my regards to Pop and the men and your Mama and the rest of the family, and, hug April from her new Papa. I miss you sorely and my anger grows daily toward this Geronimo that he keeps me away from you when you need me so much. At night when I see the stars I will be thinking always of you. Your devoted, JE.*

July 4, 1886

Today Chess fixed a broken vane on the windmill, and Harland came over and climbed up to the top with him, and I don't know who I was more scared for, the one too old to be up there or the one too young. Mama came over and said, Sarah, that Mr. Sherrill came to my house all gussied up and said he'd like to pay a call.

So I said, Well, what did you say to him?

She just looked curious, and said, I told him to sit a spell and have some watermelon with Harland and Melissa and me. And then he did.

Well, Mama, what did you expect? You told him to sit right down.

She said, Yes, but I didn't think he would. What's a man want with a old woman like me?

So we talked a long time about men and women, and Mason in particular, and she decided at first she wanted no more attention from Mr. Sherrill, but then when she got ready to go home, she asked me did I think he liked raisin cookies.

I am so glad to have Chess here. Mostly we get along fine, and he takes my mind off many worries. It's too bad his son is not so inclined. We have had many fine talks, and along with Mr. Sherrill, this little ranch has turned again into a business.

August 26, 1886

A man I hardly know has ridden up to my front porch and let himself in and sat on my rocking chair looking thinned out and exhausted.

Jack, I said, Jack?

He just looked at me, and closed his eyes, and started talking fast. I can't believe I made it, he said. Geronimo surrendered yesterday. I'm home. You're still here. Lord, I'm tired. My horse is near dead, and my back feels like it broke in half a long ways back.

Suddenly, I reached over and felt his head, and he was burning up with a fever. Jack, you come get in bed, I told him, and I pulled on his arm.

No, he said, just let me rest a minute.

Well, I scolded him good then, and told him to get his ornery hide into bed and stop arguing with me because if he only came home to argue he could just mount up and ride away. He just looked at me and kind of grinned, and I could see it was my same old Jack, but his eyes looked red and glazed, and I could tell he was bad sick.

August 28, 1886

For two days Jack stayed in bed fighting a fever, and I can tell it is from not eating and sleeping out in the weather. He said in Mexico it has rained for three weeks almost without stopping, and about as bad as the flood we had here. Every night he went to bed wet and cold. At last he is ready to get up and his fever is gone.

Now he is back, and I feel like my arm or something has been missing and now is returned to me. It is a hard feeling to describe, it is like the smell after a rain, and a paper journal will not hold the feeling of it. And we are to have sixty days together, a long leave of absence, he calls it.

When we were alone, I told Jack that his Pop told me all about him going to the West Point Academy, and it wasn't just any bend in a river either but a big, fancy school, and that I never thought he had gone to a college like that, and asked him why didn't he say so to me?

He didn't really have a good answer, except that he said it wasn't such a big thing and he was just a fair student, not good at anything.

But, I said, You went to college! You have all that learning and all those fancy things and letters and such, it is so a big thing.

He started to ask me how was the windmill working and did I mind the bunkhouse the cattlemen had built for themselves and such.

I wonder if he really knows who I am, sometimes, and that I never in all my life have set foot in a schoolhouse, because I told him that but he wasn't listening. Then I got to thinking maybe he is ashamed of me being ignorant, and the thought got bigger in my head all day long until it was all I could think about. The thought of him being ashamed of me stabbed me with every breath I took like it was a big thorn deep in my chest. It hurt so bad it hurt clear up into my jaw. Finally, just before supper I asked him those very words, Jack are you ashamed that I'm so ignorant?

He said to me, That was the only thing you ever have said that wasn't smart, Sarah. In the first place, you aren't ignorant, and in the second place . . . and then he just let the words wander off like whatever it was, was too much for him to say.

So I didn't let it be, and I said, In the second place what?

In the second place, he said again, Education doesn't keep a person from being a fool, and the lack of it doesn't keep a person from being intelligent. Then he said no more about it, but I am thinking of those words and trying to figure out just what he meant.

April got a bad splinter in her foot, and we fussed for over an hour trying to get it out with her screaming at the top of her lungs. Finally, Jack held her tight and Pop had to cut her foot with a knife, but Pop managed to get out a ragged piece of ironwood as long as my fingernail. We bandaged her up, and then Jack held her and rocked her to sleep, even though I wanted her. Jack said No, you get to hold her all the time, this is my turn.

So I watched my baby girl cuddle in his lap and go to sleep. After he put her in bed, he said, How's our second one? and patted on my belly.

Just then the little baby kicked hard at his hand, and we both were startled, and I said, Well, looks like he's pretty ornery. I wonder where he gets it?

Jack just shrugged and kissed my cheek, and then whispered in my ear, He gets it from his mother.

September 25, 1886

Fall is in the air today. I sent Mason with April to Mama's this morning. I have felt small pulling feelings all night until now, although no pain at all yet. Jack has gone overnight with the men putting up fence, so he is not home nor anyone else, but Mason will leave April with Melissa and send Mama and Savannah here. I told him not to hurry, and stay for supper if she'll have you, for if this is anything like the last one, I won't be needing her until late tonight or maybe tomorrow.

So he has been gone for awhile, and I have stayed busy collecting things we will need for the birthing. All is ready, and there is no pain, so I picked some weeds in the garden, and fed the hens and brought in eggs. Still nothing happened, so I read some and put on a roast of beef to have for supper, and put some little pies on the griddle and fried them with fruit inside.

I sat on the porch for a while, just listening. Chickens and guineas in the yard were making their little quiet chucking sounds. My biggest Buff Orpington rooster is on the small corral fence letting the world know he is in charge, all puffed up and sassy. There is nothing more silly than a rooster taking over the world, but every day he thinks he can. I wonder if we are just a little part of the world, like that rooster, and that the real things go on around us while we strut in our own yards trying to take charge of things.

Well, it happened so fast, I hardly knew what was happening. Just after noon, I felt at last a tugging feeling that I knew meant I was about to have the baby. It started out regular and even, but I felt very little except the tightness, so I sat up in the rocking chair on the porch snapping long beans, intending to go inside later after Mama got here and all. All at once, I had a sharp, terrible gripping in my insides, and I doubled over and couldn't breathe for a minute. Then there was a few more tight feelings, then another terrible pain. Suddenly I remembered everything about having a baby just as clear as yesterday. I couldn't remember not remembering.

Just at that time, here came Jack riding up and calling out that Chess had stayed on the range with the men, and I tried to stand, but instead I half stood and half doubled up, and made a moaning and dropped the bowl of beans all over the porch.

His face got all worried, and he said, Are you here alone?

Yes, I said, Mason went to get Mama, but they won't be back real soon.

Jack said he was filthy dirty, and he started stripping off clothes fast, and bathed real quick right on the front porch while I sat in the chair, kind of pained, but not too bad. He got dressed and then he said, Come on, honey, I didn't want to touch you as dirty as I was.

So he took my hand and I made two steps and then started to fall. He scooped me in his arms, and another pain came real hard. Jack, I said, Mama isn't going to come soon, and this baby is! You have to help me.

So he took a couple of deep breaths, and said Tell me what to do, so I did.

It was real strange how this peaceful feeling came over me then. I fully expected to be terrified like the first time, and to scream myself out for days and days. But Jack was here, and he let me pull against his hands and didn't even flinch through the whole thing. I counted only five more pains. Five more, and into his waiting towel came a big baby boy.

Jack was grinning, but I said, He isn't crying, he's supposed to be crying. Shake him. And then I had another pain, and Jack shook the baby, and patted his back. The baby turned dark red and then blue. Jack! Shake him, spank him, something! I was yelling, when all of a sudden, the little fellow opened his mouth and coughed, and started breathing. He cried just a little mew, and then just went to sleep.

Jack said, Do you think he's dead?

No, I said, he's fine, now. I think he's just tired like his Mama.

Jack told me what time it was his son was born, and it was only 2:45 in the afternoon. I was feeling pretty sore later, but happy, and Jack did as good a job as any woman I've seen with everything. It's funny, because Jimmy would have delivered any animal on earth, except his own child. Jack just rolled up his sleeves and smiled and took hold of his son without a second thought, and was so tender with me, I'd rather have him tend me than anyone else.

Welcome home, little son. Little John Charles Elliot. Papa already called you Charlie after your Grandpa Chess, and laid you on my breast, and declared you ate like a horse for someone only a half hour old, then he said Charlie Horse, Charlie Horse, and rocked you to sleep.

September 29, 1886

Mama and Savannah were just as surprised as they could be that there was no birthing to be done by the time they got to my house. There was Jack, sitting on the porch steps by Toobuddy, and he led them to the room and showed off the little one just as pleased as punch.

Charlie is a good little rascal, and calm, much more than April had been as a baby. She is happy with her brother, except for yesterday when he had a crying time and she was plum fed up with hearing all that and told me to send him back to wherever he came from, he was too much nuisance.

Jack has a few more weeks here, and then will be going back to the fort, and he has asked me to think of moving the family there where there are houses for the officers, and rent is below cheap, and he will come home most every evening unless he is gone out of town. It is too soon after having a baby to do any driving to town, but I told him we will discuss it later on.

December 1, 1886

Chess left two weeks ago on a train for his home in Texas. I was sad to see him go, but I knew he couldn't stay forever, and he didn't want to leave his place over the winter. I hope I have learned enough about ranching from him in that short time to know what tools the hands need to do their jobs, and how to manage them, too. The cattle are not the orneriest part of ranching. For now, these fellows are working for their bed and board, as there will be no cash from it until next year. They have put up a bunkhouse and I have my hands full keeping two pantries stocked.

For my birthday this year, Jack gave me a book of twenty-three chapters—one, he said, for all my years—A History of the Americas, beginning with the settlers in the 1600's. I can hardly wait to read it all. But it seems I don't have three minutes to rub together. Some time soon I will take it on, maybe when Charlie is a few months older.

My biggest news is that Jack has made arrangements to move us into a spacious officer's house at the fort if I would say the word, as there is one empty and waiting for us. Just as I have gotten the hang of this ranching life, I have to think about leaving it. There are just too many changes all at once, and all this week I have felt tired just thinking about it all. I wrote a letter to a patent lawyer in Prescott, and got his word that since this spring my claim patent will finally be done with, it will be okay to run these cattle and have all the men living here and only visit it now and then, too. Then, I took to thinking about how much I missed Jack, and how so much of the time when he is around, he has to spend in Tucson near the fort, and how I could be nearby instead. It would save a horseshoe or two to put a few less miles between us, I suppose.

I was ready to tell him I decided I'd rather be together as a family than always living separate like this, but when he said, You know, if we live in town, April can go to school. That was all it took for me. I want her to go to school more than anything, so we will pack up just after Christmas. I have to tell my family. We have asked the whole bunch to come for a picnic tomorrow, since the weather has been gentle so far this winter. During our supper we will tell them our news.

January 3, 1887

Although I have not seen the quarters we will move to, Jack has told me much about them, and so I am trying to decide who will sleep where and all. I do not know how I will like living with all those people around all the time. I suppose it is noisy. Every day I look at this ranch, and think of all the memories soaked into the wooden walls and the dirt and the trees around. It will not disappear, but it won't feel like mine, anymore, I don't think.

Mason is staying on, and the ten hands that Chess kept around are willing to stay too. I have made an arrangement that one of the men will ride to Fort Lowell each Friday, and we will talk over business and such. And of course, it's not so far that I can't drive back here once a month or so, and stay, too, if Jack is going to be out of town. Then, whoever Mason sends to town can take back provisions and dry goods and tools if they're needed. During roundup in the spring I want to come back and help, or at least watch, and maybe living in town I can get wind of cattle buyers sooner, and take care of business there. Jack just shakes his head at it all, and says I have a natural leaning for business, so he will let me take the reins if I choose.

I feel like I don't much belong in a town. And I wonder what kind of life I will have, different than I have known before, of that I can be sure. Jack laughed and said I'd probably take a liking to it. Still, I swept over the little blue fingerprints in the floor, and got a hard place in my throat.

January 9, 1887

Savannah came over early this morning, and we talked a long spell over the heads of the children. She has made a quilt for Ulyssa, and embroidered flowers in each square, pansies, daisies, brown-eyed susans, and in the very center was a red rose on some dark blue, which I will take to her as soon as we get moved in.

She and I kept quiet for a while, and I made some coffee and gave all the little ones a cookie and set them in the parlor. I'll miss having you close by, I said.

Savannah's face got red and her smile turned down at the corners. Sarah, she said, you have to go where your husband is. The children need their father close.

I said, I just wish Jack would come live here instead. He doesn't need to be in the Army, he wants to. Even with us living in town he'll be riding off after first one thing and another.

Savannah just sipped her coffee. She said, You'll just have to treasure the times you are together, to make up for the loss of time.

I told her I don't know how I'll manage being married to Jack, it angers me the way he takes off all the time. She held my hands, and said, The Lord gives us all gifts in the people we know, and that I was not the kind to need or want a man around all the time telling me every step to take, so having Jack was the best mix of independence and love I could want. I suppose she's right. It would take more patience than I could muster to have someone underfoot all the time and trying to tell me what to do like some men do their women. Jack is about as ornery a man as I know. Yet, all I ever wanted was to be loved like Savannah, and I wonder if Jack does care for me that way, because I'm not much like her.

Mostly tonight I feel sort of lost and alone, like now I am up on a windy hill and looking toward a new direction where the wind never blew before. I am afraid to leave all that I know, nothing familiar will be nearby to keep me going. I will have to stand on the hill alone.

January 10, 1887

All is a flurry as we pack up and load crates. I don't feel of much use and I am tending the baby and Little Bitty, and he has to do most of the work. It's how it ought to be, Jack says. Then, about noon, he rode off to Albert's house to ask for the loan of his wagon, because there is a train load of books here that must go.

The hands have loaded pretty much everything. Charlie is sleeping in my lap. In a little pile beside me is Jack's saddle and outfit, which he is going to toss in the back with this rocking chair when we pull out. I picked up that old, old leather saddlebag and looked it over, wondering just why he never made a move without it. It was stiff with age and horse sweat, and it smelled bad. There was a big hole in it, too, and it was patched with clumsy stitches that looked like a child's.

The more I felt of it, I saw the patch was thick and heavier on that side, and the leather tie was coming out. I squeezed it, and it had something sewed inside it. So I began to pull the thong out of the little holes and to unwind it, going around and around.

Finally the patch came off, and it had been sewed over a kind of pocket inside that was full of stuff. I reached in and pulled out a little raggedy book, and my mouth fell open. The Duchess of Warwick and Her Sorrows by the Sea. The gold edges were long ago worn to green and the cover was broken and creased, and just as he said, a bullet had pierced right through it. That man has had that book all along.

I opened the cover and found folded inside it each of the letters that I had sent to him asking for the return of it. Goodness, how bad my spelling and punctuation was! I thought, laughing at myself. Then I found there was another folded piece of paper, and

I pressed open the creases and pushed the gunshot frayed place back together. It was a little letter all in Jack's neat hand.

February 15, 1882

Dear Miss Prine,

I cannot hope that you would understand my forwardness and my poor manners in writing this to you, as it is unforgivable to be so common with a lady as to tell her your feelings so abruptly. However, life is so uncertain in the Territories that I hope you will forgive me this impropriety for the sake of what I am about to say.

I lost my heart to you the moment you won that rifle from that blowhard and handed it back to him. Then I lost everything else to you when you stood up with a straight face and protected your family against what you thought would be a vision of horror. You have stolen my very heart away. I see your face, I hear your voice, I watch you walk, even in my sleep. You have my utmost admiration and fondest regards. If it were not for my own cowardice, I would have told you these things in person, and not given this letter in an Animal book, hoping you would turn the pages and find it some day.

I know that you want your other book returned so badly that you just ache for it, and for that it sorrows me that I cannot return it, but you must understand it is a matter of life and death that I keep it with me at all times. For you see, you have taken all my heart with you, and there is nothing left for me but the little piece of your heart that longs for your other book. So I must have it to continue breathing at all.

Please forgive the injustice of it all. I remain forever lost to you, and sustain myself only with a memory of one night when we shared a tenderness that went far beyond mortal bonds. You shared with me your fears, and most importantly, your trust as you slept quietly and safely in my arms. Unkind of you, to brutally expose a man to the sweetest thing a woman has to offer, her trust, and then to just slip away as if you cared nothing for him at all. However, it matters not what unkindness you show me, I have no heart any longer to feel it anyway. My dear, if there is any chance that you could possibly find a sliver of compassion for me, please write me in return. I promise

The letter stopped, unfinished. He had not enclosed it in the Animals of Africa book he returned to me as he had planned. Fancy words, too, all educated and clever, and he doesn't even talk that fancy.

It seems I am bound to love this character forever, soldier or no. I just hope and pray I can put up with him for the next fifty years or so.

Tears were pouring down my face but I managed to thread the stiff and cracked cord back into the patch before he got back with Albert's wagon. Then he packed up my books and it seemed to take just ten minutes or so. In that short time, everyone came to wave us off, even the Maldonados' whole family. Jack whistled to Toobuddy and that silly dog hopped up into Albert's borrowed wagon.

We are driving away, and I look back over my shoulder with a strange feeling of parting. It is not a lonely feeling, but just as I am always sad to close the cover on a book, I feel I have finished with this part of my life and will have to begin a new book. The last thing I saw was Savannah waving her bonnet toward us. Albert had his arm around her waist. Then I looked at Jack for a long minute, then I looked toward the horizon.

Jack whistled a little song, kind of merry and happy. He turned to me as we rounded the first bend away from my ranch and said, Mrs. Elliot, what are you smiling at, are you happy to leave?

No, I said, I'm not so happy to leave. It isn't that at all.

It is bitter cold here in Tucson, but this officer's house is tightly built of adobe and wood. The morning came with a bugle call, and Jack was already gone before it sounded. The children didn't wake because of it, though. It is a nice sound, and I expect it will start many a morning in my life from now on. The town has grown plenty but is still rough as a cob, although it feels safe here in the fort.

It seems this house is tightly built as long as the wind doesn't blow or rain hit it. Rain started late last night. By mid morning the ceiling began to fall in. Water is running down every wall of this place. It turns out the whole roof is made of poles and sod, and there are even a couple of old army blankets up there with dirt packed on them. I feared all day the whole mess would fall in on the children in the big room, so we have stayed in the nursery room for safety. Someone had left curtains hanging in the windows, which I thought was because they were so soiled no one would bother taking them along. Now I see why they are streaked and stained, it has rained like this before and no one bothered to fix this blessed roof. Jack says that as soon as this wet spell lets up, he will get some men here to put on a real roof.

January 21, 1887

Jack said the post commander will not approve of spending money to fix the officers' housing. I said to him I have no intention of staying in a place like this where mud drips on my babies and into the food while I cook. I can imagine in the summer it will be scorpions and spiders falling from that nasty ceiling. I've been saving soap money for a long time, and I just told him you hire some men to fix this here, and it will get paid for, and I don't care what the commander says.

But Jack says you can't just go building on some Army fort yourself, there's something called protocol that is rules of order and command. Well, I gave him a look from the corner of my eye, and just like I'd asked it to make my argument for me, a chunk of wet dirt and grass slopped onto the Franklin stove and splashed on his uniform. Then a centipede crawled out of the slop, running from the heat, and he stomped the thing dead real quick.

While the mud dripped down the side of the stove, hissing like it was cooking, Jack looked at me and made a determined face. General Elliot, Ma'am, he says. You are about to get a new roof. Then he snapped to attention and saluted me and went off to find the commander.

February 3, 1887

It appears some of the other officers' wives are real perturbed that our family has a new roof and they have all been putting up with the mud and grass ones for years. Well, I just think that is the problem, you put up with it instead of speaking your mind.

Baby Charlie is good natured and calm, not nearly as nervous and fretful as April was. When he wants to be heard, though, he can certainly make himself known. And I declare but he goes through diapers twice as fast as April. There is always a stack to be washed and a stack to be folded. It seems my whole time right now is spent keeping this baby dry.

May 5, 1887

As soon as there was dry weather, the Army started to drill their men in the fort walls here. What a dust they raise every day. I have hired an Apache lady who comes and helps me clean and keep up with the laundry, or I would do nothing but those two things every minute of every day. Her name is Juana, she says. There is a feeling of mystery around her, and I feel like something in her ways is not as straightforward as I would like. Her eyes never look at me when she talks, but Jack said that some Indians are like that, they must know you a long time and trust you for sure, before they will let you look into their eyes.

I have been so busy with children and cleaning, some days I feel worn out before I get out of bed. Juana helps a lot, and sometimes I even take a nap when the children do. Mama visited two weeks ago and said she wouldn't know what to do, having an Apache in the house and talking about the weather with her and such. I said, Times are surely changing. It was so good to have her here for a while and hear about everyone at Cienega Creek. How I miss that place and all my dear family and friends.

Jack is leaving in two days and will be gone most of a month. I am taking the children and going back to the ranch for that time. The roundup will be starting soon, and I am excited to get to that work. If ever I have a spare minute or two between chores and making soap, I practice lassoing the rain barrel by the house. I'm not very good at it and miss more often than not. I have hired five more fellows to help with the roundup, and Jack laughs when he sees the list of things I want packed in a wagon to go on this visit.

May 31, 1887

If tiredness could be measured in buckets I am a deep well of tiredness. But it is good to see so much work being done and count all the new calves as they get their rumps branded. They didn't like it at all, and a couple of the mama cows got mean hearing their babies holler, and one of the hands got horn-hooked real bad. He will live through it, but we were a man short and glad of the extras I hired, although only four of the five showed up. My roping skill, meager as it is, was not needed at all, because those fellows could throw and tie a calf faster than I could swing a loop. Still it was weeks of hard, dirty work, and I don't think I have ever seen such filthy children as mine. They were browner than the dirt they were covered with. On top of everything, April caught a cold so she was miserable and cried during the night for our first two days. After that, though, it felt good to be outdoors all day and doing something besides sweeping and washing. My hands are toughened even with the leather gloves I've had on. My blouses are faded from the sun and my face is brown and freckled, too.

Heading back to town brought almost as much commotion as going to the ranch. Harland and Melissa wanted to come to Tucson and stay with us for a spell, and it was decided that little Clover will come along, since he is six now and big enough to be out on his own a bit. Harland is to take a commencement test at the schoolhouse, and if he passes it he will be able to continue his studies at a college. He is nervous and has been studying hard, but I think it did him some good to help with the branding and get a few calluses on his hands instead of his head.

He laughed and said did I think studying things made his head thicker and harder? So we all teased him some but we are proud.

On the way, Harland and Melissa both rode next to the wagon, and we had a fine time singing and remembering things from long ago. Melissa was on Rose, who is getting old now and has given us five beautiful foals. Melissa held April on her saddle and April was happy as a little bird to be sitting up there trotting along. As we came to the last long climb, we stopped to rest the horses and give them drinks, and we spread a blanket on the ground and sat ourselves in the shade of some cottonwood trees. In the spring this place runs with water, but now it is just low and shady, and will have to do.

Once we started up the rise, Harland noticed a rider following us. The man on a horse came a little closer after a time, as if he was not in a hurry. Pretty soon, he disappeared but then I spotted a rider off to the east. I don't know if it was the same man or not, but where he was riding made me anxious, because I knew anyone simply headed north would sooner ride on this road than through the cholla and prickly pear. As our horses put their heads down into the last climb, we met up with the man right in front of us in the road. He didn't move when he saw us, and was standing still with his horse reined in hard.

Good morning, I called out. Would you let my horses pass so they can make the top of this hill before they give out?

He just stood there. It is a habit I have never shed, carrying my little hunting rifle under the wagon seat and my kitchen pistol in my apron. The little pearl handled two-shooter, I keep in my bag with my hanky and some spare diaper pins, so it was not handy. My horses were stomping, trying to keep the load from rolling backward, so I slacked the reins and pulled back on the brake so they wouldn't have to work so hard. I said louder, Sir, we'd like to pass by, if you'll just take one side or the other. My horses are about to give out under this load. Again, the man stood there.

Next I tried talking to him in Mexican, and he perked right up. He made his horse walk slow around us, and was near Melissa and April when he stopped, blocking Rose from moving. He said something in Mexican but I couldn't hear. He had hair black as a gun barrel and straight. He had a half empty bandolier over one shoulder, and a shotgun in a saddle holster, plus two pistols stuck in his belt without holsters. One of his hands was resting on the butt of one of the pistols, and he was tapping it with his fingers. After a long time of looking at us all, the man lifted off his hat and let it hang on his back, and he grinned real big and said, Ola, señorita.

Then he began to tell me I was real pretty and that Melissa was a fine young girl, and that he was interested in finding a young wife like her. He wanted to know did Melissa know how to cook. Harland was bristling like a porcupine, but I told him to keep still. By that time, we could all tell he wasn't a real Mexican and was talking with an accent, because we'd been talking it since we were young. Melissa sat stiff as a poker, and April started to whimper and put her hands over her eyes.

It's all right, honey, I said to April.

Harland said, No, she can't cook a lick. And besides she's my girl and we're going to get married.

I suppose he thought that would turn the man's mind away, but I don't think Harland knew just what the fellow was really after. The man quit smiling and looked at us like he was sizing us up again, then just like lightning he pulled a pistol and held it right to Harland's head. He said in English, She is not engaged any more, my friend. You see, it's so sad, poor el novio is dead, and he pulled back the trigger until it clicked.

He was watching Harland and didn't see me reach for my rifle and put my right hand in my pocket. I shot the pistol right through my apron. All the children around me squealed and immediately began to cry. The man doubled over and aimed his pistol at me, so I shot again and he fell off his horse. The horse shied and bucked around, but that fellow must have been strung with barb wire because he managed to drag himself up into the saddle again. As he rode away I kept my rifle aimed at the middle of his back.

Then he headed north down the road. If he had only kept on going he would have been all right. But the man stopped, dead center in the road, as Harland and Melissa were settling the little ones and getting our breath. Over the sight of my barrel I saw him turn and raise one hand like he was waving, but when I blinked and saw the sun flicker off metal in his hand, I pulled the trigger. I saw the pistol fly from his hand just before his horse took off through the cholla with him barely alive, hanging on with his arms around the horse's neck.

Clover started hollering Whoohoo! Shoot 'em, Auntie Sarah! Then Charlie started crying at the top of his lungs. We were a sober bunch by the time we got to town, and went straight to the Marshal's office to tell him what happened. After all the times I have driven to Tucson alone, to meet someone with bad intentions on the day I had a wagon load of children to look after just set me back on my heels. If we weren't so close to town, I would have turned back and taken Clover home.

I didn't quite know what to make of his reaction, because he acted like the whole thing was a kind of excitement. He asked me if he could shoot the gun, too. I thought for a while, and then asked him to sit beside me on the wagon seat, and we talked about how dangerous it was to hold a gun, and how bad I felt for shooting that man. He is a little fellow, but I think he began to understand that what happened was not playing. My little April just stared with wide eyes while I talked. I'm fairly certain she understood without being told, and the poor child looked terrified for the last hour of our trip. She is not even four years old, but has grown up knowing some rugged times.

That night after supper, Melissa hugged and kissed me, and we talked about it all again as we bathed the little ones and put them to bed. She was still a bit shaken up, and was afraid of having nightmares later on. Jack came home about nine o'clock, and when I told him what happened, he was upset and went right away to talk to the Marshal. He found out that a man with long black hair, riding a sorrel, had come into town and the doctor took three bullets out of him before he died.

They looked, Jack said, like a familiar caliber.

Well, I said, he was tough as an old boot. And he was going to kill Harland and take Melissa away, as if I wouldn't fight back.

He must not have been from around here, Jack said, or he'd have known better.

June 1, 1887

The Marshal came to our house this morning and asked me about the fellow on the road. Then he asked Melissa and Harland to tell him what happened, too, the same story three times. Then he nodded and said it sounded like a case of self defense, which also covers defending your loved ones. Well, Jack got mad and asked him right out what call did he have for questioning my word.

I was shaking in my chair, and holding tight to a coffee cup so my hands wouldn't shake. I looked into my lap and hoped he wouldn't notice the hole in my apron pocket that I washed but hadn't patched yet.

The Marshal said that during the night someone dragged that

man's body out of the doctor's surgery room and laid him up on a board by Dunbaker's Cantina with a note pinned on his shirt reading, "Murdered on the road to Tucson." Must have been that he had some friends in town, he said.

I looked at Jack. He looked back at me.

Well, the Marshal said, all I'm saying is this is a harsh place to raise a family, and Ma'am, I'd keep that pistol handy and watch your back, even inside the fort.

July 14, 1887

Harland is taking his test today. He was so nervous he didn't sleep at all last night. I helped him study every day that he's been here, and he said he wished it was me taking the test for him, and that I'd do a better job.

I have always wondered about those tests and the gumption it takes to pass one. If I didn't have these little ones to watch, I'd sure be in there trying. So while he was writing, I happened to say that to Mrs. Fish, and she just smiled and said, I'll order one for you and you can take it, too. I tried and tried to tell her that I'm not ready and I'd never pass, but she said, You'll never know if you don't try.

As I wait here for Harland to come home, it keeps running through my mind what Mrs. Fish has done. She has gone and written the United States Board of Normal Education that I have learned enough to pass a twelfth grade advancement. I begged her not to aim so high, and she said Nonsense, nonsense. I told her I was a wife and mother and she said, Does that make you stupid?

I'll never have time to study with this houseful. My test will come in two or three weeks. Oh, blessed heavens, what have I gotten into?

July 17, 1887

They are building a university, it says in the *Citizen*. I am not sure why they need one here, as there are probably not even thirty young people in this town interested in going to it. But, the government has given the money and some ranchers have given the land, and it is in full swing. Education is a hard enough thing to come by in the Territories. The thirteenth Territorial Legislature, a pit of two headed rattlesnakes if there ever was one, had voted awhile back to allot money for the building of a University right here in Tucson. Of course, they only did it to atone for the shenanigans they pulled with all the illegal pay raises and complementary gratuities they voted in for themselves, but in the end it will be the children here who will benefit. In the calm of a morning you can hear the hammers going and men shouting orders to each other. After the bugle blows, though, all I can hear are the sounds of the fort and my children. I am glad that I speak some Mexican, because many of the other women here do not know much English.

I suppose it is known around town that I killed that bandito. Some folks are suddenly much more friendly with my family and seem downright glad to invite us in, and others turn up their noses and shy away. Mrs. Larcena Page said she'd trust me with her own grandchildren, and know they'd be safe. Well, I'd like to see the woman that wouldn't defend her kin any way possible, and see what she's made of. Anyone who hasn't got some backbone has no business trying to live in the Territories.

My two children run me ragged some days, but this afternoon I am taking them in the buggy and we are going to drive over to that university land outside of town, and have a look. I am going to tell them both that they will go to that new school house when they are bigger, and get ready. Every time I think of that test coming for me from the Board of Education, my heart jumps up and down like beans on a hot stove.

Harland and Melissa and little Clover will head back to the ranch in a couple of days. He will have to wait a long spell for his grade. But he felt confident he knew everything. I'm proud of my little brother, and I wish Ernest could be here to see how tall Harland is. When we get his score, I'll write Ernest about it. I have yet to open that history book that Jack gave me on my last birthday, so tonight while I stirred gravy and mashed potatoes, I propped it open on the table and began to read a paragraph at a time.

August 1, 1887

The children and I were out at the clothesline this morning,
and while I hung sheets they were playing peekaboo under
them, squealing merrily each time they popped out from under
a damp white sheet flapping over their heads. I chased them and
surprised them by being behind first this one then that. This
kind of silly fun pleases me and we were all winded and giggling,
when a man walked up to me sort of sheepish with his hat in his
hands.

Señora, he says, I have a message for you. He startled me good,
and I collared my little ones and held them behind me. The man
scuffed at the dirt with one foot, and then saw that the dust flew
up towards my wash and said, I'm sorry, your clothes will be dirty
again.

It was an accident, I said. What message? Who from?

From me, Señora, he said, and then put his chin down against
his chest so hard I could barely make out what he was saying. The
message, lady, is that I am not going to kill you.

Run to the house children, run fast and hide, I said.

No, Señora, there is no danger. I was real mad my brother Jaime
was dead, and I swore to many people I would kill the hombre
who did this thing. I found out it was you and I was going to
avenge his blood with the life of the murderer. But you see I was
real mad, and I had some liquor and he was my brother.

I watched him close and didn't answer. He was looking as sad as
anyone ever looked.

The man went on, After a while I buried him and then the
Marshal tells me that the niños tell the story of my brother trying
to steal the señorita. I know I made a vow to the Virgin to avenge
my brother's murder, but, lady, he was not a good man. I loved my
brother but he did some things that were not right. So I came to
tell you myself, I'm not going to kill you. I would have done the
same thing to save my little Alejandra.

Well, I said, you can't help what your brother was like. With a
brother like you, he probably had some good in him somewhere, I
heard myself say.

I don't think so, he said. Jaime did a lot of bad things. He rode with some Apaches brutos, real bad ones, and did many things that broke our mother's heart. Buenos días, Señora.

The fellow walked away, his hat still in one hand, and while he walked he rubbed the back of his head with the other hand. I took up my wash basket and held it to me, feeling the cool of the wet things, shaking all over. Lands, I had put that day out of my mind so much, that if he hadn't had second thoughts, it would have been an easy thing for him to kill me. I hurried inside to my children and found them quarreling over a toy pull cart, and I kissed and squeezed them and they were so startled they forgot their argument and went back to playing.

August 4, 1887

The hottest day of all time is the day I took my twelfth grade test. My hand is so sore from writing for five straight hours that I can hardly bear to write this journal. I did arithmetic and mathematics in the first two hours, and then history, and wrote an essay on "The Framing of the Constitution," and another one on the issue of States' Rights in regards to setting the groundwork for the Civil War, and then I had to answer some things about literature and grammar, translate some Latin paragraphs, and there was a long question about a book I have never heard of called The Iliad. Then a huge spelling test. Plenty of things I studied there were no questions about at all, and I asked Mrs. Fish if I couldn't just answer another question, instead of the one I didn't know.

It's all done now. It will be three or four months before I get my test back. The United States Board of Normal Education will have written down—someplace in the Government Capitol Building for the whole world to see—that Sarah Elliot has failed. They will write to me about each question I failed. I have not even told Mama I took this test, only Jack and Mrs. Fish know about it.

Taking a school test is a new way to be afraid, and takes the knees right out from under you. If I'm riding a horse and get thrown, it's just a matter of getting back on. And if I'm fighting for my life, there's only living and dying to choose from. But taking that test, that's like showing other people the inside of your thoughts, and just waiting for them to say, wrong, wrong, wrong, and you can have a thought that seems right but since you never went to school, maybe it isn't. It's over now, and I will just have to forget about it. I wish I'd never even gone this morning.

September 3, 1887

I have felt troubled ever since I pulled that fool stunt and took that school test. This morning I not only felt troubled but sick to boot. At first I thought I got a bad egg for breakfast, but, as I was sitting with Sterling Foster, one of my ranch hands, going over the cost of winter feed, it dawned on me to count back days. As soon as he left, I counted twice, using my fingers the third time.

Pregnant again. I am fit to be tied. This is not what I wanted now, not at all. Jack and I had agreed we'd wait a while longer. This is pure accident and just the dreariest news ever. I'm just not ready for another round of nursing and diapers and all night crying jags. I sat in my rocking chair and fretted and felt sorry for myself until I wanted to laugh. This happens when we're trying not to have children. Whatever would it be like if we weren't being careful? And Charlie will still be in diapers when this one comes. The only good thing is that I'll have Juana to help.

I left her with the children and walked to the adjutant's office to see if I could find Jack. Captain Elliot, I said, there's something urgent I'd like to see you about. He looked up and smiled, and all the men around him tipped their hats and left the room like I was some kind of royal person or something. Well, Jack, I started, I'm not sure yet, not absolutely certain, that is, but I think possibly, then I took a deep breath.

A new baby? he finished for me. I just nodded. Then I hugged him and felt my throat tighten up. Once again, he was grinning when I left him.

October 1, 1887

It has been weeks of beautiful weather, and not a hint of chill in the air. I know winter will come soon enough. Most of the time the baby sickness has been mild with this one. Little Charlie is trying to learn to walk, pulling himself up on everything and anything that won't move, and now on something that will. He has discovered, by some secret communication that must exist between his head and Toobuddy's, that the dog will let him hold his fur and stand real still, and he puts one little blocky foot in front of the other, and makes his way around the porch with Toobuddy as a helper. This is a good thing, too, as Charlie is thrilled with the partnership, and Jack and April both think it is terribly funny, and Toobuddy doesn't mind much that I can tell. So I don't have to bend over and pick up Charlie nearly as often now that he is under his own power more or less. I have been to the doctor and know for certain that we will have an addition to our family in the late spring, and I don't feel as sad about it as I did at first. Now I'm looking forward to a new little one.

When Jack came in to dinner tonight he brought with him a Sergeant Lockwood and an Indian Scout named Blue Horse. I am sure that is not his real name, but it is what he prefers to be called by the soldiers. Well, I invited them all to sit down, and although the meal was interrupted by the children, both our guests had their fill and we had some good conversation. Then the men had coffee on the porch while I cleaned up inside. It was good to hear them talking and laughing now and then. Sometimes one or the other of them would remember some sad occasion from the past, and they would fall quiet, then someone would speak up with a new tale.

Blue Horse said he liked the meal and Sergeant Lockwood agreed that he had not had such good food in quite a while. Jack said to me, Sarah, come sit here by me, and then we had some more coffee and visited until nearly nine-thirty.

October 4, 1887

Well, it is all over this post and probably all over town that I have had Scout Blue Horse at my dinner table and treated him like he was a real man. For heaven's sake. How did they think I would treat him, like a stuffed man? Two of the mens' wives actually side stepped away from me as I walked on the boardwalk to the post mail. At first I didn't have any idea what they had stuck in their craw, then Jack happened to bring up last evening that the soldiers at the fort who knew how valuable Scout Blue Horse was to their lives all thought I was a top sport to have him at my table. So I said to him, well, their wives don't seem to value those soldiers' hides as much as they do. I hope I never lose so much of my mind as that. Some folks are the trifling least when it comes to sense. I told Jack right then, You just ask Blue Horse to come here as much as he wants, and have a glass of lemonade or a cup of coffee any time. If he is your friend and is helping keep you alive, he is always welcome in my parlor.

Jack just nodded at me. You know, he said, Blue Horse is lonesome just like most of the other men. If you offer him, you'll have regular company.

Well, I said, we have plenty of coffee.

He smiled, and hung his uniform over the back of a chair for tomorrow. It is odd, how he has these little routines every night. I feel like there is a rhythm to our lives now that I have never known before. Although there are periods when he is gone, and the rhythm is missing, as soon as he returns it takes up again and is a real comfort.

The ranch is doing well and we have sold most of the new steers to a big herd being driven clear to Abilene. The heifers we'll be keeping the first few years to build the herd. Between that and selling soap, I have nearly five hundred dollars saved up in a rusty can in the pantry. Tomorrow I think I'll put some of it in the bank.

October 5, 1887

Juana has left here, mad and distressed. She was hanging some clothes on the line when here came Jack home with Blue Horse and some other fellow I hadn't met yet. When she laid eyes on Blue Horse, she looked scared and mad at once, and said to me she wouldn't work in a house where his tribe stepped. I tried and tried to ask her what happened, and why she was so mad at him. She said only that their people had been enemies since the sun gave birth to the earth, and she would be always ashamed if she even looked on his shadow. Now I was purely confused. I had no idea that some Indians didn't like each other. Jack said it's true, that is why Blue Horse will help the soldiers against the Apache. To him the U. S. Army is just reinforcements sent by strong spirits to fight his enemies.

I had a little appointment with a bank clerk this morning. I wore a brown calico let out in the middle, and a straw bonnet, and I had patched the hole in my apron with a brand new pocket so it looked good as new, but altogether I was not too fancy looking because I figured that walking through this town with a Colt revolver in one pocket and five hundred dollars in the other, it wouldn't be smart to look too prosperous. Inside the bank building there were a few men in black suits and vests, wearing little stiff collars. I went to one of the windows and introduced myself, and after I told the man what I wanted to do, he had the gall to sniff in my face and tell me to let my husband handle my money and not trouble myself with the confusion of it all.

Oh, I said, how confusing is it? If it makes you confused, I surely don't want this bank holding my five hundred dollars.

Well, he perked right up and said, Five hundred dollars? Mrs. Elliot, I believe we can be of service to you after all.

I doubt it, I told him. I made this money with the sweat of my brow and the labor of my hands and I've got the rawhide to prove it. I don't intend to leave it with any man that thinks money is confusing.

He puckered up his face kind of nervous, and said, Oh, I assure you, Ma'am, we are not the slightest bit confused about money. We have a fifteen-hundred pound safe, he says. Completely, one-hundred-percent theft proof.

He had a way of talking like I haven't heard since Mrs. Hoover left us the stake money from her wagon and took the train to Boston. I've seen a safe blown up, on a train, I said back.

We offer one point nine percent interest, annually, he said.

I stood up. Well, I told him, I can turn this around in supplies and stock and see about twenty-five percent on cattle as long as there's no drought, and a hundred and fifteen percent on soap, more if there is a drought. It's a little at a time, but it comes right in steady as a clock. In case that's confusing to you, Mister, it's called profit. Thank you for your time, and good day.

I left him there with his mouth opening and closing, and I was madder than a wet hen. Eastern fellows come out here and think they've got money so they've got all the answers, when all they've really got is soft, mushy hands and a black suit and a scratchy neck collar holding them together. I'd as soon deal with that bandito on the road, he was a lot more honest.

October 6, 1887

Blue Horse has become a regular fixture on my front porch. Any time he is nearby, he sits himself in our shade. He doesn't come in, and I expect it is because this is not a big place and the children are already underfoot, but he is pleased to just sort of bide his time near us. Part of me is proud that we have an understanding like this, and part of me startles at the sight of an Indian man out my kitchen window. Juana had started to teach me a few Apache words. But now that I know Blue Horse is an enemy to them, I daren't say a one of them.

October 7, 1887

There has been a bad disturbance of renegade Indians so close by that Jack left here with a detachment and word for me to keep weapons loaded and ready, and bar the doors and windows until he returned. He told me to listen especially to the air for a bugle call that went a certain way, and then he hummed it. It will mean we are all to be ready for an attack on the fort, but then he said it was not very likely. I asked him was the trouble going on near Cienega Creek, and he said no, but east between here and Fort Grant, and the lines are cut so they are not sure if there is a fort still there or not.

After I got my bread dough set to rising, I cleared off the table of flour and got out my gun cleaning rags and brushes and oil, and made sure I was ready for trouble. While I was counting my ammunition and checking every shell for signs of a crack, I started thinking hard about Jack being out there possibly fighting for his life. I wished I was with him, but then I wished he was here, home and safe, but also to protect us if need be.

October 10, 1887

It is a certain kind of terror to know I carry a baby and have the other two to protect. Even with the soldiers around, I feel so alone. Children are a burden to a mother, but not the way a heavy box is to a mule. Our children weigh hard on my heart, and thinking about them growing up honest and healthy, or just living to grow up at all, makes a load in my chest that is bigger than the safe at the bank, and more valuable to me than all the gold inside it.

I was plum out of diapers, and some things won't wait, Indians or no, so I did up some wash and was hanging clothes on the line when I saw the column come in the fort looking bedraggled and footsore. With them there were nearly two dozen riderless horses with Army saddles on. Jack jumped from his horse and ran to the troop wagon where there were loaded up several wounded men. He wrapped his arm around one man and helped him into the infirmary. I stood on the porch and watched the soldiers unload man after man out of a wagon. It was a sorry sight. Not all of them were still alive, and they laid the dead ones in a row on the ground to leave room for the wounded inside.

Tonight Jack finally came in the door pale and grim. His uniform was bloody, and right away I asked him, Tell me quick, is that yours or someone else's blood?

Lockwood, he said. The damn fool took two arrows through the chest.

Well, Jack, I said, that doesn't make him a fool, just unlucky.

He looked down at his shirt and said real quiet, He stepped in front of me. They were meant for me. He went to the bedroom and took off his clothes, and I told him I would pull him a bath.

While Jack was taking a bath, I sat to rock the baby and made a vow to myself to pray every day for Sergeant Lockwood, and I heard the water sloshing and thought how good to know my husband is in there in that room instead of the one across the post where those young men are groaning and dying. If Sergeant Lockwood is ever able to eat, I will make him soup every single day.

April was looking at some paper dolls cut from a catalog. Charlie snuffled because my tears were falling in his face. He is getting so big, and just wanted to go to bed, so I put him down quick and wiped my face before Jack could see it.

I asked Jack would he have some supper, but he didn't eat much. He said not to worry, and that they were pretty sure the Indians would not come this far. As soon as the Army started for home, the Indians did the same, but the men here are only home to re-group and go out again to be sure, and to re-string the telegraph lines. Jack hardly said a word all evening, and then late at night, almost ten o'clock, he went back to the infirmary.

October 22, 1887

I took a feather pillow and a soft blanket to Sergeant Lockwood, and I have been making him soup nearly every day. Yesterday he asked me if I would mind including something like scrambled eggs or fried chicken. He is so thankful for my efforts, he says. I am purely thankful for his bravery, or I might not have a husband. But I cannot bring myself to say those things, as every time I do I start to well up with tears, so I just try to smile and bring him food and leave.

I seem to always have company at home, now. Blue Horse just seems to be around all the time, and I have gotten over being edgy around him. He eats with us if he is hungry, but sometimes does not. If it gets cold outside he just walks right in without even a knock or a fare-thee-well, and sits by the fire, then when he is warm he goes away.

Every few days when we get mail, I hurry to the Postmaster's and look for the news about that test. I'm sure they must have lost it, or someone robbed the train it was on, and so it never reached that government office. It has been too long. If they ever received it I would have heard by now.

October 30, 1887

Jack is out of town again so the children and I went to church alone, and as soon as we walked in, people sort of edged away on the pews and made plenty of room around us. All this over serving coffee to the Army Scout. I was feeling mighty stiff and sorry I was there amongst them. It's a fine day when the likes of the low down, lawless hooligans that make up a place like Tucson can look down their noses at me. There is a fellow over there by the window who runs a gambling hall and saloon where there is at least one murder a month, and one there who has a saloon and seven painted floozies on the top floor. Then over there, is Mrs. Watts, who cusses her own children like a mule skinner, but she has got her nose high in the air and pretended to not look at me when I said hello. And over there near the organist's bench is Mrs. O'Rourke, who is on her fifth or sixth husband and all of the former ones died young and wealthy. Here they are in church, but folks scoot away from me as if I was a sidewinder. Well, this is just a fine bunch of good wholesome men and women around me, and all have their eyes focused just right on the Lord and His good Providence, I am sure.

The service hadn't even started yet and Charlie began to

squirm, and I was considering getting up and leaving and just sitting at home and reading to my children from the Bible instead of putting up with the likes of this. But, as I stood up and straightened my dress, here came Sergeant Lockwood, looking all spit and polished. I knew he was not gone on the campaign with Jack and Blue Horse because he has had a hard time recovering from his arrow wounds to the chest and he had taken pneumonia from it.

He took off his hat and bowed to me and smiled, and said, sort of loud so everyone could hear, as I know they were straining to anyway, Mrs. Elliot, in the absence of your husband, and on behalf of General Crook, the commander of this fort, and the many soldiers whose lives have been saved by your husband's courage, will you allow me the privilege of accompanying you in church this morning and seeing you safely home?

Well, you could have heard a pin land on a pillow in that room. Certainly, I said, if you don't mind wiggly children over much.

Then the preacher came in and the singing started. Sergeant Lockwood whispered to me that he was much improved but still couldn't draw breath to sing. He held first Charlie and then April, then Charlie again, and both of them were busy all through the service admiring and poking at his brass buttons. I remembered how hard Jack works polishing all those buttons for an occasion. It made me appreciate how Sergeant Lockwood has just now given to me a gift of his support and admiration for Jack, and also a gift of the time he would have to spend polishing those buttons again after my children got through handling and drooling on every last one of them.

I took Sergeant Lockwood's arm when the service was over, and then there was such politeness and gentility around us, you would have thought I'd walked into a different group of people. He saw me to my door and I thanked him kindly, and said I appreciated very much what he had done. It was the first time I noticed what an unusually handsome looking man that Sergeant is. When he smiles he has a real sparkle about him and he would make some girl a fine catch, and lots of handsome children. He just gallantly lifted his hat and went on back to his quarters. Jack has some real good fellows at this fort.

November 12, 1887

Jack tells me that Blue Horse is a Yavapai warrior. They live a ways from here and the Apaches have tormented them for more than three generations, but they are not Comanches or Cheyenne or any of the tribes of Apache, so I have no reason to feel nervous with him. He has continued to make himself at home and now as the weather is cooler, he lets himself in the front door as if it was his own home, and sits by the fire. He just nods hello to me, and I keep on with my work, and he cleans the rifles or mends his saddle, or sometimes even tells April little stories. They are wonderful stories, and I find myself wishing I could put everything aside and sit like a child and hear more of them. I wonder if Indian folks write books that I could get them stories in, but Jack says he thinks only a few of them have writing if they have gone to a white school, and then not in their own language.

I am amazed that Indians are not friends with each other. I asked Jack to tell me as many tribes as he knew, and I was spellbound by his words for a long time. No wonder the Army has hired him as a specialist in Indian Affairs, he has more knowledge up his sleeve than I ever would have guessed. He can name nearly a hundred tribes, and knows some of the language of several of them, and knows which are enemies of what group, and where there is trouble and where there are peaceful treaties. I asked him so many questions he got tired of explaining. And I said I would give him a recess, but I wanted to know all those things and more. He just laughed and said I was a regular taskmaster and would be a fearsome examiner in school, because there was no part of his brain I hadn't picked and sorted through.

November 22, 1887

Jack surprised me good today. It is my birthday, and we left before sunup to head for the ranch. When we got there around noon, Mama and Savannah had made about the biggest spread of fine food I've ever laid eyes on. There was some kind of carrying-on happening, and every now and then I would catch Savannah and Jack whispering together, and them winking at Mama, and Albert grinning like a hound dog. We had our fill of everything, and when I said the little ones need a nap and was going to put Charlie in the house, Jack held my arm and said, Not yet. It's time.

Suddenly they were all around me in a circle, and Jack made a big fuss at clearing his throat, and then let out with a string of words like I have never heard before. He said so many Therefores and In-as-muches and such that I was lost in it all. In the end, he was smiling, and pulled out from his blouse pocket a big fold of thick, cream colored paper. It was addressed to me, although it had been opened and resealed at least once. He didn't hand it to me but instead took a smaller folded paper out. Then he proceeded to read it.

MEMBERS OF THE UNITED STATES BOARD OF EDUCATION,
ON THIS DATE OF OCTOBER 18, 1887,
DO HEREBY CONFER UPON THE STUDENT HEREIN NAMED,
SARAH A. ELLIOT,
A FINAL EXAMINATION GRADE,
WRITTEN, FOR THE TWELFTH LEVEL OF NORMAL SCHOOL,
OF NINETY-FOUR AND ONE HALF PERCENT.

After that I couldn't hear anything but all my family hollering and hooraying and clapping. I sat in my chair, kind of dizzy. I passed even higher than Harland, and he is going to college. Oh my, was all I could say. Mama is so proud she could bust.

When we got the babies napping, we had pie and coffee and I read my document over and over. It is the best birthday of my life. I will never forget this one.

November 29, 1887

I took some time by myself today and went for a ride. It is so good to be loose from the children and the house for a spell, even a short one. I rode first out of town and up into the low hills to the west. Then as I headed back through town, I turned up to the dirt trail that leads to the new university building. There it was, almost up on one side, made of cut stone blocks. Men were working on putting blocks on one wall upwards of the third story. As I stood there, I was filled with a strange thought, that younger folks than me will be able to learn wonderful things that will always be a mystery to me, inside those walls. It was a kind of achy sadness, that here, so close, someone was going to learn from a real professor. Of course, I will never have time to go to college, and it would be foolishness, now that I have a husband and children to take care of and a ranch to run.

It seems there is always a road with bends and forks to choose, and taking one path means you can never take another one. There's no starting over nor undoing the steps I've taken. It isn't like I'd want to not have my little ones and Jack and that ranch, it is part of life to have to support yourself. It's just that I want everything, my insides are not just hungry, but greedy. I want to find out all the things in the world and still have a family and a ranch. Maybe part of passing that test was a marker for where I've been, but it feels more like a pointer for something I'll never reach.

December 5, 1887

Raining today again, and I was up since about three this morning comforting Charlie. He is cutting a whole row of teeth at once, and colicky and vomiting. Poor little fellow, I know he must have a headache. I remember being a half grown girl and getting my last teeth in and how it hurt. I don't know why it upsets his stomach so much, but this has happened with every tooth he has.

April has taken today to take leave of her senses. It must be the rain and the fussy baby, and she is not getting enough attention. She upended the sugar jar and broke it, so there was sugar all over the kitchen and glass in it so it is all wasted and dirty, then she found my sewing scissors and thought Toobuddy needed a hair cut, and there is three big patches of hair gone off the poor dog, and when I sent her outside, it started to rain again.

All day long I had been at my wit's end alone with these children, and just barely heated up some scraps of beef from yesterday and put in a little vegetable to make a stew, when here came Jack with Blue Horse and some other soldier I don't even know as company for dinner, and on top of that asked me to cut his hair and draw him a bath as he was too tired to haul the water.

I am ever thankful that soldier took one look at me showing with a baby coming along, with my hair falling down, and the broom lying at a mound of broken glass, and supper boiling over on the stove, April wearing a dirty pinafore screaming for me to hold her, and just then the baby in my arms spit up all over me, and he said, You know, Captain Elliot, I forgot to rub down my horse, but I'd be kindly obliged if you'd let me have supper some other time.

When he left, I turned to Jack Elliot and said, If you are too tired to haul water, you are too tired to bathe in it, and I am fit to be tied. Your supper is on the stove and your children are driving me to distraction and April has lost the scissors under the house through a crack in the floor so there will be no haircut tonight. If that don't please you, then I will put on a uniform and ride out of here tomorrow morning and chase around the countryside and you can wear this apron and tend these crying children and this drafty house from dark to dark and then tell me you think I should haul you a bath.

He looked real startled. It is the first time I have ever just purely lost my temper over anything Jack has done. Blue Horse laughed, but when I frowned at him he quieted real quick. I have just had my fill of men and their ways of ordering people around, lately. I handed Charlie to Jack, dripping and nasty and crying, and went to our bedroom and shut the door. Then I changed into my nightgown and went to bed. I couldn't sleep with the sound of children crying and the dog barking outside, and Jack trying to hush everyone. I knew there were burned fingers and dishes banging around and water spilling on the floor and lots of fussing, but I just stayed in bed, and before long I went to sleep.

December 6, 1887

My kitchen was clean when I got up this morning, and the children were sleeping and looked like they had had their faces washed before they were put to bed. Jack was doing something on the back porch, and before long he came in and stoked up the fire and had a big tub, and said he was drawing me a bath, and please make ready. So I was mighty grateful, and I told him so. He said as soon as the sun was up he would go under the house and find the scissors and so he would wait to have a bath after he crawled through the mud. I told him I would be glad to cut his hair then, but he said, no, it was worth six bits not to make a mess in my kitchen for me to clean, what with everything else I had to tend, and he would go to the town barber. He said for me to have a nice soak, and if the children got up, he would see to their breakfast.

Well, I was still feeling pretty starched from all the turmoil in this house last evening, but I didn't mind at all when he poured hot water and handed me the soap and then even took the brush to my back for me.

Then he said, Remember the first time I did this?

Well, I said, I don't think I'd forget it as long as I live.

He said, You are beautiful.

I just had to roll my eyes. My hair was sticking out everywhere, and wet, and I am six months into bearing this next child. I look like a watermelon on a vine, I said.

What is more beautiful than that? Jack said. You are the best thing in my life, and sometimes I forget. Give me your arm.

Jack, I said, the children will be up soon.

He just laughed kind of low. I'm not after anything but tending to you, Sarah.

I looked at him kind of sideways. And I gave him my arm.

January 2, 1888

Jack is gone down to the Graham mountains with a handful of other private soldiers and a Federal Marshal, tracking some thieves who bushwhacked the U. S. Army Paymaster and took the Army payroll. The paymaster, a Major, is laid up in the hospital nearly beaten to death, and the gold is gone which was our pay, so I have to buy goods on credit until they either catch the men who did this or the government replaces the money. I hope to goodness they post a better guard around it. I am not using ranch money for drygoods because I have placed an order for fence wire and horseshoes and a new champion bull that is coming from Kansas, and it will provide more for our future to save for those things than to have an extra pound of sugar right now. At any rate, Mr. Fish knows me well enough to trust me with it until I either make more soap or the payroll comes in.

Sergeant Lockwood asked me to allow him to take us to town for church. Well, I said that would be fine, thinking how kind he was to come to my rescue before. We drove to church yesterday in my buggy and he sat with us and again let the children practically wallow in his lap with more patience than Job. Folks around were still holding their noses in the air, but instead of ignoring me so hard their eyes would shut, they seemed to be glancing and outright staring.

I had to fix supper anyway, so I asked him to take some with us. He did, and stayed part of the afternoon, and we all had a fine visit now that he is feeling so much better. He played with the children and talked about exciting things he's seen and funny stories about being in the Army which I've never heard from Jack. It was a real pleasant evening.

January 9, 1888

I have a problem I don't know what to do about or who to ask. It has nothing to do with the payroll money being late, but it has a lot to do with Jack being gone. Sergeant Lockwood came by yesterday morning, and asked me so kindly to allow him to escort me and the children to church again today. Then this morning, when I woke, I had the strangest feeling of being out of sorts. I got dressed, and dressed April and Charlie for church, and waited for him to come. But when I heard his boots on my porch, a cold chill came over me, and when I answered the door, I told him he was so very kind, but I was suffering from baby sickness again, and was suddenly not well enough to attend church. He looked sorely disappointed, and then offered to go to the druggist for me, or to stay with me. He would keep me company, he said, or he would tend the children and bring me tea and crackers, or any number of things. To all these things I said no, no, no, until he finally gave up and left. My heart was about to jump right out of my throat before he did, though.

Oh, Lord, let what I saw in his eyes be only my imagination. Please let it be only his gallantry and not what it looked like to me.

January 18, 1888

Jack came home, and the children practically attacked him, dusty and hungry, and he played with them both until they were exhausted and went to bed early. What a pleasure to have him tuck them in their little beds.

Oh, Jack, I said, I have to tell you, before you hear some rumor. My heart was aching and my throat was dry as dust. Jack, I said again, Sergeant Lockwood took us to church again while you were gone.

Well, he said, that was nice. Then he got a look in his eye. It wasn't mad or fierce, but just real stiff.

Jack, I told him the next Sunday I was sick, but it was a pure lie. Then I told him I wouldn't be going to church until after this baby, and after it is grown some, and so I said thank you very much but please don't take us to church again.

That's it? he said. You look like you're afraid I would worry about you.

I'm not afraid of what any of those busybodies in church say about me, Jack, about anything in the world. But if there was to start a rumor about something that would come between us, why, I would go back to the ranch to live, permanently, and never come back here, to keep that from happening, I said. I sat in my rocking chair. Jack Elliot, I told him, I love you every way there is to love a man.

You know, he said, I asked Sergeant Lockwood to look out for you a little. He's a real good man.

Even though Jack said that about Sergeant Lockwood, his eyes were flashing with sparks, and it's a good thing they weren't in the same room right then. Well, I said, I'm sure he is. I suppose he is mighty lonely. He never did or said anything improper. It was just a feeling I had. Maybe I was wrong. But I'd prefer if it was some married fellow with a wife and family here, too, so that there wouldn't be any talk.

How about if I find one that's real ugly and mean, too? he said, and breathed easier.

I'm serious, I told him.

Come here, Mrs. Elliot, he said. Then he took me in his arms and kissed the breath right out of me. While he did, this baby squirmed between us and made us both laugh. Jack tried to pick me up, but he said, My, you've developed quite a girth there. Tell me that part about how you love me again.

Then he sat in the rocking chair and I sat on his lap and put my head on his shoulder, and we just sat quiet for a long time and watched the stove die down. I leaned my head against his shoulder and smelled the sunshine in his clean shirt, and the roughness of him needing a shave at night.

I said it. I told him how much I loved him and he didn't slip away. He didn't even flinch or look the other direction, but lapped it up like he'd been waiting a long time to hear it.

Thank you God, for this new little boy. He was only an hour in coming. Cute little sweet potato too, with a big thatch of wavy black hair. His name is Gilbert. He has a dimple in his little chin. We have not decided on a middle name yet.

All the time I was laboring, Blue Horse was on the front porch singing an Indian song at the top of his lungs. I held Jack's hands and groaned with the pains, and in between, hearing the sound of chanting, we would smile to each other and even laugh out loud at this curious situation. When little Gilbert cried, the chanting stopped for a minute and then changed. My neighbors must have thought we had something mighty peculiar going on here.

Later, Jack took the baby to Blue Horse, and told me the man held the baby and patted Jack's shoulder many times, then put a string with a colored bead on it around Gilbert's neck. Jack says it is to ward off evil. My Mama would have a ring-tailed fit. I will take it off him tomorrow before she comes, but I cannot let Blue Horse know, as he meant it in the best wishes for the baby.

Little Charlie is fascinated with the new brother, and April said only, Oh, another brother? Have a girl, Mama, I want a girl baby, not another brother. But she held him and cuddled him, and he made little newborn faces at her, and one of them was a big smile, so she declared he loved her best and it was okay if he was a boy after all. Jack was so good to me again. Mama will be here tomorrow. And just a week ago Jack hired a lady named Anna to help me around the house a bit. Anna seemed to get used to Blue

Horse being here right away. She is very old and plump as a quail, but pretty spry, and the children love her.

A man knocked on my door today at noon while Jack was down at the drygoods store. Coming from somewhere near him was a strange moaning sound. He nodded at me right away and said, Mrs. Elliot? Mrs. John Elliot? and I said Yes. Well, he said, he had been left with something that was rightfully mine, and although it was an accident, he has taken good care of it for several weeks, and had asked all over town to determine the rightful owner of this box of goods.

I told him I had no idea what he meant, as I wasn't aware of having lost anything except a thimble and a couple of hairpins in the last few weeks.

Nevertheless, he went on, This is surely your property, as there is no one else in the entire town with a shaggy red dog. Then he tipped his hat, and smiled really nice, and seemed just as happy as could be. He said, I'm sure you'll do the right thing, Ma'am. Good afternoon to you. Then he whistled a real happy sound as he turned and left.

I stepped out on the porch. There by the door he had left a crate without a lid, and inside the crate, like a bushel of furry pumpkins, was a passel of red, Toobuddy-colored puppies. Only one had some black spots and shorter hair, but all the rest of it was red. And he was right, I have not seen another dog anywhere around that remotely resembles Toobuddy. Five puppies. They were whining, but their eyes were open, and they were bushy with fur and smelled clean and healthy. He had surely taken care of them and the mother dog, for which I am thankful, as I know lots of people would not care for unwanted puppies. Oh, what will I do with five puppies? Then I heard tiny Gilbert start to cry, and I felt my milk come, and I knew I had to put the puppies aside for a while. A three day old baby will not wait.

I have been trying to think of how I will find homes for them all. I will write a letter to Albert and Savannah, and ask Mason Sherrill, too, and even Mama if they all could use a puppy. And I will put up a little sign on our front porch, as maybe there is someone around the post that would keep a dog. The only thing I am worried about is that usually when I have seen a sign like that, people will say, Free, Good Kittens: excellent mousers, or Cow Dog: strong herder, or something like that. Well, Toobuddy doesn't have much going for him in the way of talent except personal charm. He is playful and clumsy and will chase a rabbit or a mouse but only if it's not too hard, and he gets into as much trouble as he saves me, so he is an even balance, not a big help. At least, he is patient with children. That I could honestly say. That will have to be their selling point. Nice puppies, good natured and friendly. That will do.

March 22, 1888

There goes the last of the three puppies we will be giving away. We kept the black spotted one for a house dog, and her name is Shiner. Then we kept one of the really furry red ones, and named him Rusty. I am hoping he will live at the ranch, and we will only keep one here, but that won't be for a few months, until he is big enough to watch out for coyotes on his own. I declare if there was something I didn't need after having a baby it was having five puppies, too. But Anna is just wonderful. She is slow and patient, as loving as a grandmother.

I sat this afternoon to read during the boys' nap. I was going through the botanical theory book, and while I was reading I remembered something Blue Horse said to me back before Gilbert was born. He said wisdom is not a path, it is a tree. At the time I was too busy to give it much thought, so I nodded politely but didn't pay much attention. Now I see that he was surely right. I have been sad almost a whole year, thinking that taking that test was somehow the end of my learning and that not having that as a possibility in my future left a big empty spot in my life that the children and the ranch didn't fill. But my life is not like that, it is a tree, and I can stay in one place and spread out in all directions, and I can do more learning shading this brood of mine than if I was all alone. I declare, it is like some other part of me made up some rules about happiness and I just went along with them without thinking. My heart is lightened so much that I am amazed at how sad I felt for so long.

I have donated a box of books to the library of the university, and paid for a tree to be planted near the fountain which will be built by the front steps. Someone even wrote about it in the paper where they were listing all the names of people who gave trees, saying the books were a gift from "the extensive library of Captain and Mrs. J. E. Elliot." What a hoot. I figured it was a good resting place for the Expositional Sermons.

September 1, 1888

April's first day at school. I walked with her almost all the way there, and promised her I would be waiting to walk her home again. The pups went with us, and wanted to follow her right up into the school house. They are hardly pups anymore, big red reminders of their silly papa dog. April has got a brand new slate and a McGuffy's First Reader, and a little chalk and a new pencil tied with a string. She holds these things out carefully, in one hand, as if she knows they are real important. In the other hand she is carrying a little shiny new lunch pail with a sandwich of jam and butter and a couple of apples from Albert's place. She is walking as solemnly as she knows how, and I want to laugh at her seriousness, but I mustn't or she will think I am laughing at her.

Although these things are required by Mrs. Fish for all first grade students, April can already read well beyond the McGuffy's First, because I have taught her to read straight from some other books. After this first week of school, I will have a talk with Mrs. Fish and see if she will allow April to progress into another reader. What a glorious day to me, to see my daughter step up that walk and wave goodbye from inside a school house.

When she was gone, a strange feeling came over me, and I sat at my kitchen table and put my face in my hands. I am terribly envious of my own child. She has no idea what a blessing is being handed to her, and I can only dream of what I might have learned if I had ever lived near a school. While the little ones were playing, I got out my copy of *The Iliad*, which I found on a tinker's wagon, battered and falling apart, tied together with a string. It cost nearly four dollars.

April 6, 1889

This morning as usual, I let April and Charlie out of the buggy in front of the Feed and Grain store. I left Gilbert with Anna at home. It is only three blocks to school, and April's friends Carrie and Opal Rae usually meet her there at the corner. Charlie likes to walk along pretending he is old enough for school. Old Toobuddy often goes also, and sits by the school house door until I drive by and call him to jump up and ride home with me. When school is out, Toobuddy heads back through town to the school and waits for them, so to the children it is like he has sat there all day, rain or blistering sun, waiting for them. For such a silly dog, he has got the lay of the town smartly.

After handing them their lunches, I left them to go into the feed and grain store. They always check to see who got the biggest apple, and I saw them trade buckets. I smiled and went to pick up a sack of oats and some chicken mash. Not twenty seconds had passed when I heard April and Charlie both let out blood chilling screams. My heart felt stabbed at the sound because I knew it was them. I dropped the sack of mash and it burst on the floor as I ran to the door. I ran all the way down the street, with my bonnet blowing off and a wagon stopping short to let me pass.

There in the street was poor Toobuddy, run over by a wagon. April and Charlie were shrieking, with tears running down their faces, hovering over their dog. Up the street aways was a boy I recognized from school—one of the oldest ones who was having trouble finishing the last grades. He had turned around in his wagon and was laughing, pointing at my children to another boy sitting bareback on a horse. Both boys laughed loudly. People started to gather up and I felt sick at the sight.

I lifted Toobuddy's head, and his eyes opened, but he didn't even whimper. I could hear him breathing hard between the children's cries. Suddenly beside me is Blue Horse, who must have been standing nearby when it happened. Get buggy, Ma'am Elliot, he said. I took my children's hands and we hurried to it, and drove back there. Then Blue Horse lifted Toobuddy into the floor of the buggy for me, but he said, There isn't much to do but save him from pain, now. April and Charlie wailed louder at that. I just looked at the man, feeling helpless.

Blue Horse climbed into the buggy seat beside me, and we drove back to the house. There he took the dog out, and Toobuddy drooped, limp. Blue Horse put his head against Toobuddy's body, and said, The spirit is gone. Then he looked at my whimpering children and got a real sympathetic look on his face, and said, Little ones, bring shovel, come quickly.

They looked at me, and I said, You do what he tells you. The shovel is in the lean to.

From the back porch I watched as Blue Horse told first one child then the other to dig, and finally he took the shovel and made a bigger hole. They laid Toobuddy in it, and then stood by and Blue Horse put a big handful of dirt in both the children's hands, then he started to sing. He motioned to them, two or three times, and then they started to sing too. Mingled from the back of my house were some Indian words in a soft, wailing sound, and April and Charlie singing in their childish voices some mixed up words to Blessed Assurance. They dropped their dirt on the little grave, and made a great ceremony of filling it and piling rocks.

By the time the funeral was over, the morning was near gone, and I told April she could stay home from school for the rest of the day. It remained a somewhat somber day, but later on, when Blue Horse had taken his usual chair on the porch, I saw April walk up to him with a wild flower and kiss his cheek as she gave it to him.

April 7, 1889

Today I drove April right to the front door of the school and picked her up there, too. When she came out to go home, she said those two boys were not in school at all. Maybe they are being kept away by their parents, maybe they are truly sorry for what they did. I will be glad if it is their repentance that troubles them, and there will be an end to this hatefulness.

Jack came home just as I was pulling the buggy into the shed. He asked me if I had seen Blue Horse, but I told him about what had happened, and said I had not seen him since we went to bed last night.

April 9, 1889

The paper today reports that the doctor has seen two young men in his office, one of which will be spending a few days in the doctor's home, recovering. They are the two boys missing from school, who killed our dog and laughed. They had been asked by the Marshal if they fought each other, but both said no, and when asked who beat them, they would not answer but gave each other frightened and threatening looks.

Blue Horse has not come to our porch since the day Toobuddy died. He did not report to his duty at the post, either, and has been listed as Away With Out Leave. All are speculating about the turn of events. However, I will not join in to even raise an eyebrow over it. I know Jack's hands had no bruises because I looked for them. Blue Horse has not been seen or heard of since that day. The last picture in my mind of him is sitting on the porch in that old chair, wearing the checkered shirt I made him, and April tiptoeing to kiss his cheek.

May 26, 1889

It is commencement day at the Tucson School. April is going to wear a new dress I made her with a ruffled pinafore. Must hurry, baby is crying and I have to get the hem in April's dress.

December 25, 1889

A new decade will be upon us soon, and our family will greet it with another baby. This one was planned, but I told Jack I think this will be enough. I feel like I have been taking care of children my whole life, and unless there is an unforeseen slip up, I'd like to stop after this one. I think four children is a nice size for a family. He said that was fine with him, although he didn't mind having as many as I could manage. Gilbert will be over two years old when this one comes, and with any luck there will only be two of them in diapers for a couple of months then. Savannah and Albert have a houseful, now. Besides Clover, Joshua, Rachel and Rebeccah, there are Esther and Mary Pearl. That doesn't count one that was lost early in the fall, and Savannah thinks she may be expecting again already.

May 18, 1890

Another child has blessed us, little Suzanne, born May 14, 1890. I missed Blue Horse. I gave Suzanne Gilbert's blue luck bead to wear for a few days. My days begin before reveille and end with the coyote's hunting songs. It is a bustling, crowded house now, and somebody is wet at one end or the other all the time.

Christmas Day, December 25, 1891

I turn around and I cannot believe that six years have past since Jack and I married. What busy times these have been, too. Weeks turn into months without sitting to write my journal, and I am so thankful for all four of my children but equally thankful there are not eight. They have all put down for the night at last, and Suzy is cuddling her prized gift, a little china doll, the way April used to hold Mrs. Lady.

Jack tucked all the children in bed tonight and stoked up the fire in the Franklin until it was nearly glowing. Then he held me close and said he thanked God for our family. He pulled up two chairs side by side, and we sat and held hands and watched the fire go out.

I have bought Harland some leather gloves for his birthday, which I will send up to Tempe where he is attending Tempe Normal School. He will graduate next year, and says he wishes to become an architect of houses and bank buildings and bridges and such. Ernest has made a long career of the Army now, and has been made a Sergeant through several close scrapes and his good and willing service to his country. He has not married so far, but he is young, and maybe his time will come to settle down a bit, soon.

Mr. Sherrill calls on my Mama every Tuesday without fail. They sit and talk, or sometimes he brings his guitar along and sings some tunes, and she brings him a cool drink in the summer and coffee in the winter, and he keeps her in firewood and other things now that Harland is gone. Melissa is a pretty much grown girl now, and is wishing she had a fellow, and I know she writes to Harland every week.

It's lonely here in the fort. Mrs. Page comes by for coffee now and then. Mostly I just raise my children and cook and clean, flirt with Jack and enjoy his company, and read aloud the books he gives me for silly holidays he makes up. Like, Oh, here's a gift for The Third Tuesday in October, didn't you know that's a holiday? Well, I bought you a book. He is amazing.

I sent Mason money to buy a few new brood heifers last spring, to get new blood into our stock. Almost every cow on the place is carrying a calf, and I can't wait to see the new strain come through. I have enlarged my ranch land by another three hundred acres to the east plus a straight out purchase of the six hundred-forty acres that was the old Raalle homestead. I deeded the best quarter of that homestead to Melissa Raalle, so she will have a legacy of some sort, seeing she is an orphan and utterly alone in this world.

I have tried to write some letters for her, to retrace her family and see if there is any kin anywhere on this continent, but the name Raalle seems to start and stop with her, and no one in the state of Louisiana has the name or knows of them. She was so little she doesn't remember where she lived before that, only that it was a white house near a green field, and that they had a brown cow that her mother milked twice a day. I have written a letter addressed to a Bureau of Missing Persons in the Kingdom of Norway. It is where I remember Mr. Raalle saying he was from the very first time we spoke. I have no idea if there is such a bureau there, but I am hoping that with time it may fall into the hands of someone in an official position who may be able to help us locate some of Melissa's kin.

January 7, 1892

This morning we took a look at a piece of land on which to build a house. It is close in to town, on the southern tip, down by Sixth Street near where the Apaches used to have a regular horse race from a big mesquite tree to the fort. It apparently doesn't take much prodding to hold a horse race, as they are always eager to wager a bet on their favorite horse and rider. Anyway, this piece of land is not too big, barely half an acre, but Jack says people don't go for huge spreads in town, otherwise it wouldn't be a town, just a gathering place. As far as I'm concerned, that's town enough for me, and I don't care for the closeness of people or the new fashioned sewer system they have put in, or the taxes you have to pay each year either, for that matter.

We are going to draw up some pictures of a house, and Harland will convert them into real drawings he says will get us a grand place like we want.

January 8, 1892

That Jack Elliot is a low down cussed mule headed skunk. This is not Army business and he has no reason at all to be headed off on some bandit roundup the town Marshal has cooked up. This is just pure disregard for all reason. Why he thinks he has to go, there is no explanation, and he has not given it any thought himself either. Just that the Army is giving him leave to take some men and head off after some banditos or whatever they call them in the north of Arizona Territory, and see if they can round them up. It is one thing to be at the mercy of the U. S. Army. It is entirely another thing to take off on a whim, with me home with these four children, left to worry and now to see to the starting of a house.

I am packing up my children and going to spend a week at the ranch. That new house will have to wait until there is a man to see to it. I suppose I should be thankful for the time he does spend here, and I am, but this time I know he could refuse if he wanted to. January in Cottonwood was always a cold and wet month, and I'm sure all of the north territory is cold and wet, and he will be miserable. It aggravates me that he laughed and said, I'm glad to know you'll miss me.

You have responsibilities here, I said. Missing you has nothing to do with it. But even as I said those words, I got that old hurting feeling I have always felt when he is too far away.

January 21, 1892

We had been back in town three days when Jack came home this time, thin and ragged looking. He got angry when I brought the doctor in, but was polite to him. He stayed in bed for one full day, and then pronounced that he was well, and indeed his mood at least was improved, although he still carries a terrible cough.

Tonight Jack told us the oddest story. It seems while they were riding through some rugged country full of strange rock shapes they stopped at a trading post called Hubbell's. It was all that was left of an old Army fort on the northeastern plateau. There he spotted Blue Horse, dressed differently, with his hair grown long and acting like he didn't speak English. Jack watched the other men around to see if they recognized him, but they didn't seem to at all. Jack was going to tell Blue Horse that he understood why he left, but he went quickly out a door and disappeared.

Well, I said, did you all ever catch up to those fellows you were after?

He shook his head. Never even got a trail, he said.

I went back to drying dishes while he made some coffee. I'd never say it to him, but it seems to me soldiers can sometimes act like a pack of coyotes, and just go out in a bunch and howl up a storm and traipse around making a lot of noise, getting nothing at all accomplished. Well, at least he is home again. Handsome and ornery.

January 30, 1892

We attended church Sunday as a family, and it was an even balance as to who was harder to keep still, the four Elliot children or Captain Elliot himself. Jack kept up a stream of secretive winks at me in a most suggestive fashion, which made me blush despite the fact that I desperately tried to maintain my composure. Two year old Suzanne squirmed in my lap but was still for him, so he bounced her quietly on his knee. The boys, true to their deeply spiritual natures, snored softly through the entire sermon, and April sat still but looked out the windows, bored and restlessly shifting in her seat.

Jack waited until the preacher came to a particularly poignant story of death and despair, and he poked me in the ribs. It was terribly embarrassing to have to pretend to be moved by the preaching and cover my eyes with my hanky. Jack just sat back and grinned his secret smile, prouder than ever of himself to have yet again taken away my serenity.

I do not know why I love that man so. He tries me to the last, and torments me mercilessly sometimes. He conspires with the children and tells them to mind the General, meaning me, and the five of them all salute in a mocking way when I scold them about washing their hands and such. Thank goodness for his steady head and nurturing way with the children or ours would be a truly low and sordid life.

February 22, 1892

My life is so full of wonderful things right now. My children are happy and healthy, my husband loves us truly, and we are about to build a wondrous new house for them to grow up in. Almost every heifer on the ranch is carrying a calf, and birthing season starts next month and will get into full swing during the two months after that. I expect the herd will increase by a third to half again at least, if all of them come to term. I'm sure we'll lose a few to coyotes. I asked Mason to be especially on the watch. Savannah lost another baby but she is expecting again. Albert is losing some hair in the front of his head like Papa did. Their farm is all in blossom and heavenly.

Mama told me to make a special point to remember the best times of my life. There are so many hard things to live through, and latching on to the good things will give you strength to endure, she says. So I must remember this day. It is beautiful and this seems like the best time to live and the best place. The sky is clear but cold, here in the fort. The dust is settled, though. All seems peaceful and well inside my home, and I am anxious to move into the new one.

Jack is home for a while. He has been gone on Army business a couple of weeks. We are a noisy and blessed little family. I have made him a gift, for no real reason at all. It is a fine new cambric shirt and vest for when he is not on duty. He is real proud of them, too.

March 1, 1892

Today we went to Sergeant Lockwood's wedding to a lady named Adelita Muñoz Obregon. I don't know her at all, and when Sergeant Lockwood brought her by to introduce her yesterday, she seemed mighty stiff and unfriendly to me, although it wasn't anything I could put a name to. I hope he will be happy. He deserves some happiness.

March 22, 1892

Mrs. Sergeant George Lockwood seems to be a fitting addition to life here in this raggedy adobe fort. She fits right in with the scorpions and centipedes and poison spiders and all. Their arguments began within a week after their marriage. Poor Sergeant Lockwood looks so pained all the time now, and I am sure it will be just a few more weeks and he will be begging the General to please send him to be tortured by Apaches.

April 7, 1892

I have gotten a letter from a place called The Royal Office of Emigration and Classification all the way from Norway. It is not good news for Melissa, because it seems that Raalle is not a common name and the Minister of Emigration suggests that Mr. Raalle changed or shortened it when they came to the States. This is a fine looking letter, though, with a grand stamp and a gold seal all official looking. I will save it in my things until I can hand it to Melissa personally.

April 8, 1892

I went to Adelita Lockwood's house today. Even though she puts people off right away, and I know she torments poor George, I feel like I owe him still, so I thought if I could just break through to her maybe she would soften up towards him a little. She didn't really want me to visit I could tell, but I just sort of made myself at home, and talked a blue streak until she finally gentled a bit.

Later that night, I told Jack and he laughed a little, kind of pitying Sergeant Lockwood. He wanted a strong woman like you, he told me.

I said, Well, I hope I am not that cantankerous.

No. There is a difference in strong coffee and bitter medicine. Poor George!

April 12, 1892

What a surprise. Adelita Lockwood knocked on my door this morning. I made some coffee for us and in the middle of getting Suzanne's hair braided, we had a little talk. She told me she has been terribly unhappy here, and I said I thought as much. No one is friendly to her at all, she said, even though several people had told her they thought highly of her husband. Then she said it was all George's fault she is so unhappy.

I asked her, Why? Didn't you know he was a soldier when you married him?

She said it wasn't that, but that he didn't love her and he was a spineless coward.

Well, I stood right out of my chair. One thing I know for certain, I said, is that George Lockwood is not a coward. He is a brave and loyal man, and he saved Jack's life heroically.

But, she said, it is true he doesn't love her.

That, I said, is not something I have any knowledge about. I felt myself blushing, and went to get some more coffee. What is it that makes you say he doesn't love you? I asked her.

Well, she began to tell me, and it turns out her mother had told her any man who really loves her will not let her do foolish or bad things, and will teach her not to be foolish. I asked her what did she mean by that, and she says, He has not once so much as raised his hand toward me, even though I call him a coward right to his face. If he was a real man, and if he loved me, he would not let a wife say those things. Adelita was wringing her hanky in her hands, saying those things.

I told her if George Lockwood was found out to be beating his wife, he would likely hear from my husband for it. She should be thankful he will take all her worst insults and not raise his hand to her. Many men I know would have belted her like she was a man for saying those words.

Adelita looked real confused.

If all you want is a good licking, I told her, I'll take you out to see my Mama. She can lay a peach tree switch into your backside like you never felt before. I believe my Mama could whip the tar out of anyone alive if she chose to. Adelita laughed. Then she didn't look so mean and angry, either. So I said, If you are just trying to back him into a corner to see which way he'll strike, then you have a lot to learn about men. Sergeant Lockwood is much too clever and too proud to stoop to brute force. He wants to talk to you on a higher plane, more like he respects you and you respect him, and you can disagree without having to force your ways on each other.

I declare, but it was like she had never given that any thought before at all. She at first said, No, no, that is not the way of things. Then she got quiet and her face turned dark red like I thought she might bust out crying, but she stood up suddenly, just like she came, and said goodbye and left. I called out to her to come back any time. That woman tries my spirit, but every time I think of being rude to her, I think of arrows piercing Jack's chest, and I am not inclined to do anything hurtful to those people.

April 14, 1892

Sergeant Lockwood stopped here with a basketful of treats, little presents for everyone in the family, plus a sack of candies, a sack of good coffee, and a box of ribbons and lace for me. He had a nice smile on his face, and said Thank you, thank you, Mrs. Elliot, for befriending Adelita, thank you so. You'll never know what it means, he said, and then let the words trail off as his eyes went around the ground. Thank you, he said again, and took off.

May 25, 1892

Our new house is well under construction and appears to be a fine place. I have so much to do. Feeling somewhat ill, also, and I expect it may be a fifth Elliot child approaching. Albert and Savannah have seven children now. All pretty spunky, too, and when all these little cousins are together, it is a noisy and wondrous time of quarreling and love and ornery tricks on each other. They have added onto their house also, and it is a big rambling place that reminds me of Chess' spread in Texas.

This house in town we are building is nothing like that, but it has a fancy feeling to it. Mrs. Page helped me decide on some things so it is very formal and fancy looking. She came from a wealthy family and knows about things you can have in a house that I never heard of before. She has a way with things that I like and suggested many nice things I wrote to Harland to include, and she doesn't go in for fussiness but says real richness can be displayed in simplicity. I do like her special little touches of what Harland called artistic aristocracy, but nothing shares the homey and welcoming goodness of Savannah's scrubbed clean and simple place sprawling across the rocky ledge and filled to the brim with life.

Mama has not added on to her little place, and it suits her, she says. The ranch house isn't changed except we have added a brick fireplace besides the cookstove, and there will be warmer winter nights this year. We have moved some of the old furniture back into it and will be buying new for the house we are building. The children and I have made the ranch our second home when school is out. The herd is up to four hundred now and beef prices are high, but rustlers are everywhere. Mason even caught one of our own hands driving off a head or two each week to a canyon where his partner took them and sold them off.

May 30, 1892

Jack told me today that Sergeant and Mrs. Lockwood are expecting. He grinned real big at me and said, After you became friends, she sort of got the knack of married life. I want to know what you told her.

Nothing, Jack, I said. I don't want to know about the private side of other people's lives. But I know there have only been a few fights since I talked to her, and not the daily torment as before. He just laughed.

June 2, 1892

Went to see Adelita today. She seemed edgy and purely nervous. I told her it is just the coming baby, and not to worry, as I am on my fifth now, and I know all about it.

Later on, Jack and the children and I were just sitting down for dinner when Sergeant Lockwood came by. Something is wrong, he said. She is out of her mind. He said he was afraid she would hurt herself or the baby or something, even him.

June 19, 1892

Jack is taking the boys fishing today. There are places close by, but to make it more special, he called it the Men's Day Without Mama. They are riding three or four miles down the Santa Cruz to try to catch some fish. I told them that is fine with me. April and Suzanne and I are taking the wagon and heading for the end of town to teach April how to shoot, and we will have a little picnic and learn some embroidery stitches. We are all looking forward to the fine day and the mild weather, in addition to a little vacation from the headaches of construction.

I am glad to be away from the fort. Adelita Lockwood has gone plum crazy. She is not just staring and numb like my Mama was for a while. She seems all right one minute and the next she takes to shrieking like a wounded mountain lion. George took all the knives out of the house, and the scissors, and everything he could find with even a piece of glass she could use to cut with. He is horrified with her. I suspect that in his mind is the idea of having her put away somewhere too, but he wants to wait for the baby. Mama and Savannah have both told me they knew of women who go insane from having a baby. Some of them it is before the baby is born, and some right after. It isn't the same as having a houseful of crying children and no clean diapers left, that is a different kind of crazy. Adelita is off somewhere in a terrible place in her head.

June 20, 1892

My brave little Gilbert got a fish hook caught in his hand and his Papa cut it out with his knife. I made him wash it and wash it until he was purely aggravated. I was perturbed with Jack for letting him stay out and fish for hours without some antiseptic on it, but Jack says he will be fine. He asked me how was the target practice, and so I told him April doesn't seem to be able to manage it yet at all. She is too afraid of a gun to be safe with one. But at any rate, we had a nice picnic, and she did some fine embroidery. It is strange to have this little girl who is my flesh and bone, and yet she seems so separate from me.

We are going to be sure all our children learn to ride and shoot and throw a rope, besides being able to read and cipher and put down a proper sentence with good spelling.

September 1, 1892

Imagine that. Here is a story in the Weekly Citizen about our new house. A fellow from the paper came by last week as we were moving in, and asked around and wanted to see every nook and cranny. He wrote here about the new gas lights, which he says adorn and make lustrous few of our town's homes, and about the good design which Harland did, and the portico and the mock gables and everything. The article describes our house as "an impressive red brick structure with painted stucco around the second floor. The gabled third floor windows overlook town through gingerbread balustrades. The roof is of the latest in scientific advances with tar and slate and hammered lead gutter plates, and will not leak in heavy rains nor blow away in a storm." He even did a whole paragraph dedicated to the designed, two-colored, hardwood floors.

And there is two paragraphs about the indoor convenience. Well, that is purely embarrassing, as if we wanted everyone in the state to know about our toilet set up. He described the bathtub, and the water pump, and even the well we drilled and the small pipe. That is a fine idea, though, to drill a hole with a tool instead of with shovels. That way we are left with a small hole that no people or animals can fall into, and there is just a pipe coming out leading to the pump house. All I have to do inside to get water is work the handle, there will be no hauling of buckets in here, even to fill the bath. I am proud and embarrassed all at once. I imagine there will be a string of folks lined up now to see where we take a bath.

November 21, 1892

Besides the fact that tomorrow is my birthday, I am hurrying to clean this house because Ernest is coming day after tomorrow, and the day after that will be Thanksgiving. I feel every one of my twenty-nine years today. Jack should be home this afternoon some time and will stay around if I have any say at all. Rudolfo and Celia are here already with their two children. They are so much fun to have around. What a good husband Rudolfo is. And Celia is learning some English so she can be more independent. We have spent hours catching up on everyone's families, in between dusting and sweeping. I told them to please let me finish and they were my guests, but they said they came early to help, and if they were going to be insulted by being called guests they would leave. They both said this with a smile, but I know their feelings are too sincere to ask them to be merely guests.

The morning dawned slowly and bright, but a wind started up as soon as the sun was clear of the mountains. After leaving the children at school, I went to the Depot at 8:45, but the train didn't arrive until 9:15. In the Territories, being only fifteen minutes late is generally considered early. I waited as more and more people poured out of the cars, and I began to think Ernest had missed the train, when I heard someone holler, Sarah!

There was Ernest, swooping around me and picking me up in a bear hug. He has filled out a little, but mostly he just looked wiry and strong and lean. He also had a big, deep looking scar down one side of his jaw to the neck, and I said right away, Ernest, what happened to you? Well, I knew it was rude to say such things right out, but he is not a stranger, and since we were children, we were always able to tell each other everything.

It's nothing, he said. Just had a little disagreement with a Sioux warrior who wanted a piece of scalp. I'm so glad to see you, Sarah A. Why, wait 'til you see the surprise I've brought you!

Oh, Ernest, I said, that can wait. I'm just so glad you're here. Let's get your bags and get to the house.

No, oh no, he said. This surprise can't wait at all. Come here, Sarah. Come right on over here. He started pulling my arm, and we bustled through some people and came up to a little stack of bags and parcels, where a woman was standing right in the middle of them. Here, Sarah, he says. Here is my big surprise. I've brought you a new sister. I want you to meet Miss Felicity, Mrs.

Felicity Prine. The woman turned around when he said that and fluffed out a parasol over her head.

I know my mouth opened and nothing came out for a full minute. My eyes opened even wider. The woman put out her hand as if I was a man and would take it and kiss it, but I just shook hands very quickly. I tried to smile, and she just beamed as if she was the happiest person on earth. Standing before me was a woman the likes of which I have never before seen. She had gussied up hair in curling tassels, and a huge hat covered with ruffles and bows and little dried roses tucked into the band. She had tied it in a great big sash bow under her chin like a little child in a sunbonnet. Her face was plump and shiny looking, and flushed as if she had just run in the summer time, although it was chill out. And for a girl with plain brown hair, she had the darkest, blackest eyebrows I have ever seen.

Her dress was almost as gaudy as her hat, just miles of ruffles around her bosom and hem, and little ribbon bows every few inches. She looked just like a doll in a store, a very tight-packed, plump, cinched in, snapped and tied kind of doll, too. She shook her parasol, and just then the breeze tried to snatch it away from her. She smiled largely at me.

Oh, dear Sister Sarah! She said. Your sweet brother has told me so very much about you! I can hardly wait to see your family and your wonderful house and your ranch and all. It must be wonderful to be so rich! Ernest and I are going to come into some money of our own, soon. Won't that be grand?

Yes, I'm sure, I said. I felt completely dazed by her looks and by what she said. Speaking right up about money to someone you don't even know is beyond rude. I tried to smile, and told Ernest over and over he should have told me sooner. I was thinking in my head he should have too, because I have got him and Mason and three cousins in the room together and no provisions for a lady at the same place, so I will have to put Mason and the cousins somewhere else, even if it is on the sofa in the parlor, or maybe on a cot in the boys' room. I said again, How wonderful, you two. Congratulations and best wishes. When did you all marry?

Just last week, Ernest said. I could see he was practically beaming with pride.

We filled the short span between the depot and my house with little details about who would be coming over and when, and the room arrangements, and then there was a great commotion getting all the parcels and bags onto the back porch.

Miss Felicity, I said, why don't you go on in and make yourself at home, while Ernest helps me stow away the buggy?

Oh, that will be just swell with me, Sister Sarah, she said, and flounced into the kitchen door.

Ernest, I said, this is a real surprise. Mama will be amazed.

Won't she though? I bet not one of you ever thought you'd see Ernest Prine married to the likes of her. A real lady. A very fancy, genteel sort of girl. Why, when I met Miss Felicity, I was just bowled over that she would even talk to me. Ain't she something?

She sure is, I said. Where did you meet her?

Well, she is from back east. She is a city bred lady, not used to the west at all. I was so surprised when she agreed to marry me I could have hollered to the moon. She was just standing on a sidewalk in Taylor's Bend, South Dakota, waiting for a friend, she said, and when I offered to help her across the street, she took my arm. Well, we started up a conversation, and never seemed to quit talking for two solid days. Then my leave was up, and I had to get back to the fort, but she said she would stay in town if I cared to see her again. Ain't she fine?

Fine, I said, real fine. I'd like her not to call me Sister Sarah. It makes me sound like one of the nuns at the hospital, I told him.

Oh, sure enough. I'm sure she's just excited, he said. She's real special.

Ernest, I said, hand me that rail there. Well, Miss Felicity has got quite a special way about her. You just can't help noticing her. I patted Brownie on the rump and closed the bottom half of the door to let some sun in the top and warm the place.

I know, he said. He was fairly glowing as we left the dark of the stable for the sunlight. The wind blew dust around the yard and the chickens in the coop fussed a little. Ernest leaned over real close. Sarah, I need you to do me a big favor. You see, Miss Felicity is so very fine and genteel, she's not used to any kind of hard work or anything. She's had servants all her life, and lived a quiet and refined way. So you've got to be very patient and mild around her. There can't be any loud racket or busy-ness, or her nerves will get riled.

They will? I asked. Well, I'll try not to be too loud when I fix dinner and bathe the children.

Oh, that's right, he said, how are the children? Boy, I can't wait to see 'em. You've got how many now? I bet they're big. And smart. All in school, right? Do you think they can keep quiet while me and Felicity are here, for her nerves?

Oh, certainly, I said, feeling more than a little bit aggravated at all this fuss. I looked him square in the eyes and said, They are the quietest children ever born. Purely quiet.

And, you will try, won't you, he said, whispering, you'll try to act genteel in front of her?

Ernest, I was getting ready to scold him.

Oh, Sister, called Felicity from the porch. Sister, I've tried to make some tea and had a little accident. Can you come here? Quick?

There in the middle of my two-colored braided hardwood floor sat the teakettle, red and glowing hot, which it will only do if it had had no water in it, scorching a black hole into the wood. Felicity began to moan about having burned her fingers on the handle as I grabbed it up with the hem of my skirt around the handle and set it back on the stove.

Oh dear, oh dear, said Felicity, and she buckled up and cried.

Well, my first inclination was to slap her silly, but instead I said, Now, it'll be all right. Jack will sand the floor and it will be good as new.

Well, Felicity snuffled like a little child, If you're sure.

Before long I had made some tea and Anna left for home, so Suzy was with us, and Ernest made a big fuss over her and getting to know her new Auntie Felicity. Suzy couldn't handle that mouthful of consonant sounds, so her version of it came out like An' Flippy. I didn't expect more of a baby, but Felicity kept on and on at her to say it right, until my little girl started to worry and I knew she was about to cry. I finally scooped up Suzy and gave her the little box of colored spools and some yarn to thread them on, and told Felicity that it was better not to push her too much at first, she will learn the new name later on.

Felicity lifts her eyebrows at me and nods, and then says, Oh, I see. She's simple minded.

No, I said, she's not in the least. Then I said I had to start dinner and went in the kitchen and made enough noise to rile her nerves good. Pea brained fuss and feathers like that calling my child simple. Oh, Ernest, what a surprise you have brought me!

As soon as we ate a little something, she wanted to see the whole house, and then settled in the parlor for a minute. I knew my wash water was hot so I went to the kitchen to clean up the dishes.

I could hear her in the parlor and she says to Celia, Fetch me my hatbox, girl.

Celia shrugged at her and said back, No anglais, señora.

Then Felicity hollers to Ernest, Tell your sister to tell this serving girl to fetch my box, honey dearest, please? Well, I knew Celia had been real helpful at dinner but nothing she did put in my mind that she was anything but a friend. She ate at the table with us, what did that woman think? I know Celia knew more "anglais" than she let on just now, also.

Here came Celia with tears in her eyes and I grabbed her quick and hugged her and told her not to mind. I wasn't going to have my friends insulted. So I went towards the parlor to tell Felicity my friend is not a servant and my child is not a fool, and as I did, here she came again, saying, Sister Sarah, did I say something wrong? You mustn't judge me too harsh, after all I'm so anxious to have everybody in my new family like me and I want us to be sisters. Let's be friends, okay Darling?

Well, that's fine, I said. And inside I knew that in all she said, the words "I'm sorry," had yet to appear. All these misunderstandings have been my fault for judging too harshly. Yes, indeed. So I said to her, Would you help wash and dry these here dishes from our dinner? and held her out a towel.

She says back, Oh, how I'd love to, Darling! But I have a hand condition.

A hand condition? I said.

Yes, just can't take soap. Simply can't.

How sad for you, I said. How do you wash your hands?

Well, she says, my dear Ernest gives me this special kind he gets in the mail called Mrs. Reed's. It's the only one I can stand.

Sure enough? I said. Well, Ernest is a thoughtful fellow, isn't he?

Yes, Ma'am, she says, and lifts up a bundle of flounces in her skirt, turns around on one heel, and puffs out of the kitchen like a cloud on a frying pan.

Later on, I hear her walking around on the wooden porch. I can tell where anyone is out there. She plops herself down on the wicker settee by the back door and is just lolling around when I hear Jack's horse gallup into the yard. Pretty soon I hear the squeaking hinge on the horse shed, and Celia and I tipped over to the dining room window to watch what happened next. Well, here came Jack, stomping off dirt and dusting himself the way he always does as he comes up the back steps.

He stopped, startled, right in front of her and said, Hello. Hello, Miss.

Well, Miss Felicity perks right up and says, in a real affected, giggly voice, Oh, hello, sir. My, my, my. You have pure fluster-rated me, what with your handsomeness and all. Then up flies her hand like she did to me.

Jack has got his hat in his hands and is looking puzzled. I looked at Celia and made a face and she laughed. Jack stiffened up and took her fingers and bowed real formally over her hand, snapping his heels together, and said, Captain J. Elliot, at your service, Miss.

Well, that woman squealed and giggled like a fat child. Then she patted herself on the bosom and said, Oh, sir, you do honor me, why I might just faint with the, then she stopped quick and looked around, and stood up so she was so close to him her ruffles whipped against him in the breeze. Celia and I leaned away from the curtain so they couldn't see us. Felicity's voice got real quiet, but we could tell she was just talking up a storm, and I saw the look on Jack's face go from puzzled to amused, to kind of wary. Then he made a little step towards the door, and she grinned like a cat and pushed her hand through his arm and got up even closer than before to come in the house with him.

La muestra, whispered Celia.

I looked at the place where Felicity's big bosom was nudged up tight against Jack's arm, and I said under my breath, pescadora.

Celia clapped her hand against her mouth and neither one of us was smiling now.

Well, I went to the back door to greet them, and Jack looked me in the eyes. His voice was happy sounding, but his face was plum curious and stunned. We have a new sister in law, he announced grandly, as if I hadn't known yet.

Yes, indeed, I said. Felicity, maybe you'd like to wake up <u>your</u> husband and let him know Jack is home and we'll be having supper quick? Then I turned to Celia and said in Mexican, She has still got her corset lying on my husband's arm, and I smiled and nodded.

Celia said in English, I need some help to set a table, Felicité. Come here with me.

She let go of Jack as if it took all her strength to pull her hands off him, and I followed him quick up the stairs.

What do you make of that? Jack whispered to me as he was drying his face.

I think my brother has lost his mind, I told him.

He said, I'll bet your Mama is going to have a conniption. He was grinning as he hung up the towel, and said, Well, he's got a right to marry anyone he pleases. I seem to remember he isn't the only Prine to lasso a mustang. Seems there was this younger sister with her cap set on a soldier.

I never set my cap for you. You just followed me around like a bird dog 'til I couldn't do anything but marry you.

Oh, I see, he said. Is that the way you're telling it?

Jack, I'm serious, I said. This is nothing but trouble for Ernest. It's not like lassoing a mustang. I think Ernest has got a wildcat by the tail.

Then, that Jack Elliot burst into the most heathen laughing I ever heard, and shook the window laughing so I know everyone in the house heard. When he finally sputtered down he was red in the face and teary eyed.

Would you mind telling me what I said that was so funny, Captain Elliot?

Yes, he said, I would mind, but that was quite surely the most truthful way to describe, and then he started laughing again. Sarah, he said, enough of them. How are you feeling? Come here, he said, and kiss me and I will stop being a lowdown cuss and help you with supper, too. I have told them I want two weeks off. How's this new baby doing? Is your back still hurting? Did you tell them all the doctor said you aren't supposed to lift anything?

And so, in that frame of mind, we returned to the company, conspiring to be welcoming in spite of ourselves.

Well, it wasn't long before Savannah and Albert and Mama and Mason arrived, and the house was a jumble of noise and confusion and happiness. Of course Mama was just stunned with Ernest's new wife. She smiled, and looked at me and lifted her eyebrows, and I did the same back. We ate tamales and corn and tortillas and beans until we could burst, and Savannah's girls had each made their first pies, and they brought so much with them for tomorrow's Thanksgiving dinner that we shared the twin's good efforts tonight.

During supper, Jack looked at me across the table and the candles made us all kind of sparkly even with the gas lights burning. Once I caught him smiling at me during all the noise, and he winked like we shared a secret, and I smiled back. Then all our boys started talking loud and Celia's and Savannah's littlest both began to cry in the sudden loudness, and there was Jack, smiling through the candle flames, and he mouthed the words "I love you" across the commotion.

Pretty soon we had the children's faces washed and set them in the parlor where Ernest said he would tell them a story. Felicity followed them in and sat herself in a chair while the ladies and Jack and Mason went in the kitchen and began cleaning dishes. Rudolfo went to the shed to tend everyone's horses and said he would check for eggs in the chicken coop. Jack and Mason made some coffee and toted water pails here and there for us, and we washed and talked and dried and then began setting up for the big dinner tomorrow.

Mama asked why Felicity wasn't in here with us and I told them all, very seriously, that she had a hand condition, and wanted to but couldn't. Then I told them about the soap, and every last person in the room about split wide open trying not to laugh out loud. Rudolfo shelled pecans Albert had brought, and we heard about how Albert broke his arm trying to prune a dead branch in a tree.

Jack laughed and said, You know you aren't supposed to saw off the same branch you're standing on, Albert.

We all laughed and Albert said he was just reaching too far over his head and lost his footing, but we had to tease him about standing in a tree cutting branches anyway.

November 25, 1892

It is a beautiful day for Thanksgiving. This morning early I saw Savannah kneeling in the dining room, praying. Then she was done and she looked up, watching the sun rise over the Catalinas. It is real different for a sunrise, here, than out at the ranch. Everything was gold and pinks and glittery, and the mountains looked dark violet under the break of daylight. When I was sure she wouldn't mind the intrusion, I went and sat with her, and we talked for a little while before going in to start the coffee.

Sarah, she says to me, I'd never complain and I'm sure grateful for your home, but is there any way at all we could change bedrooms with Ernest and Felicity?

Surely, I told her. But you all have the best room. Is there something wrong? Is there a drafty spot in there?

Oh, no, she said. It is warm and lovely. But I thought, well, it might be quieter. And the children are all up on that third floor with them.

Quieter? Are the children getting up at night? Are they noisy?

Savannah blushed nearly crimson. It isn't the children. It's them. In the room over us, she whispered. It is their honeymoon, after all.

Oh, Lord, I said. And I turned my own face away.

She said, It's just that the children are on the same floor.

Oh, Savannah. Oh, oh, was all I could say. I'll have to have a reason. I'll say, maybe, that it'll be easier for Felicity not to have to climb extra stairs, she'll like that. How will that be honey?

Let's go get those turkeys started, I said. I need some coffee extra strong to get me going on all this cooking ahead.

Savannah and I hugged each other and went to the kitchen. She is sure the finest friend and sister I could ever have, and suddenly I thought, maybe next to her I am not giving Felicity a fair shake, so I decided I will just try again to see her in a better light.

We had almost an hour together in pure quiet, working, before the little ones came toddling down the stairs. The boys were having a bed-wrestling match and someone fell, then we heard tears and wailing, then just more laughing. Whatever it was, they must have made amends.

You know, I said to Savannah, as we watched Suzy and her three smallest ones working at their oatmeal, I think your Mary Pearl resembles Ulyssa.

Oh, said Savannah. Not really? Do you think so? I hoped.

See her bright eyes, the way they turn up a bit at the corners? That sweet child has more than her fair share of beauty already. She is Ulyssa Lawrence's niece for sure.

Savannah smiled and petted her little head gently. How's my little Pearl? Is that good oatmeal? Then she turned to me. Why, Sarah, I believe you're right. She does indeed. Oh, I'm so thankful. It won't even be prideful to have her portrait made to send to Ulyssa in the sanitarium to show her.

By the time we got the big ones fed and the men, the house again was a roar of voices. The boys went out to find a stick big enough to hit a ball Charlie had wound up with string and rawhide, and play a game of Baseball. Then Albert, who had somehow got his buttons done, splint and all, presented them with an India rubber ball, but they hit it so well they nearly took out a window, so I made them go to the back and get out by the shed.

As noon approached, I suddenly noticed how tired I was, and after Mama scolded me for working so hard, I went upstairs intending to rest for an hour. All the women at the kitchen table purely fussed at me and promised they would tend to everything and Thanksgiving dinner would be ready at two, so I had plenty of time. As I went up the last stairs to our room, I passed Ernest and Felicity, coming down for the first time today.

Felicity asked me what had I fixed for breakfast, and would I mind bringing it to her?

In that instant all my aggravation at her came back just like the tick of a clock had brought it on. Just as I was about to open my mouth to say something I'm sure I would regret, I heard a terrible wail from the back of the house. Downstairs, I found Gilbert and Clover and Joshua all bearing Charlie like he was a sacrificial ram into the kitchen. Charlie was fussing at them to leave him be, though was surely in some kind of distress. Charlie's arm was hanging down, and he was doing his level best not to cry, but he was about to let go. Jack and Albert and Rudolfo rushed up also, and with everyone trying to get a look at Charlie at once, it made me dizzy and I leaned on his chair for my own support.

We have put aside all the cooking to take him to see the doctor. Mama and Celia, and of course Felicity, stayed behind to mind the turkeys, and the whole rank and file of our family waited in front of the doctor's house for Charlie to come out with a splint. Charlie's arm is broken, in the very same place as his Uncle Albert's. It seems the boys all went to catch the ball at once as it was coming down out of the sun overhead, and the four oldest ones crashed together without even seeing each other.

There has been no rest today, and after Thanksgiving supper, which was purely wonderful and noisy and which we ate again as if we were sitting at a trough instead of the fancy dining table, Jack insisted almost gruffly that I had to lie down. But I didn't want to miss anything and Charlie said his arm hurt him terribly, so I convinced them all that I would rest and put my feet up in the parlor, and Charlie could sit by me. Before long, though, I was asleep and when I awoke the dishes were all clean and the house was quiet with all the family outside visiting. Charlie was asleep next to me with his poor splinted arm resting on my lap. That is how I happened to have some time to write this journal today amidst the commotion.

It is a rare thing to see that boy not moving. Even in his sleep his body seems to be quivering, trying to grow as fast as it can. He eats about five meals a day, and he is just a child. He has got a big scratch across his nose and cheek from Lord knows what. And freckles, and rambling, wavy hair like his Papa's. His hands look too big for his arms, and his nails are all broken and ragged on calloused fingers with a wart or two on nearly every knuckle.

I was sitting there trying to think how I could get up without bothering his arm, when Gilbert tiptoed into the room. Mama, are you awake? he says.

Yes. Come here, son, I whispered.

Look what I made you, Mama, he said. Uncle Ernest showed me how to whittle and gave me this here knife. He showed me a pocket folding knife and at the same time produced a long, thin, sharp twig he had peeled and put a point on.

Well, look there, I said. That is a fine thing, son, and I know what I will do with it. Next time I make a cake and need to run something around the edge to get it out of the pan, I will have a good tool for it and the knives won't go dull or scrape ashes from the pan. Just smooth wood; it will be a fine tool.

Gilbert was glowing with pride.

You know, I told him, if you could find a good sized stick that had a kind of hook in it, and smooth it pretty good and round off the ends, I could use that to pull a cake pan out of the oven. His eyes lit up and he folded up the knife, handed me his gift, and went out the back door to hunt for a stick.

Charlie looked over at me, and said, It's just an old stick, Mama.

It's a gift from my boy, I told him. A kitchen tool. Then I saw him looking kind of glum. See, I told him, You run faster and throw better than anyone in the school. You have a real hand for riding and roping, which you took to faster than any child I ever saw. And your brother is littler and not as quick to do those things. But he likes fine work with his hands. What's Gilbert going to ever do that he can claim as his own? He can't be you. He's got to find himself a talent, and maybe this is just the start of some fine whittling.

Whittling ain't nothing but a waste of time, he said.

Isn't.

Isn't. It's just a stick.

Well, you'll know it isn't just a stick when your own boy hands you a thing he made with his hands. Then we went outside on the porch with the others until the sun set.

November 28, 1892

Albert and Savannah and the children went home yesterday with Mama. The Maldonados and Mason left the day before. For four days now I have tried every way I know to be kind to Mrs. Ernest Prine but I am purely out of patience. This morning I found Felicity counting the silverware, and she asked me since Ernest told her he gave me some of it did I plan to give it back now that they were married.

That woman has not lifted so much as a finger to contribute to the work around here. I have flatly refused to do her washing and ironing as she asked, and that caused an hour long fit of wailing and crying. She wants to take a bath every blessed day even though she has done nothing to break a sweat all day, and she spends hours at a time in the bathroom so that all of us have more than once had to make use of the outhouse behind the shed because of her and it is too blessed cold to think that is no small sacrifice. She lies around and Ernest totes things to her, then she complains about them and he brings something else.

Not only that, but I have discovered because one day she was careless and forgot to do up the way she usually does, that those black, black eyebrows are painted on. That woman is a hussy if ever there was one. The one time I got her to lend a hand in the kitchen, she dished up supper and made sure the biggest piece of steak was on the bottom and started the plate around so it came to her last. Same with the biscuits. The biggest, lightest ones seem to make it to her plate every meal. Any time she thinks she is alone with Jack, she finds a way to bump against him or touch him. He has taken to following me from room to room, even if he is reading a book, just so he doesn't take the chance of being left alone where she can use him as a scratching post. All the while my brother Ernest just moons over her and eyes her like a calf looking at a teat.

Ernest, I said, we have a passel of company. There have been upwards of twenty-three people in this house and more than half of them under the age of twelve. I have cooked and cleaned for this army for days. There is washing to do, and children to tend, and floors to sweep and furniture to dust. There are lamps to clean and stoves to watch. If she needs company, she will have to come downstairs. She is not sick, and she ought to be lending a hand, not whining about her nerves.

This morning we are leaving in just a bit for the ranch. It will be a slow ride as Jack is taking me in the buggy so it is not too bumpy. My back is hurting so badly I cannot ride the wagon and certainly not on a horse. Well, we don't have an extra team for Ernest to ride Felicity in the wagon, and Jack went to get loan of some stock from the fort so Ernest and Gilbert could ride, but Charlie shouldn't because of his arm, so he will hold Suzy in the back for me and be smashed up next to fat Felicity the whole way. Poor boy.

That woman grinds my grits, and that's a fact.

November 29, 1892

This visit to the ranch may just be the very best thing I ever did. Felicity just could not say enough about our house in town, and when she found out how many hundreds of acres I have bought, and that Jack lets me run the whole thing, and how many cattle there are, she was just full of questions like how much do cattle sell for, and how fast do they have calves, and how much money did I think the whole place was worth. I asked her right out did she have in mind to buy the place out, but she said, Oh, no, it was just interesting to her.

There are always lots of chores to do and she was certainly interested in anything that had to do with making money, particularly how much money Jack and I had, not necessarily what she could lend a hand at. She asked more questions than I had answers for, and finally I got to saying, I don't even know how much land there really is, and I leave it to the hired men to count the cattle. She kept saying she would like to own a spread herself, and she and Ernest could work it, or she could buy into my place on credit, and work here and pay off the loan from us, while taking part in the profits also, as we have certainly managed to live fine in that big house in Tucson, although of course, she just couldn't do without a couple of maids and a cook. I just didn't know what to say, but luckily Jack said right out that credit was something we didn't deal in, and had no plans to.

Last night as I had just got the children to bed, Felicity let out a scream that would have split a rock. It was only an old tarantula crawled into her room from the open window, and she was cursing the fact that there was no screen on it like in town. I picked up the little hairy fellow in a newspaper and set him carefully down outside and she screamed at me to Smash it, smash it!

And I said, I will certainly not, as those nice tarantulas keep the scorpions down, and eat several of them at night. That's probably what he was doing in your room, looking for supper. Then my true meanness came out for all my family to see, because I added, Besides, if you've got tarantulas, you know you don't have rattlers, because they'd eat 'em.

Well, I have never actually seen a conniption before, until now. Ernest looked at me real mad for saying that and started to explain to her that I was just being touchy, but before long he was backed into a corner and quiet. That woman went beside herself, all dressed in the biggest, most ruffled and fluffy night dress I ever saw, with her hair up in rags, her eyebrows down to normal size, and ranting around the room like a wet hen.

Ernest fell to saying, Now, Sweetie, Now Honey, now, now, until I wanted to box his head. He was standing up in the corner of the room repeating it when I just walked out and shut the door.

December 1, 1892

Savannah's house was no escape for me. Felicity insisted on walking with me and taking the air on the way from my house. Gilbert asked me why she needs so much air, and is it because she is so pillowy? I just laughed and clapped my hand on his mouth and told him not to say things like that out loud, even if he thinks it.

December 3, 1892

We are headed back to town. Ernest and Felicity are both mad and silent and pickley looking.

She said yesterday she had figured out that if she just had a screen on her window and a bucket under each post of her bed so nothing could crawl up the legs, she was real happy staying there. In fact, between the house in town and the ranch, she said, she could just feel like staying forever, it was so homey. And so nice for a winter, as she had never seen a winter without several feet of snow in Pennsylvania. Well, by then, I knew for a fact that my brother Ernest had been shooting off his mouth to her about this ranch, claiming that he owned a share of it and the pecan farm too, and that our family was going to be the wealthiest family in Arizona Territory before long. He flat out told me that he had bragged to her before they got married, too. Not a word of that is true; this ranch was Jimmy's and now it is mine and Jack's. Yesterday, just before Felicity's sudden change of mood, she had pestered him to make Albert buy out for cash Ernest's share of the farm, and he was going to try. And he wanted me to consider her good offer of buying a share of this ranch on credit so she could help out and they would own some of it, also.

And she decided, she told me, to learn to cook, so she could be helpful at the ranch and feed the ranch hands. Even when I told her they cook for themselves, she insisted that she would feed them for me. When she thought about them, she said, her eyes just watered right up. She wanted to be sure we knew that she knew Ernest had a share of the pecan farm that Albert runs, and he intended to own part of my ranch, especially if she stayed and worked there and cooked for the hands. Cooking was something, she declared loud and long, that she could do for those poor, poor men out there living in the barn with no one to care for them.

Well, I said, They don't live in a barn, it is a bunkhouse, and they always have a man to cook for them, and they clean their own mess or they aren't allowed to stay, but she wouldn't listen. I told her it would aggravate her hand condition, but she said it is purely better from living on the ranch. I told her every way I knew how that it would never do, and then I thought of something that would fix her wagon for sure.

I did it while Ernest and Jack were gone over to Albert's where they were getting wood to re-roof part of Mama's house. I figured that's when Ernest was also going to try to put his hand in Albert's pocket, too.

I went to the bunkhouse and told my two top hands, Bud Higgins and Sterling Foster, to run up a few of the range bulls that we had missed during roundup, which they had been keeping in a section west by the Raalle land. I said, We are going to have some out-of-season branding. They didn't really want to do it and I don't blame them, but I gave them each two dollars extra for the day's work, and I told Felicity to get ready for some ranch work, as she was about to learn the one thing I needed her to do so she could live here.

Well, Bud and Sterl held the first bull still, tied him with ropes, then told Felicity how to cut the soft part on him to make him a steer, and save enough of the skin to sew shut. They handed her a sharp knife and the needle with the special catgut thread. She cried out and blubbered, and wouldn't do it. They put the branding iron in her hands and told her to punch him in the rump and she cried some more and only waved it over the fur. The bull wailed at her and she screamed. Then they got out the de-horning saw and started the cauterizing iron heating in the fire and said, Try your hand at this here, Ma'am, and commenced to explain exactly what she was to do with those things, shoving the blade in the head and searing off the horn and all, and she fainted there in the corral onto a little fresh pile of steaming manure.

They said Get up, Get up! We don't need a cook. We need someone to do this here. It takes a quick hand to get those horns out before he hooks you, and you got to plunge that red cauterizing iron in the hole. She fainted again.

We fairly tormented her until she got up and stumbled to the house, crying sort of addled, saying, Fetch my bags, Ernest, Fetch my clothes!

I just watched her run, and sighed real deep, and turned my back on her. I watched the men brand the half dozen strays, and they simply blunted the horns and didn't do anything else but leave them to be bulls and turned them into the long corral. Pretty soon here came Ernest saying he has to leave quick and get Felicity back home, clear to his post. He was plenty mad at me and made it real clear I had strained every last nerve Felicity owned.

I am sorry, I said, really sorry that you feel that way. But she wanted to live on this ranch, and I'm not supporting slackers here. Everyone on this ranch works or they don't eat. And I said, Isn't that right? to the hands.

Sterling and Bud both said, Yes, Ma'am.

Well, we can't send them to town in our buggy and have no way to return ourselves, and I don't want to put out Savannah and Albert, so we are all leaving at once for Tucson so Felicity and Ernest can take the next train out of here. It took me fifteen minutes to be packed and ready, except for five more minutes it took me to go back to the corral and give Bud and Sterling each another dollar. Hallelujah!

Two days ago Adelita and George had a tiny baby girl. The baby looks healthy although it is entirely covered with blond hair. She is a bit early, which is the reason for it and it will go away, the doctor said. Everything seemed peaceful with them when we left, and Adelita didn't have a very long labor, only seven or eight hours. The baby's name is Hannah.

Tonight it started to rain, and in a little while, the rain turned to ice and then to snow. The children are excited, it is their first time to see snow. I'm sure there won't be much, but it is beautiful and makes me feel good to be inside with a kettle of beans and ham going on the stove and everyone inside safe and warm.

Lord, look down here and let me know what to do. It is past midnight. After we went to bed, the snow had stopped and became rain again, chattering on the metal flashings on the roof as the snow-turned-ice broke and slid off. I thought I heard something, an hour ago, and Jack said, no, it is just the rain. But again I heard soft tapping, too regular, and it had a human feel to it, so I went downstairs to see if someone was at the door. The sound came from the kitchen, and when I opened the door, a man pushed his way into the house. I held the lamp high.

Mrs. Elliot, said George Lockwood. I can't go back there. She's done something, Oh, God, she's done something! He was literally sobbing, wrapped tight in his coat and poncho, all white knuckled and wet and freezing. His breath made a cloud around his head.

George! was all I could say.

Then Jack was behind me with another lamp. Come in here, man, he said.

No, George said. I'm going. I can't stay. Oh, God, he said again. God forgive her!

Lockwood, said Jack, settle yourself. Have a chair. Tell us what's wrong. Then Jack reached his hand out to pat George on the shoulder. As he did it, George backed up against the wall quick, and there in his hand was a Colt revolver and I heard the hammer nock back on the spring.

No, I'm not staying. No! He said, God forgive me but I'll kill you if you try to stop me, and then he opened the door and ran away into the dark. Then we heard hooves beating past, slopping in the wet.

So I am sitting here alone in the bedroom and Jack has ridden through the rain and cold to the fort to see what has happened, and then back here to tell me, and now he is gone to get the Marshal. He said it looked like Adelita had murdered her baby, and George found her with bloody hands, and shot her dead with a solitary bullet hole through her head.

Maybe he came here because he thought we would understand. Maybe he thought we could stop him. Or forgive him. But it was too late. He is gone. So he will be wanted for murder and desertion, also, and if he is found he will surely hang. Run, George Lockwood. Run.

December 9, 1892

It is now five in the morning and Jack is gone. He came back here and saddled up for a long ride, since he had ridden bareback to the Marshal's and the fort. He loaded up both his pistols and the bandolier he sometimes carries, and then took his old army carbine and plenty of shot for it in his saddlebags.

You're going after George? I asked him.

He just nodded.

Will you take some food? I said.

No, he said.

He might be back in a few hours. He might be gone days. So I went in the kitchen and put some slices of bread and leftover roast beef in some waxed paper. I put those and some hard candy in his saddlebags with a clean handkerchief full of dried fruit. I dread to think what is in Jack's mind. I dread to think what is in my own.

We both know there is no sense trying to follow a track through mud before dawn. But he thinks he knows where George might go. I put on a pot of coffee but he left without having any. Jack left to track down his friend.

I sat in my parlor and stared out the dark windows. I tried not to think that George might be so wrong in the head that he would lay in wait for Jack, but is just flying for his life on a fast horse somewhere.

The sun was up although it was cloudy and dim when I woke to find Suzy climbing up into my lap. I was cold and stiff.

Mama, she said, have some bed'fast.

I patted her head and went to the kitchen. April and the boys were yawning and scuffling their feet around the floor, looking dazed because the heat stove has not been warmed for them like I usually do. By the time I got a fire going, I heard a strange sound coming from the little barn we built to shelter the buggy and a team of horses. It sounded like a striking of something heavy and wet, like two men fighting, but it never stopped, it kept on and on. I told April to start some oatmeal for the others, and to keep everyone inside while I went to see what the horses were kicking.

In the barn I found Jack, swinging a shovel against a soggy bale of hay. He had already broken the shovel part off, and was beating the hay again and again with the handle. He looked weary and wild-eyed, and damp with sweat and cold rain. Over and over he swung that big handle like a machine of some sort, grunting with every beat. The horses skittered around in their stalls, fretting.

I held a lantern up high as I could. Jack, did you find him?

Yes, he said, and smashed the pole into the hay.

I felt my heart squeeze up and I couldn't breathe. I was hoping he would never find George. What did you do?

Jack spoke slowly, whacking the hay with every word. I am ashamed to tell you, Sarah.

So I knew. Jack would have been cut to the bone to have to take George in to face a gallows, but he would be purely ashamed to let a murderer go away free. He must have done something the others don't know about to let George Lockwood slip away, so he is paying this debt all by himself. That explains him coming back so soon, too.

I told him, You did the right thing, whatever it was. Come in the house when you get through, and take a warm bath so you don't get sick. And then I left him alone.

It was only a few more minutes until he came in.

All the food was gone from his saddle bags.

We haven't talked much today. Now and then I see him watching me closely, and when I look up he turns his eyes away.

April 8, 1893

My life feels like a book left out on the porch, and the wind blows the pages faster and faster, turning always toward a new chapter faster than I can stop and read it. We lost the baby I was carrying at Christmas, in February. It was a little boy almost full term, but born too small and never took a breath. I knew something was wrong. My back hurt so terribly the whole time I carried him, and I just felt sick and so tired so I tried to take it extra easy. But suddenly one night, about two months early, I started laboring, and there wasn't even time to send for the doctor. The children were asleep, and Jack was gone just until the morning, and Anna never stays the night. I didn't know what to do, but I couldn't get help on my own and I was afraid of frightening the children. I wished Blue Horse was singing on my front porch again. I patted the baby, just a little handful of a fellow, but he didn't wiggle or stir at all. I think the life was already gone out of him before he was born. I am so very sad.

For weeks afterward I had nightmares about what happened at George Lockwood's house, and my friend Mrs. Page said it is likely that a fright like that can cause the baby to drop early. The doctor said that is just an old wives' tale, and sometimes these things just happen, and not to worry. But I still felt mournful because I had felt the little one move, and was happy expecting him. We hadn't even chosen a name yet, but we had to buy a little coffin. It made me too upset. Jack had to tend to it all.

Jack and I comforted each other with thoughts that we will have another one, maybe next year. In so many things he is rough and ornery, but in ways of our family, he is always so gentle it is like I am married to two different men. I love them both and need them equally.

June 9, 1893

Just as we might have expected, Harland and Melissa declared to us that they have been in love since they were children and they married last week. Melissa had on a beautiful white dress sprigged with tiny yellow flowers, with dark blue trim and buttons. Harland had on a gentleman's suit and a bowler hat. He looked like a professional man and indeed he is, for he has graduated now and has gotten a position at an Architect's office in San Francisco. He said they will return for visits, but we all miss them so. I'm sure Mama feels lonely and I'm glad Mr. Sherrill continues to pay her calls.

August 22, 1893

Two days in a row I have been troubled by a nightmare. It is the same one each night. When I awake I am shaking and my heart is banging like a drum, but I cannot put back to my thoughts just what it is that scares me so. I wake on the verge of tears from fear, and hold onto Jack like he is my last chance to stay on earth. He just pats my hand and goes back to sleep, but I lie there fearing to shut my eyes.

I was looking at Jack this morning after breakfast, and followed him into the bathroom and watched him shave. He looked at me and grinned kind of puzzled, and said, What are you up to?

I couldn't answer. I just told him, I want to remember you real good, for those times you are gone.

I'm coming back, he said.

I know, I told him. If you don't I'm coming after you.

He just smiled and nodded. Then he said, I'm counting on that, Sarah.

September 1, 1894

Time is flying. It is Gilbert's first day of school. The boys walked to school together today, tagging after April, who walks with her girlfriends and told Charlie and Gilbert not to walk with them, only behind. The boys let her put down endless rules for them, quietly taking all her orders as if it is the natural way of things. I am sure in a few years, they will grow tired of her bossiness and have a mind of their own, and their peaceful way of doing whatever she asks will be gone for good.

I hope Gilbert pays attention. Often he comes up with the most curious questions, and he takes his time but finds some real clever answers. Charlie is fast on his feet and can throw a ball long and hard, and rides real well. Gilbert is good with little things, and he has fine, even handwriting for such a little fellow, and can put together a puzzle or work a letter box fast as lightning. His whittling has taken to looking more like animals and such, also, pretty fine for such a little fellow. They look so big to me, but walking from our front gate down the road to the school house with a little pail of lunch in their hands, they seemed mighty small.

I picked up Suzanne and we went to look at our tiny garden, and she cried because she couldn't go to school. I told her that I have shed those same tears, and one day soon she will be luckier than her Mama and go to school with the big children.

September 2, 1894

Gilbert got into trouble the first day of school. April was mortified to own up to having him for a brother and I was forced to scold him soundly.

It appears he drew a very distorted picture of his brother on his slate. Charlie took it upon himself to discipline Gil with a sound pinch right in the middle of the fifth grade recitation. Gil squealed and whacked his brother over the head with the slate, and soon the boys were rolling together across the floor, each trying to get in a good punch.

They disrupted the whole school and both got a rod and sent to opposite corners to be stared at and mocked by the other students. Mrs. Fish has little patience with nonsense of that variety, and I know she is a fine teacher, but still, when they were out of the room, I had to smile when I pictured them both in the act. Rascals to the end.

September 4, 1894

Suzanne is coming down with another cold, her third in as many months, and is whining today and following my every step hanging onto my skirts. It is so hard to get anything done this way, and so I asked Jack to please try to get her to sleep some. He sat in the big rocker and held her, telling her stories until she did sleep, but when he moved she immediately woke and cried. So he carried her with him and came out to where I was hanging out the wash. She's got a bad fever, he said, and handed me a wet shirt from the laundry basket.

I felt her little head, and pulled a wash cloth from the cool, wet clothes and put it on her head. Just another baby cold, I said to him.

For a while he stood there handing me things to hang out so I would not have to bend over as my back has been bothering me some lately. Then he said, There's a call for men to go track and catch a gang that has robbed the Southern Pacific Railroad near Lordsburg. I told the Federal Marshal I'd go.

Oh, you did, I said. Well, when do you leave?

In the morning, he said, and walked away with Suzanne and took her in the house.

I hung out those clothes and hung them fast. There's nothing I can do. Here I am not feeling well myself, and the little one sick, and Anna only comes but three days a week. I suppose I am just worn out. All I can do is pack him a couple of days' food and hope they feed him later on.

September 5, 1894

I fixed up his two saddle bags this morning just after dawn. Jack is still carrying the one I gave him for our first Christmas, and keeps his razor and extra ammunition in the old one with a bullet hole in it which doesn't hold much, but he won't go without either of them. I put in a few biscuits and some hard candy, and salt bacon and jerked meat and I added a bottle of Doctor Forthcum's Lung Elixir as Jack gets affected with a cough now and again and I warned him to take it at the first sign of a cough. I kissed him goodbye, and the children waved as they headed off to school.

I have never told him about the nightmare. It is always the same when it comes, which it did again last night. I was up with Suzy several times, and was actually glad to be forced not to sleep.

Suzanne is sicker than ever this afternoon, and I dressed her up and took her to the doctor's office. We had to wait almost half an hour, but finally, he saw her and in just a minute pronounced that she had an acute inflammation.

Well, I said, acute inflammation of what? I know enough to know something has to be inflamed, it is not realistic to say her whole body is an inflammation.

That doctor stood there and got all tight in the jaw and looked at me indignantly, and said, I will not argue my diagnosis with a woman, period, pay at the door before you leave, one dollar.

I was ready to tell that character right then and there that he was mighty high in the britches and I had read plenty of medical books and I knew that was not a genuine diagnosis. After all, it is my child who is ill, and if she were his, he might care a fig what happened to her. But I held my peace. I paid him his dollar all in pennies.

September 6, 1894

I sent April to school with a note to Mrs. Fish to please loan me those two medical study books again. Suzanne has broken out in a dark rash, and has quit crying and now just lies in bed, weak and feverish. This afternoon when April gets home I will do some diagnosing of my own. At first all I could think of was wishing for Suzanne to quit crying, but now that she is not crying I pray that she would again. At least that was a sign of some fight in her.

Something is badly wrong with this child.

September 13, 1894

I have been waiting for days. Walking this floor. Watching. Waiting for Jack. Finally, Jack came home this morning noisily stamping trail dust off his boots on the back porch like he always does. I was ironing in the kitchen, ironing the sweat that rolled off my face right into the dress in front of me, yet I didn't feel the heat, I was cold inside and out. He came in and tried to throw his arms around me, and I said to him Jack, come lets' sit in the parlor.

He got a funny look on his face, but just leaned out the kitchen door to the rest of the house. Children at school? he asks. Suzanne! he starts to call. Where's my Suzy! Papa's home!

Jack, I said again, and pulled his hand after me toward the parlor so I could make him sit down. Jack, I'm so sorry. I'm so sorry, I said, crying. Suzanne was buried four days ago. I sent men to ride to find you but they never could. We tried to find you Jack, we tried, I said.

The look on his face was like I never have seen before. It was like the fire that has always burned inside him had kerosene thrown on it, and it seemed to have taken over him. He broke the screen door banging it open, so that it hung off the hinge and swung all crazy, and he jumped onto his tired horse without even touching the stirrups, galloping off down the road towards the cemetery up north. A heavy trail of dust followed him, then obscured him from my line of sight. I finished ironing my newly dyed black dress. For days I have been stirring everything we own into boiling pots of black dye and tears.

Jack didn't come back home until nearly three o'clock this afternoon, and there was a hurting and frightening look on his face and red rings around his eyes. I was sitting in the rocking chair, staring out the front window. Every now and then the breeze would lift the corner of the black crepe bow on the front door and it would flick at the window pane. I watched that black flicking. Like a little black bird pecking at this house, trying to get inside.

He knelt in front of me and put his hands on my knees. I couldn't even look at him. What was it? he asked in a voice I didn't recognize.

Scarlet fever, I told him. Then we held each other. I felt the dirt and sweat from his clothes smudging into my stiff ironed black dress. I watched my black sleeve turn brown and smeared. I felt brown and smeared, through and through. The other children came home from school and walked somberly into the house, and as they came in, each of them patted Jack on the shoulder and said Sorry, Papa. When they had gone on to their separate places and left us alone, the most awful, hurting, frightening sound I've ever heard came out of Jack and he sobbed into my shoulder like a child.

September 18, 1894

Jack walked in this morning while the children were getting ready for school and stood in the middle of the usual uproar of lost pencils and missing buttons like a statue.

When they were gone, he said to me he has done some thinking and reckoning, and he was terribly sorry to have been gone when Suzy died. There was no way to know, he said again, echoing words I heard a hundred times since he got home. But, he said, he has decided to quit the Army for good, and has found a job as the town Fire Chief, which they were in bad need of, anyway. That last was added hopefully, as if it made sense to him to fill some kind of need in other people's lives.

Maybe the fight is over inside him, I do not know. Maybe he will be happy to be home every day, and have hot meals and eat at a table and lie in a bed. He is blaming himself for Suzanne's dying, and there is nothing I can say to him, he just looks kind of haunted and dead and pained all at once.

November 1, 1894

No wonder Mama went away in her head when Clover passed on. And then Papa. I am going to visit my Mama tomorrow and tell her I am sorry for everything I ever did that caused her sorrow or worry, and for ever wishing, during those days, that she would come back. She probably wanted to stay there. It's a wonder she came back at all. If I knew how to make myself go away in my head, I declare I would.

Christmas day, December 25, 1894

This house is just too quiet. I told the boys to bring their friends over, and they did but the weather is nice and they are all playing in the yard. It is still too quiet inside. I wish Mama had come to visit, but she takes Christmas with Albert, and I didn't feel like going out to the ranch for just a day. April says she hates the ranch anyway, and she is off to show off her gifts to her friends.

Jack said last night he wants us to think about having another child. The truth is, I don't know if I want another child or not, but I said to him, this time, let's just let nature take its course, and see what happens. We loved each other for the first time in months.

So he seems a little cheered. He has not been the same man since Suzanne died. He smiles and plays with the boys, and is cheerful around the house, but in everything there is a mood of sadness, a shadow over his face. He claims he likes being the fire marshal, although there are stretches of time where there is little to do. But he stays busy and tends the fire horses.

He has no interest in the ranch really, and I still run it all with

Mason by mail, even though Jack has the time now. I suppose he never was cut out to be a rancher, but asked his Papa for all those cattle just for me. It is good to have him home every night and know that he will be here. He spends a lot of time with the children that I have never been able to, what with the cooking and cleaning, and making soap and ranch business. Most of the time, they hurry after school to get homework and chores done then he takes them riding or they play baseball, or practice roping, or some other thing.

Mama told me it takes time, a long time to get over the loss of a child. But I don't want to get over it, I want to turn back the calendar to when it never happened and all the future is sunny. I used to complain to myself that life was so boring, that there was too much laundry to do, too many noses to wipe. Now there are not enough noses to wipe. I wonder if Jack feels as hollow as I do. We have talked about Suzy and about her last days, but it's as if our lives stopped then and there. If I say anything to him about feeling lonesome, he goes outside and does some little chore. I can't tell if he is secretly blaming me, or himself, or just too full of pain to talk. That was the one thing we could always do together.

I wish for the old days. I wish for the struggling days and the days of Geronimo, and the days of birthing Charlie with no one but Jack to help me. How happy and in love we were then. I want to be in love again, but all I feel is darkness and shadows. Everything is changed and different.

March 1, 1895

Today Jack asked me if I would like to travel this spring, maybe take the train to visit the Lawrences in Texas with Savannah and a few of her children. He said maybe a change would lift my spirits. I told him thank you, but I am not inclined to go. I will keep it in mind, but there isn't much I want to see in Texas. I find that I don't care about much of anything any more. I have a brand new book on the shelf I haven't even unwrapped. The only time I feel better is when we go to the ranch. Maybe it is because Suzanne was there only rarely, and her memory seems steeped into this house.

April and the boys have gone on with their lives. I know from my own losses that losing a brother or sister is not nearly so terrible as losing a child, and they don't have the same thoughts of Suzy that Jack and I do.

Gilbert asked me if he died would I be that sad, too.

I hugged him close and told him yes, it would be the worst thing for me.

He asked me, Mama, would you miss me the most?

Well, Gilbert, I said, there is only one boy like you in the whole world, so I wouldn't just miss any old boy. Only you can be you. It would be like someone shot a hole through my heart. I wasn't sure that made any sense but he seemed pleased.

He just said, Well, then Mama, I'll wait until I'm real old.

May 27, 1895

April is giving a recitation of an essay she wrote on The Value Of Statehood For Arizona Territory. I am so proud. She is to be the third one, right after the high school valedictorian and the salutatorian, and she is only eleven years old. I have to finish hemming her new dress this afternoon.

The University has already expanded and added a school of Mines to add to their Medical and Law departments. April says she will hate to study any of those, especially mining, but I told her there is no learning that is wasted, and all of it can be applied sometime, someplace. Besides, I said, what if, one day when you are a grown lady and are looking at a piece of property, you just happen to pick up a little chunk of quartz with a ripple of black and yellow in it? Wouldn't you like to own that land?

She said to me, What for?

So I told her, Exactly my point. If you study Mining and Engineering, you will learn what I mean, and I'm not telling you the answer, you have to look it up. Go in there to the shelves and find Striechenburg's Geological Resource and see what you can learn.

Believe me, if I found that piece of quartz I would pay top dollar for that land.

She got all high in the britches and not only wouldn't do what I told her but fussed around and cried some and then stormed off mad to her friend's house. That girl tries me to the bone, sometimes. I think her father will have to have another talk with her about respectfulness.

May 29, 1895

We have just had a telegram from Chess that Jack's sister Penelope's husband has died. She has written his Pa and begged him and Jack to come to help her set things right and she is afraid of dealing with the lawyers. So he is headed off to Mississippi and will be gone four or five weeks. While he is gone I want to take the children to the ranch, and he will join us there for a while when he is back in the Territory. It is roundup time, and these children have only seen two other roundups since they were old enough to watch. Now they are big enough to help and it will be good lessons in hard work and square living for them. I think we might stay all summer, depending on the weather.

May 31, 1895

Dear Jack. We leave tomorrow morning, and he will be on the one o'clock train east. He said last night he misses us already, and the whole family went for a buggy ride up the foothills of the Catalinas to watch the sun set over the Tucson Mountains. There is a pretty stream, all brushy and rocky nearby, with so many colored birds like little pieces of broken rainbows flitting through the branches and singing at the top of their lungs. It is a fine sight, to see the grand rocky heights around us turn violet and many shades of orange and yellow, and then the sky go from turquoise to yellow, to dark violet, to indigo. Stars start to come out even before the last light is gone.

The boys started poking each other in the back seat and wrestling. They were purely bored with the scenery. Jack held my hand.

Remember, I told him, to keep your feet dry and eat plenty. Take that lung medicine with you.

Sarah, he says, it isn't like I'm some old codger you have to coddle.

Well, I told him, I want you healthy, to be sure that someday you are.

He just smiled at me and put his arms around me. Then, right in front of the children, in the reflected orange light off the mountain, he put his hands on my face and kissed me hard.

The boys howled.

April whispered Hush, hush, you two knot-heads, to them.

I could hear this while we kissed, and Jack held me close, and I just felt like I melted into his chest.

I love you, Mrs. Elliot, Jack said out loud.

The boys giggled and twittered.

Oh, Mother, April said, exasperated.

I love you, too, Captain Elliot, I said. Fine example you're setting for our children, though.

Yes, indeed, he said. I want them to know that I love you and just how much, too. And that I don't leave you because that feeling's not there, but I stay alive because it is. Will you pack up my saddle bags for me?

Yes, I said, as long as you will promise to bring them back.

He just looked at me funny, kind of sideways, and chucked the reins. The children were quiet as mice all the way home.

July 16, 1895

Jack has returned from Mississippi, and he will be here at the ranch for two more days, then he is going back to Tucson to take over his job again. It is a bad season for fires, what with the near drought conditions and the promise of several more dry lightning storms before the rains come. Everything is settled for his older sister. She refused to return to Texas to live with Chess, apparently she is too much a part of her surroundings in Mississippi to leave.

All the boys play together like there is no tomorrow. It is fun to watch Charlie and Gilbert and Clover and Joshua riding horses, running races, catching a ball and practicing throwing lariats and all. Today Charlie begged and begged Jack to show him how to draw a sword, and Charlie managed to cut the palm of his left hand right away. I think it needs stitches in it, but Jack said no. He has taped Charlie's hand with adhesive tape, and he is helping him hold the sword in his right hand. It is almost noon and they are still at it. I told them when the cousins come over to find something else to do, as I will not be the one to try to explain to Savannah why her boys are being taught swordplay in my front yard. Her convictions about fighting and violence seem to be tempered with common sense too, but I know she would draw the line at something like that.

Rachel and Rebeccah and April are trés amigas, and scamper about just as rowdy as the boys sometimes. Savannah and I have made a pact to teach them some manners and gentility if it is the last thing we do. Often the passel of ours and Albert and Savannah's children runs from our house to theirs on one mission or another the whole day through. When night falls, they barely get through dinner and fall asleep just as hard as they have played. Sometimes the littlest ones have actually drifted to sleep and nodded right into their plates.

As I hang wet clothes on the line, April is patching holes in the boys' pant legs for me with a gift Jack has brought, a sewing machine. It is a wonder. You have to put a little wound up thread shuttle underneath, and a spool on top on a peg, and then with a flick of your foot, it will just whip that needle up and down. I am fretting every second she will get her fingers too close to the needle, but she promised she will go very slowly, and is a bit afraid of it, also, so I must trust it to her. It is a hard thing to let your children near danger, and yet, I remember my Papa teaching me to fire a rifle before I could even hold it with my own strength. And if he hadn't trusted me to be careful, I would have never had faith in myself to do it.

It is no wonder my Mama's hair was gray before her children were grown. Every time I hear that saber clear the scabbard and that sewing treadle go around, I feel my heart speed up.

January 22, 1896

A letter has come for Jack, inviting him back in the Army as a post commander up in Wyoming. Jack looked at the letter a while and studied it carefully before he told me about it, and then he watched me like a hawk on a mouse. Well, I said, do you have a mind to go?

No, he said.

Well, do you know much about Wyoming? What kind of life would there be for the children? Is there a school? Did you ever go there?

No, no, he said again. I don't know much except that it is more wilderness and rough living. And taller trees, he added.

They're offering you a fine salary, I said, watching him. You're considering it?

Jack just laughed, and said, That's how I know you are teasing, Sarah. Anything the Army could offer is just fiddling in the wind next to the cattle ranch and the life we have here.

Well, he assures me the thought never crosses his mind, but I know part of Jack will always miss the Army. He is happy here, but it is not the same, and yet it is not as if you can turn back time, either. I have wished for that to happen, myself, and I know we just have to go on. Still, he gets up every morning at reveille, even when we can't hear the bugle at the fort clearly.

Can it really be four years since I have had time to write? Each month spins past until it becomes a year without my knowing, and though I used to feel that my journal kept me going, lately I just can't bear the thought of writing in it. Mama said it's probably because of Suzanne, and that you are never the same after a child dies. That made me wonder what she was like before Clover died, because I don't think I really knew my own mother until I had children, and if she was different before, I don't remember it.

Our children are growing quickly and no more have been added to our family. After the one I lost, there was never another, even though we both wanted more and tried so hard. I spend a lot of time helping with the children's schoolwork. Mostly our lives seem pretty ordinary and all the tumult of our early marriage is gone.

Jack stays in town all day. Rusty stays by his side. He is more Jack's dog than mine, and even more than Toobuddy ever was. Every time they answer a fire call, there is Rusty right up there between Jack's legs, grinning his sparkly eyed dog grin, excited to go to the fire. Jack spends a lot of time organizing his team of firemen. He has taken to attending Town Hall meetings and speaking out, and folks respect his words. Jack has a fine reputation from his days as a soldier, and he is thought of as a hero by many people. They all tell him to run for Representative or Senator or some other office and promise they will vote for him. Then at home he tells me he thinks they are crazy.

In the evenings folks like to stroll down the sidewalks and pay calls. So we have our share of company, but it is always the same thing, little words about the weather and the health of the children, and what do we think of the statehood issue. Then there is lemonade or tea, and they go on their way and tell each other my house needed dusting or sweeping.

March 11, 1900

Had a letter from Ernest this morning. He writes pretty regularly, every month or so, although I have not seen hide nor hair of him since Thanksgiving four years ago. He says that before Christmas, Felicity was feeling poorly, and went to visit her sister in a city called Marionville, to take the air. Poor Ernest. He just doesn't see the truth of that woman. This letter says she is also having some female problems and has been to several doctors, and then he has her address and wants me to write to her. I suppose for the sake of my brother, I will, but it is a sorry thing to see him hooked up with her. At any rate, I will send her a letter this afternoon, and tell her to try some castor oil and to eat plenty of liver. I think I will also remind her of the hot summers and the tarantulas and snakes and outlaws hereabouts, lest she get the idea of visiting me again. I prefer her to take the air wherever Marionville is, than to suck it dry here in Tucson. I hope she is at least being good to Ernest. I read his letter over and over, and I wonder if it could be that he finally knows what Felicity is, but can't bring himself to admit it to me. My, that is a mixed up stew if I ever saw one.

March 12, 1900

Savannah and her precious brood came to town today. With the new baby, Zachary, that makes eight of them. What a joy. My children were sorry they had to spend the day at school, but they took their older cousins with them, and so it was not too bad. I kept the younger ones, Mary Pearl, Esther, Mark, and the baby, so Savannah could visit Ulyssa for a little while.

Then we talked until late. After supper, Jack was set upon by all the children, begging for stories and some tall tales he is so good at telling. Some of them really happened, but parts are stretched out so the truth is hard to find. I know the real stories behind some of them, and it makes me smile to hear the yarns he can spin. While he entertained the bunch, Savannah and I made up pallets and beds for all the children in the upstairs bedrooms, and then filed them in two at a time for baths until we got to the bigger ones. Then they moved the story telling up to the bedroom. Finally, all was quiet except for the sound of Jack's deep voice, and now and then the children laughing or moaning or somehow responding to his story. Savannah and I had coffee in the kitchen while she nursed Zachary and we laughed at his noisy suckling.

Ulyssa is better, she said, and is able to be out on the grounds of the asylum. And she has had a letter from Louisianna that she and her new husband have bought a farm near a little town in Texas called Lubbock. Savannah had a daguerreotype of their wedding day she showed me. Louisianna was a grown woman. I would never have known her if I met her face to face. Her husband is a homely fellow, thick set and whiskery, but she says he is gentle and quiet, said Savannah.

Then Jack came in and said his audience had fallen asleep. He took little Zachary from Savannah, and went and rocked him in the rocking chair in the parlor.

Savannah smiled at me and took my hand. Jack is a good father, isn't he, Sarah, she said.

Pretty good, I said. A little hard to hang on to, but pretty good, I said. Albert is too, of course.

Oh, certainly, said Savannah. But Albert is calm and just always there. Jack has this kind of desperateness about him, like he needs you and the children very much.

I just smiled at that and set some cream on the table. I suppose that's one way to put it. Savannah, I said, I keep wishing we'd have another baby, but it just isn't happening. For a while I didn't really want it, but now I do. Do you know anything I can do?

She looked into her cup. Not really, she said. But I'll pray for you to conceive. It seems all I have to do is begin to fit into my old clothes, and there I am swelling again. I'm a bit tired of it, actually.

Well, I said, you just have to quit having them.

Sarah, said Savannah, kind of wound up and embarrassed sounding.

Well, you know, I told her. That's how I kept from having a child every year at first. Do you know what I mean?

I don't think so, she said.

I looked at Savannah all red-faced and nearly ashamed, and wished with all my heart I could say the words that would help her not have so many babies, but I just couldn't. How could I say those things that even Jack and I never put into words? I don't know how he knew them, either. Savannah, I said, and took a real deep breath, Lean up here close. And then I put my mouth next to her ear and closed my eyes tight and told her everything I knew.

I started with, Tomorrow you go by the druggist's on your way out of town and ask him for the Lady's Preventative, and you will have to get a new one every six months or so, because they wear down. I found out that's how Gilbert came when we weren't planning. Then I told her how to use it.

I could never do it, Savannah whispered.

Do what? I said.

Ask for it, she said.

So I told her I'd go with her and I'd buy it. And, I said, it comes in a brown paper parcel, no bigger than an oatmeal cookie. It's not fool proof, but half a chance is better than none. Then I told her sometimes Jack and I just hold each other instead.

Savannah clapped her hand over her mouth at that and looked shocked. Isn't it strange, she said, how the table has turned? Do you remember when you asked me what you had to count on the ceiling? She smiled and cried, together.

Then we both cried. Then we both laughed, sort of scared and red-faced, but glad. Then Jack came in the kitchen and said Zachary was asleep in the crib he had put up in the parlor, and we women could gossip all night but he was going to turn in. Well, Savannah jumped up from the table and went to clatter around at the stove and couldn't look at him, but said goodnight over her shoulder. When he was gone she rushed back to my side and kissed my cheek and smiled.

Tomorrow after breakfast she will head for home. I hope I have done the right thing. I hope Albert doesn't think I am a lunatic. And I hope Savannah is brave enough not to have any more children than she positively wants.

And when I go upstairs, I am going to wake Captain Elliot up and tell him he is the answer to a prayer.

March 14, 1900

I was scrubbing the floor in the kitchen on my hands and knees this morning, when I heard the fire bell sound. Pretty soon, I saw some excited looking children running down the street, and I called out to one of them and asked what was burning. Whatever it was, I knew it was big, because the smoke soon blackened the whole town. I was so sorry to hear it was the new Pima County Courthouse. It is just a beautiful building, the kind I'm sure Harland is building in California. I have driven past many times just to watch the workmen, and study the plans when they will let me. Now some fool has gone and set it on fire. No doubt someone whose better interests are not served by having a courthouse in this raggedy town, where law and order might someday actually be carried out instead of wished for. There is a sorry and low element in this town that will all come to know the business end of a rope if we ever have enough law.

The school let out early, as Mrs. Fish and the other teachers realized there was no keeping the children at their studies with all the excitement and noise. My boys are now among the biggest in class, so I'm sure they led the way to where their father was fighting the fire. I was just closing the windows to keep out the smell when someone knocked on my front door like they would break it in.

The man that stood in my doorway was blacked with soot and looked like a fright, with rings of red around his bleary eyes and the smell of smoke heavy on him. Mrs. Elliot, the man said, You'd better come with me. Do you have a buggy?

I saw the look in his eyes even though he was so dirty. It's Captain Elliot, isn't it? I said.

Ma'am, he said, The fire, you know, they were painting inside and a can of varnish blew up and he's on the way to the hospital.

I can ride, I said, Will your horse take two? He nodded and I climbed up behind him in the saddle, and I didn't care if he was dirty and a stranger but I hung onto him, and he spurred that horse good and my legs showed for all the town to see.

In bits and pieces, he told me Jack had ordered all the firemen out of the building because the roof was caving in. Someone said they heard a scream inside, and Jack went in through a broken window. He went into a room where the paint cans were stored and just as he got inside the flames reached the cans, and the explosions sent metal pieces flying everywhere.

In the hospital room, all the white walls and sheets and nurses and doctors seemed to crowd in on Jack, lying blackened and sooty on the clean bed. They pulled a stretched linen curtain around us, and I sat by him. His face was black but under the sheet coverlet they had taken off his shirt and white skin showed, making him look like he wore a strange black mask. A huge bandage covered him from his shoulder to his hip, and blood seeped through it, and another smaller bandage wound around his left arm.

Captain Elliot, I whispered, do you hear me? He opened his eyes and I tried not to cry out. They were so bloodshot they looked at first as if they were bleeding. His eyebrows and mustache were singed and little curled up burnt hairs dotted his face in reddish coils against his black skin.

He struggled to breathe, and he said, Oh, Sarah, I'm sorry. I didn't mean to do this to you. I thought I heard a baby crying in there. I know there was a baby crying in there. Did someone get him out? A baby. Get the baby out.

I started to shake all over. There was no baby, Jack, it was only the hissing of the cans getting ready to pop, making a whining sound.

He just looked kind of confused. Baby? he said again, and then cringed with pain.

No baby, I said again. It was nothing, Jack, there was no baby in there at all.

I had to save the baby, he said, and shook real hard all over for a minute. Then he turned toward me and reach his hand out, groping for me, and then I knew he couldn't even see me. Sarah, my Sarah, he said, I'm sorry to tell you but I'm leaving again.

No, no, I said, No, you're not. And tears fell on my cheeks instantly, flooding out in panic.

He slowly lifted his darkened hand and reached toward my face, and with one finger brushed softly at the tears on my cheeks. Now don't do that, he said, I always liked it when you'd raise a fuss and get good and mad when I left. That way I knew you'd be all right.

Well, Jack, I said, I always cried later.

He winced then, maybe because of my words, I don't know. He seemed to be sinking into the bed, getting smaller and smaller.

Don't leave, Jack, you can't go now. You said you'd never leave me again.

Got to, he spoke with a gasp. Orders.

But Jack, you're just a Captain and I'm the General. I order you not to go.

He tried to smile, but I couldn't look at his poor burnt eyes. These orders, he whispered, come from the Commander in Chief. Then he seemed stronger for a second, and he said, That fool doctor wanted to cut on me, said it would be a good operation, and then in the same breath said I wouldn't live anyway. Damn jackass fool doctor. Damn them all anyway. Acute Inflammation. Doctors don't know a damned thing, can't help a sick child. God damn them all. Let my baby Suzy die. Sarah! he moaned, crushing my hand in his and gasping, and for a bit I thought he was gone, but then he breathed easier and I suppose he was intent on staying with me longer. April slipped into the room then. She had come behind me in the buggy.

April's here, I said to him.

Oh, April, Jack said, You're here? Well, honey, I want you to know I love you, I always have. You've been giving your Mama some gall lately and I want you to stop it and be good to her. You two need each other, and more now than ever. But don't you ever forget I love you like my own child. Don't you ever forget it was me that held you when you cried.

April started to cry. She promised she wouldn't forget, then Jack told her to go find the boys to say goodbye to their Papa, and she hurried away. When she was gone, he said to me with a look on his face I know was pure pride, She's a grown woman, isn't she?

I just nodded. Only three days ago April had scalded Jack and I both with angry words of how he wasn't her real father, and had no call to tell her what to do nor who to keep company with.

I held Jack's hand and just sat with him for a bit. It wasn't long before I heard our boys clattering into the room. Charlie is so tall now, all legs and big feet, nothing he does is quiet. He took off his hat and held it sheepishly between his hands, turning it around and around. Gil looked at his Papa and sniffed and started to cry.

Boys, Jack said, and then breathed a ragged breath. Listen to me, Men. I've gone and done a fool thing and let your Mama down, and now I can't be here to see to your raising. And you aren't done yet, so don't think now is your chance to run wild, because I'll be watching you. Both the boys started to sniff noisily and tears stained their ash smudged shirts. Now, men, Jack began again, it normally isn't right for men to say too much to each other, but this is a special circumstance. I've got to tell you I love you because it's the last time you'll hear my voice. I can't be there to show you how to grow to men, but you just ask your Mama, she knows the way to go.

He breathed a little easier then, as if he pushed on to set things as right as he could before leaving. Now, Gilbert, you have a mission. You go to the Marshal's office, and tell him, real polite, but don't take no guff from him, tell him I said to send a messenger to Grandma Prine's and to escort her to town. Your Mama will be needing Grandma for some days. Gilbert straightened up stiff. You can do it, can't you son?

Gil nodded.

Jack smiled. Go on, then. I've always been proud of you, Gilbert. Jack gasped for air. The bandage on his chest was growing redder and the sweetish smell of blood filled the little stuffy room. Now Charlie, he started again, and closed his eyes. Charlie, you're a fine man, almost grown. I've always felt so proud of you it ain't right. You look like me, you act like me, and likely that'll be a load too heavy for you to overcome. Don't worry your Mama like I've done, you hear? You've got to go to the fort, and get to the wireman's office, and you tell him to send a wire to Pop. If some shavetail tries to stand in your way, you just don't let him. You've got to tell Pop I'm going soon. Reach in my pocket here, well, they took my pants. Damn 'em. Sarah, I want my pants on.

Jack, I said, I don't know where they are.

He looked real confused for a minute and said, Well, if they tell you there's a cost for the wire, you tell them it is a calling in of a debt, and if they still stop you, remind General Crook about Mexico, Sahuarita. Now go, son, your Mama and I have to be together for a spell.

Jack held onto my hand. I held onto him. Sarah, he said after a long time, Sarah I'm so cold, is there a blanket I could have?

He had a blanket on him, and it was warm in the room anyway. Jack, it's just cold, I lied. Let me hold you closer. So I leaned upon the bed, and cradled his head next to my breast, and felt his breathing so shallow, so cool, not the hot and vital breath I knew all those years. I wet his hair with my tears, they dropped without stopping now. And there was so much gray hair on his head, I had never noticed, but he never seemed a bit older than the day he proposed to me in the shade of the peach orchard.

Sarah, he said, reaching up to hold onto my shoulder, I've been a hard man to live with, I know, he said, but I've always admired you and loved you. You are some kind of woman. You'll be fine. You keep your powder dry, and an eye on the horizon.

Then I felt him start to kind of tremble all over.

A man in a white coat and a nun with an apron came in and said to me, Mrs. Elliot you should leave now.

Leave? How could I leave him, after all we've been through,

how could they think I'd just walk away and leave him to face his last moments alone?

Jack's hand touched mine, and he held me in a strong grip that reminded me of how big and sturdy he always was. He mumbled something, then said, Sarah, don't leave my saddle bag, don't lose it. And then he shook a little softer, and he buried his face in my bosom, and then I felt one long warm breath come from his lips and no more.

I laid his head on the pillow gently, and then buried my own face on it, and I shed tears the like of which I didn't know I owned.

March 20, 1900

Rusty has lived at the fire house to be near Jack all these years of him being Fire Chief. He will not leave and come home, but waits and waits by the door to Jack's office for him to come out. All the firemen said it was fine with them if Rusty stayed, they will feed him and care for him. I petted his head and he turned toward my voice, but he would not come with me.

All through the funeral and all the polite callers and my family gathered around and my children weeping I have sat and walked and spoken politely and properly and without any tears. A hundred thoughts run through my head, about how he was always safe doing what he wanted to do, and because he quit the Army he died being a Fire Chief.

But then, Jack was always bursting through walls, always riding off cliffs, always thinking he was somehow immortal. I think at times like that he never felt pain, either, it was like he really was more than just a man. Sometimes, though, I needed him to be around, and he always just believed I would be fine, like I didn't really need him. But he refused to understand when I told him, too. It was like he only came home to prime himself up again to go out and fight the world's woes.

Stubborn man. Stupid man. Gone and left me now for good. Always before when he left I got mad in his face and then when he was over the hill I wept my heart out on his pillow. This time I cried right in front of him and held him to me to keep him from going. But he went anyway. And I am mad. It doesn't make sense. I am so mad at him if he walked in this room this minute I'd give him a piece of my mind, I would at that. I am mad as a wet hen.

I have to ask my Mama why do I feel so angry? It isn't right to feel this way.

March 25, 1900

Sunday morning. I tried to picture what I would do if I were Savannah: hold my head up and bravely take my mourning children to church in that peaceful, reverent way of hers. We dressed up for church, everyone in clothes of mourning black. I suppose there's more mourning in this life than otherwise. Chess is here and he made it for Jack's funeral but I forgot to write that down before now. Anyway, he said he will sit at the house and tend to dinner while we are gone.

I made Charlie drive instead of his Papa, and Gil sat beside him and April and I in the back. We pulled up in front of the church house and there was already singing coming from inside.

Wait just a minute, I said to Charlie. I looked at those front steps, and through the window to the people inside, and I knew most of them by name. I looked at my little family in this buggy, and I said, Charlie, turn us around and take us home.

He was grinning I know, and I saw Jack's eyes twinkle in Charlie's face. Yes Ma'am, was all he said, but he trotted that horse back home.

I sat everyone down at the kitchen table. It was not just a work table, but a fancy carved-legged thing Jack had bought for us. Most of the chairs matched each other, too. Now, I said to them all, I have come to a decision. My town days are over. We are packing up and moving to the ranch. You boys can finish out your school year by mail the way Harland did. Now, Chess, you are welcome to come and live with us, I will be glad to have you around, and I'm not trying to be rude but we are moving and we are starting tomorrow. I didn't even know I had made those decisions, but my mouth just opened and the words came out, as if saying them made them so.

April was furious. No, Mama, no! she hollered. I won't leave to go to that dirty old ranch, I hate it!

I just looked at her real cool and said, Well, you have to, so there.

Charlie and Gilbert were tossing their hats in the air and whooping like wild Indians. At the ranch? At the ranch, we get to live at the ranch! No more school! Nothing but roping and riding and we get to live at the ranch! They were both hollering at once, punching each other in the arm.

Chess looked at me, and he looks so old now, and he said real slowly, I don't know if you mean that, Miss Sarah, but I'd rather live with you if you don't mind. My ranch runs itself, I don't do a thing there anymore. And my daughters both live with their children, and they don't have room for an old cuss like me.

Well, I said, yes I meant it. Every word. We will start packing up tomorrow, and this house will rent out just fine.

April cried out with tears in her eyes, I won't go without my good furniture, I won't sleep on a nasty old straw mattress. Mama, how could you do this to me? And she ran upstairs wailing "I hate that ranch" at the top of her lungs like a baby.

We are going anyway, I said to the boys. We'll ship the furniture and everything, and decide later what to use. So now you have to help out, and you can get some wood from the shed and start building small crates today for dishes. Then tomorrow when the stores are open, we'll start in on the big things.

March 30, 1900

It took only three days to move us out to the ranch. But it is just me and the boys and Chess. The day we left with the last of the crates in a flatbed wagon, I found a note from April in the door of her room, and she has run off with Morris Winegold to get married. She says he has money and will not make her live in an old ranch house.

Well, this hurt my heart, and yet, I understand that she probably has some terrible memories of the ranch and the struggles we
had there, and that she is grown now with a mind of her own, and
although we didn't approve of Morris for her to marry, it was not
because he's not a nice family man. The Winegolds are a rich family and have high plans for their son that don't include the daughter of a soldier. I had tried to explain to April that if his mother
doesn't like her background, it will be a rough row to hoe being
married to him, no matter how much they love each other. But
she is gone now. Maybe she will be happy. I hope so. Some of the
things I tried to say to her she will understand someday when she
has children of her own to worry over. As soon as I hear from her,
I will just tell her I love her and they should come to visit any
time, as I will not turn them away for this. I will never turn away.
How fragile our lives are anyway. How quickly things can change
forever. Write me, daughter. Write me.

April 1, 1900

Mason has been letting the ranch slip. He is grown so old, I hadn't
noticed before now. All his hair is white as snow. He still courts
my Mama every Tuesday evening.

The sun was hanging low in the sky when I finally got to catch
my breath. Chess and the boys have saddled up and are out for a
ride to get the lay of the place; they just can't wait to start being
ranchers, and their grandpa Chess is a good man to teach them. I
sat on the front porch steps and just felt the homeyness of it all and
breathed in the smells I knew so well of the desert and the trees.

All is in bloom now and my little rose bush has become a big
rose bush. Mason tended it carefully and for that I will be forever
thankful. I let my eyes wander the hills and the little road that followed the stream. And I remembered Jack jostling April on his
shoulders those days after the bad flood. And I remembered him
being pinned under that horse on the ridge. Then I couldn't stop
the tears, and I cried and cried, and loved him with all the love I
have ever had. I opened up the last box, the one I had saved

because I couldn't stand to look inside. I again unwound the leather stitching from Jack's old saddlebag. I touched the ragged and scarred little book with the hole through it. Stumbling and sobbing, I put the scarlet velvet lady book, with the letters safely inside it, into my carved wooden perfume box on the top shelf in the parlor.

Jack's medals were in there, his watch, his wedding ring, and my brooch. I sat Mrs. Lady on top of the box, to guard it from intruders, and her worn and faded dress spread out across the top, her little patch of tangled hair flew around her head. Then I kissed the little old portrait of us from our wedding trip, and I washed my face and dried my eyes.

The other Elliot men came in noisily for supper, talking about the ranch, and the sun was setting fast as we ate. Every now and then I could hear Jack's voice in someone's from the table, just a word or a tone, but Jack was alive in these men around me.

Every now and then I look at Mrs. Lady and smile at her, and I know she appreciates the treasure she guards.

Jack Elliot, you are a sore trial and a wonder.

June 30, 1901

This morning I paid two men from town to move the coffins of my husband and my children from town to their resting places here, and put up a pretty carved headstone for each of them. And I planted a little tree called a jacaranda at their heads. It is a tiny stem, with only three little branches, but all the branches have a shoot of flowers on them, and Chess says that in Texas these trees get as big as a house, and will shade the entire hill eventually.

The air now is balmy and cool, and while the days are warm they are not as fiercely hot as during the worst of the summer. In the twilight here from the porch I can see, rising in the clear summer sky, a brilliant star, brighter than any other in the heavens. Every night it joins another one and the moon in a triangle, and makes a journey across the sky and sets in the hills. I have stayed up sometimes well towards midnight to watch it.

I have named the star Jack's Star. It is beautiful and bright and gives me joy when it is here and pain when it is not, and every year as the summer approaches, I have seen it coming over the hills. I used to think that maybe someday I will learn what educated people have called it and why it is only here sometimes, but now I think it wouldn't matter. It is Jack's Star, and they have only to ask me and I will tell them its name.

They will have to ask the star itself where it goes and why it is not content to stay.

Acknowledgments

I would like to thank my family and friends for their encouragement and support; my daughter, April, for keenly recognizing the good and bad in my work; my son, Sterling, who listened and laughed in the right places; and my husband, John, who refused to cast opinion until I asked, and was there for the rejection as well as the acceptance.

None of this would have appeared in print without the hard work of a patient yet tenacious literary agent. John Ware has proved himself beyond the call of duty in every respect.

I extend special appreciation to those faculty members of the Writing Department at Pima Community College, Tucson, Arizona, whose goal is the fanning of the flame. Otis Bronson first told me I was a writer and sent me to the forge. Meg Files, a remarkably gifted writer and quite likely the most extraordinary teacher I've had the pleasure to study under, showed me how to refine the blade and polish the edge, and cheered me onward at every turn.

NANCY E. TURNER has been a seam snipper in a clothing factory, a church piano player, an aide to a paleontologist, and an executive secretary. She lives in Tucson, Arizona, with her husband and two children. This is her first novel.

ARIZONA

AND

NEW MEXICO

SCALE OF MILES
10 20 30 40 50 60 70 80 90 100